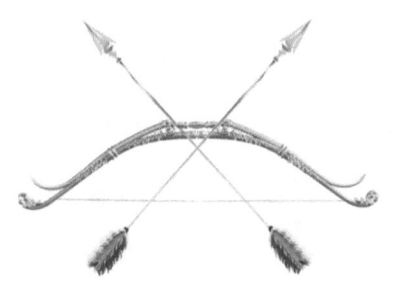

CROWN OF DUSK

MEGAN GILBERT

CROWN OF DUSK
First published in Australia in 2026
by Crafted Press, an imprint by Megan Gilbert

Cover design by David Gardias: bestselling-covers.com

ISBN (Paperback): 978-0-6458553-4-0
ISBN (eBook): 978-0-6458553-5-7

Megan Gilbert
megangilbert.co

A NOTE TO READERS

This is the second book of The Crystal Crown Trilogy.

Please be aware of the following content before reading *Crown of Dusk*:

Anxiety
Battles and hand-to-hand combat
Blood
Death
Misogyny
Murder

To enhance your reading of *Crown of Dusk*, why not listen to the official Spotify playlist? Visit megangilbert.co, or scan the QR code below, to find the playlist and listening guide.

To every woman who has ever been told she has to earn the crown she's already wearing; you don't need to wait for permission to use it.

THE WETLANDS

THE EDGE

THE SHADOWED COAST

THE HOOK

THE STARLIGHT MOUNTAINS

THE VALE

THE ENDLESS SEA

THE MIDLANDS

WHARF TOWN

SILKSHELL

BEAR JAWS VALLEY

THE SOUTHERN SHADOW

ELDERGUARD

THE ISLE OF CRYSTAL

THE QUEENDOM OF CRYSTERRA

NEW MOON

I

THE WINDS BELLOWED THROUGH THE WETLANDS, SHAKING EVERY TREE and window in their wake. The gale had not calmed since the return of the army in the days prior. The hordes of soldiers barrelled past the rocky border of The Edges and down into the familiar marshes. The citizens of the Wetlands could hear the army's return before they appeared on the crest of the mountain range. It was not the battle cries or the pounding of horses' hooves that announced their arrival, though. It was the piercing whistle of the unnatural wind that accompanied them.

To drive their forces home faster, and to push through unfriendly towns and provinces without issue, Valah Pyrin propelled her allies through the kingdom of Crysterra with a gust that held the strength of a hurricane. Citizens of the Midlands took cover in their homes, shielding themselves from the dust, leaves, and ash that were stirred up as the army passed, no one daring to approach the force that moved eerily quickly through the kingdom. No one had ever witnessed a Wind Wielder of such power before. Valah's strength was legend across Crysterra, and many either feared it or believed it to be merely a myth. Given the isolated life she had lived for many decades, hiding in the Wetlands away from the eyes of the rest of the country, no one could confirm its truth until she swept through on the Sixth Day of Mourning, hurtling her thousands-strong army forward with her.

When they made it back to their home, the wind subsided, but it didn't still completely. Although the days were getting cooler as they neared winter, the wind was unseasonal, and many believed that Valah's temperament was likely keeping it around. No one in the province could escape the whistle of the wind as it travelled through the city streets and over the marshes. Eyes watered, lips cracked, and trees lost their leaves quickly. Even below the Pyrin manor—deep beneath the layers of beaten earth and the dark granite floors, in a locked chamber—the piercing winds could be heard.

Drystan Allard was awoken more than once by the shuddering sounds of wind that rattled through the building above him.

He thought that the manor might collapse on him at any moment, and he questioned whether that would be the worst end for him. The room he was in had no windows to the outside world, only a wooden door with a small metal chute at its base. This was locked from the outside and, he assumed, heavily guarded. The only light he could see by was a small lantern set by the door; it could not be opened from the outside and seemed to be kept alight by the abilities of a Fire Flourisher on the other side of the door. The flame cast shaky shadows across the small room, Drystan's own shadow warping across the back wall like a deformed phantom.

He could have travelled across the room in three strides if his ankles weren't shackled together and connected to the wall furthest from the door, allowing him very limited movement. His wrists were also manacled to one another, a short chain tethering them. The room was cold and damp, and he could even hear a light trickling coming from one of the corners of his prison cell. The dribbling stream landed in one of two pails, which he assumed were his lavatory and his only source of fresh water. He had been given a bed of clumps of dry straw, but as his skin itched in irritation in the night, he wondered if he'd have better luck sleeping on the hard, damp floor.

Drystan had been dragged into his cell unconscious, and given the lack of sunlight that his cell provided, he didn't know what time it was or how long he had been held captive. Based on how many meals he had received, he estimated that at least five days had passed since the attack on Elderguard. When one such meal of stale bread and uncooked beans was pushed through the chute in the door, he overheard one of the guards uttering Valah's name beside the phrase "the prisoner", so he felt it was safe to assume he was being held in the Wetlands, likely beneath Valah's home. His chains only just allowed him to reach the food, and he devoured it in seconds, a deep pit of hunger sitting in his stomach, never fully satisfied.

At the mention of Valah's name, memories of the previous days came flooding back to him. The attack on Elderguard; fighting defected Royal Guard soldiers from the east, the Wetlands, and Lund; being attacked and dragged by his neck beyond the walls of Elderguard; Galdinia.

Suddenly, he was outside the Northern Gates once more, beaten, bloody, and broken, unable to hold up his own weight without support. He could feel the glint of metal of a blade against his throat. As the sound of Galdinia's voice ripped across the chasm, he looked up, wanting nothing more than for his ears to have deceived him.

She couldn't be here, not now.

Across the stretch of land between the Bear Jaws Valley and Elderguard, he glimpsed Galdinia as she stood in front of the burning gates of the capital's walls, Captain Ilyon by her side. Drystan's vision had become blurry after multiple blows to the head, so he wasn't sure if he could truly believe what he was seeing, but through squinted eyes, he saw the most magnificent scene: Galdinia had harnessed the power of the fire that had burned through the city gates and created great spheres of flames that were suspended in the air behind her. They sizzled and cracked as they grew in size at her will, their ferocity mirroring her own. Drystan had never seen anything like it. She was so powerful—it was spectacular. She was spectacular. The Gods had finally blessed her, and she could be queen.

Again, Galdinia's voice travelled to him, low and hot on the wind that now surrounded them. Galdinia was demanding for Drystan's life. His heart dropped in his chest, making him feel unwell. He needed her to turn around and run in the opposite direction.

Valah's velvety smooth and condescending voice followed, offering an exchange: Drystan for the crown.

It's a trap, Drystan thought, not quite able to find his voice. Valah wouldn't let Galdinia quietly walk away from this. After everything she had been through, Gal could not give up the crown—her life—for him. This was not an exchange she should even consider!

His words formed in his mouth before he could think about the consequences: "Don't do it, Gal—"

As he uttered her name one final time, a blinding pain ran through his jaw and to his already injured head, rendering his vision dark and his limbs loose.

The next time he opened his eyes, his head was throbbing and he was on the floor of his prison cell, chained to the wall, in near pitch black. The armour he remembered wearing was gone, and he was left only with his tunic, trousers, and boots.

While it took him hours to regain complete consciousness as the pain in his head shuddered with every beat of his heart, and although he was bound in a chamber without sunlight, Drystan held on to some hope.

Galdinia was a Fire Flourisher, and she had proved herself worthy of being Queen of Crysterra. The Gods had ordained her.

Drystan prayed that she was as far away from the Wetlands as possible, crown firmly on her head, fortifying Elderguard. As he imagined what Galdinia would look like with Queen Anae's crown resting on her head, the biting chill in the air of his cell seemed to dull.

She could finally be who he'd always seen her as: the most spectacularly powerful queen that Crysterra would see.

Finally.

Across the kingdom, over the ranges of The Edges, beyond the Midlands and the Shadowed Coast, in the depths of the soldiers' barracks of Elderguard, sat a prisoner in an equally perilous position, yet in an arguably nicer cell.

Bentley Penrose, now stripped of his deceptive finery and fraudulent title, sat slumped on a stretcher that was pushed up against the wall, his hair far less lustrous, wearing clothing fit for a prisoner and traitor of the crown. He was sitting on the edge of his poor excuse for a bed, his elbows resting on his knees, his hands and feet shackled to an impossibly thick bar of metal on the floor below him. The door to his cell had a small frosted glass window set in it at eye level, and a dull, cool light from the room outside cast into the cell. Try as he might to harness a nearby flame, Bentley couldn't feel the familiar heat in his periphery or in his fingertips, so he assumed the light in the underground bunker was that of Peacelight.

After spending far too long searching for a flame, Bentley hung his head and looked down at the steel bar on the floor. The refraction of light through the door's window lined up with the piece of metal; this was his true guard. He wasn't sure if he would be able to melt it even if he were able to find a flame. It would likely take him hours, and then what would he do? He'd be trapped beneath an army of soldiers in a cell that he very much deserved to be thrown into.

As he studied the metal, his eyes tightening on the bolts and welding that kept it attached to the stone floor, his light was suddenly obscured. He looked up to his door and saw the head of a figure through the glass, silhouetted by the dim light behind them.

The person themself was otherwise unrecognisable, aside from the outline of a crown that sat atop her head.

2

QUEEN GALDINIA ELDERWIN SAT IN THE BASEMENT TRAINING ROOMS OF the barracks, sweat dripping down her temples and neck, her skin hot. Her crown of crystals and gold sat beside her atop a cushion reserved for the headpiece, shimmering in the firelight.

The cool of the underground room, made more intense by the lowering temperatures of the autumn day, was welcome. Galdinia pulled her long golden hair off her shoulders, twisting the waves in on themselves at the nape of her neck and securing the ends within the twist. She relished the sensation as she wiped the sweat from her neck, her warm fingers absorbing it instantly. Galdinia's hands had quite literally been on fire for the previous three hours, and around her stood torches of different sizes, periodically placed throughout the room. They were now extinguished, but moments earlier they were all alight, burning with the power of the queen's fury.

After her coronation five days prior, Galdinia had insisted on being trained by Captain Ilyon once again. The Captain of the Royal Guard gladly obliged, spending hours with Galdinia in the underground bunker, teaching her to use the skills he had introduced to her during the Week of Mourning. Today's session had Galdinia hurling balls of flames at the torches that were scattered across the room.

They were working on her target practice, and she'd had a reasonable amount of success.

At first, she had struggled to reach the torches further than ten feet from her, the flames overshooting or missing the torches completely. She recalled her success when sending her gift out in the entrance hall during the attack on Elderguard, telling Ilyon about how she'd sent arrowheads of fire into the hearts of their enemies, not missing a shot.

"You were driven by many factors that night, Your Majesty," Ilyon explained, walking slowly between the torches, pacing in front of Galdinia as she caught her breath after a particularly unsuccessful barrage of flames. "You were desperate to protect your home, your veins were on fire with adrenaline, and you didn't stop to take stock of yourself or those around you. You had no choice but to hit with accuracy. You had faith that you could, so you did."

"But I believe that I can now," Galdinia protested, feeling the flickering heat in her palms, the feeling now second nature.

"I'm sure that you do. But there's a different desperation that comes with the attacking onslaught of enemy soldiers." Ilyon stopped by a nearby torch, surveying the queen, his dark eyes firm as ever. "Your body and your gift respond to that. We just need to learn to tap into it again in our sessions."

Galdinia nodded, bringing her palms together, rubbing them against one another slowly, the heat in her hands building.

"This time, I want you to try to hit every second torch only," Ilyon said, walking to stand behind Galdinia.

"Alright," Galdinia said simply, feeling the newly familiar warmth of the fire in her veins, trying to tap into that same energy she'd felt during the battle.

"Don't turn around. Focus on the torches." As Ilyon spoke, Galdinia heard the distinct sound of a sword being unsheathed. She didn't need to look at her captain to know that he now held his sword at her back. He tapped the tip of it against the training leathers that wrapped around her arms and torso.

"Is that really necessary?"

"I need you to find that same place you were in during the attack," Ilyon said simply, as though holding a blade to his queen's back was a commonplace training strategy. "If you'd like to, you could imagine me plunging it into your side if you don't hit the torches."

Galdinia shook her head, letting out a short chuckle. She was always taken aback when the captain tried his hand at humour. Captain Ilyon was a stolid man who was two decades older than Galdinia and had been serving in the Royal Guard since before she was born. Her father had appointed him as Captain of the Royal Guard himself, which was all the seal of approval Galdinia needed to trust him. But after showing Galdinia such unwavering support during the Week of Mourning when she was on the brink of giving up on herself, she knew she didn't need to fear the blade in her side. At this point, she'd walk off a cliff face if Ilyon assured her it would be safe to do so.

"Here we go, then."

Galdinia sucked in a deep breath, feeling her diaphragm expand into the side of the blade, its point pressing into her leathers. She looked across the room, her eyes darting from each of the torches she needed to hit.

Every second torch, she reminded herself.

She raised her right hand and sent out two balls of flames, both landing on two of the torches closest to her. Quickly, she raised her left hand and threw it in an arc, sending two more balls flying through the air to their perches in the second row, another ten feet away from her. Two to go.

Galdinia brought her hands back in front of her, pressing her fingers together. Her eyes focused on the two torches furthest away; they were positioned in line with the others that were now on fire, so Galdinia carefully readjusted her stance to get a better view of each of them. She felt the pressure of the blade in her side as she moved. Her final two targets were at least forty feet from her. The flickering flames from the already lit torches cast dancing shadows over the last two. She hadn't yet successfully landed these marks in this training session, as she struggled to send the flames with both accuracy and enough fervour to set the torches alight.

Once again, Galdinia felt the sword on her training leathers and tried to concentrate on how she felt during the attack; the betrayal-fuelled rage that had allowed her to set her beloved library on fire, the desperation to save her home, the internal demand to find Drystan alive and well. The onslaught of the enemy soldiers had not deterred her rampage. It spurred her on, and she could still hear their screams of pain echoing in her mind. Galdinia scrunched up her eyes in protest, trying to block out the ghostly cries and distinctly metallic smell of blood that lingered in her memory.

Instead, she focused in on the anger she'd felt, remembering how Valah had made her feel in the library: inadequate, powerless, and juvenile. The devilish woman's scornful words about her father scratched in her ears, and Galdinia felt them as close as the whispers in the chasm beyond the Northern Gates. She could see the sheer satisfaction on Valah's face when she declared Bentley one of her allies and not the suitor he had claimed to be. The curl of Valah's lips and the shadows in her eyes as she shared Bentley's betrayal would be imprinted on Galdinia's mind forever. The thought of him set Galdinia's veins alight.

Bentley.

Galdinia's eyelids snapped open, and she homed in on the torches. With one swift movement, she threw her arms out at her sides, sending two fiery orbs through the air, twisting and weaving between the other torches. They collided with her targets in an explosion of crackling light, her flames now sitting atop every second torch.

"Well done," Ilyon said, the pressure of the sword relinquishing as he sheathed it at his hip once again.

Galdinia smiled at the sight of her achievement, finding solace in the six flames that she had landed safely. Another bead of sweat trickled down her back as she moved to sit along the benches at the side of the room, still watching her handiwork flicker.

"Those early training sessions are paying off," Ilyon said as he came to stand beside Galdinia, his usually firm features softening slightly as their training came to an end. "You're learning quickly."

"You were right about the need for preparation, though," Galdinia noted, wiping the back of her hand across her brow. "I don't imagine I would have been able to do half of what I did in the attack without your lessons. Finding my connection with the flames was almost easy. Controlling it, on the other hand…"

She trailed off, thinking of the pressure in her chest she'd felt when she pulled the balls of flames from the Northern Gates. That was the last moment she saw Drystan, and he had seen her with her gift. Did he know that she was going to fight for him? Did he know that she would do everything in her power to rescue him?

"Again, you're learning quickly. We will continue our training, though. Should we face our enemy again, I need you to be prepared."

Galdinia had every intention of facing Valah once again, and only once. She would bring that woman to her knees for all she had done to Elderguard. Galdinia tried not to imagine what she may be doing to Drystan right now. She couldn't let her mind wander to those dark imaginings where her deepest fears festered.

"I will be," Galdinia said, looking up at her captain, the edge of a smile flickering over his lips. "We all will be."

Ilyon turned and went about tidying up the space, extinguishing the flames, and rearranging the torches along the edge of the room. As he did, Galdinia reached into the pocket of her trousers and pulled out a piece of parchment. It was barely larger than her palm and had been folded and unfolded so many times that it practically fell open as it lay in her fingers. The day before, a silky black raven had delivered this letter to the castle. It was rolled up neatly and was tied to the bird's leg with red twine, not a crease in sight.

The raven had found Galdinia on the castle terrace. It landed on the bannister and stared at her, its eyes harsh pools of ink. The young queen approached the bird carefully, then untied the parchment and stepped back from it quickly. In seconds it flew away, beyond the walls of the castle towards the west. The then-pristine letter was simple.

You have until the next new moon to relinquish my crown before I suck the air from his lungs.

A cry had escaped Galdinia's lips as she read Valah's note, the words bombarding her mind with a painful image: Drystan, lying on the ground, eyes wide, lips white, chest still. The reality of watching Valah inflict this punishment on someone was all too familiar to Galdinia, and it wasn't difficult to place Drystan's figure over her uncle's,

Draven, who had fallen victim to Valah's fury and life-extinguishing gift. This vision had infiltrated Galdinia's subconscious as she slept, and each night she felt powerless to stop it. She knew there was only one way to erase the phantom image from her mind: rescue Drystan.

Since she received the note, Galdinia had reread the letter dozens of times, always keeping it on her person, a tiny fragment of a connection to Drystan. She prayed that air continued to flow through his body each time her eyes scanned the words.

By way of response, she called for a Syndicate meeting, which would occur in mere hours in her throne room. It would be the first time she held court as queen. The next new moon was less than four weeks away, and they needed a plan of attack. No one knew if Valah was in the Wetlands or in hiding elsewhere, and Galdinia wondered if Drystan was with her or if he was being kept somewhere remote. There was only one person that Galdinia thought might have some idea of where she may find Drystan, but she had not yet approached him.

Galdinia's best friend, Neryda, had convinced her that speaking with Bentley would not bring about any good. Neryda doubted that Galdinia would leave Bentley's cell without his blood on her hands, and while the queen wouldn't disregard that suggestion completely, she herself didn't even know exactly what she wanted to say to him after he was captured. It had been six days since she'd seen him, and she had hoped that this made him stew in fear and questions. Was he expecting her to visit him? Was he waiting to be brought out of his cell and executed in the square at any moment?

With hundreds of questions but no real sense of direction in her mind, Galdinia had resolved that it would be foolish not to question him about Valah, so she would start there.

As she sat in the cool of the basement, her face finally drying off and her core temperature lowering, she folded up the paper and put it in her pocket again.

"I want to see him," she said simply, looking at Ilyon as he moved the last of the torches from the centre of the room. His dark eyes became hard again as he stared at her, the harsh lines of his jaw and slicked back black hair framing his concerned expression.

"I'm not sure that's a good idea, Your Highness."

"Why not?" Galdinia asked, her brow creasing into a frown. "Are you afraid that I can't protect myself against him? I think I've proven that I can."

Now was not the time for Ilyon to lose his confidence in Galdinia.

"Aside from the fact that there aren't any flames in his vicinity and he is under constant guard by two powerful Water Weavers, I'm more concerned about what you may do to him." Galdinia raised her eyebrows at her captain. "He is a valuable prisoner, and we need him to stay that way."

"Exactly," Galdinia countered as Ilyon approached her. "Who better to squeeze out information from him than the person he promised to love?"

Ilyon pondered this before replying. "He manipulated you, Your Highness. He manipulated all of us. I don't imagine he will be quick to spill Valah's secrets."

"All I'm asking for is a few minutes with him," Galdinia said, standing to her feet and walking to her crown that was still perched at the end of the bench. "I need some indication of his mindset before court with the Syndicate."

Galdinia picked up her crown and placed it on her head before pulling her twist of hair loose, letting it cascade down her shoulders and back. Aside from during her training sessions, Galdinia refused to be seen outside of the castle walls without her crown. She'd gone long enough without it; she wouldn't squander her opportunities to wear it now.

"I'd prefer not to order you to take me to see him, Captain," Galdinia said as she turned to face Ilyon once again. "But we both know that I have no problem doing that if I need to."

On the opposite side of the barracks, beyond the central training yard and at the end of a guarded hallway, sat a staircase similar to the one that led them to the underground training rooms. This one was accessed through a heavyset iron door, which was guarded by two soldiers who both held a key that allowed access. At the sight of their queen and captain, they unlocked the door and stepped aside.

Upon entry at the top of the landing, Ilyon took hold of a lantern that hung on the wall. Its green-blue glow lit their way down the spiral staircase that seemed a bottomless pit of darkness beneath them— Galdinia couldn't see further than a handful of steps in front of them.

"It's a form of Peacelight," Ilyon explained, referring to the lantern. "High Priestess Saena lends us some light when necessary."

"You mean for when you have a Fire Flourisher in your cells?"

"Exactly."

"How is she keeping it alight from so far away?"

"The priestesses take shifts maintaining the light."

"From the Isle of Crystal?"

"They're more powerful than you may realise, Your Highness."

Galdinia had always thought that those of royalty held the most power in the kingdom. Perhaps she was wrong.

Finally, Ilyon stepped down onto the basement floor and walked along another hallway, still illuminating their way with the enchanting light. They encountered yet another heavily guarded door, which they were allowed entry through immediately. Ilyon left the lantern at this door before they stepped through into a chamber that was lit by more lanterns that emanated a similar glow.

Galdinia had never been in Elderguard's prison before. Aside from not being allowed in the barracks at all as a child, she had no reason to ever come down to this part of the city. Had she lived in some false hope that Elderguard never had prisoners? Perhaps. But as she walked through the chamber, she had to remind herself that she was queen of this room, just as much as she was in the castle above ground; this was not a moment for her to lose her wits.

The room was lined with heavy doors, and soldiers of the Royal Guard paced up and down the room, bowing as they passed their queen and captain. Galdinia counted at least thirty cell doors as they walked through the chamber. There seemed to be hallways leading off in all directions, burrowing deep and wide beneath not only the barracks, but also deeper below Elderguard. Ilyon reported that the Royal Guard had captured upwards of two hundred prisoners after the attack on the capital, so Galdinia could only imagine how many cells lay within the prison.

Ilyon led Galdinia to the end of the room, and they turned down a smaller chamber. This one held only five doors. The one at the end of the room was guarded by another two soldiers. Although she felt entirely safe with Ilyon by her side and guards stationed throughout the underground stronghold, the warning of worry that crawled up the back of her neck at the thought of stepping into a windowless room with Bentley, without access to her gift, could not be ignored. Just days earlier she had been in a very similar situation, though ignorant to the circumstances that awaited her behind the castle library's door. Now she was entering such a space willingly.

Reminding herself of the crown that now lay on her head and the lethal nature with which Ilyon could swing a sword—or more importantly, hone his gift as a Water Weaver—set her mind at ease.

"I will be right outside the door," Ilyon said, as though reading Galdinia's thoughts. His face held a shadow of concern as he spoke. "If I get even a whiff of danger, I will be removing you from the cell, understood?"

"Understood," Galdinia said, nodding. "Even if I'm the cause of said danger?"

"In that case, especially so," Ilyon said, looking across at Galdinia with narrowed eyes. "You don't want that blood on your hands."

Perhaps I do, Galdinia thought.

They walked towards the guards, who bowed to Galdinia and then promptly saluted their captain.

"Soldiers," Ilyon said firmly, "anything to report on the prisoner?"

Galdinia noted the small, frosted glass window in the door and stepped forward between the soldiers to look through it.

"Nothing out of the ordinary, Captain," one of the soldiers replied. "He has been eating every meal, and we haven't heard anything from him."

Through the cloudy pane of glass, Galdinia could just make out Bentley, who was perched on the edge of his bed across the room. His hands and wrists were chained to the ground between his feet. He looked up at her. Galdinia didn't know if he could see her clearly in the dim light and murky glass, but she felt her insides recoil as he faced her.

"Very well," Ilyon replied to the soldiers. "Queen Galdinia is going to speak with the prisoner."

Galdinia did not look away from Bentley as the soldiers unlocked the door. They pushed it open, and she stepped into the cell.

3

If there was ever a time for Galdinia to feel secure about her new title, this was it. Without the glass between them to cloud her vision of him, Galdinia was struck by just how dishevelled Bentley appeared. His blonde hair fell flat against his scalp, lacking its usual buoyant volume. He was wearing a light-coloured under-shirt that was ripped at his forearms, and his trousers were made of a brown, scratchy-looking material. His fingernails were covered in dirt, and his wrists were bandaged beneath the manacles that shackled his arms to his ankles; one bandage ran up his right fore-arm, covering the spot Galdinia had burnt him in the library. His skin appeared lightly singed in areas, and a still-healing cut ran along his neck. It seemed he hadn't bathed since the battle, as he was covered in soot and smelled like he'd been rolling around in days-old kitchen waste.

And yet, despite all this, his bright eyes cut through his hopeless exterior. They seemed to be the only remaining feature of him that outlived the battle. His watchful eyes quietly reminded Galdinia of the moments in which she'd been so easily lured in by him: by the docks, in the ballroom, in the gardens, on the terrace.

Galdinia hated that.

Bentley's expression communicated very little as the door closed behind her, though Galdinia thought she detected an element of surprise in his face. Or perhaps it was fear.

Neither of them said anything for a long time as Galdinia stood just inside the doorway, arms firmly crossed over her chest, her gaze burning into his. Instinctively, her body searched for a flame, wishing to feel the comforting warmth of fire. She felt naked and vulnerable without her element close by, and it was thanks to this man that she couldn't hold one now. She tried not to focus on how they shared this gift, a similarity between them that made her feel unbalanced, crooked.

For days, Galdinia had imagined herself barging through this door and doing any number of things: yelling at him, punching him in the nose, sending a wall of flame in his direction. But now that she was standing in front of him, she didn't want to do any of that, and she started to question why she'd come here at all.

Then, before she could stop herself, one word came tumbling from her mouth. "Why?"

Galdinia wasn't sure if Bentley heard her as he merely continued to stare, his elbows on his knees, casually observing the new queen. She felt the weight of her crown atop her head, and she hoped it made him feel restless.

After a few long seconds, he finally replied. "Because I didn't have a choice." His voice was hoarse and pained, as though he hadn't had a sip of water in days. Perhaps he hadn't.

Galdinia tightened her eyes on Bentley, not expecting this response.

He took this as his cue to elaborate. "My parents were desperate for a way to escape the obscurity they were living in." He looked away from her, his gaze trailing along the floor. "My family barely survived the aftermath of the Battle of the Midlands, and they felt abandoned by Elderguard despite their loyalty to the crown. When they heard of another that was vying for the throne, they found a glimpse of hope. That's when they met Va—her."

Galdinia practically snarled at the hint of Valah's name.

Bentley caught himself and kept speaking. "She promised a fairer world order and a throne that would protect all its citizens. She made it sound so easy."

"And how did you leading me to my death factor into this?" Galdinia asked, her voice hot.

"When the Syndicate started looking for suitors for you, she took it as an opportunity for an easy way in. My parents quickly agreed to her plan to send me as a suitor. Sending their son into the hands of their enemy paled in the shadow of promised riches and glory." As Bentley spoke, Galdinia glared down at him, so angry with herself that she'd been deceived by this man. "I didn't think she would abandon me so immediately, though. I soon realised that I was foolish to trust her, but it was too late by that point."

No, no, no, Galdinia thought. *You don't get to be the victim.*

"Of course she left me behind the minute I wasn't of use to her anymore," Bentley said with a shrug, sitting up straight and looking at Galdinia again. His voice had an air of helplessness. "I suppose I'm getting what I deserve, but you knew this would happen to me, didn't you? The moment Valah made her plan clear, you knew I didn't have long left."

He let out a rasp of a laugh, the sound of it scratching through the cool air. It didn't emanate the bell tone Galdinia was used to hearing from him, and it unnerved her. Was this a reflection of his current physical situation, or was she just now seeing the real Bentley?

"I was following my parents' wishes—well, their orders, I suppose. I believed what they said about you, your father, and Elderguard, that Elderwins are self-serving, arrogant, and inconsiderate. The more time I spent with you, the quicker their lies unravelled, though. I trusted them, and I wanted to help." Bentley's voice was even as he spoke. "So that's why. That's why I did it. And I'm sorry."

Again, Galdinia glowered at him, his words catching her off guard, yet searing through her like a branding iron.

"You're sorry?" Galdinia asked tempestuously. "You can't possibly think that I'll forgive you after this."

"No, of course I don't," Bentley said, his tone direct and candid. "I just need you to know that my objective was not to hurt you. I didn't even know you when my family struck this deal… not who you really were, at least."

Galdinia looked upon the man who had betrayed her, the man who had walked her to her intended death. He knew what the consequences were, and yet he lured her in, seduced her, and held her hand as he led her to her enemy.

"You didn't *mean* to hurt me?" Galdinia was incredulous, her eyes searching his for more answers. "What exactly did you think would happen when you took me to Valah? I was lucky to get out of the library with my life."

"I said that it wasn't my objective to hurt you." Bentley seemed to steel himself before he continued. "Of course I knew there would be potentially fatal repercussions, but that was not my goal. This was a way to help my family. It was a gateway out of the scarcity we had been living in, but I can't expect you to understand that."

"I understand desperation, Bentley, I really do. I may not have experienced it the same way you have, but I'm no stranger to it." Galdinia's face warmed as she thought of the decisions she'd had to consider in the previous week, as well as the apex of her pain and anger that she'd felt in the Crystal Temple on the Sixth Day. "And I would never put someone else's life—thousands of lives—in jeopardy for my own selfish gain."

Bentley's eyes bore into hers. Galdinia could see a mix of guilt and pain within them. She decided that she needed to change the subject; she couldn't guarantee she'd be able to restrain herself against harming him if she had to keep listening to him pity himself.

"Where is she now?"

Bentley looked taken aback by the sudden shift in topic. "Who, Valah? In the Wetlands, I suppose."

"You suppose?"

"I'm not sure if you've been listening to me, but she left me for dead in that burning library. She didn't tell me about this other plan with Dryst—"

"Don't say his name," Galdinia hissed, glaring at Bentley. "So the only arrangement that she told you about was taking the throne?"

"That's right. As far as I was aware, that was the only outcome she would accept. She didn't make me privy to any contingency plans."

"Where in the Wetlands does she live?"

Bentley once again looked surprised by Galdinia's line of questioning. Instead of giving her an answer, he simply asked, "You're not planning on going to her, are you?"

"Of course I am."

Bentley let out another pained laugh, shaking his head. "You've got to be kidding." When he realised that she wasn't joking, Bentley quickly added, "It'll be your funeral."

"I've fought her off before," Galdinia said simply.

"And she won't let you get away again."

"How can you be so sure?"

"The only reason I'm still breathing right now is because she thought the library had fallen down on top of me the minute she fled the flames. You saw what she did to your uncle." Galdinia was confronted with the mental image of Draven writhing on the floor, the oxygen being ripped from his lungs by Valah's lethal gift. "If he and I were her supposed allies, I can't imagine she'd allow you, her greatest enemy, to go free again. She's ruthless, Galdinia, and so is her army."

Hearing her own name on his lips caught her off guard. He might not be the jovial young man she had laughed with on the terrace or danced with at the feast, but the glint in his eye still shimmered. The air he carried when he made her smile was still evident, and she could feel it when he said her name.

"And why do you care if I get out alive? After everything that's happened to you, surely you'll be glad to see me in my grave." Galdinia hurled the words at him from across the dim room. As if by habit, Bentley reached up both hands and awkwardly ran them through his greasy hair, his movement restricted with the chains that kept him attached to the floor.

"Perhaps I don't want to see you dead," he said with a sigh, averting his eyes as he spoke. "Perhaps what happened over the last week changed how I felt… about you."

Galdinia glared at him.

"No," she hissed, bringing her hands to her sides in fists as a darkness rolled over her.

She tried to feel for any sign of a flame, her instincts telling her to protect herself immediately. How could he possibly suggest that he cared for her? How foolish did he think she was to believe such a lie? Her heart raced, and she needed the fire and its comforting warmth. Her senses stretched out as she searched for the familiar heat. It was useless. There wasn't a lick of warmth in the air beneath the barracks.

"There's no fire," Bentley said, looking from her face to her clenched hands and back again. "Trust me, I've tried."

Acting on impulse, Galdinia strode forward, taking Bentley by surprise. She slammed a foot down on the chains that lay on the floor, creating another anchor. This pulled Bentley's arms tight to his knees, Galdinia's foot taking any extra slack that he'd had at his disposal. Her left hand found his throat quickly, and her right hand leaned against one of his imprisoned wrists, keeping him firm on the stretcher. Bentley's eyes widened at her movement, but he didn't fight against her, seemingly stunned frozen.

"There's no way you actually care about me," Galdinia said fiercely, her eyes ablaze, her hand tight around his neck. "Don't think you can lure me back in like that. What we had meant nothing."

"Why do you think I let you get away in the library?" Bentley winced as her grip tightened in warning. "I know it's hard to believe, Princess, but I am in fact capable of emotion."

"I'm the queen now, you miserable traitor." Galdinia didn't need flames in her hands; her words were fire enough. "And I will not be sucked in by you again. I'm not the fool you and Valah made me out to be."

"Perhaps there's a reason it was so easy to believe me," Bentley wheezed. "Because it was true."

Bentley's words cut through Galdinia, and she squeezed his throat firmer. He let out a strained breath, and she could feel the tightening sinews and muscles in his neck.

"Then why would you try to have me killed?" Galdinia asked, teeth bared.

"I already—" Bentley's voice strained against the pressure of her hand. "I already told you. I didn't have a—a choice. That doesn't mean I don't regret it. It doesn't—change how I feel."

Galdinia could feel her blood rising up her neck, her anger manifesting within her skin as she grasped his throat, feeling his thundering pulse in her fingertips.

She could do it now, she knew she could. With a little more pressure, she could end his life in a matter of seconds. It would be easier knowing someone so deceptive was no longer breathing. As his words rang in her ears, taunting her, trying to make her believe that he truly cared about her, she seriously considered it. After an intense few seconds of staring into his reddening face and watery eyes, Galdinia relinquished his neck and stepped back off his chains.

Bentley coughed violently, taking in rough breaths. Galdinia faced the door and raised her hand to knock.

"You know you won't be able to get into the Wetlands without an attack," Bentley croaked, his voice strained and his breaths ragged. Galdinia's hand remained suspended in the air. "Her army has been weakened, but so has yours." Galdinia didn't reply. She merely looked over her shoulder at him as he heaved in air. "You need someone to get you in, beyond her patrolling soldiers and into the heart of the Wetlands."

Galdinia could hardly believe what he was suggesting—he thought he could be the person to take her to the Wetlands. "You said she doesn't care about you. You said she left you for dead."

"But if I show up at her door, hell-bent on getting my revenge on the crown that I had lured in so easily, she might very well take a powerful Fire Flourisher if she thinks she can have her way."

"There's no way she will believe you."

"She doesn't have to," he said, leaning forward on his knees once again, one hand rubbing his neck, his voice still hoarse. "It would be a fine distraction, though, while your armies surrounded her. And if my parents are still loyal to her, then I certainly stand a chance."

The tone of his voice was easy, but Galdinia saw a desperation in his eyes.

"So I'll follow you, once again, into Valah's clutches so you can have her finish the job," Galdinia said, glaring at Bentley from the corner of her eye. "Do you really expect me to trust you again?"

"You and I both know that captain of yours would lop my head off without a second thought," Bentley said. "You don't really think I have a leg to stand on in order to betray you, do you?"

"I don't know, Bentley," Galdinia said, rapping her knuckles on the door. "It would seem I don't actually know anything about you, and I simply don't care to."

The door of the cell swung open, and Galdinia stepped back out into the hallway without another glance in Bentley's direction. The door slammed with a thud behind her, the heavy bolts of its locks echoing through the chamber.

Galdinia closed her eyes as she stood in the hallway, regaining her breath, her composure, and her sense of self. Bentley admitting his lasting feelings for her—whether true or fabricated—had caught her off guard. Upon entering the cell, she thought he may have laughed in her face or ignored her or even tried to kill her himself, but never in her imaginings could she have predicted what he'd said. And had she really responded by threatening to strangle him with her bare hands? All kinds of anger and confusion flooded her mind, drawing a distinct pain to her temples.

"Your Highness?"

Ilyon's low voice broke Galdinia's reverie, and she opened her eyes.

"I'm fine," Galdinia replied, knowing the question hidden beneath his words.

"Are you sure?"

Galdinia turned to face her captain, inhaling and exhaling slowly. "Yes, Captain," she replied, her jaw tight. "I have to prepare for court, so we best leave."

Ilyon watched his queen carefully, his eyes scrutinising, boring into her face, seeking more information than she was willing to share. Galdinia turned away from his gaze and walked down the hallway before he could ask her any more questions.

4

After bathing herself and changing into attire suitable for court, Galdinia finally felt as though she'd reclaimed some semblance of peace. The pain in her temples remained, but her heart had settled, and she felt she could breathe evenly again. Being surrounded, once again, by her element also helped to set her at ease.

Once she left her rooms, Galdinia decided to take a detour on her way to the throne room. After winding through the western wing of the castle, she stepped into her once inviting sanctuary for the first time since the attack on Elderguard. The library was full of black ash and tainted with the hazy smell of smoke. She walked over dozens of books that were barely holding their shape in their blackened state. The smell of the fire was still prevalent, the scent seared deep into the walls. The great oak table that once stood in the centre of the room had collapsed on two of its burnt legs, while the rest of the piece of furniture lay awkwardly on top, resembling a horse that had stumbled mid-gallop.

While some of the books on the highest shelves of the library were still intact, the majority of the Elderwin literature collection had been burnt to a crisp, now strewn on the ground at the queen's feet. She knew much of the damage was her fault, as she had used the fire her uncle had started to protect herself, and now, after finally facing the damage, a deep pit of grief and guilt opened within her.

Who else would be affected by the state of the library, though? Galdinia was the only Elderwin left alive—aside from her mutinous aunt—so the burned collection belonged to her alone. Her grandparents had spent decades collecting and archiving many of the books in the library, and now that most were ash, she felt her connection with these people she never met sever even further. It was the books her father had gifted her over the many years, which he often brought back from his travels, that she was grieving. And, more importantly, the memories they held.

Glancing across the room, she saw the space in front of the fireplace where she, Neryda, and Drystan often found themselves studying—or distracting each other from such study—had also given way to a charred rug, collapsed armchair, and crumbled books.

Galdinia's heart hung heavy in her chest. So many memories had gone up in flames in her desperate attempt to save her own life.

As she walked through the room, inspecting the damage, she heard the crunch of coals by the library door.

Galdinia turned to see her best friend, Neryda Fleur, step into the room. She was lit by the warm light of the corridor behind her, illuminating her deep russet curls that trailed over her golden-brown shoulders.

After the battle, Neryda and her family had made it back to shore after fleeing to the sea with a number of other noble families. When the girls reunited later that night, they both broke down in tears, holding each other close and heaving into one another's shoulders. They had both been so frightened to lose each other that to have their safety confirmed let loose the emotional weight of their fears.

When she learned of her best friend's gift, Neryda began to cry all over again. They wept and laughed, and Neryda squeezed Galdinia tight. After the loss Galdinia had experienced that week—from her father's passing to Drystan's capture—she didn't want to let go of Neryda. Galdinia promptly insisted on Neryda staying in the castle with her again, to which she gladly obliged. These two friends had forged a sisterhood over many years, and neither could afford to lose the other.

"It's a bit bleak in here," Neryda noted, stepping into the library somewhat haphazardly. She cradled a mug of tea in her hands, presumably making her way from the kitchens.

"That's one word for it," Galdinia said with a short, pained laugh; Neryda could make any painful situation light, even in the midst of tragedy.

"Your attendants are going to have a year's worth of work just trying to clean this up," Neryda said, looking around the room.

Cleaning up the destruction I caused, Galdinia reminded herself. The thought of starting another fire anywhere near this room made her feel unsteady, so she crossed her arms, tucking her hands into her sides.

"I should be the one to clean it," Galdinia mused, looking from the charred fireplace to another crumpled armchair.

"Gal, this isn't your fault," Neryda said quickly, coming to stand by her friend, placing a warm hand on her shoulder. "You didn't start this fire."

"But I perpetuated it."

"To save your life," Neryda added, looking pointedly at her friend. "You can't possibly blame yourself for this. You did what had to be done."

Galdinia considered everything else that she'd had to do in order to save her life and the lives of her citizens. She could hear the pained cries of the enemy soldiers as she sent bursts of fire into their chests. She felt the warmth of a dying soldier's blood soak into her sleeve at her elbow as he took his last breath after trying to take her own. If it weren't for her, the city wouldn't be in such disarray. If it weren't for her, Valah, her aunt, and her uncle would never have attacked. And Drystan would be here with her now.

"How was training this morning?" Neryda asked.

"Good," Galdinia replied simply, looking back to her friend. "I'm starting to find some precision in my attacks, which is encouraging. I had to do it with a sword trained on my side, but it was effective."

Neryda raised a brow of concern at Galdinia as she sipped her tea.

"Ilyon thought it would help to put me in the same mindset I was in during the attack. He said that if I could achieve that level of accuracy in a battle, then I could do it again."

"That feels a bit... callous," Neryda said with wide eyes.

"Well, it worked," Galdinia said, a small smile growing over her lips. The sense of power and accomplishment she had felt at the end of their training session had remained, even after her encounter with Bentley.

After a moment's silence, Galdinia said, "I went to see him after training today."

Neryda's head snapped to face her friend. "You what?"

"Bentley. I went to see him." Galdinia spoke so casually, as though she'd said she had visited an old friend.

Neryda looked like she was going to throw up. "Why? What happened? What did you say?"

"Not too much; I wrapped my hands around his throat, for one."

"Figuratively?"

"No, very much literally," Galdinia said, almost indifferent. Was she trying to convince herself that it was a mere triviality?

Neryda let out a harsh laugh.

"Heavens, I wish I could have seen that," Neryda said, shaking her head in disbelief.

"He told me he still cares about me, so I thought it best to warn him that that kind of sentiment is not welcome around me."

"He said *what*?"

"That he cares about me. That his feelings for me were real and perhaps he didn't hate me as much as I may have assumed."

"What a disgusting pig."

"Hence the choking," Galdinia replied, a small smirk pulling at her lip. "He also told me that he could get me into Valah's manor."

Neryda took pause and stared at Galdinia, a frown settling into her brow. "Why in the heavens would you want to go to the Wetlands?"

Galdinia looked taken aback; was it not obvious? "You know exactly why."

"To save Drystan?" Neryda asked, and Galdinia replied with a short nod, her raised eyebrows telling Neryda how obvious that fact was. "Gal, you can't do that."

"Shall I let him rot in the Wetlands then?" Galdinia asked, incredulous.

"Of course not, but you can't go wandering around Valah's home."

"What do you suggest I do then? Sit back and wait for Valah to deliver him to Elderguard and tell me I've won? That isn't going to happen."

"I certainly don't think the Queen of Crysterra should be walking into her enemy's territory," Neryda said defensively. "You can't possibly think that's a good idea."

"Why not?" Galdinia asked.

"Because you will be risking your life to save one person."

Galdinia winced against Neryda's words and said, hushed, "Ner."

How could Neryda suggest that Drystan was just some other solider?

"I didn't mean it like that," Neryda said quickly, shaking her head so as to organise her thoughts. "He's my friend too, Gal. I want him back as much as you do. But you're the queen now. You can't go waltzing into the homes of your enemies. You need to think about the greater good."

"I am thinking about the greater good," Galdinia retorted, bringing her hands down by her sides instinctively. "If I don't give up my crown in the next twenty-four days, Valah will murder Drystan. We know I can't do that, so we have to find a way of getting him out. And either way, she's going to come for me, so I might as well beat her to it."

"But what if...?" Neryda scrunched up her nose as she trailed off, looking as though she was deciding whether she should say her next words.

"What?" Galdinia pushed, staring at her friend with a furrowed brow.

Neryda sighed before continuing. "What if... you don't save him?" Neryda's words hung in the air before them like a foul smell. "If you engage in a conflict with Valah again, you'll risk the lives of countless soldiers and civilians, both here and across the country."

"So you're suggesting I should let Valah kill him?" Galdinia asked in disbelief.

"When you say it like that—"

"There's no other way to say it!" Galdinia could feel the heat rising in her chest. Her hands started to yearn for the flames that danced in the lanterns set around the room.

"Gal, I love Drystan. He's like my brother. Saving him should be a top priority of the crown." Neryda tried to speak evenly, keeping her voice soft. "But you need to consider the greater implications of this. There's got to be a safe way to rescue him that doesn't involve you forgoing the crown or unnecessary bloodshed."

"So we'll find a way," Galdinia said, pained.

"We will," Neryda said, nodding in agreement. "But you've got to worry about the rest of the kingdom as well, not just Drystan."

"I am, Neryda," Galdinia replied quickly with a frown. "That's all I've ever been doing."

Neryda's words hurt Galdinia more than they should have. The suggestion that she was being selfish and hadn't considered the fate of her kingdom felt like a punch to the gut. She sensed that all-too-familiar feeling of inadequacy, as though she were a child trying to make an adult's decision. A pressure started to rise in her chest, the thick taste of ash coating her throat.

"I need to get some fresh air," Galdinia said hurriedly, turning to walk towards the library door.

"Gal—"

"And I'm due in court with the Syndicate shortly," Galdinia cut in.

"We're going to save him," Neryda said, drawing her friend's attention back to the charcoal room behind her.

"I know that, Neryda," Galdinia said bluntly. "I'm the queen, and *I* will save him."

With that, she turned out the door and strode down the long hallway away from her best friend.

5

GALDINIA SAT ON HER THRONE FOR THE FIRST TIME SINCE BECOMING queen. Although it felt right and natural to be sitting in what was, until very recently, her father's throne, she couldn't suppress the quick sensation of a shiver that climbed up her spine as she laid her bare arms on the armrests. The delicate and intricately woven golden vines spread out from where she sat, making it appear as though she were almost glowing. She sat up straight, poised with her crown on her head, looking across the throne room.

The Syndicate members sat in their usual seats before their new queen. Governor Ryden Calcutter and Captain Ilyon were front and centre as Galdinia's second- and third-in-command. High Priestess Saena was beside the governor, her easy elegance practically radiating as she sat amongst those in otherwise dull dress clothes. The high priestess wore delicate robes of white, which trailed along the dark brown skin of her arms and pooled at her feet; Galdinia thought she practically personified her role as the most powerful Light Lender in Crysterra. The other members of the Syndicate looked up at their queen with a mixed array of emotions; some were obviously pleased with her crowning, while others appeared to still be sceptical of her place on the dais.

"Thank you for joining me for my first court as queen, Crysterra

Syndicate." Galdinia addressed her governing body warmly, but her expression remained firm as she sought to channel the air of confidence her father once held. "It has been a week since we were attacked by a savage enemy, and while I appreciate the efforts that have been taken to begin to restore the damages made to our city—both physical and emotional—it is time that we regroup and set our course for the future."

No one else spoke; many nodded, others stared at their queen. Galdinia steeled herself before continuing.

"As you know, Valah Pyrin continues to set her sights on obtaining the Elderwin crown, which is, put simply, unwise on her behalf. Rest assured, I will not give up my crown so easily to such a woman." Galdinia considered her words for a moment before adding, "I will not give up my crown for anything."

This elicited a smile from many in the room. Ilyon's face, however, remained as solid as sandstone. He was as difficult to read as ever.

"With that said, she has taken one of our own, and so we have two priorities that we must contemplate in order to set our plans moving forward: we must rescue our soldier from the Wetlands and protect the capital from Valah." Galdinia was careful not to utter Drystan's name; even at the thought of him, she felt an ache in her chest, and after her interaction with Neryda in the library, she didn't know what response may befall her if she said his name again. Regardless, her resolve had not changed: he had been captured because of her, and she would return him home safely at any cost.

"By achieving these priorities, I believe we will be able to neutralise the threat from the west. Taking Valah as our prisoner will be our first priority, but if it came to a battle, I would not fear causing bloodshed. With Valah out of the picture, I will be able to rule a unified kingdom and bring it back to its former glory."

"Your Majesty." A voice broke through the momentary silence, and a Syndicate member in the second row stood to his feet. Serril Oryn, Master of Coin, awaited the queen's response before continuing.

"Yes, Serril?" Galdinia said with a bow of her head.

"I wonder, Your Highness, what was made of your aunt after the attack. Is she another threat we must factor in?"

Galdinia had not thought much of Edana after the battle. Draven's body was not found in the aftermath of the attack, nor was Edana's. Galdinia assumed that Draven's body had been burnt with the kindling of her library, and she had not been made aware of what happened to her aunt. Although she was a powerful Water Weaver and likely still hell-bent on taking the crown, Galdinia had not heard anything from her or her allies. Did she flee safely from Elderguard back to her home in the Shadowed Coast? Or was she lying at the bottom of the sea?

"Edana was not found, dead or alive, so we must assume she lives until we can confirm her whereabouts," Galdinia said thoughtfully. "We will need to send informants to the Shadowed Coast in order to secure that information and to further inform our decisions."

Serril nodded and sat down again.

"While we send for information from the Shadowed Coast," Galdinia continued, "I suggest that we increase our resources in rebuilding the outer walls of our city, fortifying it stronger than it was before, in case of another attempted attack before we can vanquish Valah ourselves. In the meantime, we can begin planning our rescue in the Wetlands. Valah has given us until the next new moon, so we will make the most of this time. I can foresee myself and a select group of soldiers infiltrating Valah's walls before the end of next week."

A hum of murmurs buzzed in the room as frowns were set in place and heads shook. Galdinia had anticipated such a response.

She cleared her throat, and in the moments of silence that followed, Governor Ryden took this as his opportunity to stand to his feet and address the queen.

"Your Highness," he said with a bow.

Galdinia had been, if she was honest, avoiding the governor for the last five days. The day after her coronation, Galdinia threw herself into training with Ilyon. She was desperate to put her gift into practice, and she yearned to start proving herself as the true protector of the crown that she was. She wasn't angry with her governor, per se, but she couldn't vanquish a simmering feeling of hostility when she was in his presence.

At the start of the Week of Mourning, he had promised to protect her, ensuring that the Syndicate would do right by her as they prepared for her coronation. She had agreed to their terms about finding a suitor to legitimise her on the Seventh Day, and then, just an hour before she was given her gift, Ryden informed her that the Syndicate had gone back on their word. They didn't think she was good enough to rule, and a suitor wouldn't change that. She had gone as far as to almost accept the proposal of an unknown traitor—someone the Syndicate had presented to her—in order to stay within the bounds of their wishes. She was sick of abiding by their rules and laws, and she couldn't help but hold some contempt for the man who led the governing body.

For that reason, she hadn't felt compelled to speak to Ryden, so she rose before the sun and arrived back at the castle after sundown. Although Ryden requested an audience with her, she declined and settled on speaking to him in court. She'd struggled at the thought of facing him, almost predicting how he would respond to her priority of rescuing Drystan. Now that they were face-to-face again after multiple days, Galdinia inhaled a deep breath and addressed him, unable to shake the air of contempt that she felt towards him.

"Yes, Governor?"

"Firstly, as this is your first court as queen, I humbly welcome you to your esteemed position." He bowed briefly, his eyes not leaving Galdinia as he looked up at her from beneath his silver eyebrows. "Secondly, as your governor, I appreciate your direct and straightforward approach to your future planning." Although he was respectful in his tone, Galdinia could sense the approach of an interjection. "However, we cannot send our newly crowned queen into the clutches of our greatest living enemy. It would be, respectfully, a fool's errand."

"I appreciate your thoughts, Governor," Galdinia said easily, keeping her hands perched on the armrests of her throne, trying to ignore the tingling in her fingertips as they yearned for the fire in the torches around the throne room. "But respectfully, I disagree." The governor went to speak again, but Galdinia continued, cutting him off. "The last place Valah would expect me to be right now is the Wetlands. As far as I see it, she is waiting on two scenarios: I sit right here and wait for her to attack once again with a larger army. Or I attack her with my own forces, surrounding her and forcing her to surrender. Unfortunately, both of these scenarios will see the loss of our captured soldier, which is not an option for me. Therefore, by the element of surprise, I will infiltrate the Wetlands with a small but mighty force that can be easily disguised."

Again, murmurs fell upon the room, this time louder in response to the queen's plans.

"I may be new to this role, Governor," Galdinia said, speaking over the rumble of voices as they slowly died down, "but I am more than capable of making such a decision for myself."

Ryden looked at Galdinia with guilt in his eyes, which Galdinia returned with stoicism that would rival Ilyon's. She had spent the Week of Mourning bending to the whims and decisions of the Syndicate, striving to become queen; now that her mother's crown was rightfully on her head, she was ready to shift the narrative. The tension that followed her words was evidence enough that this group of powerful individuals would need to start adjusting their expectations of her.

"Your Majesty." The voice of Marcel Killeen rose from the second row as he stood to his feet. He was Elderguard's Master of Infrastructure and was the longest standing member of the Syndicate, having served Galdinia's grandparents, even before Ryden. This was evident by his thin grey hair, hunched back, and creaking voice. Despite this, he was not a man to be taken for granted: he was firm in word and adored in Elderguard as a powerful Wind Wielder.

"Yes, Marcel?"

"I understand that the soldier in question is of grave importance to the crown." Marcel's voice was quiet yet commanding; all in the room watched on intently. "However, he is but one soldier, and I don't know that we should risk the life of our queen to save him."

Many Syndicate members nodded in agreement, taking this moment to support someone who the queen may struggle to denounce. Galdinia's eyes crossed the room as she watched her Syndicate waver, Neryda's identical sentiments from earlier echoing in her mind.

"Thank you, Marcel," Galdinia said quickly, trying to recapture the attention of the room once again. "As far as I see it, though, no matter who Valah took hostage, I would consider them our highest priority, despite their perceived importance to the crown."

"But Your Majesty," Wynsten Yole, the Master of Economy, inter-jected, his deep voice commanding the room; Galdinia could feel herself losing control of the conversation. "Although any citizen's life is of importance, yours far outweighs anyone else's. If we were to send a small troop of soldiers into the Wetlands, we couldn't possibly include our queen. Our soldiers are more than capable."

More voices of agreement rose, now louder than ever. Galdinia wondered if her father had ever struggled to maintain command of his court. She could feel the heat rising in her chest, her skin itching for the flames around her and the comfort they would bring her.

"I agree that our soldiers are capable of undertaking such a task," Galdinia said, raising her voice to cut through the noise, forcing herself to push against the fear and pain within her, "but I am the queen, and if I'd like to accompany them, I will do so, with or without the Syndicate's support."

All at once the voices rose again, mostly ones of outrage and incredulity.

"Surely not!"

"We can't afford to lose another ruler!"

"And who would we be left with?"

Galdinia's eyes darted around the room, moving from face to face as they denounced her suggestions. Her eyes flickered up to the flames around the room once again, wishing for nothing more than to take hold of their warmth and run from this room immediately.

She glanced to the back wall of the throne room where, hanging behind the Syndicate, was a tapestry that was older than herself. It had been hanging in that very spot since her grandparents took the throne, and it depicted an intricate map of Crysterra, labelling each province and—

That's new, Galdinia thought as her eyes roamed along the bottom right edge of the sprawling tapestry.

Galdinia couldn't remember the last time she properly looked at the tapestry—it could have been during the Week of Mourning, or when she snuck into the throne room during one of her father's final moments commanding the country from the same throne—but the words that were embroidered along the base of the map no longer read *The Kingdom of Crysterra.*

"The Queendom of Crysterra." Galdinia read the words under her breath.

Had there been another map ready to replace the old one in the event of a ruling queen? Or had some handy attendants altered the tapestry after Galdinia's coronation? Either way, at the sight of this change, Galdinia felt compelled to sit up straighter—they were sitting in her queendom, after all.

I am in control, Galdinia thought. *I do not need to run.*

By way of controlling the longing to reach out to the fire, Galdinia pressed her palms into the armrests. Her eyes shifted from Ryden and then to Ilyon; the former was speaking with Serril behind him, but the latter was watching Galdinia carefully.

"May I suggest, Your Highness," Captain Ilyon said as he stood to his feet, bringing the room to a hush, "that we consider another vital element in achieving your goals?"

"And what might that be?" Galdinia asked as a silent relief rested on her shoulders. Each day her gratitude for the Captain of the Royal Guard grew exponentially.

"Allies." Although there were short murmurs from the Syndicate, Ilyon's commanding tone and stature dimmed the noise almost instantly. "I agree, we need to rescue our soldier, but we also need to build up our army. Valah hopes to lure you in with her hostage in order to take your crown. None of us are under a false pretense, and we know that Valah won't go down without a fight. I think a physical conflict is inevitable, so numbers will be vital. Therefore, we need to build our allies."

Ilyon raised his eyebrows to the queen, as though asking for her permission to continue.

"Go on," she said quickly, eager to capture Ilyon's support and hopeful the support of others would follow.

"The Shadowed Coast and the Wetlands are undoubtedly compromised," Ilyon went on, his shoulders square and his hands firmly clasped behind his back; everyone in the room was hanging on his every word. "We know that there are soldiers in the east who swore their affinity with Valah. The Midlands are certainly available for us to make connection with, and thankfully, some of our powerful guests from last week may prove useful in our ventures."

Galdinia knew, of course, to whom he was referring: her suitors. Galdinia had not given the suitors much thought after the battle, as their initial purpose became inconsequential the moment she was given her gift. While Dillian and Evarius had taken their leave shortly after the attack simmered, both Kell and Kaedric remained in Elderguard, making their availability known to the queen.

"Our greatest asset would be making contact with Lund in the North," Ilyon continued. "It is still unclear why they aligned themselves with Valah, but we would be foolish not to investigate."

"Are you suggesting we send troops into the Starlight Mountains, Captain?" Wynsten asked in disbelief.

"Of course not," Ilyon replied coolly. "I suggest we make a connection with the only other province they have aligned themselves with in the past: The Hook."

Again, voices began to rise, some chuckling at the captain's suggestion, others shaking their heads. Galdinia frowned, not fully understanding the connotations that others seemed to catch on to. Galdinia knew that The Hook was a secluded province of the kingdom, situated in the southwest. Her understanding of any political or loyalty ties with the province, however, were lost on her. It seemed the list of details her father had not entirely shared with her was growing.

"Lord and Lady Lidel haven't concerned themselves with the matters of Elderguard in decades," Serril chimed in, his voice cutting through the voices of the Syndicate.

"I'm aware of that, Master Serril," Ilyon replied, pulling the attention of the room once again. "But they also didn't align themselves with Valah or Draven and Edana during their attack. The Lidels are known for their privacy, and they don't get involved in the conflicts of their neighbours, but I highly doubt they would want to see a Pyrin on the throne once again. I suggest that we make contact with The Hook and propose a treaty between the crown and the Lidels. They have been the governing family of The Hook for many years, and I would be surprised if they refused an opportunity to at least consider a treaty with a new ruler."

Galdinia watched Ilyon carefully, taking his suggestions into consideration. He was right. Establishing allies was their best bet to rebuild a strong enough force to take on Valah and ultimately rescue Drystan.

"What do you propose be included in this treaty?" Ryden asked, his voice steeped in curiosity, far more sceptical of the captain than Galdinia was. Perhaps she was just glad that Ilyon hadn't shut down her own suggestion straightaway.

"First, we should make it plain what has transpired in the capital this week. They should know that most of the country has aligned itself with either the crown or Valah, so it would be remiss of them not to be our ally. Secondly, in the event of a battle, we will ensure their protection in exchange for their military support and help in liaising with Lund."

As Ilyon spoke, Galdinia found her heart swell with gratitude for this man. He didn't always have a lot to say, but when strategy and military power were involved, she was reminded just how considered and well-spoken he was.

"Have you forgotten the last time a treaty was made with The Hook, Captain?" Marcel asked, doubtful. "Or shall we just ignore their inability to hold up their end of a bargain?"

Galdinia's eyes narrowed at this. Yet again, she felt in the dark about her own country and was quickly realising how much more she needed to learn before she could govern it with the wisdom she truly required. For now, she stayed quiet and tried to glean as much information from the conversation as possible.

"It has been ten years since our agreement with them during the famine, and I'm sure they want to move on from it just as much as the crown does," Ilyon explained, motioning towards Galdinia. "Mending the broken relationship between Elderguard and The Hook would go a long way in establishing allies that Valah won't be able to secure herself. She, too, lost vast numbers."

Again, the group whispered between themselves, and Galdinia watched as Ryden's brow furrowed in contemplation. She still didn't have enough information to fully grasp the events that transpired a decade ago, so she made a mental note to ask one of her advisors after the meeting.

Ilyon went on. "It is hard to say what Valah's true intentions or strategy are regarding Allard, and presumably her next attempt to take the throne." Galdinia felt her stomach flip at the sound of Drystan's name, and she saw the flames in the torches on the walls flicker briefly; she hoped no one else noticed. "It would be in our best interest to make haste to The Hook to begin negotiations with the Lidels. We should also utilise our connections to the Midlands to ensure our ties there are strong also. Both Evarius Wrynn's and Dillian Othid's families are loyal to the throne, so we will make contact there."

The Syndicate considered this, and all eyes turned back to Galdinia. After a heartbeat, she realised that they were awaiting her response. This would take some getting used to.

"This is a sound plan, Captain," Galdinia said quickly with a short nod. "I'm sure you will disagree with me, but I'd like to be the one to negotiate with the Lidels. I think it's important that I make my own first impression."

"On the contrary, Your Highness, I absolutely think you should accompany us."

Everyone in the room turned to look at the captain, and even Galdinia's eyes widened.

"Ilyon," Ryden said in a hushed but frantic tone, "you can't be serious."

"Who better to sway the reclusive Lidels than a fresh-faced queen with a very impressive gift? I think Queen Galdinia is exactly the right person to negotiate with them, not a handful of Syndicate members who haven't spoken to them in a decade."

A small smile tugged at Galdinia's lips.

"And who will accompany her?" Ryden asked.

"I will, of course," Ilyon went on. "I have a small company of hand-selected soldiers who would act as her personal guard. I suggest that Lord Kell Ly and his family secure our allies along the Shadowed Coast, and perhaps their soldiers can scope out Edana's whereabouts. Young Lord Kaedric Novus should be sent to investigate the east. His family is highly respected there, and my hope is that they will be able to distinguish defected soldiers from our allies. We can send each of them with a battalion or two of the Royal Guard, while you, Governor Ryden, remain here to watch over Elderguard in the queen's stead."

A quiet chatter flitted through the throne room once again, and Ryden turned from Ilyon to Galdinia as the queen considered the plan. In short, she was convinced.

"What do you say, Your Highness?" Ryden asked, and all eyes turned to Galdinia.

"While I still believe it is a priority to rescue Drystan"—she sucked in a quick breath—"the captain is right. Valah will be planning another attack, whether she believes I will succumb to her demands or not. We need to secure our allies across the kingdom before we try to execute a rescue mission. I will go with the captain and his soldiers to The Hook, while Kell and Kaedric, along with our soldiers, establish a hold in their respective provinces."

Most in the room nodded in agreement, while a few others looked at the queen, stone-faced.

"Ryden, please send word to the Lidels that I will be arriving in two days."

"Of course, Your Highness," Ryden replied with a curt nod. "There is one other item on our agenda that we must discuss in haste."

"Is it more important than preparing for our trip west?" Galdinia asked, brows raised.

"Unfortunately, it is." Ryden's tone was grave, and Galdinia didn't like it for a second.

She nodded slowly, inviting Ryden to elaborate.

"It's about our prisoner," Ryden said carefully as Galdinia's eyes narrowed. "Our most controversial prisoner."

Galdinia could feel Ryden's discomfort as he mentioned the traitorous man that he had brought into Galdinia's life. Of course the governor couldn't take full responsibility for Bentley's deception; the Penrose family had been loyal to the Elderwins for decades, so he couldn't have known that they had shifted their alliance in recent years. Ironically, had the capital maintained closer contact with the far reaches of the kingdom, they probably wouldn't have defected. Bentley may have been a pawn in Valah's plan, but he had put on a good show to draw the Syndicate—and Galdinia—in.

"Yes, what about him?" Galdinia asked, disdain thick in her voice.

"We have allowed him to sit in our prison for a number of days now, hoping that little food and sunlight, as well as no access to fire, would coax information about Valah and her plans from him. However, as of yet, none of our soldiers have been successful in obtaining any such information. I wonder if our best course of action would be to—"

"I've already spoken to him," Galdinia said candidly. For the first time, Galdinia's words brought a response of silence from the room. She liked it.

"You've spoken to him?" Ryden's words choked out of his lips.

"Yes, just this morning," Galdinia said, a casual air to her words.

"And what did he say?"

Galdinia could tell that the governor was far too preoccupied with the potential for information, as he bypassed questioning her access to Bentley. Now that she was queen, maybe she didn't need to explain herself so much. This was something they would both have to adjust to.

"Not a lot," Galdinia replied. "He showed some remorse for his deception and behaviour on the night of the attack, but I merely took that as his attempt to sway me to release him. He also told me about how Valah primed him as a suitor when his parents shifted their loyalty to her. And he believes he could assist the crown in breaching Valah's stronghold in the Wetlands."

At this, Galdinia expected more whispering, but it didn't come. The room remained deathly quiet.

"I asked him where Valah would be now, but he didn't know for sure. His assumption is the same as ours. I don't know that I believe him when he says he can get us beyond Valah's walls to rescue our prisoner, but he seemed quite sure of himself."

"What is his suggested strategy?" Ryden asked, his forehead creasing.

"He said he could be a distraction, meeting with his parents and drawing Valah in with the promise of his powers and vengeance in order to help in her next inevitable attack. He assured me that he knows the lay of the land in the Wetlands well and could get us into her prison to rescue Drystan without detection." Surprisingly, Galdinia moved past Drystan's name with an ease she'd not thought she was capable of. "He doesn't recommend it, but he said he can."

Ryden's eyes shifted to Ilyon, and the two conveyed silent communication with mere glances before turning back to the queen.

"We must assume that he is lying for his own sake," Ryden finally said, taking in a deep breath before continuing. "But of course we can't know that for sure. I think it would be worth the captain and me having a strategic conversation with him while you prepare for your leave in the morning, Your Highness."

Before Galdinia could protest, Ilyon spoke.

"We will inform you of any new information learned, of course." Ilyon spoke evenly, putting Galdinia's concerned mind to rest with ease. "I do not think it would be wise for you to speak with him again before our departure. The governor and I can be far more... ruthless, if need be."

Galdinia didn't want to know the practicalities of such a conversation, so she accepted his instruction with a short nod. She knew she could trust Ilyon; he wouldn't exclude her from such a meeting because he thought she wasn't strong enough, but rather to protect her from unnecessary and unpleasant exchanges.

"We can reconvene in the morning then, before we set sail," Galdinia said to her governor and captain, looking pointedly at them both. "I expect a full report on your communications with him."

The last time the Syndicate met with Bentley in private was the day she found out that five suitors had arrived in her home to vie for her hand in marriage, and that hadn't worked out so well for her.

"Of course, Your Highness," Ryden said with a short bow of his head.

"Then all I'll say is good luck." And Galdinia felt as though her sentiments were true, despite the undercurrent of sarcasm that accompanied them. If all Bentley had to say to her was the same warning she'd received from Ryden, as well as a brief confession of affection, she hardly thought they'd be any more successful in drawing out information from him. Maybe she did want to go with them, she began to think, if only to see them employ those ruthless tactics on Bentley when their interrogation inevitably came up short. Galdinia thought that a powerful Wind Wielder and Water Weaver could bring the amount of destruction in that prison cell that might make her feel an ounce better about her current circumstances.

"That's appreciated, Your Majesty," Ilyon said, also bowing to Galdinia, a knowing expression on his face; Galdinia could tell that even Ilyon was dubious of an interrogation.

Sitting up tall in her throne, mindful of the weight of her mother's crown, Galdinia addressed the whole Syndicate once again.

"With that being said, court adjourned."

6

It didn't take long for the governor to find Galdinia soon after she left the throne room. Galdinia had called for lunch to be brought to the terrace, hoping for a quiet moment on her own to turn over her plans for the coming days. She hadn't intended on being joined by Ryden immediately after court.

"Your Highness," he said as he stepped out onto the terrace, coming to stand beside the queen as she sat at the table, looking across the city. Although much work had been done to repair the damage caused by their enemy, she knew it would be weeks until the wreckage was no longer visible. Her eyes roamed over the broken roofs and crumbling walls. There were signs of fire in the streets—scorched flags, burnt bricks, and ashen windows—and Galdinia wondered how much of that damage was caused by her newly received gift.

"Hello, Ryden," Galdinia said simply, watching him with questioning eyes as he pulled out a chair beside her.

"May I?"

After a moment's hesitation, Galdinia replied, "Of course."

Ryden settled in the chair beside her, looking across Elderguard, seemingly contemplating his next words carefully. Galdinia made the conscious decision not to speak first; if he wanted to address her, to reprimand her for what she'd said in court, or to tell her what a mistake she was making, he didn't need to wait for an invitation.

"I'm sorry, Your Highness."

Galdinia's questioning expression remained, taken aback by his apology. This wasn't what she had expected from him.

Although Galdinia could quickly come to multiple reasons for his apology, she felt the need to ask, "What for?"

"Where do I begin?" Ryden turned to look at the queen, his dark eyes full of regret and disappointment. "After your father's passing, I promised to look after you, and I feel like everything I did during the Week of Mourning was decidedly in opposition to that promise. I'm sorry for forcing you to meet with the suitors; I'm sorry I was fooled by Bentley; I'm sorry I went back on our deal at the eleventh hour; I'm sorry if I made you feel as though you weren't—aren't—good enough to sit on your throne." He let out a long breath. "I'm so sorry, Galdinia."

Instantaneously, a lump rose in Galdinia's chest, moving towards her throat. She tried to ignore it, hoping to hold the frustration against Ryden; she found a strange comfort in it.

"Thank you, Ryden, I appreciate it." Galdinia's words were far softer than she'd hoped they'd be. She took note of his words, though, and how he chose to lay the blame on himself only. Galdinia knew that the Syndicate were a significant part of every decision made regarding her future, so it couldn't have all been Ryden's decision alone.

"I was foolish not to trust you—I was foolish not to trust the Gods! I suppose I was fearful of what might eventuate if your gift didn't arrive. I couldn't bear seeing your aunt and uncle—or, Gods forbid, Valah—take the throne." Galdinia could see the anguish in his expression. "I need you to know that I do trust you and I will do everything to serve you wholeheartedly moving forward. You are my queen, and I will not forget that."

With each word that he spoke, Galdinia felt her contempt dissipate, becoming nothing more than steam in warm air. In her heart she knew she couldn't hold her frustration—whether righteous or not—against Ryden forever.

He's not the enemy, Galdinia reminded herself.

He was her second-in-command, but he had become family to her, so holding a longstanding grudge against him was not a prudent decision as queen. Perhaps that was why she became so easily frustrated by him and ultimately could forgive him just as easily. He was family, and by all accounts, he seemed truly sorry for his actions.

"Thank you," she said again, allowing a small smile to flicker over her lips. "I'm sorry I've been so cold towards you. I was hurt, but you're my governor, and you're certainly not my enemy."

"There's no need to apologise," he insisted, a small crease forming on his brow. "You have every right to be angry. I just hope that we can move beyond it and work together to rebuild what we've lost."

"Of course," Galdinia said with a nod. She wouldn't let her past hurt control her; if she wanted to be an effective queen, she needed to forgive quickly and move on even faster. And she felt there wasn't a better way to do that than to seek advice from her own advisor. "Speaking of which, I'm glad to be leaving for The Hook tomorrow, but based on the conversation in court today, I fear I'm underprepared. Are they likely to be hostile?"

Ryden seemed pleased with the change in subject, obviously glad to be moving on to discussions of strategy, and with that relief, the air around Galdinia became all the lighter.

"I don't think you'll be faced with hostility, no, but they can be... indignant," Ryden explained. "They don't enjoy choosing sides in conflict and have managed to become self-sufficient, so when they're asked to ally with the crown, don't be surprised if they refuse. They're not easily persuaded."

"Why is that?" Galdinia asked. "Why have they secluded themselves?"

"The Lidel line has lorded over The Hook since before the Pyrins were on the throne. They have passed their lord and ladyship down to each generation without objection from their civilians or the crown. They've become their own ecosystem, happily providing for themselves—they don't ask for anything from the crown with the expectation that the crown will not ask anything of them."

"That seems quite self-serving," Galdinia said, frowning.

"And it is," Ryden agreed with a nod. "The Lidels do not pretend to be a welcoming bunch, but as Ilyon said, being faced with the new queen may sway them. It's certainly worth trying."

"And what caused this silence from them? I fear I'm not privy to the events of a decade ago."

Ryden sighed as he internally reflected on the past; Galdinia could see the shadow of a time long gone in his eyes.

"About twelve years ago, the west suffered a great famine due to a lack of rainfall and low tides: their crops weren't growing, and their access to fish was dwindling. The Hook was, and still is, home to many of the country's strongest Water Weavers, and even they struggled to survive in the west during that time.

"Your father offered them a trade deal to provide them with necessary provisions, but being the proud pair that they were, Lord and Lady Lidel declined, determined to sustain themselves. After two years of this, however, the Lidels became desperate at the threat of their population waning, but they were also desperate to maintain the stronghold and refused to leave The Hook. Your father graciously offered the trade deal again and sent them more than enough food to sustain the province every month. All he asked in return was that they provide a deposit of sorts to show their good faith, which would be returned once they were able to pay back the cost of the provisions— at a far lower rate, mind you. The Lidels insisted on paying for the provisions, but your father only requested a return of fifty percent. The Lidels must have thought that insulting, so they proudly agreed to pay back the capital in full within one year."

"But they didn't pay it back?" Galdinia asked.

"Worse than that: they never sent the deposit." Ryden shook his head, the frustration of the situation lingering still all these years later. "Your father sent three ships to collect their deposit, and being the honourable man he was, continued to send them provisions on ships across the Southern Shadow for three months, but before the fourth lot was sent, he sent a message with a raven to The Hook and questioned the whereabouts of the deposit and his ships. Lord and Lady Lidel guaranteed that they sent a set of three jewels on his ships across the sea before they received the first allocation of food, but we never received them. Both their deposit and your father's ships were never seen again by the capital. The only conclusion we could come to was that the Lidels had the soldiers onboard captured—or worse—and kept our ships and, of course, their deposit.

"Your father ordered for the provisions to halt, and all communication between The Hook and Elderguard ceased. They took much needed reserves from us without payment, and in return, spread rumours about how deceptive the capital was, suggesting that we stole their jewels and didn't hold up our end of the bargain. They've wanted nothing to do with us since, which is a sentiment that was reciprocated by your father and the Syndicate."

While Galdinia wasn't shocked by the tale—her father often made quiet comments about the Lidels—she was surprised she hadn't heard it before. Ryden's story caused a bubble of apprehension rise within her.

"So that's how this rift began? They used us for our crops and lied to other provinces about the exchange? All over some jewels?"

"You'll be surprised what people go to war for, Your Majesty," Ryden replied, a knowing expression on his face. "What seems petty to a queen may be the end of existence for a king."

"So it would seem," Galdinia said, pondering. "Do we really think they'll listen to me?"

"Honestly, I'm not sure how good your chances are," Ryden replied, "but with Ilyon by your side and the threat of a Pyrin attack, they may be swayed to agree to becoming our allies. Venturing beyond the borders of their province to help establish our relationship with Lund, however, may be a greater obstacle. I don't think they've left The Hook since their first son was born twenty years ago."

"I know my short existence has been quite sheltered, but I would go mad if I never strayed beyond the walls of Elderguard."

"When you see The Hook, you'll understand why they never leave," Ryden replied, smiling. "Our capital is beautiful; we are lucky to have our perfectly manicured gardens, this castle, and such well-maintained buildings. The Hook, though, it's a sanctuary."

"It's really that special?" Galdinia asked, sceptical.

"I'll admit that it's been a long time since I visited," Ryden said, nodding, "but it can only be described as glorious."

Galdinia's eyes roamed to the west. Beyond the horizon, on the other side of the Southern Shadow, lay The Hook. She was intrigued, and if she was being completely honest with herself, she was ready to leave the capital for a time. She could feel the walls of the castle starting to encroach on her, and she needed to come up for air. While she hoped that their visit to The Hook would be politically fruitful for them, she also needed to get away from the ashen remnants of the battle, the towering walls of her home, and most importantly, from their prisoner beneath the barracks.

"What do you intend on asking him today?" Galdinia asked, breaking the silence.

Ryden knew exactly who Galdinia was referring to. "I hope we can extract information about Valah and her plans."

"I don't think he has any such information."

"It's still worth us investigating," Ryden said thoughtfully. "As I said to you before, while rescuing Drystan is a priority, we need to prepare for another attack. Valah isn't going to roll over and accept defeat so easily. We need as much insight into her plans as possible."

"I agree," Galdinia said, trying to pretend that Drystan wasn't her first priority. "However, I think Valah kept Bentley in the dark about most of her plans beyond the attack. But by all means, use whatever tactics necessary." Galdinia's tone was dark.

"We certainly will," Ryden said, matching her expression.

"And I expect to be informed on anything learned," Galdinia reiterated.

"Of course. Ilyon or I will share any and all information." Ryden nodded, meeting Galdinia's gaze. "Like I said, you are my queen, and I will not forget that."

A maidservant stepped out onto the terrace, and she approached the two.

"Your Highness, your lunch," she said timidly, curtseying as best she could with a tray of food in her hands.

"Thank you," Galdinia said as the food was set before her. A steaming bowl of soup, a few slices of bread and a handful of cherries lay before her. "Do you care to join me, Ryden? I can have another plate sent up."

"Thank you, Your Highness, but I will have to regrettably decline," Ryden said as the maidservant moved back through the door into the castle. "Ilyon and I will be travelling down to the barracks together shortly, and heaven forbid I'm late."

"He runs a tight ship," Galdinia said with a smile.

"He certainly does," Ryden agreed, pushing his chair back and standing to his feet. "If I don't see you before your departure tomorrow, all the best. Please, stay safe."

The governor reached out and placed his hand on the queen's shoulder, squeezing it briefly.

"I will," Galdinia assured him, placing her hand on his. "Keep my home in one piece while I'm gone, won't you?"

"Of course," Ryden said with a smile before turning to leave Galdinia on the terrace.

After lunch, Galdinia went back to her rooms. All she wanted to do that afternoon was train. She'd had such success over the last few days as she learned to hone her gift, and she wanted to be as physically prepared as possible for when she faced Valah again. Given her trip the following morning and her trainer's necessary plans that afternoon, she resigned herself to going back to her rooms to rest.

As she stepped into her bedroom, she felt a wave of relief wash over her. Neryda was sitting in the bay window, wrapped in a blanket, a cup of steaming tea in her lap and a book of Galdinia's in her hand. Galdinia hadn't had much time to contemplate their argument earlier that day, and while she knew that forgiveness would be easily attained —their arguments never lasted more than a few hours, at most—she was glad to see that her best friend had not abandoned her.

"You really enjoy this kind of story, don't you?" Neryda asked, not taking her eyes off the small, tan cloth-bound book in her hand.

"I do," Galdinia said with a smile, undoing her cloak and draping it over the chair by the crackling fireplace. "In fact, that's one of my favourites."

"This?" Neryda asked, raising an eyebrow, not an ounce of humour on her face. "'If I could profess my love for you a thousand times every day, I would. You are the sun to my horizon, the moon to my waves. You are my morning and my evening; you are every moment in between. I would use my final breath to say your name so you were the last thing on my lips.'"

Neryda made a retching sound as she screwed up her nose, giving Galdinia a look of utter contempt. Galdinia smirked as she came to sit with Neryda on the cushioned seat in the window.

"You're better than that, my friend," Neryda said with a shake of her head, shutting the book with a thud and discarding it to the side.

"It's romantic!" Galdinia insisted, picking the book up and holding it carefully in her hands.

"That isn't romance," Neryda retorted. "That is sick-inducing."

"You're ridiculous," Galdinia said with a roll of her eyes.

"I'm pragmatic," Neryda countered. She lowered her eyes to her tea, the brightness in her face dulling for a moment. "I'm also sorry."

A silence hung between them, and Galdinia let out a long breath. "Me too," she said quietly, reaching out to take Neryda's free hand in her own. "I shouldn't have been so defensive. I know you were just trying to be helpful."

"You're right, I was," Neryda said. "But I shouldn't have said what I did. Of course rescuing Drys should be your priority. I'm sorry for suggesting it shouldn't be."

Galdinia let these words sit before responding. Both Neryda and Ryden had said that travelling to the Wetlands would be dangerous and ill-fated. While her best friend was apologising for what she had said, an ounce of doubt rang through Galdinia's chest as she considered her priorities.

"I was blinded by my anger and desperation," Galdinia replied. "Rescuing Drystan is still a priority of mine, but it isn't my only one."

"Oh?" Neryda asked.

"In court today we decided that we need to focus on securing our allies and existing armies," Galdinia explained to a wide-eyed Neryda. "We're going to start in The Hook with the Lidels. They're notoriously reclusive, so I don't expect it will be an easy negotiation, but the Syndicate believe they have a strong army, and their numbers would support us exponentially."

"When are you going?" Neryda asked.

"Tomorrow morning. We should arrive the day after next."

"Fantastic," Neryda said with a smile. "I've always wanted to visit The Hook."

"Perhaps one day you will."

"Yes, I will," Neryda said with a short nod and bright eyes. "In two days."

Galdinia frowned at her friend. "Ner."

"Don't *Ner* me," she replied, mimicking Galdinia's furrowed brow. "If you think I'm letting you go by yourself after what happened last week, you've lost your marbles. Which, I might add, may already be missing, given the literature you consume."

Galdinia rolled her eyes again. "Irrelevant arguments aside, I'm not going alone. Ilyon and a small company of his finest soldiers will be with me."

"All the more reason to come if Ilyon will be there!" Neryda's eyes glinted as she smirked at Galdinia.

Years prior, Galdinia had made the mistake of overreacting when Neryda made a comment about her adolescent crush on Ilyon; it was a passing comment, but Galdinia felt the need to reprimand her friend for seeing someone who had known her since she was a child in such a light. Ever since, Neryda's perceived interest in the captain seemed to withstand any serious conversation the two girls had. Galdinia could only imagine how mortified Ilyon would be to hear such a thing. Although Galdinia knew that Neryda only made such comments to rile her up, she couldn't help but react each time she did, reminding her friend how it made her squirm. The smile on Neryda's face only grew each time she did.

"Firstly, you must get over this infatuation with my captain," Galdinia said pointedly. "And secondly, I don't know how this meeting with the Lidels will go. Gods forbid it ends tumultuously; goodness, I don't even know if they'll let us through their gates. I can't risk your safety."

"You won't be risking anything; I know how to protect myself," Neryda said simply, placing her cup of tea on the windowsill. In a moment she had used her gift to raise the liquid in a small whirlpool in the air. With a flick of her fingers, the tea swirled between the women, snaking its way around Galdinia's neck before dancing up beside her face. She could smell the distinct peppermint and aniseed scent as it travelled by her nose, but not a drop landed on her face. With another swift movement, the tea returned to Neryda's cup, as though being poured from a jug. "Imagine what I could do with an entire sea."

Galdinia knew that arguing with Neryda would be futile. If she really wanted to join them on their travels, she could stow away in the ship and announce herself once they were hours from the capital. It would be easier and cause far fewer headaches to concede.

"We're leaving before dawn," Galdinia said with a sigh. "You and I both know that you haven't seen that time of day in years."

"That's because pre-dawn is still nighttime!" Neryda feigned frustration and went on in a softer tone. "But for you, I'm willing to lose my precious beauty sleep."

"If you're still asleep, I'm leaving without you," Galdinia warned, pulling the end of Neryda's blanket over her knees.

"If you leave me here, I will swim across the Southern Shadow myself and hunt you down."

"What a spectacle that would be," Galdinia said with a laugh as she settled into the window seat with her friend.

FIRST QUARTER

7

GALDINIA AWOKE AND DRESSED WHILE IT WAS STILL DARK. THE ONLY light filtering in through her chamber's curtains was from the glow of the stars and the moon. The ever-present reminder of Valah's demands hung in the sky, already in its first quarter, making Galdinia's stomach tighten uneasily. In just a few weeks, the moon would have vanished from the sky again and Valah's threat would be imminent.

In her dressing room, as she adjusted the buckles on her boots, tightening the thin straps around her calves, Galdinia inspected her robust ensemble: her battle leathers. She had insisted Ilyon provide her with a soldier's uniform, which he maintained wasn't appropriate for the queen. After a stern look from Galdinia, the captain reluctantly agreed, and she was fitted in the barracks with her own uniform of fighting leathers, which she had been breaking in the last few days during training. He had also agreed to having a set of armour made for her, which she had still yet to receive.

She looked down at her uniform; it clung to her curvaceous figure, accentuating the line of her waist, hips, and thighs. The fresh leathers were still firm against her, but she could start to feel their give as she bent to tighten the strap on her other boot before standing up straight. There was something about the uniform that made her feel stronger, more confident in her power. And this was a feeling she gladly welcomed.

As Galdinia clipped her hair in a twist at the nape of her neck, she turned at the sound of Neryda rousing awake.

"You're not leaving without me, are you?" her best friend mumbled from the furthest side of Galdinia's bed, which she had claimed as her own.

"I would never," Galdinia replied, pushing one final clip into her hair, securing her golden waves into place. "I'm going to the kitchen briefly before we leave. I'll meet you at the castle doors in ten minutes. Will you be ready?"

"Plenty of time," Neryda said without opening her eyes, waving at Galdinia groggily.

Galdinia picked up her cloak and satchel, in which were the bare essentials she needed for their trip. A trunk of clothing for both women had already been transported to the docks the evening before. Galdinia exited her rooms, passing the guards at the door, who stood to attention as she walked down the hallway.

The castle was so still at this time of the day; her footsteps on the marble floors echoed lightly as she made her way to the grand staircase and down to the kitchens. The dim light from the nightly lanterns flickered along the walls, the heat from the flames bubbling beneath her skin, waking her tired body. She noticed that the pull of her gift was more effective at drawing her out of her sleepy disposition than a cup of freshly brewed tea or a croissant slathered with pistachio cream. It was an experience she wasn't prepared for before she received her gift, but it was one of the unexpected perks. Her Flourisher gift called to the flames, and she felt at peace knowing they were so nearby.

As she approached the main door of the kitchens, she could already hear the only other people in the castle who would be working at this hour, other than the patrolling soldiers.

Miss Giles was standing over one of her stoves, a wooden spoon in hand, mixing a concoction that smelled very much like tomatoes, beans, and garlic. A basket of eggs lay beside her, and she began cracking them into the bubbling mixture. Two of Miss Giles' attendants were furiously mixing a batter in too-large bowls; one of them had her entire arm wrapped around the bowl, trying to keep it steady as she worked. Another attendant stood at the sink washing dishes, but he seemed caught in a tired trance as he absentmindedly scrubbed at the crockery while he stared out the vine-covered window behind the sink.

Aside from the noise, Galdinia was always struck by the warmth of the kitchens, which was maintained by the stove, ovens, and fireplace. The fire in the corner, which Galdinia had hoped to control on numerous visits to the kitchens, was ablaze, boiling the water in the pot that hung over it. Now that she had her gift, she felt an instant pull towards it.

"Good morning, Your Highness," Miss Giles said, drawing Galdinia's attention away from the fireplace. Having not turned to see the queen's entrance, it always amazed Galdinia how Miss Giles knew she was entering the room.

"You always know it's me," Galdinia said with a smile, placing her cloak and satchel on the table by the fire. "How?"

"I would know your footfalls anywhere, Your Highness," Miss Giles said, turning from her eggshells to smile at Galdinia before returning her attention to her attendants. "Back to work."

Galdinia hadn't noticed, but the three others in the room had stopped work to bow at her entrance. She tried to offer them a reassuring smile as they worked again, expressions of trepidation and apprehension painting their faces.

"And Tomin," Miss Giles added, looking to her dishwasher, "put a little elbow grease into it. I'd prefer it if the queen wasn't tasting yesterday's dinner this morning."

By way of response, Tomin started to scrub feverishly, not taking his eyes off the task before him.

"To what do I owe such an early visit, Your Highness?"

"Must you insist on calling me that?" It hadn't escaped Galdinia's attention that the woman who had been like a grandmother to her had called her by her title three times since entering the kitchen.

"I really must," Miss Giles replied as she scooped a few spoonfuls of her mixture to two freshly washed bowls before turning to bring them to the table. "Now, are you going to tell me why you're up earlier than most of my staff?"

Galdinia glanced at the attendants on the other side of the room, unsure whether they should be privy to information about the queen's whereabouts for the foreseeable future.

"You needn't mind their wandering ears," Miss Giles assured Galdinia, taking up a seat beside her, placing a plate in front of each of them. "My little birds have already informed me of the trip you have planned."

She shouldn't have been surprised that Miss Giles knew about her plans; she and her kitchen staff were often privy to the goings-on in the castle, and one such occasion even before Galdinia. During The Week of Mourning, Miss Giles had been preparing breakfast for Galdinia's suitors before Galdinia knew they even existed.

"Always well-informed, aren't you?" Galdinia asked with a smile, picking up her fork and breaking the egg yolk atop her breakfast. "I suppose the surprise of why I'm awake so early has burst then. We set sail at dawn."

"I didn't realise you were leaving so early," Miss Giles commented, eyebrows raised as she took a mouthful of her food.

"We wanted to leave with plenty of time to sail today. We hope to arrive by midday tomorrow, which shouldn't be too difficult with Ilyon at the helm." Galdinia took a spoonful of her breakfast, the warm mixture heating her from within, the scent of the spices engulfing her. Miss Giles' cooking almost had the same effect on her as wielding a flame.

"And I imagine you've already been told about what to expect of the Lidels?"

"At great length, actually."

"How are you feeling about your meeting?"

"Apprehensive... anxious... concerned." Galdinia listed her feelings as she took another bite; she would miss Miss Giles' cooking while she was away. "Could I bribe you to join us? One of your hearty meals a day should keep the anxiety away."

"While I'd like nothing more than to cook for my favourite royal, I don't have the greatest sea legs, and I don't intend on finding out how strong they are anytime soon." Miss Giles smiled at Galdinia, taking another bite of her food.

"It was worth asking," Galdinia said with a shrug, trying to ignore the all too familiar surmounting pressure that was building in her chest.

"You've not got anything to worry about though, Your Highness," Miss Giles assured her. "The Lidels may be self-absorbed, but they're not fools. Once they have their very powerful queen standing in front of them, I don't know that they'll be hard to convince."

"I hope you're right," Galdinia said, staring at the mouthful of food on her fork. "I hadn't anticipated my first foray into queenhood being so daunting."

"Have hope, Your Highness. The Gods have orchestrated so much of the last two weeks; you must trust them with the future too."

Galdinia knew Miss Giles was right; the Gods had brought her to this point. They had arranged her steps all the way to her coronation. Ten days ago, she didn't understand why her powers had not yet come or why she was apparently not good enough for the throne. Mere days later, she was able to understand that striving for greatness in her own strength was done in vain; it wasn't until she relinquished control and followed the Gods' path that she found herself in a slipstream, being granted her gift and protecting her city, as she was meant to do.

She supposed that she needed to lean into that trust again now; the unknown was terrifying, but not trusting the Gods was even more so.

"You're right," Galdinia conceded before taking her final bite of breakfast. "And what's your fascination with suddenly calling me Your Highness? If I expected anyone in this castle to treat me the same as always, it was you, Miss Giles."

"Can't an old woman show respect to her queen?" Miss Giles scraped the edges of her bowl before consuming the final dregs.

"I'd feel far more respected if you called me by my first name."

"I'll consider it," Miss Giles said, her face not giving anything away as she picked up their bowls and placed them beside Tomin with his already mountainous pile of dishes. How he already had so much work to do at this hour was beyond Galdinia, and she wondered if he had neglected his work the evening before.

"I should probably head to the docks," Galdinia said, standing to her feet and retrieving her satchel and cloak.

"Before you go," Miss Giles said quickly, moving to another bench, where she began wrapping something in a piece of parchment. "Take these for your journey. If I can't be there with you, at least you'll have a taste of home to take with you."

She handed Galdinia a small parcel, wrapped up with a piece of twine. The package was still warm.

"Your oat and cocoa biscuits?" Galdinia asked, her eyes widening in delight. These were her favourite treat of Miss Giles'.

"Of course," Miss Giles replied. "They would have ended up in your rooms anyway, so you should take them."

"You know they won't last five minutes around Neryda," Galdinia said with a raised brow as she stowed the biscuits away carefully in her satchel.

"Neryda is going with you?"

"She wouldn't let me go alone."

"I suppose I shouldn't be so surprised," Miss Giles said with a smile.

"Thank you for these," Galdinia said, patting her satchel. "And for everything. I don't say it enough, but I'm so glad to have you."

"Of course," Miss Giles said, placing a hand on Galdinia's shoulder before pulling her into her arms, squeezing her close. "I'll see you soon, Galdinia."

Galdinia wasn't sure how long she'd be gone from her home—she knew that was dependent on how she would be received at The Hook —and even with all her excitement to leave the capital's walls for a time, being wrapped in Miss Giles' warm embrace brought on a pre-emptive homesickness. Some home comforts were harder to leave than others.

"I'll be back in no time," Galdinia said, her assurance unconvincing, even to herself.

Miss Giles stepped back and looked at Galdinia for a long moment, her hands still resting on her shoulders.

"I'm so proud of you," she said quietly with a small smile. "You're a wonderful queen."

"Thank you," Galdinia said, a warmth in her chest making her feel more like a beloved adoptive granddaughter than the most powerful individual in the country. "I'll see you soon."

"That you will," Miss Giles replied, taking her hands from Galdinia's shoulders and stuffing them in her apron pocket.

Galdinia gave Miss Giles one final smile before turning to leave the kitchen, stepping back out into the early morning chill of the castle.

~

"I told you I'd be ready, didn't I?"

Neryda's pride was palpable as Galdinia approached her from across the entrance hall of the castle. Neryda stood in the doorway, leaning against the frame and looking like a miniature doll in the mighty entrance. Beside her stood two guards who had been on patrol that evening.

"You certainly did," Galdinia said with a smile. As she came closer to her best friend, she noticed that while she was fully dressed and had a satchel of her own slung over her shoulder, Neryda was only barely awake. "You haven't quite woken up yet, though, have you?"

"Ready, yes; awake, less so," Neryda agreed, her final word morphing into a yawn.

"Your Majesty," one of the guards said as they stood at attention. "Your carriage is ready."

"Thank you," Galdinia said with a smile. While she would have loved to have freely walked through Elderguard before she left for The Hook, she wasn't sure that Neryda would make it all the way to the docks without collapsing out of exhaustion.

The girls walked arm-in-arm down the castle steps and boarded the carriage. As soon as they were seated, Neryda nestled into Galdinia's shoulder, making herself comfortable for their brief trip through the city. Before she could drift off, however, Galdinia could hear Neryda sniffing.

"You have biscuits," Neryda said, her tone accusatory. "Miss Giles' biscuits!"

"My goodness, you have a strong nose," Galdinia said with a sigh.

"Hand them over."

"They were a gift for me."

"Hand them over."

"Miss Giles made them for her queen on her treacherous journey to the west."

"You're not fooling anyone, sister," Neryda said before lolling out a lazy hand to her friend. "Hand them over."

Galdinia rolled her eyes before retrieving the package of biscuits from her satchel and placing it into Neryda's eager hands.

"Please don't eat them all," Galdinia said as Neryda quickly untied the parcel. "I'd really like at least one of them."

Neryda didn't have time to reply before she took a bite into one of the biscuits. There were six in the now unwrapped parchment, and she could only hope that she'd get a morsel of one.

The girls rode in silence as Neryda nibbled on the biscuits, her eyes still closed. Galdinia watched the sleeping capital pass her by as they travelled down Main Court. There were few lights in windows and even fewer people on the streets. She imagined that Raff would already be well into baking today's treats, while Madame Moya would be fast asleep in her home above her tailoring shop. It was such a peaceful morning, and the sky was clear, cast in a deep shade of purple as the morning sun prepared to rise.

As they reached the southernmost tip of Elderguard, they passed the barracks before moving through the gates to the docks. A cold shiver ran down Galdinia's spine at the thought of their prisoner, Bentley, who sat underground beneath them. She forced her eyes away from the barracks and looked out across the dark sea, seemingly endless as it stretched south.

The carriage rolled to a stop, jolting Neryda awake, who must have fallen asleep mid-bite on Galdinia's shoulder. She sat up straight and chewed the piece of biscuit still between her teeth. She seemed to have saved her friend three and a half biscuits. Galdinia smirked as she tied the package back up, placing it in her satchel again.

"Time to go, sunshine," Galdinia sang, pushing Neryda's crown of red hair behind her ears as she yawned again.

"I'll need a few more of those treats before I really wake up," Neryda warned, rubbing her eyes hastily.

The door to the carriage opened, and Galdinia stepped out, the fresh ocean breeze greeting her instantly. Before them sat the royal ship, its sails unravelling, being readied to head westward. On board she could see the shapes of a handful of soldiers moving about the deck. She didn't want to imagine what time they awoke to prepare the ship.

Galdinia and Neryda walked to the ship, flanked by the two royal guards who travelled with them from the castle. As a crisp gust of wind picked up the hem of her cloak and sent goosebumps along her neck, she wished she'd brought a small flame with her from the castle. She'd have to draw one out from a lantern aboard the ship.

Standing close together, Galdinia and Neryda walked up the gangway and onto the deck of the ship. Onboard, the soldiers came to stand in a line and at attention, their chests high, helmets on, and hands clasped behind their backs. Ilyon moved from the helm, coming to stand beside his soldiers to greet the queen.

"Your Highness," Ilyon said, bowing at the waist, his soldiers following suit. "Lady Neryda."

"Good morning, Captain," Galdinia replied.

"We're just about ready to set sail," Ilyon explained. "We're just loading the last of the cargo and will be ready in two minutes."

"Excellent," Galdinia replied, smiling. She cast a glance down the row of soldiers beside her, all in their full armour, helmets on and swords on their hips. She counted twelve in total. "And this is our party?"

"My most trusted soldiers, yes," Ilyon replied, nodding. "We may save introductions for later this morning when we are comfortably on the water and perhaps a tad livelier."

"Good plan," Galdinia said with a smile, turning back to her captain.

"Captain!" A familiar voice came from the gangway. Galdinia turned to see Governor Ryden step onto the deck of the ship, surprise lighting his features as his eyes caught the queen's. "Your Majesty, I wasn't expecting you to be here already."

"I'm nothing if not prompt," Galdinia said, smiling. She was glad to be able to see Ryden again before she left.

"I suppose this is good timing, then," Ryden said, looking from Ilyon, then back to Galdinia.

"Good timing for what?" Galdinia asked, her expression quizzical.

"We have one final piece of cargo to bring on board, for which we need your approval," Ilyon said carefully, and Galdinia glanced back at him, her brows furrowing.

Footsteps echoed up onto the quiet deck of the ship from the wooden gangway, and in moments three figures appeared. Two guards stepped with heavy feet onto the ship, bringing with them a third man. In the light of a nearby lantern, Bentley's features were illuminated, his dirty face and matted hair brought into focus. His wrists and ankles were chained together from arm to foot, keeping his hands close to his body. Another precaution seemed to have been added: a sphere of water was twisting around his bound Flourisher hands.

Galdinia's heart stopped, her mouth went dry, and the tightness in her chest returned. Her body longed for a flame, yearned for it. She instinctively searched for it but couldn't feel a lick of heat in the air, nor a morsel of fire. She glanced desperately at the lanterns before realising they were not housing fire, but rather Peacelight—they couldn't bring Bentley onto a ship filled with fire, so they'd extinguished every single one in the vicinity. Galdinia couldn't speak, she couldn't think, she couldn't move.

Neryda, on the other hand, didn't appear to feel the same. In a second, and with a renewed sense of energy, she was lunging through the air, hands out, reaching for Bentley's throat.

8

"Let go of me!" Neryda's voice rang out over the silent dock as she snarled.

She moved so quickly that Ilyon barely managed to wrap his arms around her waist and pull her away from Bentley before her hands made contact with his neck. Bentley stumbled back, but the guards held him up; one of them even attempted to shield him from his attacker. Ryden appeared shocked, and the line of soldiers didn't move from their posts. Had they been trained to only move at their captain's command? Or did they know what Bentley had done and were glad to watch someone attempt to rip his head off?

Galdinia stared at Bentley, her other senses numb at the sight of him. How she longed for a flame at that moment. As he regained his balance, which seemed all the more difficult with his chained limbs and encased hands, he looked up at Galdinia. There was a shadow of something in his eyes. Was it remorse? Guilt? Surely not. Galdinia thought she must have been imagining it.

"What is he doing here?" Galdinia asked, her voice low.

"What are you thinking bringing him here?" Neryda yelled, kicking her legs in every direction as she tried to twist back towards Bentley, writhing in Ilyon's arms.

After this moment, when she was no longer shellshocked by being blindsided by Bentley's presence, Galdinia would be grateful for the fight her best friend was putting up for her honour, however drastic her reaction.

In the moment, though, she watched Bentley and wondered why her own reaction wasn't to launch into an attack against him, with or without her gift. Was she searching for a flame with which to attack or to protect herself? She'd already had her chance to strangle him, so she couldn't be surprised that Neryda had a similar reaction upon seeing him for the first time since his betrayal.

"You need to calm down, Lady Neryda," Ilyon said, his voice strained as he tried to contain Neryda's movements; if it weren't for the circumstances, Galdinia knew that Neryda would have made endless jokes about being wrapped in Ilyon's arms. "He is a prisoner of the crown and mustn't be harmed." As he spoke, he lowered her to the deck, still standing between her and Bentley.

"Mustn't be harmed?" Neryda scoffed, glaring at Bentley from over Ilyon's shoulder. "I'm sorry, Captain, but have you forgotten already what he did? He's lucky to have been in your prison! Otherwise, I would have drowned him days ago!"

"Ner," Galdinia said quietly, her voice breaking through the anger that surrounded Neryda. Everyone's eyes were fixed on her, including Bentley's, who was standing upright now, yet seemingly not as tall as he once was. He stared at her from beneath his brows, apprehensive and tired, looking like a shell of the man he once was.

Galdinia didn't believe his facade for a second.

"Perhaps we could speak about this more calmly in your quarters, Captain?" Ryden suggested, raising his eyebrows to Ilyon.

"Yes, let's," Ilyon agreed, still keeping Neryda in his peripherals. "Soldiers, take the prisoner to the brig for now. You are to both guard his doors and keep his hands weaved." The guards nodded in unison, and Ilyon turned to Galdinia, his command giving a name to the sphere of water swirling around Bentley's hands. "Your Majesty, Governor, Lady Neryda"—Ilyon's voice dipped into a tone of warning as he addressed Neryda—"please, this way."

Ilyon gestured to the doors to his quarters beneath the helm, staring Neryda down until she finally yielded and turned around to walk with Ryden across the deck. Galdinia glanced back at Bentley, his gaze on hers, still having not uttered a word. His eyes were pained. Galdinia forced herself to turn from him, not willing to give him the satisfaction of seeing her question his presence without first hearing from Ilyon and Ryden.

She followed them into Ilyon's quarters, and she heard the heavy footsteps of the guards as they walked Bentley towards the stairs that led below deck. She tried to ignore how painfully aware she was that he was now in her vicinity, but she struggled to shake the encroaching feeling. He was much easier to disregard when he was beneath the ground of Elderguard.

Through the wooden doors beneath the helm, they entered a narrow hallway that led to two doors. They entered the door with Ilyon's title on the front, and it felt like they were stepping into his drawing room at the barracks. In the centre of the room was a large table, over which were sprawled a number of maps of the Southern Shadow and the coast of Crysterra. Everything else in the room, however, seemed to be in its perfect place. There was a small collection of books that were neatly stacked on a shelf behind the desk, a carafe of water on a side table with a spotless glass beside it, a carefully draped throw over the back of a lounge chair, and in the corner of the room by the window, a bed, pristinely made, as though no one had ever slept in it.

Galdinia didn't know what to expect from Ilyon's quarters, but she supposed that this was exactly what she should have assumed. Everything was in its place, and it was unbearably clean.

"Please, take a seat," Ilyon said, extending his arm out to the chairs around the table. He and Ryden took seats on one side, while Neryda and Galdinia sat opposite them. She felt like they were school children about to be disciplined, but she quickly remembered that Ryden and Ilyon were the ones who needed to explain themselves.

The four of them looked at each other for a moment, no one quite sure where to begin. Ryden eventually broke the silence.

"We promised you that we would keep you informed of our plans and any information we became privy to," Ryden said, looking to Galdinia, his tone careful. "Yesterday, the captain and I had an illuminating discussion with Bentley."

"And?" Galdinia asked, her fists already balled in her lap.

The two men glanced at each other momentarily.

"We have come to believe that Bentley may in fact know more than he is letting on," Ryden said.

This piqued Galdinia's interest. Of course he kept information from her; all he cared about was his own neck.

"Oh?" she asked, hoping to seem nonchalant about it, but just about every muscle in her body was tensed.

"We know we cannot believe everything he has to say," Ilyon went on, "but we think he may have insight into not only Valah's where-abouts, but her plans moving forward."

"What else could he possibly know?"

"That remains to be seen, unfortunately," Ryden replied. "But he assured us that he has information that could help keep you alive. We think he may be an asset as we gather more information about the Midlands and its provinces that we think could be valuable."

"Okay," Galdinia said, still dubious. "Then why is he here? Can't you extract the information while we're gone, Ryden? You can send a raven with your findings."

"That would be the far simpler plan, yes," Ryden agreed, nodding. "However, Bentley had some demands of his own."

"Oh, here we go," Neryda said with a huff, breaking her silence and crossing her arms over her chest.

"He requested to be taken on the journey to the Wetlands if and when the queen decided to travel," Ryden said carefully.

"But I'm not going to the Wetlands," Galdinia countered. "You were decidedly against that."

"Yes, but he doesn't know that," Ilyon replied.

Galdinia raised her eyebrows.

"He thinks we're going to the Wetlands now?" Galdinia asked.

"Correct," Ryden said with a curt nod.

"And you think he'll talk between now and when we arrive at The Hook?"

"We hope so," Ilyon said. "If not, we will tell him that we are making a necessary stop in the southwest to secure allies before moving to the Wetlands."

"Don't you think he could be using this as a means of trying to escape?" Galdinia asked, her brow furrowing.

"That is a possibility," Ilyon replied. "If we are successful in retrieving information from him, though, he won't step on land again until you return to Elderguard. We don't intend on him leaving his chains in the brig."

Galdinia considered this plan. What information might Bentley hold that would actually be worth risking him escaping their grasp? Would he try to run when they docked in The Hook? If he could get out of the cell, Galdinia imagined that it wouldn't be hard for him to swim ashore once they were close enough to land. He could even bribe his way off the ship the moment he harnessed a nearby flame.

"What about fire?" Galdinia asked. "What if he got his hands on a flame? He's a powerful Flourisher."

The men exchanged another look, this time longer and painfully silent. Ilyon held Galdinia's eyes for a moment before answering, causing an apprehension to forge in her stomach.

"We have removed every flame from the ship in anticipation for his arrival."

A weight landed somewhere deep within her as her fears were confirmed.

"I see," Galdinia said slowly.

"We can't risk him harnessing a flame, so we have employed a priestess to join us on the ship and keep it lit at night with her gift by drawing on the light of the moon and stars. We will need to go without warm food or hot water for a few days while we travel, but at least we will be able to see in the dark by way of the priestess' lanterns."

Galdinia's hunger for a flame grew as they spoke, and she was becoming acutely aware of just how restricted she felt without it. As they sat in the captain's quarters, she instinctively searched for a nearby flame, but she knew there were none to be found.

"I don't think a hot meal should be our main concern here," Galdinia said, careful to keep her voice even. "If we don't have a flame onboard, I won't be able to protect myself."

"We considered this," Ryden said even more carefully. "The journey will take a day and a half, and the risk would be far too high to allow Bentley access to a flame."

"It's a risk to bring him at all," Neryda said, her words scathing.

"How am I to protect myself if he tries to attack me?" Galdinia asked, the image of Bentley leaping at her amongst the flames in the library coming back to her.

"One of my soldiers will always be shadowing you," Ilyon assured her, his expression firm. "Every gift is among them, so some of them will have to go without their gift for the next few days also. With Weavers, Wielders, and a heavily armoured guard, we hope that your need for fire will be considerably diminished."

"It's not just about needing to protect myself," Galdinia said, trying to explain her feelings. "I may be new to my gift, but I under-stand just as well as anyone how necessary it is to maintain a regular functioning life. Imagine if the sea were sucked dry and the skies never shed rain on our land, Captain. You would feel like you were suffocating."

Ilyon looked as though he was struggling to think up a rebuttal.

"Or what if the breeze went still and you couldn't feel the air dance around you?" Galdinia asked, now pointing her words at Ryden. "I don't have the luxury of having constant access to my element. I have just been given my gift. I don't need it ripped away from me so quickly."

"We know this is a monstrous request, Your Majesty," Ryden said, his eyes drawn from her own.

"We recognise it is a great sacrifice for you to go without your gift for the next two days," Ilyon began, "so if you'd prefer us to keep him in Elderguard, Governor Ryden can work on drawing out information from him while you're gone. It is entirely your decision."

Galdinia looked to each of them, their expressions reflecting varying degrees of gravity, hope, and contempt. While she knew that she should simply forgo her gift in the hopes that Bentley would share whatever information he might or might not hold, she felt uneasy about willingly surrendering her gift for thirty-six hours. It felt like a betrayal against herself.

"And what if Bentley doesn't have any information for us?" Galdinia finally asked, turning back to the men.

"Then it will have wasted a short—yet significant—amount of time that our queen could have been flourishing her gift," Ryden said, sincerity behind each word. "We don't ask this of you lightly, Your

Highness, and please know that we would never request this of you if we didn't think it was worth it."

Galdinia contemplated this and turned to Neryda. Her friend was telling her with her eyes that it was Galdinia's choice to make, and Galdinia knew she would support her no matter what. Plus, if she kept Bentley around for a few more days, perhaps Neryda would actually drown him, and then one of her more immediate problems would be solved.

"Fine," Galdinia finally said, bringing a smile to Ryden's face. "But I don't want to have to see or hear from him."

"Absolutely," Ilyon agreed, nodding.

"Thank you, Galdinia," Ryden said quietly. "We both pray that this will be a fruitful journey and worth your sacrifice."

"So do I."

The four of them shared a brief moment of silence before the captain spoke up. "I think it's time to introduce you to my soldiers, Your Majesty."

9

AFTER THEIR DISCUSSION, RYDEN DISEMBARKED AND STOOD WATCHING the royal ship leave its dock just as the sun started to appear over the horizon. Galdinia watched him shrink in the distance as Elderguard eclipsed the sun's rays. As the wind picked up with their speed, Galdinia's heart knotted with so many emotions: her excitement about leaving the walls of the capital had dulled since Bentley's arrival and the loss of her gift; her confidence in Ryden to watch over Elderguard in her stead was muted at the sight of the crumbling seawalls, which brought an unease at the thought of leaving her home so soon after such a brutal attack. Galdinia tried not to let the discord within herself mar her judgement or allow her mind to waver on the decisions she'd already made. She had to believe that she was making the right decision for her people, despite the friction in her chest.

You're going to find a way to avenge them, she reminded herself as the ship sailed into open water. She wasn't leaving to take a vacation or run away from her problems; she was leaving her city to protect it. She was leaving to rescue a piece of her heart.

"Your Highness." Ilyon approached Galdinia, drawing her attention from Elderguard and back to the main deck. "I'd like to introduce you to my best soldiers and, moving forward, the Queen's Guard."

Galdinia's ears pricked up.

"The Queen's Guard?" Galdinia asked, hoping her expression reflected her curiosity instead of her convoluted feelings about leaving Elderguard.

"Just as your father had his own guard, so you will too," Ilyon replied.

Four soldiers stood at attention behind Ilyon, their arms firmly clasped behind their backs. The other eight soldiers on the ship were keeping the vessel moving and constantly patrolling the deck. While all twelve were part of the Royal Guard, Galdinia welcomed the idea of having a dedicated group of soldiers, particularly while she couldn't flourish fire.

"These are four of the most skilled soldiers I've ever had the pleasure of training, and they will be by your side for the remainder of our trip. Should you find their protection useful and… successful, we can instate them as your guard full-time."

"You mean if they keep me alive?" Galdinia asked, raising a brow at her captain.

"Well, yes, I suppose so," Ilyon replied, his voice briefly grave. "Moving on." He approached the first soldier, who was lean and stood taller than Ilyon by a few centimetres. "This is Kayd, the most powerful Wind Wielder in the capital."

Kayd removed his helmet and tucked it under his arm. His expression was serious, though his features were somewhat boyish—flushed cheeks, slightly upturned lips, and a round chin. He bowed briefly before uttering, "Your Majesty."

Galdinia nodded to the soldier.

"Kayd's father was in the Royal Guard before him, so he has been training since he was a child. Kayd is in his sixth year of service to the crown."

Galdinia knew that soldiers could be drafted into the army from the age of eighteen, and given his family's involvement, she imagined that Kayd signed up as soon as he was able to.

"Next is Raia," Ilyon said, taking a step forward to the next soldier.

Galdinia was shocked as she watched Raia remove their helmet, beneath which was a long ponytail of blonde hair, rosy cheeks, and full lips. Galdinia recognised her instantly as one of the soldiers that Ilyon had chosen to train with them in the barracks during the Week of Mourning. At the time, Ilyon had informed her of their plans to publicly open the Royal Guard program to female soldiers; Ilyon, Ryden, and her father had personally invited potential candidates for five years, without the knowledge of the Syndicate or the public. Of course Galdinia was in full support of this, especially after she had trained with Raia in the barracks. Despite this, Galdinia was still pleasantly surprised to see a woman standing before her, fully armoured and considered one of the most powerful soldiers in the Royal Guard.

Raia bowed, addressing Galdinia similarly to Kayd. Galdinia smiled in response.

"Raia and Kayd are cousins, and she followed in Kayd's footsteps when she turned eighteen four years ago," Ilyon went on, drawing Galdinia's attention to Raia's and Kayd's similarities—pale complexion, wide eyes, and light hair. "Raia is a Water Weaver and gives me a run for my money daily with her gift."

Raia's stony expression faltered for a moment as her lips curled in response to her captain's compliment. Galdinia would be giddy to hear Ilyon speak about her gift with such high praise.

"This is Evander," Ilyon said, stepping forward to the next soldier. Evander removed his helmet, revealing short, cropped dark hair and deep umber skin, before he followed suit, greeting the queen in the same way his comrades had. "He is our resident Fire Flourisher, and he's been in my service for eight years. He's about as happy to be separated from his element as you are, but he is also a master swordsman, so I don't foresee him slowing down while he is without access to his gift."

Evander's dark eyes darted from the captain's and back to Galdinia. His face was stern, which was possibly his response to being without his gift or simply his usual demeanour.

"You met these three during our training last week," Ilyon explained, validating Galdinia's memories, "albeit in a less formal manner."

"I'm glad to put faces to the gifts, as it were," Galdinia replied, looking back at the first three soldiers. "It's lovely to meet you all officially."

While she had only glimpsed Raia's face during their training session in the Week of Mourning, now that she looked at the three of them again, all standing at attention, their builds and stances were unmistakable.

"Finally, this is Vega." Ilyon gestured to the final soldier, who removed her helmet. Two long black braids ran down Vega's back, and despite the fact that most of her tawny brown skin was covered by her armour, Galdinia could tell that Vega was muscular and strong. "Vega has been in our service for five years. She was our first female soldier in the Royal Guard program, and unlike her companions, she does not possess a gift."

Galdinia was surprised by this, but she tried not to show it on her face. She didn't think she was doing a fantastic job of hiding just how pleased she was about the Royal Guard not only accepting female soldiers, but those without a gift in their new program.

"Vega is an expert in hand-to-hand combat, a trained archer, and if given access to even the smallest dagger, could climb the rigging, lay waste to the sails, and end our lives in less than twenty seconds."

At this, Vega finally bowed.

"Thank you all for accompanying me on this journey," Galdinia said, her eyes scanning the soldiers before her, the morning sun glinting off their onyx-coloured helmets, which were tucked under each of their right arms. "I understand the captain didn't likely give you a choice"—Galdinia glanced at Ilyon, a smile on her lips—"but your service is greatly appreciated, and I hope your presence will surmount to nothing more than a precaution in the coming days."

The soldiers bowed once again to their queen, this time in unison, not an ounce of humour in their faces.

"Given the lack of flames, Your Highness, I brought you something to make you feel a little more at ease." Leaning around the mast, Ilyon picked up a sheath of arrows, which was attached to a brown leather belt with a golden buckle, and an elegantly crafted golden bow. The bow was stunning, Galdinia thought, gratefully taking it from Ilyon.

"Thank you, Captain," Galdinia said, inspecting the bow as it gleamed in the early morning light, the sunrise making visible intricate carvings of vines beside the grip. The weapon was heavy in her hands, but she instantly felt a sense of calm with it in her possession.

"Of course," Ilyon replied, also handing her the quiver of arrows. "Your father kept these on his person when travelling beyond the walls of Elderguard. Thankfully, he didn't need to use the bow often, but it can certainly put one's heart at ease."

Galdinia took the strap and secured the quiver to her back.

"Vega will run you through a training session later this morning when we're all feeling a little more limber." Although Galdinia knew that she was the least limber among them, she was thankful that Ilyon insinuated that everyone else might still need time to wake up their bodies. She didn't imagine these soldiers slept much, yet they all seemed entirely composed and prepared for a long day. "I'll show you to your quarters with Lady Neryda. Soldiers, you're dismissed."

Ilyon turned, and Galdinia followed closely, leaving the soldiers watching her as they walked away. He led her to the door beside his own rooms, pushing it open for her to enter. This room, while a mirror image of Ilyon's quarters, was far more lavishly decorated with tufted throws, heavy drapes over the windows, rich velvet and intricate candelabras. On the bed across the room lay Neryda, having pulled a book from Galdinia's satchel, holding it in the air above her as she read.

"I can't believe you considered this one of your essential items to bring with you," Neryda said with a scoff, rolling over to look at Galdinia and the captain standing in the doorway. In seconds, Neryda was on her feet, discarded the book to the side, and appeared incredibly sheepish. "Captain, hello!"

"Hello, Lady Neryda," Ilyon said, raising his eyebrows in response to her movements. "If you can move that quickly in combat, I could use someone like you in my army."

Neryda stood up straighter and grinned.

"Let's not give her any more ideas," Galdinia said pointedly before drawing Ilyon's attention back to her. "Thank you for organising the Queen's Guard. I'd say that I look forward to training with Vega later, but I'm not sure that would be entirely honest."

"She's a ruthless competitor and outstanding soldier, but she wouldn't dream of hurting the queen," Ilyon said assuredly. "But perhaps this will put your mind more at ease. May I?"

The captain gestured to a large cabinet behind the desk. Galdinia stepped aside, and he strode across the room and opened the cabinet doors.

Inside stood a suit of armour resting on a female form, and atop it sat a helmet. The armour matched those worn by Ilyon's soldiers in its deep onyx colour. The only difference that Galdinia noticed was that this suit had a small flame encircled by a crown etched in the breast plate, right above the heart.

"You got me my own set?" Galdinia asked, placing her bow on the desk and approaching the armour, eyes wide. She wasn't sure if he would have abided by her request, given the connotation that came with it: the queen in battle.

"Of course. The blacksmiths in the armoury have been working on it day and night this past week. I also took the liberty of having Madame Moya sew you three fresh sets of fighting leathers too. Lady Neryda, she made a set for you as well. She wasn't too pleased about the short notice, but we all know that she'd do anything for you, Your Highness."

"I don't think many things please that woman," Galdinia said frankly, not taking her eyes off the armour as she reached out and placed her fingertips over the breastplate; it was cool and strong to the touch.

"There's one other thing," Ilyon said, stepping forward to pick up the helmet; his fingers were gentle and careful as he handed it to Galdinia. "Look at the name plate inside."

Galdinia took the helmet from her captain and turned it over in her hands, inspecting it. At the back of the helmet, a small metal plate had been bolted over the inner lining, identifying the owner of the armour. As she read the inscription, Galdinia's heart tumbled in her chest.

D. Allard, Elderguard Royal Guard.

"This is Drystan's helmet?" Galdinia asked, running her fingers along the words, her voice thick and her eyes glassy.

"It was found near the Northern Gates on The Seventh Day of Mourning," Ilyon explained. "I thought you may like to have it."

"Thank you so much, Captain," Galdinia said, her voice shaking as she turned the helmet over, now noticing a few small dents and scratches in the metal that Drystan had received during his short time as a Royal Guard soldier. It had obviously been cleaned and buffed in the days after it was retrieved, so the surface shone, making it appear fresh from the armoury from afar. Had this piece of his armour kept him alive during the attack?

"You're welcome, Your Highness," Ilyon said, gracing Galdinia with a brief smile. "Rest for an hour, suit up, and meet Vega on the deck." Ilyon's words came out more like an order than Galdinia thought he intended, so he quickly added, "When you're ready, of course."

"Will do," Galdinia said, and then Ilyon turned to leave.

Neryda was at Galdinia's side in a heartbeat, peering to look at the evidence of Drystan in the helmet.

"He'd want you to have it," Neryda said, wrapping an arm around Galdinia, who just continued to stare at his name.

"Mm-hmm" was all Galdinia could manage as the tears swelled in her eyes.

"He'd be glad to still be protecting you," Neryda added, squeezing Galdinia close.

No matter how far away Drystan was, no matter how weak or battered he was, of course he would still have a hand in keeping her safe. Although the inner lining had been cleaned, Galdinia could smell the faintest hint of Drystan's warm scent in the fabric. The hairs on the back of her neck prickled, causing her to reluctantly place the helmet back in its place in the cabinet for fear of losing all sense of herself in the memories of her last moments with Drystan in the castle.

"So where's mine?" Neryda asked as Galdinia pushed the door of the cabinet shut with a click.

"You won't need one," Galdinia replied with a sniff, not looking away from the cabinet. "You won't be in combat."

"You don't know that."

"Yes, I do," Galdinia replied firmly, no amount of humour in her voice. "I won't have you anywhere near a battle, should it come to one."

"I don't think you get to decide that, Gal." In response to Neryda's objection, Galdinia turned to look at her friend, frowning and still fighting back tears. "If we are suddenly thrust into a battle while on this journey, I should be just as prepared to protect myself. And I don't think fighting leathers will be enough. I know I'm not the queen or anything, but confidant and royal food tester feel like pretty important roles to protect."

"Royal food tester?"

"You didn't know if those biscuits were safe this morning until I ate them!"

An air of levity returned to the room, and Galdinia smiled in spite of herself.

"Yes, because Miss Giles has been working on a decades-long plot to take me down with sweet treats."

"Either way, I'm important and need armour too!"

"Ner." Galdinia placed her hands on Neryda's shoulders and looked at her square in the face. "Trust me when I say that you will be miles from a battle, should one arise. At the slightest whiff of conflict, I'll be sending you as far away as possible."

"Maybe I want to fight too. You can't stop me."

"I already let Drystan slip through my fingers, Neryda. I can't let that happen to you as well." Galdinia could feel her voice tightening with every word, the very possible threat of losing another friend crashing upon her. "You have no idea the guilt and pain I carry with me every day when I relive the moment Valah took him away from me. You're lucky I even let you on this trip in the first place. Your safety is the most important thing to me, and I will put you on a ship back home in an instant before I let you in a battle. I couldn't possibly survive without you too."

"Don't you think I want to keep you safe as well?" Neryda argued, a scowl forming on her brow, her expression communicating that this should have been obvious to Galdinia.

"Let the soldiers protect me with their weapons and gifts," Galdinia said, pulling Neryda into her side, wrapping her arms tightly around her best friend. "You can keep testing my meals before I eat them."

What had started as a good-humoured conversation to improve

Galdinia's spirits had quickly divulged into the pain that came with the possible reality of losing each other. While neither Galdinia nor Neryda had any siblings, they both found familial comfort with each other. Knowing that another conflict with Valah was inevitable, Galdinia couldn't help but feel emotional at the thought of losing her best friend.

"I'll be the best royal food tester ever," Neryda said, leaning her head against Galdinia's shoulder.

Galdinia looked back at the cabinet, the image of Drystan's name on the helmet etched into her mind. The longer she was without her gift, the more she wanted to strap her armour on.

"And an even better confidant."

10

An hour later, after she and Neryda clumsily wrangled her armour on, Galdinia stepped out onto the deck of the ship, Drystan's helmet tucked carefully under her arm. She felt simultaneously awkward and strengthened in her armour. Although the pieces of metal were made to her exact specifications, fitting her as well as her new fighting leathers, she would need to learn how to move more gracefully in them. The added weight and rigidity would take some getting used to.

As she walked across the deck, the eyes of the surrounding soldiers turned to watch her. Galdinia was glad for the cool ocean breeze that ran through her hair; the dark armour radiated with the warmth of the sun as it rose higher still in the air. The sensation was almost akin to how she felt when she was using her gift.

"How does it fit?" Ilyon asked as she came to stand by him at the mainsail.

"Perfect," Galdinia said, moving her arms by way of demonstration. She chose not to mention how stiff she felt and hoped her movements appeared natural and fluid.

"Excellent," Ilyon said with a nod before turning to the raised deck where Raia was behind the helm, Vega at attention by her side. "Vega!"

At her captain's command, Vega made her way down the stairs and came to stand beside Ilyon, hands clasped behind her back, eyes forward. Although Vega's expression was stern and unreadable, Galdinia couldn't help but notice just how striking her face was. Her high cheekbones, defined Cupid's bow, and thick lashes were made all the more apparent now that Galdinia wasn't distracted by introductions or the fact that she was standing in front of a team of soldiers who had been handpicked to keep her alive. Her sword hung easily at her hip, and her posture was impeccable; there wasn't an ounce of apprehension in her stance. Although she tried to stand tall, Galdinia didn't think the armour would be enough to supplement her confidence.

"Your Highness, Captain," Vega said, greeting them both.

"You're very skilled with a bow and arrow, Your Highness," Ilyon explained, "but I'd like to see you work on your sword and shield skills. You can take these."

Ilyon handed her a sword and shield, which were similar to those she had trained with during the Week of Mourning, but they would take some adjustment to manoeuvre in her new ensemble.

"Are there any particular drills you'd like us to run?" Vega's voice was low and silky smooth.

"I'll leave that up to you," Ilyon replied, "but let's get our queen moving in her new armour."

"Good to know you won't be reducing the intensity of my training," Galdinia said, looking knowingly at Ilyon, hoping some humour would dull the rising concern in her chest.

"Neither of us want that." Ilyon returned her expression before turning to join Raia at the helm.

"Alright, Your Majesty, let's—"

"Galdinia is fine."

Vega paused, her countenance firm, before continuing to speak. "Your Majesty," she went on, ignoring Galdinia's request, "let's start by warming up your arms. I want you to make your way across the deck, moving your arms up and out, shield on one, sword in the other. You need to get used to the weight of the weapons first."

In normal circumstances, Galdinia might have questioned why Vega refused to call her by her first name, but given the weapons in their vicinity and the pain she assumed she was about to feel, Galdinia didn't think this was the best time to scrutinise her new ally. Instead, Galdinia strapped the shield to her left arm and lifted the helmet to her face, slipping it onto her head. She was immediately overcome by the familiar remnants of Drystan's scent, and her pulse quickened beneath the armour in one breath of warmth and comfort.

This was not the moment she wanted to be distracted, so without hesitating another second, Galdinia did as she was told.

After twenty laps of the deck, Vega changed the exercise, instructing Galdinia to move her arms in a forward motion instead. Once she had completed twenty laps of that movement, she was told to rotate her torso from side to side as she lunged over the deck. By the time she finished, her body was certainly warm—sweat was trickling down her neck as the sun beat down on them. The fresh autumn air was only able to cool her so much when she was wrapped in metal.

"Now that you're limber, we are going to walk across the deck, facing each other. I'll go backwards, you go forwards. With every other step, I want you to swing your sword and—"

"At you?" Galdinia asked, thinking it prudent to clarify.

"Yes. You can—"

"But what if I hit you?"

Vega paused again, clearly thinking carefully about her words before she said them. "You won't."

With Vega's definitive tone, Galdinia reminded herself that she was talking to the person who Ilyon had described as an expert in hand-to-hand combat. Perhaps Galdinia should have been surprised that Vega didn't simply laugh in her face.

"As I was saying, you can swing your sword in either direction, but be mindful of the placement of your feet. Depending on your positioning, you'll find it more comfortable moving in some directions than others. This is a good way to learn to listen to your body and use your strength strategically."

Galdinia simply nodded as Vega positioned herself in front of Galdinia and took a step backwards. Galdinia followed suit and stepped forward, swinging her sword awkwardly at Vega. It was a weak swing, and Vega didn't even need to use her shield to defend herself. She merely leant backwards to avoid it.

"Come on, Your Majesty," Vega said, her voice almost a drawl. "I think you can do better than that."

Galdinia didn't have the relationship with this soldier to respond with a quippy reply, but it seemed that for the same reason, she felt she couldn't swing her sword with all her strength. She wasn't a soldier, and it didn't feel right to attack one of her own, even in training.

Galdinia took another two steps forward and swung her sword again, this time putting more energy into it.

"You'll have to do better than that to keep up with Valah's armies, Your Highness," Vega said, again easily avoiding the swing with the quick twist of her shoulders.

Galdinia felt a frown form over her brow and irritation bubble deep in her chest. This spurred her on to slash the blade through the air once again, still not quite connecting with Vega's shield.

"You just lost against a soldier from the Wetlands," Vega muttered, once again easily avoiding the attack.

Galdinia's skin was getting hotter with each word that came from Vega. Vega hadn't seen how good Galdinia was with a flame or a bow and arrow. She'd used a shield during the battle in Elderguard, but her gift was the far superior weapon, and her longing for it grew with every swing of the sword. If only Vega had seen her in the battle, she wouldn't be hurling such insults now.

Another two steps forward, and Galdinia swung her sword out from her body, and Vega used her shield to deflect it this time, the metals feebly clattering.

"Well done." Vega's voice was monotonous. "You may have just given someone a paper cut."

It seemed like such a contradiction that Vega wouldn't call Galdinia by her first name but was willing to spout such blatantly rude words at her. Did she not realise that Galdinia wasn't a soldier?

As Vega took another step backwards, Galdinia twisted her body so she was perpendicular to the soldier. With a mighty backhanded swing, Galdinia hurled her body towards Vega, arm outstretched. Her sword sent a cascading metallic ring across the ship as it collided with Vega's shield, which she held firmly in front of her face. Galdinia stumbled back as the shock wave reverberated up her arm. With the extra weight of her armour, she lost her footing and fell to the ground with a thud, her sword clattering by her side. A deep burning rose in her cheeks as a heavy weight of humiliation settled over her.

"Well done, Your Majesty," Vega said, her voice noticeably gentler. "That's more like it."

Galdinia pushed the helmet up from her face with a huff, utterly exasperated. Vega stretched out her hand towards the queen, which Galdinia scrutinised—her hesitation palpable—before accepting it. Vega easily lifted Galdinia to her feet, and they were again standing face-to-face. Although Vega's expression was still firm, there was a new softness in her eyes.

"I've got to say," Galdinia said, picking up her sword and inspecting it, "the negative motivation strategy doesn't really work with me."

She wasn't sure she'd agree to more training sessions if they'd end up like this.

"It got you to do that, didn't it?" Vega asked simply.

"Yes, but I don't need to be made frustrated by one of my soldiers to land a successful blow to an enemy," Galdinia assured her, attempting to keep her tone even and amicable.

"Trust me, Your Majesty, when you're in a battle with hundreds of enemy soldiers who want not only your blood but every ally and friend that stands around you, you'll be feeling all sorts of frustration. It's not something to run away from, it's something to harness; why not practise that now in a safe environment?"

To this, Galdinia didn't have a reply. She wasn't sure this felt like an entirely safe environment, not while she was falling on the ground and feeling like a sideshow for the soldiers who patrolled around them on the ship.

"I'd prefer that I stayed on my feet," Galdinia said, as though offering a possible compromise.

"We'll see what we can do about that," Vega replied, her strong body imposing and very much suggesting such a promise could not be kept.

"Let's keep going, then." Galdinia pushed the helmet back down onto her face before readying herself to swing her sword again, determined to stay on her feet.

Two hours later, Galdinia was covered in a layer of sweat, her arms ached, and she was about ready to throw her sword, shield, and Vega overboard. However, swinging her sword was becoming only more comfortable, and a fresh fervour burned in her stomach each time she connected her weapon with her soldier's.

"You're beginning to tire," Vega said after Galdinia landed a less powerful blow to Vega's shield. "I think it's time we take a break."

"No, I can keep going," Galdinia said between great gulps of air. It wasn't lost on her what Vega was suggesting: she wasn't strong enough to continue. The burning in her gut was urging her to continue.

"I don't make it a habit of training new soldiers beyond their limits," Vega explained, sheathing her own sword. Her expression was resolute.

"I know my own limits," Galdinia pressed, her frown deepening.

"I'm sure you do, Your Highness, but I know soldiers. And you'll thank me tomorrow when you're actually able to move your limbs."

With a sigh, Galdinia sheathed her sword and replied with a terse, "Fine."

Vega's dark eyes watched Galdinia carefully, her expression unreadable. "A pleasure, Your Majesty," Vega said, before turning to move below deck to her quarters, moving as though their training had had little to no effect on her.

The moment Vega was out of sight, Galdinia turned, pulled Drystan's helmet from her head, and placed her free hand on her waist, taking in deep breaths, her exhaustion very much showing on both her face and body now that she was alone.

Despite Vega's initially abrasive strategies, Galdinia had to begrudgingly admit that she had elicited successful results. For all her skills in archery and her training in using her gift, the sword and shield had been foreign to the young queen. After training with Vega, however, she felt her confidence grow ever so slightly.

"How did it go?" Ilyon asked, approaching Galdinia from the helm. "I could see a lot of improvement from where I was."

"Yes, it went well," Galdinia replied, her words still curt. "But I don't think Vega likes me very much. Nor do I think I like her."

"Don't be put off by Vega's demeanour," Ilyon said.

"It's hard not to be," Galdinia retorted, wiping the sweat from her hairline with the back of her armoured hand.

"She's like that with everyone," Ilyon replied. "She works hard, and she expects the same of those around her."

"Well, that's just it; I wanted to keep working, but she said it was time to stop. I know when I need a break."

"Respectfully, Your Highness, if Vega suggested you needed a break, then she's probably right. She has trained a dozen battalions, and they're the strongest groups I've ever seen. She knows when to work hard, but she also knows when to rest."

"I still didn't appreciate her tone," Galdinia said, letting her annoyance sit with her.

"I'll talk to her about it," Ilyon replied, "but remember that she's here to protect and train you, not to be your friend."

Galdinia nodded, sucking in another deep breath, her heart rate finally lowering.

"I think I need to get out of this armour," Galdinia said, her arms very much feeling the weight of the metal wrapped around her.

"It's about time for lunch anyway," Ilyon said, changing the subject. "Go rest up, and I'll send a guard into your rooms with a plate for you and Neryda shortly."

"Thank you, Captain," Galdinia replied.

With that, she turned from Ilyon back to her quarters. At the sight of her bed, she was ready to peel her armour off and take a nap.

Perhaps, after all, Vega was right.

II

Galdinia was walking through Elderguard at dusk, wading through a heavy mist. As she walked across the square, she watched as attendants and civilians started setting up the decorations for the Commemoration Banquet. They were singing jovially to themselves, excited to celebrate their incoming ruler. After the Week of Mourning, they were glad to be able to celebrate together, to laugh, to drink, to dance.

One civilian turned and saw the princess approaching, and their expression dropped.

"You haven't got your gift yet?" they asked as she walked past.

"How do you expect to rule without your gift?" another spat, their voice dripping with disgust as their smile turned to a frown.

"No, I do have my gift, I…" Galdinia looked down at her hands, reaching out for the familiar warmth of a flame, but she couldn't do it; she couldn't draw on the fire. She stared at the flames in the nearby lanterns and torches on the street; they moved, flickering, but not at her command. They were mocking her. Her body yearned for the fire as she stretched her desperate hands out to the flames, but they merely shifted in the breeze. She couldn't control them.

"You're an imposter, a liar!" the first person said, frowning at her and turning away.

"You'll never be queen," the other replied, also turning their back on Galdinia.

Before she could refute their claims, Galdinia watched as smoke rose in the north.

The gates were burning. She had to extinguish it.

Galdinia ran up Main Court towards the gates, watching the billowing smoke rise into the air. She tried to run faster, but her legs felt heavy and tired, as though she were running through thick, wet sand. As she strode forward, her throat began to itch as she inhaled the smoke; it tightened her lungs, making her breaths shorter.

When she finally made it to the gates, she found Ilyon, who was covered in ash and blood.

"Princess!" he exclaimed, running to her side. "Princess, Valah has him, she has—"

"Drystan." She whispered his name as she watched the gates burn higher and higher. Through the flames she could see the shadowy figures of people far across the plane. Drystan was out there.

She reached her hands up, urging the flames to shift, to make a path for her, but they simply raged on, taking no notice of her efforts.

"What are you doing?" Ilyon asked, looking at her with disbelief.

"I need to move the flames. I need to get to him…" She trailed off, losing her breath as she inhaled more smoke, her chest aching and her eyes watering.

"You can't," Ilyon said, putting his hands on Galdinia's shoulders, trying to stop her. "You don't have a gift."

"But I do! I'm a Fire Flourisher!" Galdinia said, sweat now dripping down her temples as she stepped closer to the flames, arms still outstretched, aching in the heat on the fire. "I can do this! I can save him!"

"Princess, you need to give up," Ilyon said softly, his brows furrowed.

"I'm not a princess anymore, I'm the queen," Galdinia said breathlessly, her eyes becoming heavy. "I'm the queen!"

Galdinia woke with a start, sweat coating her brow, her hands clenched and her breaths heavy.

She quickly oriented herself in the wake of her dream, the rocking of the vessel beneath her on the water reminding her where she was.

She was on the royal ship, on her way to The Hook. She was a Fire Flourisher and Queen of Crysterra.

She was safe.

She stared up at the ceiling as she tried to catch her breath, attempting not to wake Neryda, who lay beside her, sound asleep.

Galdinia's chest was sore, her hairline was damp, and her muscles were aching, though she didn't think she could attribute the latter to her dream, but rather to her training session with Vega.

Feeling as though she were still surrounded by smoke, Galdinia yearned for fresh air, not sure she could spend another second in her stuffy, suffocating quarters. With that thought, she quietly slipped out from under the sheets, pulled her cloak from the back of the desk chair, and threw it over her shoulders, tying it up close to her collarbones.

Galdinia stepped out of the door of her rooms into the crisp night and gladly welcomed the autumnal weather. Tilting her head backwards to look into the sky, she inhaled deeply, the residual feeling of smoke dissolving in the clean air. She stretched her pained arms over her head, revelling in the release it gave her. Gleaming in the inky black sky, the moon cast its shimmering light over the deck, reminding Galdinia she had only three weeks to meet Valah's demands. As she scanned beyond the railing of the ship, all Galdinia could see was the sea—the endless, formidable sea. They were well on their way to The Hook, and she could no longer see the safety of land behind them.

A guttural sound that somewhat resembled a human drew her attention across the deck to the port side.

"Hurry up," a gruff voice said from the shadows of the mast.

"Sorry my ailment is inconveniencing you," a weary yet snarky voice retorted.

Despite its lack of usual vibrancy, Galdinia would know Bentley's voice anywhere.

She stepped cautiously towards the port side, her heart racing at the thought of Bentley having left the brig.

A guard stood by the railing, his back to the queen. He looked down upon who appeared to be Bentley, his torso well and truly over the railing. Galdinia heard him retch, followed by a distant splashing sound.

"Alright, let's go," the guard said, pulling Bentley back up and turning him around, Bentley's chains in his hands. "Your Majesty!"

The guard halted as he spotted the queen, his eyebrows raised and eyes wide. Galdinia glimpsed Bentley's face, and he looked more unwell than she had seen him in his cell in the barracks. His hair was still matted, his eyes were set in deep shadows, and his face was pale. She wasn't sure if it was the moonlight playing tricks on her, but he looked almost green.

Bentley was seasick.

That fact instantly put Galdinia's mind at ease, replacing her concern with pure delight.

The guard bowed without hesitating, pulling Bentley into a bow with him. Bentley didn't appreciate the sudden movement, and when he came back up, he wrenched himself from the guard's grip and emptied more of the contents of his stomach over the railing. The guard raced after him and held on to the back of his shirt tightly, pulling him from the edge of the ship.

"I was just taking the prisoner back to his cell, Your Majesty," the guard explained hastily, pulling a very ill-looking Bentley in close to him. "I didn't anticipate seeing you on deck so late."

"I couldn't sleep," Galdinia said simply, watching Bentley as he looked at her with drooping, exhausted eyes. "It looks like you haven't been able to either."

"Unfortunately not," the guard said, answering for Bentley. "But we'll be out of your way now."

"Why don't you leave the prisoner here with me?" Galdinia suggested, stepping in front of the guard's path.

"I'm sorry, Your Highness, but I couldn't do that. I—"

"You most certainly can. He doesn't have access to his gift, and even if he did, I don't think it would be much use to him right now. Why don't you leave this with me?" Galdinia said, reaching out to take the guard's sword from his hip. He flinched as she did so, taken aback by the queen's casual approach. "I can protect myself in case he musters up the strength to try to throw me overboard."

The guard seemed to contemplate this for a moment. Galdinia

knew he would be in direct opposition of his captain's orders, but was it worse to deny the queen's wishes?

"Alright, but I'll be just over there, keeping watch," he said quickly, pointing to the stairs that led up to the helm where Raia was steering the ship, her gentle eyes watching them silently. She observed Galdinia carefully and looked as though she may say something but seemed to think better of it and kept her eyes trained on the queen.

"Of course," Galdinia said with a sweet smile, turning back to the guard. "I'd expect nothing less."

The guard relinquished Bentley's shirt with hesitation before marching to the other side of the ship. He stood at attention and watched the queen from the bottom of the stairs. Without the stability of the guard's hands, Bentley swayed, the chains binding his ankles and wrists softly clinking. He and Galdinia stared at each other, and a small smile lit up Galdinia's face.

"You get seasick," she said plainly, raising one eyebrow.

"Well observed," he replied groggily, his voice thick with pain and exhaustion.

"And it was your idea to come on this boat."

"I thought you were going to the Wetlands by land, so I assumed I'd be taken to a horse or cart," Bentley said, still swaying as he tried to balance himself against the movement of the ship. "I think I was less pleased to see the ship than Neryda was to see me."

"How poetic," Galdinia said, her smirk deepening. "You get seasick." She repeated herself out of sheer amusement and disbelief. She was thoroughly enjoying herself.

Bentley didn't reply—or rather, he didn't have time to. His eyes widened, and he turned quickly to retch once again over the side of the ship. Galdinia's smile was now a fully-grown grin.

She approached the edge of the ship slowly, coming to stand beside Bentley as he coughed. She didn't imagine he had anything left in him to empty into the sea. After a few long seconds, he turned slowly and slid down the wall of the ship's railing, sitting on the deck and leaning his head back against the wood. His heavy breaths were ragged, and his hands trembled.

Galdinia realised that his hands were no longer wrapped in water as they had been the previous morning. Galdinia supposed it didn't matter—there was now a sea between them and the nearest flame.

"How did you manage to talk your way out of your cell?" Galdinia asked, looking down at him.

"I didn't need to say anything," he said between two long, shaky breaths. "I filled up a bucket, and they didn't have any interest in cleaning up after me anymore."

"You've been sick all day then?"

"It would appear so."

Even when ill, Bentley's natural inclination for sarcasm prevailed.

"You must realise how much I'm enjoying this," Galdinia said, leaning against the railing beside him. Although she maintained a few safe feet between them, she kept the sword close by her side as a warning.

"I can only imagine," Bentley said, his voice hitching on his final word as he held back another sick spell. After another deep breath, he peeled his eyes open and glanced sideways and glimpsed the blade just a few feet from his face. "You know, you won't need that."

Galdinia's fingers tightened around the hilt.

"Better to be safe than sorry," Galdinia said pointedly. "You never can know who to trust."

"You can trust me." Bentley's voice was small and frail.

Galdinia stifled a disbelieving laugh; she didn't want to disturb the quiet deck and potentially rouse her captain from sleep.

"Trust you?" Galdinia asked, looking across the deck, averting her eyes from Bentley. "In what world could I trust you?"

"Well, if you don't trust me, I think we can both at least agree it would be fairly impressive if I could stand still right now, let alone attack you," Bentley said before quietly adding, "Not that I would."

Galdinia briefly peered down at him, her eyes as suspicious as her heart. She didn't need to hear his lies about how he wouldn't push her over the railing of the ship in a heartbeat if it weren't for his ailment, so she changed the subject.

"Alright, if I'm to trust you, then explain to me why you didn't appear sick when you were staying on your ship last week." Galdinia's words were sharp and icy. "I think I would have noticed if you were staggering around Elderguard, a slightly pale shade of green."

Bentley hesitated; Galdinia couldn't tell if this was due to his churning stomach or if he was actually contemplating telling her the truth.

"That wasn't my ship." Bentley took a long intake of breath. "I made it appear as so by staying in close proximity, but I was lodging in one of the inns by the docks. It's far more impressive to be a lord in a great ship than to be one in a small room that smelled of mildew and the innkeeper's cat."

Galdinia frowned, the word "impressive" making her skin crawl.

"I'm not easily impressed by such things," Galdinia said tersely, staring across the deck.

"So I soon learned," Bentley replied. "But it didn't matter because the next thing I knew, I was staying in the castle."

Galdinia watched him. His eyes were shut as he faced the sky, the ocean breeze dancing in his hair, flecks of seawater dotting his face. His breaths were long and trembling as he tried to calm his stomach. She watched him flinch with each shudder of the ship as it travelled over the waves. He was broken, helpless, and more vulnerable than she'd ever seen him. A week ago she wouldn't have recognised the man before her.

"Why are you here, Bentley?" Galdinia finally asked. His blatant revealing of the truth burst the bubble of humour she'd been in after seeing him in such a state.

After a brief pause, he answered. "Didn't your two trusted advisors already inform you of this?"

"Oh yes, you have some special information to share with me that you refused to divulge in Elderguard. How convenient." If he could be sardonic, so could she. "Why are you really here?"

"For that very reason," Bentley said, opening his eyes briefly to peer at Galdinia. He caught her gaze, and she quickly looked away out to the abyss of water that surrounded them.

"Go on then," Galdinia said, not meeting his eye. "You're here, I'm here; out with it."

"You can't go to the Wetlands," Bentley finally said with a long exhale. Galdinia quickly looked back down at him, and his eyes were closed again. "Given your choice of vessel, I don't think that's where we're going anyway. But nevertheless, you can't go."

"Why?" Galdinia asked, her frustration with him resurfacing, quickly superseding the mocking joy she'd felt moments earlier.

"We've already discussed this," Bentley said with a sigh, swallowing deeply as the ship crested a small wave. "Going to the Wetlands is a death sentence."

"A death sentence?" Galdinia scoffed, crossing her arms over her chest, bringing the sword to her opposite side so it now dangled between her and Bentley. "A death sentence is leading someone into a windowless room full of books with a Fire Flourisher and a Wind Wielder who loathe her. A death sentence is luring a vulnerable, grieving girl into a relationship with the intention to kill her. I know all too well about death sentences, so don't for a second think you can try to tell me that I shouldn't go somewhere out of fear for my life. You must realise how truly asinine it is for you to say something like that to me."

"I'm just trying to warn you that it would be foolish to run to Valah," Bentley said, his eyes still squeezed shut, either trying to avoid Galdinia's gaze or another retch.

"Stop pretending that you care about me," Galdinia practically spat.

"But I do," Bentley said with another huff, steam billowing out of his mouth into the chill of the night air. "It would be far easier for both of us if I didn't, but unfortunately, I do."

"You don't," Galdinia almost whispered, the anger inside of her beginning to bubble. How she longed for a flame to calm her or to attack him.

"Do you think I'd warn against you going to the Wetlands if I didn't?" Bentley asked, peeking through his eyes up at her. "If I wanted you dead, I'd have thrown you overboard by now, or I would have encouraged your trip to the Wetlands yesterday in my cell. Whether you accept it or not, I care about you, Galdinia, and I'd much rather see you on the throne than Valah. So don't go to her, don't walk into her trap. You'd be far better off waiting for her to come to you."

"And I'll just let her kill Drystan and finish what she started in the capital?"

"Forget about him," Bentley said, his voice still uneven. "You've got to protect Elderguard and your kingdom from her. Hurtling into her clutches won't help you do that."

"Don't tell me what I need to do. You haven't any idea what I need to do."

"Of course I do," Bentley said, his breaths finally coming to him more evenly. "Everyone knows what you need to do. You need to establish allies and be prepared for another attack from Valah. You need to forget about saving Drystan and think about the greater good of your people. Everyone knows that."

Galdinia started having flashbacks of conversations with Drystan mere days ago in the same library where she nearly lost her life. She could hardly believe she was having an almost identical conversation with Bentley now. What's more, he was giving her the exact advice the Syndicate had insisted upon. This made her blood boil, not because he was right, but because he thought he had any say in her decision-making.

"Well, not everyone is the queen."

"You're right, they're not. You are. You're the one who has to make these decisions. You're the one who needs to put their people first before their own self-interests."

Galdinia took pause and looked across to the endless sea around them, her frown deepening the longer she stood there beside Bentley.

"Where were these sentiments last week, Bentley?" Galdinia asked, avoiding looking at him. "Why didn't you believe I was of such importance before you almost had me killed?"

Bentley didn't reply straightaway, and the silence of the night, only interrupted by the splashing of the water against the hull of the ship, stretched out between them. Galdinia glanced up at the helm where Raia was still watching them closely.

"Ignorance," Bentley finally said. "And fear."

Once again, Galdinia looked down at Bentley, his eyes still closed, face turned towards the sky.

"You know how terrifying she is." Bentley didn't need to name Valah for Galdinia to know who he was referring to. "I believed her lies, but what's more, I was terrified of her wrath. I was selfish in that moment and chose to save myself and my family before you, who I learned too late was far more innocent than I'd been led to believe."

Putting one's family first was a sentiment Galdinia could understand.

"But I'm done with being selfish," Bentley went on to explain. "And I'm not afraid of irritating you by insisting you put yourself first —I know you couldn't possibly hate me more than you already do. I don't have anything left to lose at this point, so I'll continue to insist that you shouldn't run into the clutches of the woman who wants you dead, even if it pushes you further away from me."

The silence again hung between them as the spray of seawater crested the railing and gently showered them both.

"I have to save him," Galdinia said quietly, her breath billowing around her as she spoke. "I can't let her kill him."

Bentley let out another drawn-out breath before replying. He seemed thoughtful and contemplative as he spoke.

"If you really want to get him out of the Wetlands, you're a fool," Bentley said. Before Galdinia could retort, he added, "And you'll need me."

Galdinia looked down at him, and his gaze was already on her. His bright eyes had not lost their sparkle; they seemed to be the only quality that remained true to his former self.

"You're going to help me save Drystan?" Galdinia asked, incredulous. "You've now professed your concern for me twice in a matter of days—which I still refuse to believe—and yet you think I will trust you to help me save *him*?"

"Would I rather him stay in Valah's clutches? Perhaps. But if you intend on going after him and facing Valah, then you'll want my help, trust me."

There were those words again: *trust me.*

One conversation of perceived honesty wasn't enough to convince Galdinia of Bentley's loyalty, but she couldn't help but wonder if he could be a helpful pawn in her plan of rescue.

"I'll think about it," Galdinia finally replied. "I have other matters to attend to before I can even plan breaking Drystan out."

As she spoke, yet another wave crashed into the ship, causing them to shudder as the vessel steadied itself beneath them. Before he could reply, Bentley scrambled to his feet and lurched his torso over the railing once again. Galdinia smirked, glad to have been able to experience his sickness once again, leaving her with a moment of levity.

"Feel better, Bentley," she said in a mocking tone as she turned to walk back towards the door to her quarters. She handed the guard his sword before looking over her shoulder at Bentley, who was turning from the railing, wiping his mouth, and staring at Galdinia with a glimpse of longing in his weary eyes. "He's all yours."

Galdinia turned from the deck of the ship and walked back to the warmth of her quarters. Her muscles throbbed as she climbed into bed beside Neryda once again, the memory of her dream having floated away on the ocean breeze.

12

THE FOLLOWING MORNING, GALDINIA STIRRED WEARILY FROM HER sleep. Her intrusive dreams continued to rattle her as she tried to sleep, so when the sun started to peek through curtains of her quarters, she pulled herself from her bed, dressed, and stepped out onto the deck, her legs still tired from her training the day before.

The ship was sailing smoothly through the sea as the now-risen sun warmed her against the biting breeze. Despite this, Galdinia pulled her cloak tight around her, protecting herself against the cold sea air, missing the accompanying warmth of her gift.

"You're kidding! You must be cheating!" Neryda's voice travelled down from the quarterdeck.

Galdinia turned and saw Vega at the helm of the ship, her stern eyes on the water ahead of them. Somewhere behind Vega, Galdinia's best friend was making a lot of noise.

Galdinia climbed up to the raised deck, and Vega bowed to her briefly as she reached the top of the stairs. Behind the helm, Neryda, Kayd, Raia, and Evander sat around a makeshift table made from a stack of produce pallets and a sheet of wood, which was strewn with cards and glistening gold coins. Neryda threw her small handful of cards into the centre of the table and crossed her arms over her chest in frustration. Galdinia knew that expression well.

"No cheating here, Lady Neryda," Raia said with a grin. "Pure skill."

"And a little luck," Kayd added as he, too, threw his cards into the discard pile. His feet were propped up on the edge of the pallets, and he sat comfortably among his comrades and new friend.

They all looked so casual in comparison to when she met them yesterday. Even Evander was resting his elbows against his knees and smirking at his friends; he hadn't even broken the edge of a smile with her the day before.

"Not so fast, Raia," Evander said quietly, discarding one card before placing his cards face up on the table for all to see. He must have had a good hand because Raia hung her head in disbelief, her long blonde ponytail draping over her face.

"Now I know that you're cheating," she said, eyes wide, looking at Evander in disbelief.

"You know I would never," Evander said simply with a smirk, collecting his coins and stacking them in neat piles before him.

"Counting cards is just a form of cheating," Kayd pointed out, collecting the cards.

"Keeping track of everyone's plays isn't cheating," Evander replied, eyeing his winnings. "It's a strategy."

"One that none of us can do!" Raia countered, still clearly annoyed by her friend's success.

"I don't remember that being my fault," Evander said, smiling briefly at Raia. As he turned to look at the blonde woman, he caught a glimpse of Galdinia, who still stood at the top of the stairs, watching them. "Your Majesty."

Raia and Kayd looked up from the table and quickly stood to their feet, following Evander's movements. Kayd abandoned the cards in a heap on the table, and their faces all fell uniformly as they stood at attention. The only person whose countenance didn't change was Neryda, who remained in her seat.

"Morning, Gal," Neryda said casually from her seat, smiling up at her friend, utterly out of place beside the soldiers.

"Good morning, everyone," Galdinia said with a warm smile, approaching the group. "What are you playing?"

"This card game Raia was teaching me," Neryda said almost hopelessly. "I'm convinced they're cheating, though."

"Or maybe they're just a little more practiced?" Galdinia questioned with a smile to her friend. The three soldiers were still standing at attention, expressions impassive. "Please don't stop on my behalf."

"I think we'd best get to our posts," Raia said quickly.

"It's about time," Vega said off-handedly from her position behind the helm.

"Come on, one more game," Neryda said, looking up at the soldiers who now resembled statues.

"I'd love to see how to play," Galdinia said, hoping for a chance to get to know her new guard and ignoring the deflated feeling that came with seeing their countenances shift so suddenly.

Raia looked briefly to Evander and Kayd. Her cousin shrugged, and Raia turned back to the queen. "We probably have time for one more round."

Evander offered Galdinia his seat, and he pulled over a barrel to sit on, while Kayd and Raia sat once again, looking arguably less comfortable.

"So what are the rules?" Galdinia asked, taking her seat between Neryda and Evander.

"This is called Trader's Triumph," Kayd explained as he shuffled the deck. "You'll be dealt nine cards, and you need to make either three sets of the same value card, a run of at least three cards of the same element, or a mix of both. Each round you bet based on your current hand, and you can only pick up a new card and discard another each round if you raise the bet. It can become quite expensive quite quickly, so you can fold whenever you wish."

"I see," Galdinia said, nodding.

"Here's something to get you started," Raia offered, drawing from a pool of coins on the edge of the table. "I'm sure you're good for them."

There was a glint in her eye, and Galdinia was warmed as she lowered her defences.

"I promise that I am," Galdinia replied with a smile, stacking the coins in front of her.

Kayd dealt the cards to each of the players, and Galdinia fanned hers out in front of her. She already held a pair of eights and a four, five, and six of wind, but she tried to keep her face expressionless as she moved the cards around in her hand to start to build sets.

"Lady Neryda," Kayd began, offering for Neryda to start the round.

"I've told you already, if you call me that one more time," Neryda said, picking up a new card before throwing a ten of fire into the middle of the table, "you'll meet a grisly end at the bottom of the Southern Shadow."

Kayd smirked at Neryda as she rearranged her cards.

"So now Raia can either take from the discard pile or risk it with the main draw pile," Kayd continued to explain, pointing to the cards at the centre of the table.

Raia proceeded to pick up Neryda's discarded card before discarding a six of wind.

Play continued until it reached Galdinia, and she matched Evander's bet before looking at her options. She could take Evander's discarded eight of wind to complete her set of three, or she could take her chance on the draw pile. She decided to take the eight, and she watched Evander closely as his eyes travelled with his abandoned card, then followed Galdinia's discarded nine of light.

The game continued much in the same way for multiple rounds: Neryda's shifty eyes watched Evander closely; Kayd started to ease back into his chair as he raised the bet; a hint of a smile flickered over Raia's lips with every turn; and Evander quietly played his hand, no hint of success on his face. Galdinia soon held two twos and was only one card from winning. She watched Kayd sigh as he picked up an undesirable card from the pile. Kayd discarded it immediately, leaving the eight of water out for all to see.

With an emotionless expression, Evander picked up Kayd's card and discarded another: the two that Galdinia was waiting for. Her eyes widened. Before she could pick it up, however, Evander placed his hand face up on the pallets, an air of ease about him. Three fours, and a water run of five, six, seven, eight, nine, and ten.

"Triumph," he said simply, announcing his win.

"Absolutely not!" Neryda said, gaping at the soldier, her red curls billowing around her face in the salty wind.

"Yet another win for Evander," Kayd said, tossing his hand into the pile.

"You've got extra cards in your sleeves, surely!" Disbelief stained Neryda's face.

"Nothing here," Evander said, indicating to his arms, which were wrapped in his fighting leathers. "Just years of practise in the barracks."

"I'm watching you," Neryda said with sharp eyes.

"You'll spend years trying to catch up with him," Raia said, tossing out her hand.

"And I will win every last piece of gold back from you," Neryda warned, her eyes narrowing on Evander.

"Be my guest," Evander replied, picking up the coins and sliding them into a small pouch at his waist. "My hip is getting quite sore from carrying all of this around."

Kayd rolled his eyes as he collected everyone's cards, shuffling them.

Before Neryda could retort again, the sound of firm footfalls travelled up the stairs by the helm as Ilyon approached the group. His soldiers instantly stood at attention, all humour leaving their faces, cards and coins abandoned on the table. Vega remained at the helm, and she, too, stood firmly in place.

"At ease, soldiers," Ilyon said, his hands clasped behind his back. "Good morning, Your Highness, Lady Neryda."

"Good morning, Ilyon," Galdinia said with a smile, joining the soldiers on her feet.

"Sorry to interrupt you," he said, looking at the remnants of the game.

"We just finished, actually," Galdinia remarked. "Evander took everything we had."

"Ah yes, he's got a particular skill at that," Ilyon replied, looking pointedly at Evander; a gleam of pride glistened momentarily in the soldier's eye. "I don't think there's a soldier in the Royal Guard who hasn't lost at least a milligram of gold to him."

"You have a reputation," Galdinia said, looking at Evander, who held his stoic stance, a flicker of a smile dancing over his lips.

"I see it as more of a status of honour," Evander replied.

"Well, now that you've finished taking Kayd's life savings," Ilyon began, looking pointedly at Kayd as the soldier rolled his eyes, "can we discuss today's travels? I'd like to arrive at The Hook by noon, which I think is possible given the currents. Raia, we will work from the bow to help the ship cut through the water; Kayd, can you fill the sails and push us forward?"

"Yes sir," Kayd said with a nod.

"Can I help, Captain?" The question came from Neryda as she stood. "I have my own reputation."

Neryda was known in Elderguard as a capable Water Weaver, having not been quiet about her gift from a young age. As best friend of the princess, most in the city knew who Neryda was, but her abilities as a Weaver often preceded this.

"Of course, Lady Neryda," Ilyon said. "You can join me and Raia at the front of the ship. Evander, you can relieve Vega at the helm, should she need it."

"I'm fine, sir," Vega replied, her stance not wavering for a moment.

"As you wish," Ilyon said with a short nod. "To your stations."

Galdinia watched as Kayd walked back to the stern, and Raia and Neryda followed Ilyon to the bow, all of them ready to use their gifts. Evander remained where he stood, also watching his comrades move about the ship. Although she knew that his gift wouldn't have served a particular purpose in this moment, Galdinia felt a pang of guilt sink in her heart.

"I'm sorry there isn't any fire on board," Galdinia said, turning to her fellow Flourisher.

"No apology needed, Your Highness."

"I've only had my gift for a week, and I'm already going crazy without it," Galdinia said, watching Neryda take up her place beside Raia and Ilyon as they reached their hands out to the sea to manipulate the water. "I can only imagine how unbearable it is for you."

"It's uncomfortable, yes, but not quite unbearable yet." Evander glanced at Galdinia, and his face softened. "It isn't your fault, Your Highness. It is a necessary evil that we go without our gifts for just a few more hours. You have nothing to apologise for."

Galdinia nodded, a sad smile forming on her face.

The two of them stood together as the ship gained speed. Kayd stood behind them, his hands outstretched towards the sails as he drew the wind into the great panels of fabric. The building wind danced around Galdinia, picking up her hair and the hem of her cloak. The Water Weavers at the other end of the ship pushed their hands towards the sea, making a deep cut in the water before them, clearing the ship's path. The cut was so long that even with the bow in the way, Galdinia could see the track before them that was being made.

Watching the others use their gifts caused Galdinia to bundle her hands into fists, the desire to connect with a flame becoming almost painful. The sense of comfort that even the smallest of flames gave her was unparalleled. It was like taking a deep breath upon breaking through the surface of the ocean after a long swim. At the moment, however, Galdinia was still very much sitting beneath the waves. In a few hours, she wouldn't feel that itching sensation in her hands as she sought the flame that she so desperately needed.

"So where did you learn to play cards like that, Evander?" Galdinia asked, hoping to distract herself from the longing feeling in her palms.

Evander, looking somewhat taken aback by the queen's line of questioning, turned slowly to Galdinia. "My grandmother, actually. She taught me and all of my brothers to play cards before we could form full sentences."

"All of your brothers?" Galdinia asked.

"I'm one of seven," Evander replied. "My grandparents helped my parents raise us, and my grandmother took it upon herself to teach us the finer skills in life."

"Thank goodness for that," Galdinia said with a smirk, which Evander returned.

"I attribute much of my ability to bluff and keep a straight face to that woman. You'd be surprised just how helpful that is in combat."

"Oh?" Galdinia raised her brows.

"You can't give your opponent even an inkling of what you might do next. If you look to your hands for a moment or even shift your back foot, they can anticipate your next move."

"And playing cards with your grandmother taught you that?"

Evander paused before answering.

"Earlier, before I put down my cards," Evander replied, motioning towards the makeshift card table, "you told me in a heartbeat that you wanted the two I had discarded, all by the look on your face."

"But I wasn't looking at you," Galdinia said, surprised he remembered.

"It was precisely because of where you were looking that I knew what you wanted," Evander said casually. "You had been waiting for me to discard a two, so your eyes lit up when I finally did."

"But it was too late anyway," Galdinia replied, catching on.

"Exactly," Evander said with a nod. "I wasn't going to risk giving you a card I believed you wanted until I knew I could win. Nor was I going to let on how close I was to the win before I had already captured it."

"You knew which card I needed," Galdinia said, her eyes narrowing on Evander.

He nodded. "A good soldier keeps track of their opponent's earlier moves."

"So it would seem."

"Your opponent will always be looking at what they want—be it your cards, your crown or your heart—but to protect yourself, you must focus on your own next move while keeping track of theirs. If you give too much away, they'll anticipate it and do all they can to cause your downfall."

"How could I have stopped you from winning, though?" Galdinia asked. "I wasn't keeping track of the cards you held, and I had to wait for the other three to go before it was your turn again. My next move was unlikely to affect you."

"Sometimes it's worth losing if it means you can bring down your opponent."

"So I could have let someone else win?"

"If your goal was to ensure that I lost, then someone else's victory could have easily been your key," Evander said, cocking an eyebrow at Galdinia.

"But what if *I* wanted to win?" she asked.

Evander smiled at the queen. "Then you need to get better at cards."

13

"LET'S EASE OUR SPEED," CAPTAIN ILYON CALLED FROM THE HELM.

They had been sailing forward all morning at a steady pace, and now, less than two kilometres from their destination, The Hook came into view. The Hook was aptly named; the peninsular province drew out from the southwest and carved into the ocean in a brilliant arc. At the entrance of The Hook stood two towering stone pillars, which had been intricately chiselled with images of the seas, their waves, and the sails of ships.

Listening to their captain's instructions, the Weaver and Wielder soldiers on board either drew the water up as a barrier at the bow to slow the ship or pulled the wind back into the sails to slow it down. Galdinia felt the ship glide as it slowed, the motion smooth despite its weight. These soldiers were very well practised at controlling this vessel with their gifts.

"We must first be accepted entry," Ilyon explained to Galdinia as they stood on the quarterdeck, watching this marvellous feat of the soldiers. Ilyon called out again, "Hold fast! Let's bring it to a halt."

"But they know we're coming." Galdinia's words were almost a question.

"This is The Hook, Your Majesty," Ilyon said, steering the ship as it slowed further. "They scrutinise everyone who enters their gates, even if the queen has already announced her arrival."

"What would happen if we just sailed into the bay? This is my land after all." Although Galdinia doubted she'd ever do such a thing, the self-assurance of the Lidels that she was being met with made something new rise within her.

"We'd be very sorry if we did that," Ilyon explained as the ship slowed to a stop. He pointed over the bow towards the water at the base of the entrance. "We are metres away from a robust and formidable coral reef. The Lidels have Weavers stationed at the entrance day and night, ready to deny or accept any visitors who try to enter by water."

Ilyon now turned to Vega, who was also stationed on the quarter-deck, and he nodded to her. With this signal, Vega pulled on a rope that slowly drew a golden flag to the top of the nearby mast. Once in place, it fluttered in the wind, bold and imposing. Upon it was stitched the Elderwin crest of an owl with outstretched wings sitting on the shoulders of a roaring lion.

"How do we know if they will accept our entry?" Galdinia asked, looking back at the pillars before her. High above them, she could just barely make out a group of people at the top of each pillar, their movement barely perceptible.

"Watch," Ilyon said knowingly.

Almost instantaneously, a deep rumbling came from below the ship as it started to shake and tilt beneath Galdinia's feet. She steadied herself against the movement, holding her arms out by her sides for balance. Galdinia watched as the water around the ship surged, a bubbling whitewash suddenly covering the ocean's surface, the strength and power of the water echoing below them. The water wasn't moving towards the ship, though, but rather towards the entrance of The Hook; they were merely at the centre of the sea's movement. As she balanced herself on the railing of the quarterdeck, Galdinia realised what was happening.

The Water Weavers atop the pillars were raising the tide of the Southern Shadow to allow safe entry to The Hook.

Galdinia watched in awe as the water levels rose. The reef soon disappeared from view below the surface of the rising water, and the ship slowly ascended with it.

"This is remarkable," Galdinia said, eyes wide.

The most impressive display of a Weaver's power she had witnessed was when Ilyon alone sent a rainstorm from above her out to the seas. Watching the outworking of these Weavers' gifts was a close second but just as enchanting.

"Quite incredible, isn't it?" Ilyon asked, looking at Galdinia expectantly.

"I've never seen anything like it," she replied, peering over the railing to the water.

As the rolling of the sea halted beneath them, Ilyon looked to the pillars, and Galdinia's eyes followed his. Moments later, a green flag appeared at the top of the left pillar.

"And now we have been accepted entry," Ilyon said to Galdinia with a smirk before calling out to his soldiers, "Onward!"

Once again, the Wielders and Weavers onboard used their gifts to move the ship forward, towards the entrance between the pillars. Galdinia strained her neck to inspect the towers of stone as they passed them. Now seeing the carvings in more detail, she noted that each level depicted various scenes at sea, from great coral reefs to mythological sea creatures, from ships at battle to Weavers controlling the waves. Their intricacy was as impressive as the Weavers' abilities to shift the tides.

As the royal ship entered The Hook, Galdinia tore her eyes from the pillars, and she was taken aback by her surroundings; very quickly she realised why Ryden said the residents never leave.

The Hook was plentiful in trees and flowing gardens, the greenery covering much of the mountainous land masses that rose above the bay. Perched atop the hills and cliffs that made up much of the bay were buildings of bright colours, seemingly piled on top of each other. At the tip of The Hook, which curved to point back towards Crysterra, was a structure that was almost comparable to the castle in Elderguard in its beauty and opulence. From her position at the bottom of the cliff, Galdinia could only see so much of the structure as they sailed by, but even so, she would have best described it as a mansion made from blocks of opalescent marble and surrounded by climbing vines and a sprawling garden. She assumed that this was the Lidels' home.

They passed the tip of The Hook and sailed into the bay, which was full of ships of all shapes and sizes as the citizens made the most of the warmest part of the day. Despite the chill on the water and the sea mist hovering over its surface, there were children splashing in the shallows and families enjoying the sun. As they caught a glimpse of the royal flag hoisted in the air, people paused and stared at the incoming vessel. It had been some time since the royal ship had visited these waters, and now it did so with a new ruler.

Ilyon directed the ship to a vast dock at the southern end of the bay below the mansion. Here they laid anchor. The soldiers of the Royal Guard quickly drew in the sails and dropped a mooring line to the docks, saving the Weavers among them from needing to keep the ship in place. Once happy with their position, Ilyon led Galdinia and Neryda to the gangway, the Queen's Guard close behind. Galdinia instantly felt a sense of ease and comfort with her newly appointed soldiers standing in her shadow. She looked down at the gangway and the path that lay ahead: this appeared to be a private dock, and there was a set of steep, winding stairs that led up the cliff face to the mansion above.

From the mist that lingered over the wharf and stretched up the cliff face emerged a man shrouded in white and gold, his azure eyes and neatly trimmed silver beard peeking out from beneath his hood.

"Welcome, Your Majesty." The man bowed deeply as the queen and her entourage stepped off the gangway. As he stood up straight again, he removed his hood and smiled politely at Galdinia. "I am Feyroy Varant, governor to Lord and Lady Lidel."

"A pleasure to meet you," Galdinia said warmly, returning his smile.

"The pleasure is all ours, Your Highness," he said, standing up straight, his billowing cloak swaying lightly in the breeze. "Welcome to The Hook."

"This is my Captain of the Royal Guard, Ilyon Trunder; my advisor, Lady Neryda Fleur; and my Queen's Guard," Galdinia said, motioning to those around her. She noticed a smirk spread over Neryda's lips at the mention of her new title.

After courteous bows, Feyroy turned once again to Galdinia.

"If you'll follow me, Your Majesty," Feyroy said, gesturing to the length of the dock, "Lord and Lady Lidel are awaiting your arrival."

This was not the reception Galdinia had expected, particularly after Ryden's warnings. She thought she may have been welcomed by armed guards or even refused entry altogether—perhaps things had changed in The Hook since Ryden last visited.

The group followed the governor along the dock and to the stairs that towered above them. Steeling herself, Galdinia began the almost vertical climb behind Feyroy and Ilyon.

When they arrived at the top of the long staircase, Galdinia felt a trail of sweat trickling down the back of her neck, and she could hear Neryda taking deep breaths beside her. Her soldier companions, on the other hand, weren't perturbed in the least.

"That would certainly keep you in good health," Neryda said, taking a moment to pause at the top of the stairs to catch her breath.

"And it does, Lady Neryda," Feyroy replied with a smile. Despite his age, he seemed perfectly unaffected by the climb. "Some just avoid leaving the manor instead."

"I couldn't imagine why," Neryda said breathlessly, wiping her brow with the back of her hand.

"Right this way," Feyroy said, leading the troop through a winding garden that led to the entrance of the manor.

Up close, Galdinia could truly appreciate the beauty of the lavish structure before her. It towered before them and practically shimmered in the light of the sun. The entrance was decorated in potted plants, sturdy columns, and snaking vines. Two guards stood by the doors, which they opened upon arrival of the group.

The manor's interior matched the outside with its glistening marble, soaring ceilings, and brass decor. The round entrance hall was bordered by two curved staircases that led to a mezzanine balcony above them. The warmth of the sun carried into the building through the glass dome that made up much of the ceiling of the hall. Feyroy led them through an archway on the other side of the entrance hall, drawing them into the depths of the beautiful building.

As the young queen walked through the sun-drenched manor, attendants and soldiers bowed, their faces astonished by her presence.

Galdinia returned courteous smiles as she moved through the building.

Feyroy guided them through one more doorway, and they stepped into a vast room at the rear of the manor. Almost the entire back wall was made up of windows that looked southeast over the Southern Shadow. Somewhere beyond the horizon sat Galdinia's home. She hoped and prayed that it was recovering swiftly under Ryden's watch.

Galdinia could only take in the view briefly, however, as the hairs on her arms stood on end as the warmth and pull of a flame demanded her attention. An oval table sat in the centre of the room, and an attendant approached it, then placed two lit candelabras on the tabletop. In the presence of the open flames, Galdinia finally felt like she could breathe again, as though she'd undone a particularly restricting corset. Her veins warmed instantly, and she felt all her muscles relax. She hadn't realised just how much pressure had built in her body in the absence of her gift. A smile flickered over her lips as she watched the flames dance in their perches. She turned to look at Evander, who, like her, had felt the flames as soon as they entered their vicinity. They shared a brief glance and a reassuring smile. She wanted nothing more than to draw them to her palms, but she didn't want to alarm her hosts so soon after arriving.

"Welcome to The Hook, Your Highness." A bright, friendly voice broke Galdinia's concentration, and she turned to face two people who approached from the doors of the room.

"Queen Galdinia, this is Lord and Lady Lidel," Feyroy announced, stretching an arm out towards the couple.

Lord and Lady Lidel wore robes of a similar colour as Feyroy's: pearly white with gold detailing.

"Thank you for accepting our request, Lord and Lady Lidel," Galdinia said as her hosts approached and bowed to her.

As they stood up straight, Galdinia saw their faces clearer. Lady Lidel had a friendly face; her eyes were dark and warm, and her high cheekbones made her appear as though she was perpetually smiling. Her lustrous brown curls framed her face, and her dark sandy brown complexion was dotted with freckles. Lord Lidel, however, had a stern face with permanently pursed lips; he did not look like a man who was easily impressed. His eyes were what stood out to Galdinia though;

while they were scrutinising, they glistened green against his deep olive complexion.

"It is a pleasure to have you," Lady Lidel replied, her voice as warm as her countenance. "I am Ravenna, and this is Bael." She gestured to her husband, who still hadn't spoken. He merely watched the queen.

"You have a beautiful home." Galdinia smiled. "It's truly spectacular."

"Thank you," Ravenna replied, leading Galdinia and her company to the table at the centre of the room. "It's our pride and joy."

"I can understand why," Galdinia said, taking a seat at the table. Ilyon sat to her right, Neryda to her left. The Queen's Guard took up their position behind her, and the Lidels crossed the room to sit opposite them, Feyroy taking his place beside them. Galdinia took note that there were guards stationed at the exit.

"Now, I know that you haven't come all this way just to talk about architecture," Ravenna continued, smiling warmly at Galdinia as she settled in her seat. "Governor Ryden was vague in his correspondence, so your arrival has been highly anticipated."

"Ah, yes," Galdinia replied, glancing at Ilyon as she spoke. "We didn't think we could trust such a sensitive matter in the clutches of a raven, so I apologise for our ambiguity. I'm sure you are aware by now of the attack on the capital last week. Valah Pyrin of the west, and my aunt and uncle, Edana and Draven, laid siege on our city in an attempt to take the crown from me before the end of the Week of Mourning. While they were obviously unsuccessful"—Galdinia motioned briefly to her crown atop her head—"they took many lives and caused significant damage to our infrastructure. Valah took a soldier of ours hostage, and while Draven lost his life, we believe Edana is still alive and likely back in her home on the Shadowed Coast. They did not achieve their goal, but they wounded our side."

"I'm very sorry for the losses you have experienced," Ravenna said, her voice low and grave.

"Thank you," Galdinia replied. "That being said, we can only assume that Valah is planning another attack on our city, so we must start fortifying our allies now to prepare for what may come."

At this, Bael's eyes narrowed slightly, and his lips creased even further.

"So what you seek is our loyalty?" Bael's voice was deep and hard as he spoke, bypassing any niceties and speaking plainly.

"Put simply, yes," Galdinia replied. "We need to rebuild our army, and in order to do that, we need allies. While we know The Hook hasn't engaged in battle for many decades, we also recognise that a conflict of this magnitude hasn't occurred in far longer."

"You mean since your grandparents took the throne from the Pyrins?" Bael's words were cutting, but Galdinia maintained her composure.

"Yes."

Ravenna looked at her husband briefly before he spoke again.

"You are correct in saying that the army of The Hook, or any governing Lidel family for that matter, hasn't engaged in combat in decades, and we don't intend on starting now." Bael leaned back in his chair, his viridian eyes fixed on Galdinia. "Many years ago, we made peace with your father, agreeing that while we recognised him as King of Crysterra, we would not align ourselves with any armies, be it the Royal Guard or otherwise. If others stayed out of our way, we would stay out of theirs. Frankly, it has been working out just fine for us. We gladly extend the same courtesy to you, Queen Galdinia."

Galdinia could guarantee that Bael wasn't glad about any part of this situation.

She stared at the Lidels for a beat, trying to rally her thoughts. While the smile remained on Ravenna's face, she did not make an attempt to add to her husband's words or offer any consolation. They were on the same page about this issue, and Galdinia didn't even know where to begin.

"If I may," Ilyon said from beside Galdinia, leaning forward to speak. Galdinia attempted to communicate her full support of Ilyon stepping in as she tried to think strategically about how to respond. "Lord and Lady Lidel, I am Ilyon Trunder, Captain of the Royal Guard. I understand wanting to maintain the peace and solitude you have worked so hard to establish here, but I fear that might be in jeopardy if you don't align yourself with the crown today."

"Thank you for your concern, Captain," Ravenna said pleasantly. "We are well fortified and are not fearful of any oncoming battle."

"With all due respect, Lady Ravenna," Ilyon went on, his voice careful, "Valah Pyrin has established a strong alliance within other provinces, and I don't think your army alone could stand against her force. I foresee a significant battle across this country, and you will be forced to choose a side or perish. Given how Valah treated her supposed new allies when they attacked the capital, I don't see your chances of survival being all that high if you do not accept Queen Galdinia's offer of an alliance."

"Captain," Bael interjected, "we know all too well how she treated the people of Lund. Our friends were used as a battering ram to breach your walls, and they lost many soldiers. But if you don't think I'm just as wary of you and your army, then you are gravely mistaken."

"Lord Bael," Galdinia joined, hoping to soften the tension in the room, finally organising her thoughts, "I understand that there is damage in the relationship between The Hook and Elderguard, but I hope to help mend that. In fact, I want to help unite our country once again. If you are not willing to align yourself with us for now, I understand that, but we would like to approach those in Lund and speak with them about their loyalty and hopefully encourage them to join our side in this conflict. It is time we come together as a country."

"And you want us to help you approach them?"

"You are their only known allies and connection to Crysterra, and accessing their home in the mountains is almost impossible without a guide, so—"

Galdinia was interrupted by a harsh laugh that erupted from Bael's lips. The sound echoed in the cavernous room, the mocking tone reverberating deep within Galdinia. The first smile she had seen from Bael appeared on his lips, and it was painted with ridicule.

"My dear girl," Bael said, his words condescending, "I know you've only been queen for barely more than a week, but even you can't be that ignorant."

A familiar heat started to rise in Galdinia's chest, and her breaths quivered slightly as she tried to maintain her composure, all too aware of the flames sitting atop their candles between her and the Lidels.

"Be careful how you speak to our queen, Lord Bael," Ilyon said fiercely, his voice severe and bitter.

"I am merely questioning how many of the relationships between the capital and the other provinces you are aware of," Bael forged on. "To expect not only our allegiance, but also our help to connect you with our wounded and incredibly private friends in the north, merely highlights your lack of awareness of the relationship between The Hook and Elderguard. We recognise you as queen, but you should not expect anything else from us, just as we do not expect anything from you."

Galdinia stared at Bael, her eyes narrowing on the man.

They don't know you.

The words seemed to intrude upon her mind, guiding her.

She contemplated her choices in that moment. She could leave it at that, accept the Lidels' lack of loyalty, prove herself to be seen as inferior and ignorant, and go home to try to find another way to Lund.

Or she could remind herself, and everyone in the room, who the ruler of this country was.

"You're right, Lord Bael. I have only been queen for nine days," Galdinia began, her voice calm and even as she pushed back against the tightness beneath her ribs. "And the day before my coronation, I had to defend my city from a deadly enemy who wanted my head. An enemy who wasn't afraid to kill both enemies and allies, as long as their purpose was served. So before I was given my mother's crown, I had already fought in the kind of conflict many rulers before me never experienced. So yes, my experience may be limited, but I am not ignorant to the political machinations of this country. I know you and my father lost trust in one another a decade ago, but I would hope we can move on from such unpleasantness to serve the greater good of our country. But if you are truly that self-serving and arrogant that you won't even consider my offer, you may need to consider who the ignorant one is here today, Lord Bael."

Galdinia felt Neryda shift in her seat beside her as she sat up taller. Galdinia's gaze did not leave Bael's as he stared her down. She wasn't willing to give up just yet.

"We have been burnt by the crown before, Your Majesty, and we don't intend on being burnt again."

"And yet Elderguard also felt something similar in return from The Hook," Galdinia said, eyebrows raised.

"We sent our payment," Bael replied, his voice low and dangerous. "We needed help. Your father agreed to a deposit and then kept our payment for himself and stopped sending supplies. He was greedy and showed how little he cared for the provinces outside his own."

"I can assure you," Ilyon interrupted, his voice just as stern as ever, "we never received your deposit. Three gems never made it to our shores."

"They were not merely gems, Captain," Ravenna said, a shadow of pain cast across her features. "They were precious jewels that were of significant personal value to us."

"What did they look like?" Galdinia asked, attempting a different tack; the Lidels both appeared wary of her line of questioning. "I don't believe we ever received them, but if you think they made it to Elderguard, then perhaps I have seen them in the castle."

Ravenna and Bael looked to one another before turning back to the queen.

Ravenna answered her question. "The first jewel, which was named Victory, was deep amber in colour, and it represented knowledge and wisdom. It was discovered in the foundations of The Hook when the first Lidels built our grand city. The second was an amethyst jewel of rich purple, named Admont, representing beauty and prosperity. This one was passed down from generation to generation in my bloodline, and it became a Lidel heirloom when Bael and I were married." The two shared a moment as Ravenna reached a hand out and placed it on her husband's beside her. Her eyes sparkled with nostalgia. "Finally, the third and largest jewel, the Leian, representing tradition, was gifted to us from our friends in Lund. It was a glistening starlight crystal. The monetary value of the jewels was great, yes, but their sentimental value was far greater. Having them taken from us was heartbreaking and far more damaging than any battle."

Galdinia listened to Ravenna's description and couldn't help but be struck by the unique quality of their colours. Amber, amethyst, and starlight. She tried to imagine the jewels in her mind's eye, and while there was a glimpse of a shimmering memory, she could not place it. Suffice it to say that she had encountered many jewels over her nineteen years, but she was drawing up a blank.

"Perhaps in the catacombs?" Galdinia asked Ilyon quietly. "I wonder if Ryden ever saw such jewels."

"But the ships never laid anchor at our docks," Ilyon said, whispering to Galdinia. "We could never have received them."

"How were they transported?" Galdinia asked, turning back to the Lidels and searching for more information.

"One each on a different ship provided by your father," Bael replied, his words slow. "We did not want to risk them all being on one ship. You must see now why it is hard to believe that all three never made it to your shores."

"Those ships never arrived back to Elderguard," Ilyon pressed. "I oversaw every vessel that entered and exited the docks at that time, and I can assure you that our ships never returned, with or without your deposit."

"Perhaps they docked elsewhere and transported the jewels by foot," Ravenna suggested. "Regardless, we farewelled them at the gates of The Hook and never saw them again."

Galdinia and Ilyon held the gazes of Lord and Lady Lidel, seemingly in a stalemate.

"If I could replace these jewels, I would," Galdinia urged. "But it would seem that they are irreplaceable."

"That they are," Bael said, his expression harsh.

"If there is something else I can give you in return to help mend this rift between us, I would very much like that."

"We are not in the business of being bought, Your Majesty," Bael replied.

"What my husband means is that nothing can rival the value of these jewels, no matter the cost," Ravenna said, her voice gentle. "Regardless of the whereabouts of the jewels, we recognise you as the Queen of Crysterra, but that will be the extent of our association with the crown. An alliance is not a priority for us."

Galdinia looked at them both, becoming irritated. "So you won't even help me make contact with Lund?"

"Our friends value our honesty, and we have built a firm foundation of loyalty with them," Bael replied. "We cannot in good conscience send to them a queen whose father may have taken our most treasured possessions from us, especially not after how they were treated in the battle with Valah."

Galdinia held her tongue from speaking up against how their friends had treated her home in return; she didn't think Bael would take kindly to her pointing out his hypocrisy.

Feeling defeated, Galdinia let out a long breath.

"Very well," she finally conceded. "Thank you for your time. We will take our leave immediately."

"That isn't necessary," Ravenna replied, a brightness returning to her voice. "We may not be willing to give you our alliance, but we are not beyond being hospitable. You and your crew may stay in our home, and you can leave tomorrow whenever you are ready."

If it was possible, Bael's expression became even more stern at Ravenna's suggestion.

"Thank you, Lady Lidel, but we can sleep on the ship," Galdinia replied.

"Certainly not," Ravenna said with a shake of her head. "You are to stay in our home and join us for dinner this evening. We insist."

By the look on Bael's face, Galdinia wasn't entirely sure that was how he would describe how he felt, but he didn't contradict his wife's offer.

"In that case, we would be pleased to stay," Galdinia said, holding on to an ounce of hope that she may be able to sway the Lidels before they disembarked. "Thank you, Lord and Lady Lidel."

"We will have rooms made up for you in the southern wing," Ravenna said. "How many of you will we be hosting?"

"Seven," Ilyon replied. "We have another ten on board the ship, but they can remain there for the evening."

"Certainly not," Ravenna said again, frowning. "I will not have any guests of The Hook sleep on their ship, be they soldiers or the queen. They are more than welcome to stay in our home also. We have ample room."

Ilyon glanced sideways at Galdinia before he continued.

"Eight are soldiers, one is a priestess, and… one is a prisoner. To be frank, we don't want him to leave the ship, so our remaining soldiers will stay with him."

"Is this prisoner dangerous?" Ravenna asked.

"You have no idea…" Neryda said under her breath.

"As long as he is kept away from fire and is heavily guarded," Ilyon said, speaking over Neryda, "he would not be considered dangerous, no."

Galdinia glanced at her captain; was he really suggesting that Bentley should also stay in the Lidels' home for the evening?

"Your prisoner can stay here for the evening too. The western wing is easily secured, and all flames in the vicinity will be extinguished," Ravenna explained. "It will be far safer than leaving him on a ship where just about anyone could board… or disembark."

"What if he manages to access fire and escapes, or worse?" Galdinia asked, frowning, looking from Ilyon to Ravenna. A seasick Bentley was one thing, but he could be lethal with a flame.

"He's in a city full of Water Weavers, Your Highness. I'd like to see him try." With that, Ravenna stood, closely followed by Feyroy. "Let me give you a tour of our home while your rooms are prepared. You may also like to take a walk down into the town or down to the coast —this truly is the most beautiful place in Crysterra."

Galdinia, Neryda, and Ilyon stood, following Ravenna as she walked towards the door, sharing about all the sights of The Hook as though she and her husband hadn't just delivered Galdinia a generous helping of disappointment. Galdinia's soldiers followed closely behind, and she noted that Bael stayed in his seat.

As she walked out of the room, Galdinia felt a heaviness on her shoulders. They had come to The Hook with two goals in mind: settle an alliance with The Hook and be given an escort to Lund. And yet, she hadn't achieved either. She tried not to think about the conversation with the Syndicate she would be having in a matter of days when they arrived back in Elderguard.

In that moment, it felt as though her mother's crown became ever so slightly heavier on her head.

14

GALDINIA LAY ON THE BED IN HER ROOM, HER HEAD HANGING OFF THE edge, staring out the palatial window at an upside-down view of the coast. In her right hand, she was swirling around a ball of flames, having taken it from a lantern in her room the first chance she had, deciding it wouldn't have been appropriate to borrow the fire from the lanterns in the hallways during their extensive tour of the Lidels' home. Once her door was shut, however, she beckoned the fire to her palm and released a long breath of relief. The moment the flame skimmed her skin, it brought a calm to her spirit that she had longed for since leaving the castle the morning prior, warming her entire body and easing her tense shoulders. How had she managed to go so long without it?

The room she had been given was almost as nice as her own in Elderguard Castle. The strong, glistening marble continued into each room and was contrasted with the billowing linen curtains, tufted rugs, and golden detailing on the doorknobs, window frames, and chandeliers. Her crown, which she had placed on a table by the window, blended in seamlessly. Drystan's helmet, however, stood out starkly against the gentle shades and textures next to Galdinia's crown. In the corner of the room stood a large clawfoot tub, which Galdinia had been anticipating asking Neryda to fill, but she hadn't yet managed to pull herself from the bed since collapsing on it seconds after she was sure Ravenna was out of earshot back down the hallway.

The dread and doubt that had seeped into her veins weighed her down. She couldn't escape the harsh reality that was partnered with the Lidels' rejection: without allies, she couldn't confidently face Valah.

And without facing Valah, she couldn't save Drystan.

Perhaps it was time for her to consider her original plan again: infiltrating the Wetlands alone, finding a way into Valah's manor, and rescuing Drystan on her own. It would certainly result in far less bloodshed than a violent battle, and it may be the only remaining option to attempt to ensure Drystan's safety. Galdinia knew she'd have a tough time convincing Ilyon and Ryden of such plans—let alone Neryda—but perhaps they wouldn't need to know. She could take her leave under the cover of night and be in the Wetlands by the beginning of the following week.

Galdinia estimated she'd been contemplating her plans while staring at the misty inverted coastline for at least thirty minutes before Neryda let herself into her room.

"It's a shame these people don't really like you," Neryda said by way of greeting, closing the door behind her. "I could see myself staying here indefinitely if they let me."

"That seems doubtful," Galdinia replied, her voice low and sluggish, still lost in swirling thoughts of Drystan, the Wetlands, and the Lidels' dismissal of her offer.

Neryda's legs appeared in front of her face as she came to stand in front of Galdinia.

"What are you doing?" Neryda asked, hands on hips.

"Wallowing," Galdinia replied, the defeat settling in her chest.

"Well, okay then," Neryda said in agreement, coming to lie beside Galdinia, mirroring her position and hanging her head over the side of the bed. Neryda's bundle of auburn curls dangled down to touch the floor. "You know, we can't do this for very long."

"I know," Galdinia replied, her eyes fixated on the coastline, watching as the sea mist blurred her view of the ocean. "I just need to give in to the self-pity for a little longer; I'll pretend I know what I'm doing again shortly."

"Oh no," Neryda said, shaking her head. "I mean we can't do *this* for long." She motioned to their place on the bed. "We're going to give ourselves headaches."

Galdinia couldn't stop her lips from curling at the edges. She could always count on Neryda to make her smile in such moments of grave uncertainty. Galdinia knew the feeling of insecurity painfully well, but Neryda knew exactly how to distract her from it.

"The headache sounds less painful than having to go out there and face… well, anyone at this point," Galdinia said with a sigh.

"Who?" Neryda questioned. "The Lidels? Please, they're conceited and self-important, nothing more. Their opinion is of little consequence."

"It's actually of quite great consequence if I can't convince them to align with us as allies," Galdinia replied, her fingers briefly tightening around the flame.

"Well, if it's not them, you'll find other allies," Neryda countered. "Let's not put all our hopes and dreams on these people your family hasn't spoken with in years."

"Perhaps," Galdinia replied, though she was unconvinced. "They may be difficult, but they're our only chance at making it to Lund."

"Is there any reason we can't just go ourselves?" Neryda asked, turning to look at Galdinia. "You are the queen after all."

"I don't think they'd let me anywhere near the city," Galdinia replied, glancing at Neryda from the corner of her eye. "And the journey there is too difficult without a guide. Ilyon has told me about the mountains before, and no one can survive it without one."

"I see your predicament," Neryda replied.

"Hence the wallowing."

"Hmm," Neryda mumbled. "They're ridiculous though, aren't they?"

"Who?"

"The Lidels," Neryda said. "They offer to have you stay and share a meal with you, but they won't align themselves with the crown, and for what? A couple of misplaced gems and a decade-long grudge? This is not the hill they want to die on."

"Ryden warned me about them," Galdinia added, her eyes still fixed on the coast. "But I didn't really believe they'd be so shallow."

"Do we think they understand just how problematic their peaceful little life will become if they don't make nice with you?"

"I don't think they care," Galdinia replied, closing her eyes momentarily. "They think their forces and natural barriers are strong enough to protect them."

"I don't think a coral reef would stop Valah if she wanted to attack."

"Neither do I," Galdinia agreed, opening her eyes again. "The Royal Guard could barely hold off an attack; I don't know how the Lidels think they could do it alone."

"Maybe their hubris will be their downfall before an enemy," Neryda suggested. "That might do Bael some good, actually. He's painfully arrogant."

"I've had people look down on me for years," Galdinia mused, her gaze trailing along the hazy coastline. "The Syndicate were long wary of a princess without a gift, and I know much of Elderguard felt the same, especially after my father's death. But Bael…" Galdinia paused to take in a slow, considered breath. "He's something else. He simultaneously hates me for everything my father did or didn't do, and he patronised me, making it abundantly clear that he doesn't think I'm worthy to wear the crown."

"He did have a penchant for being deprecating, didn't he?"

"In some ways he's worse than Valah," Galdinia muttered. "She wants the crown, and she wants to torment and hurt me, but I can understand why she wants to kill me." Galdinia's voice was low, almost a whisper. "But Bael, he doesn't want my crown. He just doesn't think I should have it. He doesn't want to kill me, but he wouldn't give it a second thought if someone else did. I think I'd rather deal with Valah alone than try to convince him to align with us again."

Galdinia could feel Neryda's eyes on her, boring into the side of her face. Galdinia glanced at her friend, who wore an expression of concern.

Neryda held her stare for a few long moments before stretching her arms up into the air. "Well, I can't keep lying like this." She hoisted herself up into a seated position. "Come on, it's time."

Galdinia groaned in reply, squeezing her eyes shut and allowing herself to succumb to her childish response to her situation for another moment. She didn't have any choice, though, as Neryda took hold of her fire-free hand and pulled her upright. Galdinia's head spun as she righted herself, all the extra blood in her head flooding back down towards her neck. It wasn't until she was upright again that she realised just how heavy her head had become.

"Isn't that better?" Neryda asked, a grin spreading across her lips.

"Mildly," Galdinia replied, stretching her neck from left to right before opening her eyes again, small grey spots appearing in her vision.

"It's going to be okay, Gal," Neryda replied, taking Galdinia's free hand in hers. "You're not going to face Valah alone, and we're going to secure allies." She hesitated for a moment before finally saying, "We'll get Drystan back."

Galdinia halted mid-breath at hearing Drystan's name. She could convince anyone—other than Neryda—that the only reason she was so disappointed by her interaction with the Lidels was because of their rejection of her offer, but she knew that rescuing Drystan was her driving force. At night her dreams were plagued with images of him in a dungeon, or trapped in a cage, or left in some wasteland to die. He was always in pain, always on the brink of breaking. And it was because of her.

She had to do all she could to rescue him, even if it meant somehow convincing people who took a disliking to her to take her as an ally.

"I have to," Galdinia replied, her voice pained.

"We will," Neryda replied, resolve in her tone. "For now, let's get some fresh air. Sitting in this room isn't going to do you any good."

Galdinia considered her options. She could refuse, lie back down on her bed, and go in circles in her head trying to conceive a new plan, or she could force herself up, convincing herself to do something more productive.

"I think I want to train," Galdinia replied with a nod, making a decision before she could persuade herself out of it. "I need to put all this nervous energy into something."

"Why don't you test your new bow?" Neryda suggested. "You might feel better after shooting something. I can fetch Bentley for you!"

Galdinia cracked a smile at Neryda's proposition, gratitude for her friend bubbling up.

"I don't think that will be necessary," Galdinia replied, "but I have another idea in mind."

She looked down at the flame still resting in her palm and swirled it around in her fingers.

~

Thirty minutes after Galdinia's request, Ilyon and Evander had set up a training ground for her outside the walls of the Lidels' manor. Their home was the only structure for kilometres on the stretch of land that curved around to the south that gave The Hook its name, allowing the Queen's Guard plenty of space to set up targets, a sparring circle, and a handful of lit lanterns across the misty grounds.

Kayd and Raia had decided to work together in the circle while Vega stood silently between the group and the trail that led to the city of The Hook, constantly scanning the area, her hands resting on the hilt of her sword at her hip.

"I barely would have made it up those stairs in the time it took Evander to fetch the targets from the ship and set them up," Neryda pondered aloud as she, Galdinia, and Ilyon watched Evander secure the final target in place.

"And that's why he's one of Ilyon's best," Galdinia replied with a nod. "Merely because he can carry heavy loads."

"Yes, that's what I look for in a good soldier." Ilyon's tone was flat and sardonic. "Priority number one is to be able to fight. But number two is definitely their ability to heave targets up a cliff face."

"Thank goodness for that," Neryda said in mock agreement.

Galdinia smiled at her friend as she tightened the binding of the sleeves on her fighting leathers. She'd contemplated dressing herself in her full armour, knowing it would do her good to get used to the ensemble, but Galdinia felt ill at the thought of moving clumsily about the Lidels' home while wrapped in sheets of metal. If Bael didn't respect her with her crown atop her head, he certainly wasn't going to revere her if she looked like she was masquerading as an awkward soldier. Galdinia reluctantly left Drystan's helmet and her crown in her rooms, instructing the guards at her door to protect both with their lives.

"So what's the plan, Your Highness?" Evander asked, approaching Galdinia once all the targets were in place.

"I haven't done much training yet with my gift and a bow and arrow, so I thought you could teach me some skills," Galdinia explained, pulling her bow from her shoulder. If she was being completely honest, she just needed a distraction. She thought there was no better way to stifle her anxiety than using her gift and doing something she felt she was actually skilled at. She needed to supersede her performance earlier with Bael and Ravenna.

After a few minutes of stretching the fresh bowstring and loading up her quiver with arrows, whose heads were wrapped in cotton, Galdinia was ready to start firing. She fired a few practice shots to start, easily hitting the bullseye on the targets they had set up around the perimeter of the training ground. Once her body and bow were warm, she started to incorporate the flame. Ilyon placed Neryda on standby to extinguish any flames with the water she kept in a bucket by her side.

"It's not difficult to light an arrow," Evander said before he took a cotton-tipped arrow of his own and held it in the flame of one of the lanterns. It took to the fire quickly, erupting in a sizzle. "However, in battle, you don't have time to put every arrowhead in a lantern before you fire it. Instead, you need to simultaneously nock your arrow, draw out your flame, and light the tip before firing."

Again, he demonstrated. This time, Evander called his flame back to the vessel at his hip, leaving the end of his arrow blackened. He re-sheathed the arrow before taking his stance, his body facing Galdinia, his head turned to the target. In one swift movement, Evander pulled a fresh arrow from his quiver, arched it over his head, and nocked it into his bow. Before the arrow landed in his bow, though, a portion of the flame in his vessel flew from its perch and struck the arrowhead, engulfing the cotton. Had Galdinia blinked, she would have missed it. A moment later, he was pulling the arrow back and shooting it at one of the targets. His flaming arrow landed right next to Galdinia's previous shot.

"Wow" was all Galdinia could muster as she looked, dumbfounded, at the target ahead of her, now sizzling with the fire. To avoid turning the target into ash and having to replace it, Neryda drew the water up out of the bucket and extinguished it in seconds.

"*That* is why he's considered one of my best," Ilyon said quietly to Galdinia. She just continued to stare at the now extinguished target in awe.

"That was amazing," Galdinia said, turning to look at Evander.

The usually stolid soldier cracked a smile.

"It takes some practise, but you'll be able to do that shortly."

"Show me again."

15

FOR TWO HOURS, GALDINIA WORKED ON THE SKILL EVANDER SHOWED her. At first, she found it almost impossible to coordinate nocking an arrow and calling upon a flame without the use of her hands. Her instinct told her to let go of the arrow feathers before coaxing the fire from its perch, but that only left her with an arrow-less bow. Soon, she got the hang of beckoning it by wriggling the fingers that were wrapped around the grip of her bow. Ensuring it landed on her arrowhead without moving her gaze from the sight of the bow, however, was the true test.

While her gift protected her from burning herself with a flame she had control of, Galdinia sent the fire blindly into her neck, against her cheek, and grazing over her fingers multiple times in attempting to cast it to the arrowhead, leaving a warm glow on her skin and a pang of frustration each time. Although she'd picked up the use of her gift quickly, she was still such a young Flourisher, and it was showing.

"Visualise it," Ilyon said, having suggested this at least fifteen times as she continued to attempt to land the flame.

Galdinia had to keep her lips sealed against telling her Water Weaver captain that she'd like to see him blindly control a flame.

Pushing resentment aside—resentment that she knew was only fuelled by her increasing self-doubt and not by Ilyon—Galdinia closed her eyes. She took in a deep breath as she imagined the movement of the flame for what felt like the hundredth time. In her mind's eye, she saw it flicker off the lantern, twist through the air, and land on the tip of her arrow, engulfing the cotton.

"Well done, Your Highness." Ilyon's voice pulled Galdinia from her concentration, and she opened her eyes.

Astonished, Galdinia was face-to-face with her flame, sitting exactly where she had commanded it to be.

A smile spread across her face as she pulled back the arrow and let it fly through the air, sticking into the bullseye with a fiery thud. If there was one thing she was confident in doing, it was accurately landing an arrow in a target.

Neryda clapped, letting the flame linger for a few extra seconds, and Evander and Ilyon greeted Galdinia with similar expressions: subdued smirks that were full of pride.

"Let's go again," Galdinia said, smiling.

Neryda extinguished the flame and removed the arrow from the target as Galdinia prepared to repeat her work.

After landing five more flaming arrows, Galdinia found her pace and strength in lighting the arrow with minimal help from her hands. With a barely imperceptible twitch of her fingers, Galdinia could replicate the action, growing in her confidence each time she sent another lit arrow to the target. She couldn't wipe the grin off her face as she started to aim for different targets across the training grounds, adding her own level of difficulty.

Neryda was right; this made Galdinia feel significantly better.

As Evander wrapped a handful of arrows in a fresh bundle of cotton, a rumble in the sky above them broke her focus. The clouds had slowly rolled in as the day went on, quietly warning them of the weather to come.

"It might almost be time to pack things up," Ilyon said, glancing at the sky.

"We can keep going until the rain hits," Galdinia said, taking one of the arrows Evander had just placed in her quiver.

"Not that you'll have any choice once it does," Neryda pointed out.

Once again, Galdinia called on the flame beside her, and it flickered and shot through the air, colliding with the arrowhead as she pulled it back. Instantaneously, she let go of the arrow, and it landed on the target the furthest across the grounds. It was the quickest she had landed the shot, and her confidence was growing, replacing the vulnerability she'd held earlier.

"Your Majesty, it's time to return to the manor." Ilyon's voice was low and firm as he spoke to Galdinia.

"I think we have time for a few more before the rain sets in," Galdinia said, reaching to retrieve another arrow from her quiver, not ready to abandon her practice after only just starting to master her new skills.

"Vega." Ilyon's voice was still low as he spoke. "Please escort the queen and Lady Neryda back to the manor."

Galdinia caught Neryda's eye before promptly rolling her own. Neryda, however, wore an expression of confusion.

"Captain, I don't need—"

Galdinia's words died on her lips as she turned to face Ilyon. From the cliff edge behind them, a thick blanket of sea mist had risen unnaturally high from its position above the water and far thicker than it had appeared earlier, now resembling a fog. Having been too focused on the targets, Galdinia hadn't noticed it rolling in, but she could no longer see the horizon to the south. And glancing down at the ground beneath her, she saw her feet were washed in the foggy mist.

Glancing around at the group, Galdinia could see that each of the soldiers were already poised in a calm readiness.

"This way, Your Highness," Vega said quietly, approaching Galdinia, sword in hand.

"Captain, what's going on?" Galdinia asked, standing firm in the grass, pointing her nocked arrow towards the ground.

"Kayd, can you push it back?" Ilyon asked, his voice hushed, ignoring Galdinia's question.

Without a word, Kayd raised his hands and faced his palms towards the fog as it snaked between trees and moved almost undetectably faster towards the group. He pursed his lips as he tried to draw the breeze around them back against the fog, but it seemed futile —the cloud of white continued to roll in, unaffected.

"Ilyon," Galdinia said, her voice carrying with it concern.

"I estimate at least ten Wielders," Kayd whispered, continuing to try to push his gift against the fog. "Or five very powerful ones."

With this Ilyon turned towards Galdinia, a sudden haste in his expression and movements.

"Someone is pushing this fog towards us," Ilyon explained quietly, standing close to Galdinia and looking around the area furiously. "Without knowing who it is, I need you to go inside, now."

At the mention of Wielders, one who wanted her dead came to mind immediately: Valah.

"Whoever it is, I'm not leaving my soldiers here to potentially fight alone," Galdinia said, frowning at her captain. If someone—Valah even—wanted to attack them and there were in fact ten Wielders, they'd need all the extra hands they could get, even if she was surrounded by the Royal Guard's best.

"Your bravery is noted, Your Highness, but you are not here to protect us, we are here to protect you." Ilyon's words were rushed as they both watched the fog gain pace and mass.

"Captain, I—"

"Galdinia." Ilyon's voice was harsh as he spoke her first name, something he very rarely did. "Go with Vega to the manor now. That's an order."

Startled by Ilyon's words, Galdinia stared at him. Arguing with him further would be useless and his serious concern raised her own, so she slowly nodded and beckoned Neryda towards her. Her friend was at her side in a moment, and they turned to walk with Vega, their eyes darting wildly around them into the fog and surrounding trees.

The moment Galdinia stepped in the direction of the manor, however, a great gust of wind pressed in on them, whipping her hair in her face and sending the thick fog between them almost instantaneously. It was unnatural and came at such a force that Galdinia found herself immediately disoriented. Instinctually, Galdinia reached for Neryda, taking her wrist in her hand, pulling her close. Within seconds she couldn't see the manor's gates, nor the trees around them, and Vega had become a hazy blur in front of them.

"Stay close and keep your bow at the ready, Your Highness," Vega said as she stalked forward. "Take this, Lady Neryda."

Without taking her eyes off the fog in front of them, Vega reached back to hand Neryda a dagger, which she gladly accepted.

Quickening their pace, Galdinia and Neryda followed close behind Vega, and Galdinia kept an arrow nocked in her bow, scanning the area around them for any kind of movement. They weren't far from the gates of the Lidels' manor, but with barely any visibility, it felt as though one wrong step could have them plummeting off a cliff face any moment.

"Who do you think it is, Vega?" Galdinia asked, her eyes straining for a sign of movement. "Could it be Valah?"

"I'm not sure, but I doubt it's the Lidels playing a cruel trick on us," Vega said quietly, sword held out in front of her in one hand, a painfully sharp dagger in the other.

"That seems unlikely," Neryda agreed.

"Whoever it is, I don't think they're our friends," Vega added.

As Galdinia took another step forward, a low whistle could be heard. Then, suddenly, an arrow shot through the fog from the direction they were walking, barely missing Galdinia and flying past her ear. In an attempt to move out of the way, Galdinia misplaced a foot, which sent her tumbling to the ground, her cheek colliding with the grass, her skin burning against the ground.

"Gal!" Neryda said with an exhale.

"Get down!" Vega frantically whispered as she bent down in the grass.

Neryda did as she was told, and Galdinia pushed herself up to a crouched position, wincing against the sharp stinging sensation travelling across her cheek. As she ran her fingertips over the now broken skin on her face, two more arrows flew above their heads, whipping through the thick air.

Without taking another second to think about her actions, Galdinia aimed her own arrow in the direction from which the others had come, sending it into the hazy white abyss. She wasn't sure if she made contact, but she immediately pulled another before sending it in the same direction. A soft thud told her she had landed it, whether in a tree or an attacker, she couldn't be sure.

A sound to their right made Vega stand up from her crouch on the ground.

"Keep moving due north," Vega said, pointing in the direction they'd been moving, "and stay low."

With that, Vega ran into the fog, getting lost in the haze in a matter of seconds.

"Let's move," Galdinia said hastily as she nocked another arrow.

"Light them," Neryda said, and at Galdinia's questioning expression, added, "The heat from the fire might help to dispel some of the moisture in the air. I've been trying to push against it, but there are some Weavers out there too, holding control of it."

"The fire could cut through it," Galdinia said with a nod.

Using Evander's previous instruction, Galdinia clumsily beckoned the flame from its vessel at her hip and sent it to the tip of her arrow. She shot it forward, and unlike her previous arrows, this one momentarily left a thin path through the fog in its tailwind. Although it didn't alight the surrounding area, Galdinia could at least see grass ahead of them, rather than the edge of the cliff.

"Let's go!" Galdinia said, moving as quickly as she could across the grass in her crouched position, Neryda fast beside her.

Another barrage of arrows flew through the fog above their heads, now coming from another direction. Whoever was attacking wasn't short on weaponry. Galdinia sent three more flaming arrows towards their attackers.

"I think I hit them," Galdinia said as the onslaught of arrows suddenly stopped.

"Keep moving, then!" Neryda replied, and they started to shuffle forward, still bent over.

Before they could take even ten steps forward, though, Galdinia could make out a dark mass in the fog, moving towards them at pace. Emerging from the fog in fighting leathers, their assailant was a formidable shadow of muscle, the lower half of their face covered in a mask, their eyes severe and ferocious. Neryda gasped, staggering backwards. Galdinia immediately reached for another arrow, then quickly lit it and fired it at the attacker before he could reach them. The arrow struck the leather at his shoulder, causing him to stumble back a few feet. Without a moment's hesitation, Galdinia let fly another arrow, this one embedding itself in the other shoulder. Again her attacker halted in his movements, but he remained on his feet. Through the haze she could see his eyes alight with a furious hunger.

Galdinia reached back for another arrow, but her fingers did not find the familiar silky feathers. Her quiver was empty. The attacker seemingly sneered at her beneath his mask as he reached up with both hands and forcefully wrenched the arrows from his shoulders with a pained grunt, then threw them into the mist behind him before continuing towards Galdinia. He pulled his sword from its sheath, raising it, and Galdinia instinctively held up her bow in front of her as he bore down, slicing forward with his blade. Shock waves shot up Galdinia's arms as he made contact with her bow, the heavy metals colliding with each other. Again and again, he slashed the blade through the air, but Galdinia held up her bow as a shield, managing to hold him off.

"Gal!" Neryda yelled from behind Galdinia as she parried another slice of his sword.

Despite the rattling pain in her arms from each blow of metal on metal, Galdinia gritted her teeth and pressed against the attacker's strength, digging her boots into the ground beneath her. Her muscles may have been tired from training, but he'd just removed two arrows from his shoulders. They held each other's pained and desperate gazes as he pushed down on his sword against her bow, the blade inching closer to Galdinia's face.

Rushing forward from the fog behind her, Neryda appeared in a whirlwind of russet curls and recklessness. As Galdinia quivered beneath the weight and strength of their attacker, Neryda sliced her dagger through the air, landing the small blade in his side, striking him somewhere between the layers of leather covering his body.

He let out a cry of pain, tipping on his feet briefly, relinquishing his hold against Galdinia. Taking the opportunity, Galdinia furiously twisted the end of her bow towards him, the thickest part of the weapon colliding with his jaw, sending him stumbling backwards.

He looked at them both with disdain and rage, yet clearly weakened by the blade in his side.

He lifted his sword again and charged with what strength he had left. Galdinia stepped in front of Neryda and held up her bow again, shuddering as his blade made contact. Again, Galdinia pressed against him, but his wrath seemed to be spurring him on, and she took a slow step backwards, her feet slipping in the grass.

Neryda leapt forward, reaching for the dagger in his side—whether to retrieve it or twist, Galdinia didn't know. But before she could grasp it, in a swift movement, their attacker threw his elbow through the fog towards her, landing a cracking blow against her temple, sending her stumbling backward and onto the ground.

"Ner!" Galdinia screamed, her friend lost somewhere in the haze.

Galdinia pressed harder still, her knuckles becoming white as she used every inch of energy she had left to push against the man's sword. With the slight flick of her fingertips, she beckoned the flame at her hip—which had decreased in size since sending a number of flaming arrows through the fog—and sent it leaping across her attacker's fingers, willing him to let go of the sword.

"Nice try," he sneered, his gravelly voice malicious.

From his own belt rose a ball of water, which he sent towards Galdinia's flame, extinguishing it in a plume of steam, disappearing into the fog.

She now had no fire and no arrows, and she didn't know how long she could hold him off as she was.

He lifted his sword again, and after an angry slice from the side, Galdinia desperately jumped backwards, falling to the ground and narrowly missing his blade. Although she wasn't touched, her bow was caught in the strike and was sent tumbling from her hands. Galdinia's heart thumped in her ears as she watched him raise his sword again, the blade cutting a long river through the thick fog.

"Goodbye, Your Highness," he said in a mocking tone. "Long live Queen Valah!"

Galdinia sucked in a breath when his sword reached its height, anticipating the painful death that awaited her. She could only hope it would be quick and that Neryda, somewhere beside her in the fog, would be spared such an end.

Before she was sent into oblivion, another blade appeared through the mist. Two hands and a dagger wrapped around his neck as the metal made contact with his throat, slicing over his pale skin in a swift movement, a torrent of blood cascading from the cut. Her attacker's eyes widened briefly as his sword fell from his hand before his expression went blank and he crashed to the ground at Galdinia's feet, revealing a bloodied and furious Vega behind him.

Galdinia released her breath and felt a choking pain in her throat as she watched the blood continue to pour from her attacker's wound, flooding the grass around her feet and soaking the soles of her boots. His lifeless eyes stared at her without seeing, his body crumpled and the last remnants of life oozing from his neck. Galdinia's joints felt locked, her limbs unmoving, and her heart racing. Had Vega not returned when she had, Galdinia would be the one dead and bleeding on the ground.

"Your Highness, we have to move," Vega said desperately, sheathing one of her blood-covered daggers and helping a frozen Galdinia to her feet.

Galdinia reluctantly stood and mumbled something to the effect of "Neryda", struggling to find her voice. She felt as though her tongue were stuck to the roof of her mouth and her jaw were bolted shut.

"Where is she?" Vega asked.

With a shaky hand, Galdinia pointed in the direction Neryda fell, and she watched Vega disappear into the fog before reemerging seconds later with Neryda over her shoulder, her legs dangling over her chest.

"Can you walk?"

Galdinia looked down at her feet coated in her assailant's blood, his dead body lying beside her toes. Could she walk? She felt like she could barely breathe. She moved a foot backwards, away from the body, the sole of her foot feeling unsupported on the grass beneath her, as though she were walking in soft, dry sand. Reluctantly, she looked up at Vega and nodded.

"Take his sword and follow me."

Galdinia glanced at him one more time and felt as though she may be sick. She turned her face from the man, an acrid taste rising in her mouth. Watching the queen closely, Vega bent down, picked up the sword, and thrust it into Galdinia's hand. It had been sprayed in its previous owner's blood.

"Take it, Your Highness," Vega said, shaking the sword in Galdinia's palm, practically begging her to take hold of it. "We need to move."

With a quivering nod of her head, Galdinia managed to agonis-
ingly wrap her stiff fingers around the hilt of the sword. Without hesitating another moment, Vega brought two fingers to her mouth and
let out a piercing whistle before she started to move through the fog
once again. Sounds of metal on metal and cries of pain echoed
around them, muffled by either the fog or the blood pulsing through
her ears, Galdinia couldn't tell. All she knew was that she wanted to
get away from the violence as quickly as her stiff legs would take her.

She was aware they had made it through the gates of the Lidels'
home when the grass beneath them turned into a pebbled path, and
Vega navigated them through the gardens that surrounded the manor.
The next thing she knew, Vega had wrapped an arm around
Galdinia's waist and was helping her traverse the front stairs of the
mansion before pounding a fist onto the front doors. Almost immediately, the door swung open, and they tumbled into the entrance hall,
Galdinia's muscles tight and her chest cleaving. Vega slammed the
door behind them, and suddenly, Galdinia could see her surroundings
once again.

Now away from the suffocating fog, Galdinia became acutely
aware of the restriction of her fighting leathers as they seemed to have
been pulled tighter against her body. Frantically, she threw the sword
and her quiver to the ground with a shattering crash before clumsily
loosening the ties on the sides of her leathers, her breaths coming in
short bursts. She desperately tugged at the restraints, managing to
awkwardly pull her chest piece off, releasing some of the pressure that
had built. She was vaguely aware of Vega's indistinct voice as she
spoke to the guards in the hall, but Galdinia couldn't make out the
words through her hammering heartbeat and misty mind. Next she
worked on her arm pieces, pulling on the knots and ripping them from
her hands, abandoning them on the floor.

Standing in her billowing undershirt, Galdinia felt like she could
finally breathe, her torso free from the constraints of the training
armour.

She turned to look at Vega and saw her leaning over her best
friend who was still unconscious, now lying on the floor of the
entrance hall. Vega was pointing and gesturing at the guards, her
voice wordlessly echoing in Galdinia's mind. One guard sprinted

down a nearby hallway, while another looked out a window towards the gardens. He shook his head in response.

"Your Highness!" Finally, Vega's voice cut through the stifled quiet of Galdinia's mind, and she felt her senses catch up with her, the room coming into sharper focus. "Your Highness, I need your help!"

Galdinia searched for her voice, but it had not yet returned; her jaw was locked tight. By way of response, Galdinia moved as quickly as her body would allow to Vega's side and crouched beside Neryda's head. She could see a bruise forming on the side of her head and blood trickling out of one of her ears. Her breath caught in her chest, and Galdinia had to remind herself to breathe. She couldn't help Neryda if she stopped breathing.

"Cradle her head," Vega urged her.

Galdinia gently lifted Neryda's head, her crown of long russet curls cushioning her in Galdinia's lap. Galdinia held Neryda's face straight as she lay in front of her, her chest slowly rising and falling, necessary proof of life. Against Neryda's warm cheeks, Galdinia realised just how cold her hands had become, as though all the blood from her body had drained from her along with her attacker's.

At the thought of the blood that still stained her boots, Galdinia held back a lurch of bile that threatened in her stomach.

"It's clearing!" The soldier by the window broke Galdinia's thoughts, and she glanced at him as he drew his sword.

Vega joined him by the window and peered through the glass. Galdinia watched as Vega moved to the manor doors and hurled them open. Ilyon, Raia, Kayd, and Evander stumbled through the doorway, a haze of mist following them into the entrance hall. Galdinia caught a glimpse of the gardens and saw that the fog had very much turned back into a mist and was slowly dissipating in the air. The soldiers were breathing heavily, and each wore varying degrees of injuries, with Kayd's being the most severe: he was cradling his left arm, which seemed to be dripping with blood.

Ilyon's eyes darted around the entrance hall, noting the discarded leathers and weapons before landing on Galdinia. He flew to her side and crouched to inspect her face, arms, and neck, checking for any infirmities or injuries of her own. Once he was satisfied with his inspection, he finally breathed.

"You're okay." It wasn't so much a question as a confirmation to himself that Galdinia was alive, and given the circumstances, well.

Galdinia nodded, her hands still clasped on either side of Neryda's face.

Rushed footsteps could be heard down one of the hallways, and the guard returned, bringing with him Ravenna, Bael, and five more soldiers.

"What happened?" Ravenna asked, breathless, looking around at the injured soldiers and the shock-ridden queen.

"We were ambushed," Ilyon said, turning to the Lidels but remaining by Galdinia's side on the ground. "Soldiers of Valah's blinded us with a fog and attacked us."

"How did they know you were here?" Ravenna asked, concern painting her expression.

"I have no idea," Ilyon said, shaking his head. "No one was aware of our movements except the Syndicate and our soldiers on board."

"And your prisoner," Bael added contemptuously.

"He hasn't had access to any foreseeable way to communicate with the west."

"It doesn't matter, anyway," Evander cut in, still catching his breath. "The point is that Valah knew we were here and they were watching us. And now we are weaker for it."

Galdinia looked down at Neryda again, her best friend's face peaceful in her unconscious state. Knowing that everyone was alive, she felt her senses strengthen again, and she could feel a tickling dampness on her cheeks. Reaching up with one hand, Galdinia wiped at her cheek—she was crying. When had she started crying? The tears stung her grazed and broken skin, and the pain helped ground her in her body again as an ache rose at her temples.

"We need your soldiers to go retrieve the bodies," Ilyon said.

"*Our* soldiers?" Bael asked, incredulous. "An enemy was just lured to our land thanks to your group. You can clean up your own mess."

At this, Galdinia looked up at Bael, her eyes flaming. Still, however, she couldn't find her voice, but her anger at his reaction helped her mind and heart catch up with the world around her.

"Do we look in any condition to go clean up your land?" Kayd asked, stepping forward with his injured arm, lifting it in Bael's direction.

"We need to see your healers immediately," Ilyon added. "The queen could be injured, and Lady Neryda is clearly hurt beyond any of us. So if you want to make sure none of their soldiers survived our superb protection of *your* home, you'll send your own guards out there to count the bodies. There should be twelve of them."

"Thirteen," Vega said quickly.

Thirteen? Galdinia wondered, staggered that her guard of five managed to stave off so many attackers.

Bael stood in a silent battle with Ilyon as they glared at one another.

"Yewan." Ravenna finally spoke, drawing one of her soldiers to attention. "Take your troop out to the grasses and find the thirteen bodies, please."

After a quick nod, the soldier and five companions exited out the main doors without another word.

"Thank you," Ilyon said with a breath.

"Now let's get you to our healers," Ravenna said, gesturing to another hallway beyond the main staircase.

"Evander, take Lady Neryda," Ilyon said, and Evander stepped forward and easily scooped Neryda up in his arms; Galdinia could now see the cut on his eyebrow and his muddied armour. "Your Highness, are you okay?"

Galdinia looked up to meet Ilyon's eyes, which were swimming with concern and relief.

"Yes." Galdinia finally spoke, her voice coming out on a long breath. "But Captain, I think Neryda is going to need her own suit of armour."

With those words, Galdinia's muscles finally relaxed. The room tilted briefly, and Galdinia felt herself lean forward. Her vision went dark before she landed in Ilyon's arms.

16

GALDINIA THOUGHT SHE'D BEEN WALKING THROUGH THE FOG FOR DAYS. Every step she took led her no closer to the Lidels' manor, and she just kept walking in twisted lines, circling her own path. Somewhere beyond the mist she could hear murky whispers hissing through the air. Her feet were starting to drag, as though she had sandbags hanging from her hips, but she had to keep moving. They were under attack, and she had to move.

In the distance she heard the clashing of metal and shouts of agony—where were her guards? Where was Neryda? She had to get out of the haze, but which way was she to go? Among the sounds of chaos, the whispers grew louder, beckoning her in different directions, some familiar, others strange to her. Soon the voices had drowned out the sounds of violence until they were shouting at her, crying for her attention.

Galdinia couldn't bear it any longer.

She clasped her hands over her ears and sunk to the ground, crouching in a ball and accepting her fate.

After a few seconds, the voices died down, leaving her heart crashing in her chest and her eyes watering. Warily, Galdinia looked up.

A clearing in the fog had been created, perhaps five meters wide. And there he was, standing on the other side of the circle of clear air. He was still wearing his black Royal Guard armour, sword at his side, brown eyes lost in concern.

"Drystan!" Galdinia called as she leapt to her feet and rushed towards him.

"Gal, no!" Drystan raised his hands, and as he did, she hit an invisible wall at the centre of the clearing, bruising her cheek.

Galdinia stared at him, and while she couldn't see the barrier between them, she could press her palms against it. Mere centimetres away, Drystan mirrored her action, but the invisible wall—thinner than glass and stronger than stone—kept him from her.

"Drystan." Galdinia sighed, her voice desperate as she looked at him, pressing her hands harder against the barrier, hoping to feel his warmth, but all she felt was the cool of the air.

"I'm right here, Gal," he said gently, his warm and familiar voice an enveloping hug. "I'm right here."

"But I can't reach you."

"I know," he whispered, his face dropping. "I'm sorry."

A blade appeared out of the fog behind Drystan. Galdinia frowned at the sight, confused. The fingers wrapped around the hilt of the dagger were long and spindly, the skin pulled taut against the bones. Before Galdinia could say another word to alert Drystan to the danger, the dagger moved towards Drystan's throat, and in one fell swoop, it sliced.

The noise that came from Galdinia could only be described as a guttural animal shriek. Not only had the scream echoed in her subconscious, but her physical body also cried out—her own scream woke her from her horrific dream.

Galdinia opened her eyes as her voice reverberated around her room in the Lidels' home. She sat up in her fright, her heartbeat hammering through her body, her hands shaking, and her throat dry.

She heard her name echo somewhere beyond the sound of her heart as her surroundings came into focus, the fog of her dream dissolving.

Galdinia's clammy left hand was wrapped in two golden-brown hands—Neryda, who was sitting in a chair beside her bed with an expression of terrified concern painted over her features, held her friend in a firm grip.

"Gal, are you okay?"

Before she could find her voice, someone opened the door to her rooms, their gentle face one of concern. They wore robes of pale blue, and they were holding a fresh towel draped over their arm. Galdinia didn't recognise them, but they appeared to be there to help her.

Behind them, Ilyon entered the room, an air of distress about him. His eyebrows were upturned, and he appeared far less rigid, as though anxiety had weighed down on his usually immaculate posture. Galdinia had never seen her captain like this.

"Your Majesty?" Ilyon's voice was laden with worry.

"A nightmare," she said, her voice hoarse. Galdinia sucked in a deep breath, trying to calm her thrashing heart.

"You look warm," the person in blue said, their voice calm despite the obvious fear in the room. "Here, this may help."

They approached her bedside and dipped the towel in a bowl of water that was stationed there. After wringing it out, they pressed it to Galdinia's forehead, which she gladly accepted before leaning back into her mountain of pillows. The towel smelled of spearmint, and she could feel the herbal concoction cooling her sweat-drenched skin instantly. *They must be a healer*, Galdinia thought.

"That's better," the healer said, gently pressing their hand on the towel, smiling down at the queen. "I will give you your privacy, but do call out if you need anything."

"Thank you." Galdinia exhaled, watching them almost float through the room and out her door, closing it behind them.

Galdinia then turned her attention to her troubled captain and distressed best friend. Ilyon stood at the end of her bed now, and while his hands were clasped behind his back, as they so often were, his face communicated his worry.

"I'm sorry to have frightened you," Galdinia said, pressing the towel to her forehead with her free hand, looking from Ilyon to Neryda.

"It's fine, Gal," Neryda assured her.

"I'm just glad you're okay." Ilyon's voice was stilted. "You are okay, aren't you?"

"I think so," Galdinia replied as images of Drystan with a blade to his throat, eclipsed with fog, crossed her mind. So many of those images were steeped in a reality that now felt so far away, as though he were still being held by Valah and Reynard beyond the Northern Gates of Elderguard, helpless. As though she were still surrounded by a dense fog as blood fell at her feet. "What happened, Ilyon?" She was trying to separate truth from her horrid imaginings. "And Ner—are you okay?"

With a smile of reassurance, Neryda said, "Aside from a lingering headache, I'm perfectly well."

"Thank the Gods," Galdinia said, returning the smile. "And everyone else? My guards?"

"All accounted for," Ilyon said with a curt nod. "Some bruised and battered, but nothing worth writing home about."

A wave of relief fell over Galdinia as she tried to remember the last she'd seen of the Queen's Guard—had they all come back to the manor with her? Had any of them appeared hurt? Images of Kayd cradling his arm and a cut on Evander's brow came to her.

Galdinia scrunched up her eyes, trying to locate the order of events in her mind. "The attack earlier, who was it?"

Ilyon glanced briefly at Neryda before replying. "The attack was yesterday, Your Highness."

"Yesterday?"

"Yes. You've been asleep for about sixteen hours."

Galdinia's eyes widened. "Sixteen hours?"

"Your body went into shock," Neryda explained.

"Vega explained to us what you saw, and I'm not surprised," Ilyon added. "I'm sorry you had to see that."

Again, visions of blood and blades and lifeless bodies invaded her mind. She felt her hand involuntarily tighten inside Neryda's.

"It's fine," Galdinia said, shaking her head of the images, attempting to embody some semblance of strength. "I'll have to get used to seeing such things. It feels inevitable as queen."

"Except that it isn't, Your Majesty."

"Of course it is," Galdinia retorted, pressing the towel against her forehead, relishing the cool sensation against her hot skin.

Ilyon averted his eyes as he said, "I think it best you rest a while longer. We can discuss this later."

Galdinia was put off by Ilyon's uncharacteristic retreat from the conversation.

"I don't need to rest," Galdinia said shortly—had her voice been lost the day before, she had well and truly found it again. "I've been asleep for sixteen hours. Whatever you want to say, just say it."

"Your Majesty," Ilyon said cautiously, "Valah attempted an assassination, and we don't know how she learnt where you would be, but we can't risk that happening again. I know that we have been training and preparing you for all kinds of attacks, and I trust the Queen's Guard entirely, but you shouldn't be in active combat."

"I don't plan on seeking out more enemy soldiers, if that's your concern."

"That isn't my concern at all because I don't intend on having you anywhere remotely near enemy soldiers."

Beneath the towel, Galdinia furrowed her brows as she stared at her captain. "I think that's a fairly impossible plan to enact."

"Well, moving forward, I'll do everything in my power to keep you away from any such violence."

Sitting up and pulling the towel from her face and her hand from Neryda's, Galdinia looked at her captain, questioning.

"What if I want to go to the Wetlands?" Galdinia asked. "Or perhaps to Edana in the south? I could be ambushed anywhere I travel. Conflict is inevitable."

"For us, perhaps, but not for you."

"'For us,' you mean—"

"Myself and my soldiers."

It was then that Galdinia realised that he wasn't just suggesting he'd force her to retreat at the hint of an attack or change their travelling routes when necessary. No, his plan was far more restrictive than that.

"So you'll have me locked away in the castle or the catacombs in an attempt to keep me safe?"

"Perhaps not such extreme measures, but I would like to see your return to Elderguard as soon as you are well enough."

"Last week, our greatest enemies were in the heart of the castle," Galdinia pointed out. "I'm not necessarily any safer there than I am here."

"Perhaps Lady Neryda should give us the room," Ilyon said tentatively.

"Neryda can stay," Galdinia quickly replied, frowning at her captain.

After a brief pause, Ilyon continued.

"The attack on Elderguard has already informed a new strategy of protection moving forward." Ilyon's posture was shifting the more he spoke—his back was straighter and his neck stiffer.

"I have no interest in hiding away in my throne room while you fight my battles for me, Captain." Galdinia's voice was low as she spoke, reflective of her emotions. "I'm not that kind of queen."

"I know you're not. That's why you refused to retreat when I asked you to, which was noble. Your loyalty to your soldiers is not lost on us, Your Highness."

Galdinia's stomach started to feel heavy, tying itself in knots. She thought that by being given her mother's crown she'd be able to make these decisions for herself, and she couldn't believe that Ilyon—of all people—was going to try to take away that freedom. Galdinia started to wonder if his perception of her had started to warp after he watched her collapse into his arms in the entrance hall.

"Although loyalty was much of the reason I insisted on staying," Galdinia started to explain, not prepared to budge on this issue, "it wasn't the only one. It is my duty to protect my people. What kind of queen would I be if I deserted them when they needed help?"

Ilyon clenched his jaw, and Galdinia could see frustration starting to simmer just beneath his surface.

"A good one!" Ilyon's voice echoed in the room, and Galdinia saw Neryda tense in her periphery. "I said this to you yesterday, Your Highness, but we are here to protect *you*. *You* are the Queen of Crysterra, *you* are the true ruler of this kingdom, and *you* have to stay alive in order to remain that way."

"And as ruler, I can't shy away from situations that may result in violence," Galdinia countered. "I should be meeting with my people and making allies in person, no matter the risk."

"And you can do that by writing via attendants and soldiers," Ilyon replied.

"While I'm safely bound up in Elderguard, under constant watch of my guards?"

"Exactly."

A scowl crept over Galdinia's brow.

Although she understood why the Captain of the Royal Guard would insist upon such an argument, she simply did not agree with him. She glanced across the room and eyed her crown sitting on the table by the window where she'd left it before training the day before. It was still accompanied by Drystan's helmet.

"Yesterday you ordered me back to the manor, and I complied because I trusted you. But today, I'm going to pull rank and give you my own order." Galdinia looked back at Ilyon, who had returned to his usual state of stoicism. "Despite what the Lidels have said, I'm going to continue to make allies and build our forces, and I will do it in person."

"Your Highness, I don't think—"

"I'm not done, Captain." Galdinia's voice took on a new weight as she spoke. "No one is going to swear their loyalty to a queen who sends attendants or soldiers to pass on notes and letters requesting allegiance, so I will do it in person. If another attack comes in the process, so be it. I'll be better prepared. But you do not decide how I am to rule. With that being said, I charge you to do your best to keep me alive as I make such contact. I have full faith in you and the Queen's Guard to do as such."

With that, Galdinia smiled at her captain, making it plain that this conversation was well and truly over. Galdinia was not going to be dictated to anymore—she'd succumbed to the whims of the Syndicate before, and that only led to her being trapped in the castle library with her greatest enemy. She had to make her own decisions and use the power of her mother's crown to make it plain to these men that she would make her own decisions.

Ilyon didn't appear at all pleased with being given such an order, but if someone was to honour the orders of the queen, Galdinia knew it was him.

After a very long pause, Ilyon finally conceded. "As you wish, Your Highness," he said, clenching his jaw.

"Thank you, Captain." Galdinia leant back in the pillows and placed the towel on her forehead again, welcoming the soothing, cool sensation that came with it, the ache in her head still present. "I think perhaps I will rest a while longer."

"I'll come back later, Gal," Neryda said, patting her friend's hand and standing to her feet, surreptitiously raising her eyebrows in Galdinia's direction.

Ilyon, however, didn't move. "There's something else."

Galdinia peeked at Ilyon from beneath the towel. If it was possible, he looked even more displeased about what he was about to say than having to accept his new order.

With a heavy sigh, Galdinia said, "Yes?"

"I really think this is better said in private," Ilyon suggested, glancing sideways at Neryda, who had stopped in her movements to leave, now eyeing Galdinia.

Five minutes ago, Galdinia's response may have been more gracious to such a request, but after Ilyon's jarring suggestions, she instead decided to lean into the resentment that lingered.

She refused to speak but instead pulled the towel from her face and crossed her arms over her chest.

With a heavy sigh, Ilyon spoke. "It's Bentley."

The mention of his name should have made Galdinia's skin crawl, but instead it sent her heart thumping in her chest again—*what was that?* Neryda's countenance, on the other hand, changed entirely, as though a dark cloud had passed over her eyes.

"Oh?" Galdinia said, attempting to mask her physical reaction with a tone of indifference.

"It seems that last night some of the guards were talking about the attack, and when one of them mentioned you'd been hurt, he... well, he seemed to have had a bad reaction."

"A bad reaction?"

"Yes."

"Can you be more specific?"

"He's been asking after you—loudly—and is refusing food and peace until he sees you alive and well."

"Did you tell him she was asleep?" Neryda's words were vitriolic.

"Not in so many words, but yes."

"Well, you can go tell him I'm awake, breathing, and will live to hate him another day," Galdinia replied through a false smile.

"As believable as I'm sure it will be to hear that from me, he is insistent on seeing you with his own two eyes."

"Perhaps you could be a little more persuasive," Galdinia suggested.

"If threats of suffocation won't do it, I'm not sure what else will."

Galdinia frowned at her captain. "Do you really think I need to see him?"

"Regrettably, yes."

"Why?"

"He is causing quite a stir in the manor, and our hosts are becoming irritable, which I don't think bodes well for our already volatile relationship with them."

Both Galdinia and Neryda stared at Ilyon, their expressions mirroring each other's bitterness and disbelief.

He isn't being serious, Galdinia thought. Surely this was the captain's attempt at humour.

"You want to chain me to my throne and barricade the doors of the castle to keep me safe against hypothetical attacks, but you're willing to let me walk into a chamber with someone who has proven they want me dead?" Galdinia couldn't help but let out a sarcastic laugh. "I hope the irony of this isn't lost on you."

"It isn't, no," Ilyon said, standing firm in both his body and words, looking utterly displeased with the situation.

"Good."

Galdinia contemplated her options: she could refuse and stay in bed, relax back into the pillows, and sleep for another few hours; or she could prove Ilyon wrong and show him just how strong she could be in the presence of her enemies.

"Shall I go deliver the news to him that you're awake, or…?"

"Give me thirty minutes." Galdinia's voice came with sigh.

With a nod—and a barely perceptible smile of gratitude—Ilyon turned from the room and closed the door.

Galdinia glared at the door after her captain, annoyed she felt compelled to prove that she wasn't a fragile child while she was still experiencing the effects of the attack. She wasn't mad at Ilyon, per se, but rather his idealistic view of how she was to rule. And if she truly wanted to disprove his concerns, she needed to face Bentley.

"Am I missing something?" Neryda asked, looking back at Galdinia in disbelief.

"I can't have him be proven right about my ability to look after myself," Galdinia explained, reluctantly pulling her legs from under the covers and tossing the towel into the bowl of water. "And if it keeps the Lidels on our good side, then it's worth it."

"Are you sure you want to do this?" Neryda asked.

"No, not really," Galdinia replied, "but that's something else I'll have to get used to as queen—doing things I don't want to do."

"Do you want me to come?"

"I think you and I both know that if you come with me, there won't be anything left of Bentley afterwards," Galdinia said, a hint of levity to her words. "I'll be fine."

Neryda looked into Galdinia's face as she so often did, searching for any hint of dishonesty or deceit. Galdinia was used to her friend doing this, and to avoid her finding anything Galdinia would prefer to stay hidden, she reached out and squeezed Neryda's hand reassuringly, her lips slightly upturned.

"If you change your mind, or if you decide that locking him in a cell isn't enough of a punishment, you know where to find me," Neryda said, her voice sullen.

Galdinia knew she didn't need to ask her friend twice to let loose on Bentley if needed. Though Galdinia didn't think that would be necessary this time.

"At first evidence of any treachery, you'll be my first port of call," Galdinia assured her. "I'd better get dressed."

With a squeeze of Galdinia's hand, Neryda exited her rooms, leaving Galdinia alone.

Am I making a mistake? Galdinia asked herself, her thoughts far more honest than her words.

Galdinia could only assume the room Bentley was held in was somewhere deep in the mansion or beneath the surface of The Hook, and for some reason that sent a slithering shock of terror sliding up from her stomach to her chest.

She'd been so determined to prove her strength and dependability as queen, Galdinia had been ignoring a misty cloud of fear that had been looming. Now that she was alone, though, she could feel it creeping in around her. If she wanted to prove Ilyon wrong, she couldn't let it descend upon her entirely.

Standing to her feet, she was surprisingly steady; her joints were stiff, but her legs had a stability that they didn't have when she had crashed into the entrance hall the day prior.

Steering quickly away from gruesome reminders of the attack, she made her way to the bathtub, which had been filled with water and was ready for heating. Using one of the flames in a lantern by the door, Galdinia pressed the fire against the edge of the metal bath, heating the water inside within minutes. She relished the feeling of the flame in her hand and sadly left it in the lantern thirty minutes later when she was bathed, dressed, and exiting her rooms—meeting with Bentley meant she'd have to go without fire.

Ilyon waited for her outside her door, and they walked silently through the manor. Galdinia still felt unsettled by their conversation, and she found herself glowering into the back of his head as they walked.

During the Week of Mourning, Ilyon had often believed in Galdinia more than she believed in herself. He was one of her greatest encouragers, and he trained her with patience and grace despite her growing frustration and her occasional irreverence towards the Gods who Ilyon so honourably respected. So to hear him propose that she should be protected at the cost of her freedom, suggesting that she couldn't protect herself, felt like an arrowhead to the heart. As she wordlessly followed him through the hallways, she wondered if perhaps Ryden's concerns about Galdinia's ability to rule had influenced Ilyon's words; the governor hadn't been subtle when he questioned Galdinia's ability to lead during the Week of Mourning, a conversation that had been perpetuated by the Syndicate. Was this now just an extension of their concerns? If they didn't trust her ability to lead or fight for herself, how much more would they struggle to trust her plans moving forward?

Ilyon turned a corner, leading Galdinia down a dark, windowless hall. She now became aware of a persistent clanging sound echoing from somewhere at the end of the walkway. Without a conscious thought, Galdinia paused, as though suddenly cemented in the tufted runner beneath the soles of her boots. Just as abruptly, Galdinia's heartbeat quickened, the thumping of blood rising in her ears, her palms becoming slick, the dark cloud of fear creeping toward her again.

At the silence of her movement, Ilyon turned to look at Galdinia, the muted light from behind her casting his concerned features into view. "Your Highness?"

Galdinia opened her mouth, but her throat was dry, and her tongue felt caught up again.

"Galdinia, what is it?" Ilyon's voice was low as he took a few cautious steps towards her.

No windows, no light, no fire.

She knew that already—Bentley couldn't be kept somewhere that he could escape from or somewhere he could access fire. This was well-established. She wasn't surprised by this fact.

And yet, as she walked into the unfamiliar space without her gift— the fog of the day before still lingering in her mind, as well as flickers of her moments with Valah, Bentley, and her uncle in the library—a paralysing terror gripped her.

This was what Ilyon was afraid of.

"I'm fine," she said finally, sucking in a long, deep breath, closing her eyes against her surroundings as she released it. The metallic clanging continued to beat through the air, goading her.

"You're sure?"

Her eyes fluttered open, and she tried to imagine she was walking through her own home or even in the hallways of the barracks, some-where familiar, somewhere she felt like she had control. She wished she'd have brought Drystan's helmet with her, even just to hold between her clammy hands as she walked to the room.

"Yes, I'm fine," Galdinia said before stepping forward again, forcing her feet to move. "You don't think he's a real threat, do you?"

"I'm sorry, Your Highness?" Ilyon asked, taking slow steps forward to Galdinia's side.

"You don't see Bentley as a threat to me; that's why you asked me to see him. You wouldn't have otherwise."

As they walked, the path ahead became considerably darker as they left all firelight behind. A chill ran through Galdinia at the absence of a nearby flame.

"Given the volume and fervour with which he's been requesting your presence, I would say he doesn't plan on hurting you," Ilyon said carefully. "So no, I don't think he's a threat."

Galdinia didn't think her captain would enjoy hypothesising why Bentley wanted to see her so desperately, so she simply said, "Right."

Perhaps this was part of Bentley's plan to get her back on his side and lure her into another trap of his own making—putting on a show of considerate concern.

Although her heartbeat hadn't slowed to its normal pace, Galdinia hoped her steps wouldn't betray her as she tried to walk with the confidence she needed, convincing herself that she didn't have to fear what was at the end of the hallway. Valah wasn't waiting for her in a windowless room. She wasn't being deprived of her gift entirely; she merely needed to survive a few minutes without it.

She was safe, or at least that was what she tried to tell herself.

Two soldiers came into view as they approached, standing in a soft wash of blue from a lantern of Peacelight that hung from the ceiling above them. Galdinia glanced backwards at the warmth of the minimal light that refracted into the hallway. Turning back to the guards, she watched one of them place a key in the keyhole of the door, their other hand lingering on the handle.

"I'll go in first, Your Highness."

"I can go alone," Galdinia replied, swallowing in an attempt to loosen her tongue.

"Not this time." While in dim light, Galdinia couldn't mistake the resolute expression on Ilyon's face.

"Captain."

"Your Highness," Ilyon said, lowering his voice so his words wouldn't be perceived by the guards, "although I believe he wouldn't dare lay a finger on you, I do not trust their restraints like I trust the ones in my own barracks, so I do not feel comfortable sending you in there alone."

Finally, Galdinia nodded in agreement. She wouldn't win this one, and—although she hated to admit it—a gentle warmth comforted her heart, knowing Ilyon would be with her. Being a strong queen didn't mean she had to be an entirely independent one.

Without another word, Ilyon instructed the guards to open the door, and he stepped into the chamber, Galdinia following close behind.

17

Of all the people in Crysterra, Bentley Penrose was in no position to complain about his living quarters. The room in which Bentley was secured was far nicer than his cell in the dungeons of the barracks. Lit by the glow of Peacelight, he had been given a proper bed, an armchair, and even the luxury of an adjoining lavatory. Although the room didn't house any other comforts and was otherwise bare, it was certainly an upgrade from the barracks and far more agreeable than the ship—even the thought of the ship made his stomach twist in unpleasant remembrance.

When the Royal Guard soldiers came to relocate him from the ship, he hadn't questioned it, desperate for stable land beneath his feet. Had he known what emotional torment lay ahead for him in The Hook, though, he would have gladly remained on the sick-inducing vessel.

After being transported to the manor and taking advantage of the amenities in his quarters, Bentley lay on the bed, feeling as though his muscles—mostly abdominal—could rest for the first time in two days. With eyes scrunched and arms spread out beside him, he felt as if the bed tilted and swayed beneath him for at least an hour before he finally found some semblance of rest and stability, the remnants of the effects of the ship lingering in his body.

Some time later, once the room was upright again and he didn't think the thought of sitting up would cause him to run for the lavatory, voices carried from the hall outside his chamber, pulling Bentley from his stupor. As his evening meal of bread, steamed vegetables, and fish was being deposited into his room, he overheard a conversation between the guards that made him forget all about the hunger deep in his stomach.

"No one knows who it was yet." One guard's muffled voice travelled through the door as they worked at unlocking it. "But it must have been Valah's people."

At the mention of Valah's name, Bentley sat up, sending his head into a spin. He firmly gripped the mattress, trying to focus on the voices through the murky haze that overwhelmed him.

"And they attacked her?" the other replied as the door inched open, their voices far clearer now.

Bentley's eyes tore across the room.

Attacked who? Galdinia?

A waft of steamed vegetables and fresh bread billowed into the room with the guards. Bentley had been instructed to remain on his bed when his food was being delivered, and now he had to force himself to stay seated, not because he was ravenous for food after their trip—in fact, food had suddenly become the last thing he wanted to see in that moment—but because he wanted nothing more than to rush to the guards for more information.

"Presumably, though no one has made an official statement," the first soldier said, holding the door open for his companion to enter with the meal, glancing at Bentley momentarily. "But Seamus said he saw the captain carry her to her rooms, and no one has seen or heard from her since."

Carry her? What happened?

Bentley's gaze was fixed on the soldiers, who seemed entirely unbothered by his presence. As far as prisoners went, his behaviour had been nothing but perfect—aside from the sickness that befell him on the ship, which the guards begrudgingly cleaned up. His incarceration felt like fair punishment after the events of The Week of Mourning, especially considering the fact that he was positive Neryda would have drowned him herself had he been let free. Being imprisoned by the Royal Guard also brought with it an extra advantage: close proximity to Galdinia.

A heavy guilt had weighed on Bentley since the Sixth Day of Mourning, when he finally admitted to himself that he'd been wrong about Galdinia and her family, and yet he'd still spinelessly led her to almost certain death that very same day. When he was taken in by the Royal Guard soldiers who'd found him in the burning library, he went willingly. He deserved any punishment they saw fit to dole out. And if being taken prisoner by them kept him in Galdinia's vicinity where he could at least try to make reparations for his actions by keeping her alive, he would have locked the shackles to his own wrists.

But was he too late?

"Surely Kayd knows," the second soldier said as he absentmindedly bent down to leave the plate of food on a small stool by the door. "We'll be able to get him to talk."

"He is most likely to—"

"Is she okay?" The words fell from Bentley's lips on their own accord. He balled up his hands in the sheets, firmly tethering himself to the bed. With the door to the dark hallway now open, he instinctively sought the warmth of a flame, but the air was cool and stagnant with no fire in his immediate proximity to draw upon.

Both guards stared at Bentley, equally surprised and displeased by his interjection.

"How nice of you to show concern." The first guard's voice was heavy with sarcasm as he glowered at Bentley. "Isn't it a little late for you to be worried about the queen?"

Bentley shook his head—he didn't need their contempt, he needed answers. "What happened to her? Is she alive? How did Valah get to her?" The questions flew out of Bentley's lips as he ignored their scornful words.

"Prisoners are not privy to such information," the second guard replied.

Neither are you by the sounds of it, Bentley thought, tightening his jaw so as to force himself not to utter the words out loud.

"Just tell me if she's okay." Bentley's voice was hoarse as he spoke, desperation clawing at his throat.

The soldiers glanced at each other before the first one said, "I don't think so."

With that, they stepped back into the hallway and pulled the door with them. Bentley was already off the bed, sheets relinquished and charging for the door.

"Wait! I just—"

The door slammed in his face.

Bentley strained to hear them confirm if Galdinia was alright or not, but he was only met with their muffled laughter. The pain of his residual guilt wrapped around his heart, strangling it from within, his lingering nausea paling in comparison. If it weren't for him, Valah wouldn't have had such easy access to Galdinia during the attack on Elderguard. If it weren't for him, Valah wouldn't have known any number of intimate details about Galdinia's plans as queen or her father's political movements prior to his death.

If it weren't for Bentley, Galdinia may have been able to do away with Valah during the battle and she wouldn't be hurt—or possibly dead—right now.

Bentley raised his chained hands and desperately pounded his fists against the door, ignoring the lightheaded sensation he felt.

"Is she alive?" he cried out, his fists repeatedly crashing into the wooden door. "Answer me!"

For a straight minute, Bentley cried out at the door, his hands going red. Eventually he stopped to see if he could hear anything beyond the door, but he received no reply other than the echo of his own voice in the room.

If they wouldn't answer him, he'd just have to force them to.

For hours, Bentley howled at the silent guards, slamming his fists, chains, and shoulders against the door, his desperation bringing a fresh clarity to his senses. No matter how hard he pleaded, however, nothing seemed to loosen the guards' tongues. With his appetite all but gone at the thought of Galdinia being hurt, he picked up the stool and threw it, dinner and all, at the door in a fit of fear and frustration. The plate crashed into hundreds of pieces, scattering across the floor with his meal.

He stared at the mess he'd created, but all his mind could concentrate on was Galdinia and if there was breath in her lungs.

Sleep evaded Bentley during his first night in his new quarters. He attempted to sleep, his body drained after expending so much physical and emotional energy, but he found himself plagued with images of Galdinia tangled in battle with faceless enemies. Deciding there was only one way to confirm her safety, Bentley spent much of the night pacing the room with nervous energy and crying out to the guards every few minutes, demanding their attention.

Hours passed like this before his door opened the following morning. Captain Ilyon stepped into his room, causing Bentley to pause in his pacing. The captain took in his surroundings and looked at Bentley with an expression of disdain.

"Our hosts would appreciate it if you could keep the noise down." Ilyon's voice was low and tired.

"Is she okay?" Bentley repeated the question for the hundredth time, disregarding Ilyon's concern.

"You need to be quiet."

"You need to tell me if she's alright."

After scrutinising Bentley briefly, Ilyon replied. "She's okay," he said, his jaw set tight. "Now, you need to be quiet. And clean up this mess. Otherwise you can go back to the ship."

"I want to see her." Bentley didn't miss a beat. It wasn't enough for him to take the word of someone who hated him—he needed proof. He needed to see her with his own eyes.

"That's not an option right now."

"Make it one."

The slight tilt of Ilyon's head and the tightening of his eyes told Bentley he didn't seem particularly pleased to receive an order from someone else.

"I'm not sure who you think you're talking to, but you do not get to make such demands," Ilyon replied, jaw set. "Or do I need to remind you that you're the prisoner in this situation?"

By this point, Bentley had well and truly thrown caution to the wind, which resulted in the Captain of the Royal Guard paying attention to him, so he didn't see what else he had to lose by continuing such behaviour. Maybe Ilyon would drag him through the manor and back to the ship; so be it. Bentley might be able to make a break for it and find Galdinia himself.

"And I might have valuable information about your little ambush yesterday." Bentley's words were steeped in condescension as he held his head high, hoping to bait the captain into removing him from the room. "Let me see Galdinia, and I'll tell you what I know."

Nothing, Bentley thought. *I know nothing.*

Ilyon's lips almost curled at the edges as he glowered at Bentley, his fists tightening by his sides.

"If I get another report of your noise or mess, I'll come back and make it impossible for you to do such a thing, understood?" Ilyon's voice was stony and his eyes lethal.

And yet, Bentley did not take this as the necessary warning that it was.

He needed to see Galdinia alive and breathing, and he wouldn't let the captain's aggression stop him. Whether courage or stupidity, something else took control of Bentley in that moment.

"I'd like to see you try."

Stupidity, it would seem.

At that, with a storm in his eyes and an easy flick of his wrist, Ilyon drew out the water in the vessel on his belt and sent it flying towards Bentley. Before he could avoid it or even take a breath, the water spread across Bentley's nose and mouth, blocking any air from getting in or out, both silencing and smothering him. Bentley stumbled backwards, and his shackled hands flew to his mouth as he tried to wipe the pool of water from his face, his fingers frantic. It was no use, though; the captain's control of his gift was far stronger than Bentley's wild fingers. The cool of the water travelled up his nose and slowly down the back of his throat—he wanted to cough or sneeze, but he couldn't force out a breath, causing his eyes to water and his fingers to stiffen. The liquid had created a dam within the crevices of his face, and his throat quickly became hot and rough as his frenzied movements had him reeling against the metal bars at the end of his bed.

He was being suffocated.

Then, just as quickly as the water had attacked Bentley, Ilyon was calling it back towards him, releasing Bentley of the torment. He doubled over as he coughed, painfully trying to release the agitation in his throat while simultaneously sucking in fresh air.

With body heaving and hands braced on his knees, Bentley looked up at Ilyon with glassy eyes, the water hovering in the air between them.

"Nobody puts the life of my queen in danger and then thinks they can make such demands," he said pointedly before letting the water crash to the tiled ground. "Do you think you can be quiet now?"

Bentley continued to heave urgent breaths.

"I still want to see her," Bentley said, his voice raspy and broken.

With a subtle shake of his head, Ilyon turned away from Bentley and exited the room, the door slamming shut again.

Once he'd regained his breath and a clear mind, Bentley finally settled on the edge of his bed. Although he didn't wish for another such interaction with Ilyon, his desperation to see Galdinia alive only grew. Instead of shouting or hurling himself at the wall, though, he repeatedly swung his hands between his legs, sending the chains of his shackles crashing into the metal bed frame, the shrill sound echoing around his room, and presumably, into the adjacent hallway.

Hours passed like this, and the clanging soon gave Bentley a headache. He convinced himself that it couldn't be worse than the delay of seeing Galdinia, so he continued all the same. Two more meals arrived for him, and the soldiers who delivered them didn't even bother stepping into the room—they haphazardly shoved the plate through the door straight on the floor. Notably, his meals were now being served on metal plates.

Bentley watched as each one sat on the marble floors, untouched. He knew Ilyon wouldn't want a dead prisoner on his hands, so if the noise didn't annoy him into submission, Bentley's starvation might.

When the second meal arrived, the soldier let it clatter to the ground, sending his bread roll tumbling across the ground to his feet. Bentley kicked it away as he continued throwing the chains against the bed frame.

As the day stretched on, Bentley lost any real sense of time without seeing the sun. Despite this, he thought it was too early for them to be serving him dinner when the door opened for the fourth time that day.

"Don't bother leaving another plate," Bentley said, preoccupied, trying to ignore the rumbling hunger in his stomach by closely studying the threads of the fraying bandage that was wrapped around his still-healing arm. "I'm not going to eat it."

When the sound of the door closing didn't come, Bentley glanced across the room.

Once again, Ilyon stood in the doorway, frowning down at the plates and still-scattered food at his feet before slowly looking up at Bentley, his expression fierce.

"I thought you were going to clean up," Ilyon said, tempestuous.

"I've been busy," Bentley replied with a sardonic smile, nodding to his hands, sending another metallic crash through the room.

Ilyon's jaw tightened as he glared at Bentley.

"Let it be known that I'm not doing this for you," Ilyon said, causing Bentley to frown at the captain.

With that, Ilyon took a step to the side, revealing Galdinia behind him.

Bentley's breath stumbled in his throat, and he let go of his chains. Without taking a moment to think, he stood and rushed towards her, his instincts taking over—he needed to see that she wasn't hurt—but he halted to a stop the moment Ilyon's threatening pool of water was hanging in front of his face again.

"Don't even think about it," Ilyon snarled, holding the water mere inches from Bentley.

Tilting his head away from the water, Bentley repositioned himself so he could see Galdinia clearly from his position across the room. Her skin was covered by long sleeves and trousers, but she didn't seem to have any bandages on her limbs, and she was standing on her own. That was a good sign. His eyes wandered up to her face, inspecting it as best he could from this distance. Her frown was deep as she looked at him, an expression he'd seen plenty of times. But something was missing—her usual radiance had been dulled.

"I'm fine," Galdinia said, but her voice betrayed her. It hitched as she spoke, and she tried to cover it up by lifting her chin and swallowing hard.

As she readjusted, a curl of her hair shifted from her face, revealing a noticeable wound on her cheekbone. Bentley's eyes widened, and he took a hesitant step forward, trying to see more closely the damage that had been done.

"What—what happened?" Bentley asked, his voice thick, guilt snaking its way through his veins again. "Who hurt you?"

With a cursory glance at her captain, Galdinia stepped into the room and shut the door behind her.

"One of Valah's soldiers," she finally said, her eyes fixed on Bentley.

Was there concern behind her eyes? Or was it apprehension? Bentley's mind was so dizzy with questions that he struggled to translate her facade.

Finally, he asked his most pressing question: "Are you okay?"

Galdinia reached up to her cheek with her fingers and let them sit there briefly.

"This is the worst of it," she replied before lowering her hand back by her side. Bentley didn't trust her words—he could hear an edge of doubt in them. "But as you can see, I'm alive and well. Do you think you can stop antagonising our hosts now?"

"I wasn't trying to antagonise anyone—" Ilyon's scowl deepened at Bentley's words. "Well, maybe him. But I needed to see you. I needed to see for myself that you were okay."

"And here I am, perfectly fine."

She's lying, Bentley thought as he looked at Galdinia. He'd seen her lie before on multiple occasions: when she tried to convince him that she wasn't worried about becoming queen, or when she was preoccupied with the thoughts of someone else when she most needed to put herself first.

Now she was trying to be strong or courageous, but something in her eyes left Bentley unconvinced.

"No, you're not." Bentley could see she didn't like this, but the bewilderment that showed on her face rendered her speechless. "You're breathing, you have all your limbs, and your head is still attached to your neck, all of which are good signs," Bentley continued, his tone frank. "But you're not really fine."

"I don't think that's for you to say."

"It probably isn't, but someone should."

Bentley held her stare for a long moment before she spoke again.

"Keep the noise down," she said, glancing from Bentley to Ilyon and back again. "And eat something. Otherwise I'll put you back on that ship."

Bentley had to wonder if she and Ilyon had agreed on the same threat of punishment.

"You won't hear from me again," Bentley said quietly, lifting his bound hands in surrender.

Galdinia, with one more scrutinising glance at Bentley, turned from him, opened the door, and walked out into the hallway. Ilyon, however, paused by the door.

"You and I both know that you have no information about the ambush," Ilyon said, his voice quiet but lethal. "If you ever try to use the threat of Galdinia's safety as a bargaining chip again, I'll leave you alone on a ship in the middle of the Southern Shadow, understood?"

Bentley stared at Ilyon, and he knew that there was no exaggeration in his threat.

"Understood," Bentley replied with a curt nod.

Ilyon left Bentley with a threatening glower before following his queen out the door, shutting and locking it firmly behind him.

With a deep breath, Bentley relaxed back into the bars of his bed frame.

She was alright, for the most part. She was alive, which was all Bentley could have hoped for.

This brought a rush of comfort to his body, and he finally felt like he could rest. He glanced at the bread roll on the floor, still sitting in the middle of the room, discarded.

Nothing could have possibly looked more delicious.

18

FOR HOURS AFTER LEAVING BENTLEY'S QUARTERS, GALDINIA COULDN'T shake the distinct feeling of being watched. No, it was more than that; it was the feeling of being perceived.

The fact that Bentley could see through her flimsy attempt at strength after the attack wasn't surprising, but the way his blue eyes bore into hers, cast in concern as he tried to decipher every minute movement and mannerism, had made her want to run from the room. In spite of this, she'd held her ground, just as she'd charged herself to moments before entering the room.

Although Neryda tried to convince her that there was likely nothing of true concern in Bentley's perception of her ("He's just trying to get under your skin, that slimy snake" were her exact words), Galdinia was still acutely aware of every move she made and each word she spoke, fearful of how even the attendants in the Lidels' home would discern her, let alone her closest confidants and those she was still yet to convince to ally with her. Even when in the safety of her rooms, her best friend by her side and any number of guards perched outside the door, she refused to let any sign of the lingering fears show.

As a result of such a decision, Galdinia quickly accepted the Lidels' invitation to dinner that evening, not giving herself even a second to consider taking the easy route of holing up in her rooms and avoiding another potentially prickly situation. Although Ravenna had insisted Galdinia needn't feel it necessary to accept, Galdinia smiled pleasantly and assured her that a good meal could only help her recovery. And Galdinia couldn't refuse an opportunity to convince the Lidels to join her cause.

After Neryda left Galdinia's rooms to get ready for the evening, Galdinia did her best to cover up the graze along her cheekbone with the help of rouge and some strategically pinned curls. Once in a long sky-blue satin dress that hugged her full figure, framed by its billowing sleeves, she started to feel more like a queen than a soldier. Placing her crown back in place on her head, Galdinia observed herself in the mirror. With a deep breath, she steeled herself for the meal ahead.

Accepting defeat the previous day was one thing, but dining with people who considered her father a traitor—no matter how polite or impolite they may be—was not her idea of a pleasant evening. Particularly not when she hoped to continue to push them to see beyond their selfish ways and seal an alliance with her even though the shadow of an attack that threatened the security of their safe haven loomed.

Attempting to leave the heaviness of the previous two days behind her and instead donning her new sense of courage, Galdinia went to step out of the door of her room and came face-to-face with Raia.

"Good evening, Your Majesty," Raia said, her smile wide.

"Good evening," Galdinia replied, caught off guard. "Galdinia is fine, Raia."

"Oh, yes, of course." Raia stumbled over her words.

"Can I help you with something?" Galdinia asked, raising her eyebrows expectantly.

"Captain Ilyon has asked me to escort you this evening. I am to shadow you."

"Of course he has," Galdinia said. "Well, I'm just going to get Neryda on my way to the dining room. Care to join me?"

"Certainly! It seems I have no choice..." Raia's face faltered. "Sorry, that came out wrong. I just mean I will be coming with you anyway, but I would be glad to—"

"It's okay, Raia," Galdinia said with a smile. "I'm not that easily offended. I wouldn't be queen if I were."

Raia exhaled and said, "Thank you, Your Maj—Galdinia." Raia then turned to lead Galdinia down the hall to Neryda's room.

Galdinia noticed that Raia also looked more prepared for a dinner party than she had the previous day, though only marginally. The hair in her usual ponytail was twisted into four long plaits, each tied off with a white ribbon, and she had forgone her usual weaponry; there wasn't a blade in sight, though Galdinia wondered if there were one or two concealed somewhere beneath her fighting leathers.

"Let's go, Ner!" Galdinia called once they reached Neryda's room.

"I'm coming!" The muffled and hurried shout from within told Galdinia that Neryda was far from ready.

"If you don't mind me asking," Raia said from across the hall, "how are you doing?"

Galdinia took in a long breath—this was her opportunity to cement her strength. Of all people, she didn't want her Queen's Guard to think she couldn't recover quickly after an attack.

"I'm much better than expected, or so the healers tell me," Galdinia replied, pushing back her shoulders. "I'm honestly feeling good—a little tired, but well."

"I'm glad to hear that." Raia's smile was warm and inviting. "By all accounts, you held your own during the attack. You should be really proud of that."

Ilyon had been so concerned with Galdinia's wellbeing that he had hardly recognised that she had successfully kept both herself and Neryda alive in the face of such a vicious attacker. She didn't realise she needed that vote of confidence until Raia uttered the words.

"Thank you, Raia," Galdinia said sincerely, returning the smile. Hoping to move on from discussions of the attack, she asked her own question: "You don't feel you need weapons this evening?"

"The captain assured us it wouldn't be necessary, though I'm sure Vega will have stored a dagger or two in her leathers," Raia explained, shrugging. "And either way, I'm far more lethal with this."

Raia motioned towards a small glass vessel at her hip, in which about a cupful of water swayed.

"I bet you are," Galdinia said with a nod.

"Even the sharpest blade isn't as strong as one's affinity with their gift. I'm sure you understand that feeling." Raia's words seemed to come out as more of a question.

"I'm starting to learn that. Although, I'm not great with a sword to begin with, so it probably isn't much of a competition between that and a flame."

"I'm not sure about that," Raia said. "You managed just fine on the ship with Vega, and you were a natural with your new bow yesterday."

"Archery may be the exception," Galdinia conceded. "Though I'm no soldier."

"Captain Ilyon did give us a very detailed recount of the flames you were able to produce on the Sixth Day of Mourning. He said he's never seen anything like it."

"Unfortunately, I've not been able to replicate it since."

"You will." There was something so disarming in Raia's countenance, as though her expression alone radiated a sense of assurance and loyalty.

"I've become so reliant on the feeling it gives me when I make a connection, but I have to concentrate very hard to make it obey my wishes. That night came with the fuel of many emotions."

"You're still a baby Flourisher," Raia assured her with a grin. "You have to learn to walk before you can run. Just because you stood up quickly doesn't mean you won't be able to again."

"And in the meantime, I'll have my bow."

"Perhaps flaming arrows will become your specialty." Raia raised her brows expectantly. Galdinia liked that idea. "May I ask you a question, Galdinia?"

"Of course."

"I hope you don't think I'm speaking out of turn, but for someone who is so committed to that piece of gold on their head," Raia said, nodding towards Galdinia's crown, "I'm surprised by your insistence on being called by your first name. I'm curious… why?"

Galdinia paused before answering.

"I've never loved my title, so much so that I barred my friends from using it. They always called me by my first name," Galdinia admitted, putting into words an agreement she hadn't thought about in a long time. This brought back memories of her seizing this right from Drystan in the armoury of the soldiers' barracks; the betrayal she felt led her to act so rashly. Had she known what would happen in the following hours, she never would have robbed herself of hearing her name on his lips. "I didn't like the wall that my position as princess seemed to surround me with, so I tried to remove it. It's hard enough convincing people to consider you as your own person when your father is the king, let alone them being forced to call you by a title. So I try to maintain a semblance of humanity with the people closest to me by asking them to call me by my name instead. I want my Queen's Guard to respect me as Galdinia, not just as the queen."

"So not everyone is afforded this privilege then?"

"Certainly not," Galdinia said, a smirk tickling her lips. "Those Lidels can keep calling me Your Majesty until it really sinks in for them."

"I support you entirely in that decision."

Suddenly, Neryda's door swung open, and her friend's voice came from within.

"Alright, I'm ready." She walked out while hopping on one foot, slipping the other into her shoe.

"What took you so long?" Galdinia asked.

"Perfection takes time, my friend," Neryda replied, finally getting her shoe in place and standing up straight, her shimmery copper dress falling gracefully around her.

"Is that what we're calling it?"

"You have eyes, don't you?" Neryda asked, gesturing to her hair and ensemble with the flourish of both hands. Neryda did, in fact, look radiant.

"I certainly do," Galdinia said before winking at Raia, who looked amused herself.

Walking down the hallway back towards the entrance hall, Neryda slipped her arm through Galdinia's, and the pair walked with Raia close behind. If anyone glimpsed them now, Galdinia was sure they'd be surprised to learn both women had been rendered unconscious after a frightening attack just the day before.

"Do we think dinner will include a lot of seafood?" Neryda asked. "I know that's their delicacy of choice here, but I don't think I'm in a particularly fishy mood."

"I'm not sure how much say you'll have over your meal," Galdinia warned.

"I should have put in a special request and asked for pork or potatoes. Oh, potatoes would be fantastic right now. Like the cheesy ones Miss Giles makes!"

"Careful, Ner, you're starting to drool."

"Do you think it's too late to ask for cheesy potatoes?" Neryda's eyes were hopeful and desperate.

"I don't think another request after the events of the last two days would be well-received," Galdinia replied before donning a veil of sarcasm. "'I know you won't give me your alliance or take me to Lund, but could you avoid serving fish this evening? My friend would really appreciate it.'"

"Perhaps in light of your other requests, they would have said yes." Neryda shrugged as they stepped down onto the large staircase that wound down into the entrance hall.

Galdinia could hear the sounds of voices from the hallway beneath the stairs. With it drifted the smell of fresh bread, wine, and seafood. Neryda wouldn't be pleased.

The three women moved down the stairs and towards the hall to the dining room. The entrance hall was bathed in the warm light of the sunset that washed the glass ceiling. To her right, she glimpsed the shadowy hallway she travelled down earlier in the day, the absence of fire painfully obvious. Once they had snaked down the adjacent hallway and entered the dining room, however, Galdinia was instantly met with the warmth of fire, which sat in perches around the elegant room, evidently far enough away from Bentley to not be considered a threat. The room looked much like it had the day before with its palatial windows and immense dining table, but with the flickering flames and the orange sunset, the room not only felt warmer, but it also glowed, the light of the fire shimmering at different angles on the marble of the walls, floors, and ceiling. Across the sea to the south, Galdinia could see the rumblings of a storm slowly making its way towards Crysterra.

Ravenna, Bael, Feyroy, Ilyon, and the remainder of the Queen's Guard were already in the room, awaiting the queen's arrival. Ilyon and Feyroy were speaking by the door, and the Queen's Guard appeared to be stationed around the room, very much on duty. Ravenna and Bael stood by the table with a young boy, talking quietly among themselves.

"Welcome, Your Highness," Ravenna said, breaking away from her husband and the boy to walk to the door to escort Galdinia into the room. There seemed to be no residual animosity after their tense meeting—perhaps her near-death experience helped garner some sympathy—although Galdinia didn't think Ravenna would ever show such an emotion. While it was clear she could hold on to a grudge, she did so without fuss and with a smile on her face.

"This looks lovely," Galdinia said as she walked across the room with Ravenna, looking at the spread on the table. Her nose had correctly guessed the contents of their meal as all manner of seafood, leafy greens, fresh bread, and wine took up much of the centre of the large table.

"We are glad you are well enough to join us this evening," Ravenna said sincerely. "Yesterday must have been quite the scare."

"It was certainly a shock, but I'm recovering just fine, thank you," Galdinia replied, before quickly adding, "I am sorry to have been the reason for such distress in your home."

"No need to apologise. I'm just glad you're all safe," Ravenna said, moving to stand by Bael and the boy once again. "Let me introduce you to our youngest son, Luan."

The young boy, who looked to be about ten years old, beamed up at Galdinia, his dark curls sitting loftily atop his head and his deep brown eyes reflecting the warmth of his mother's.

"A pleasure to meet you, Your Majesty," Luan said as he bowed deeply. He obviously took after his mother in more ways than one. "Welcome to The Hook!"

"Thank you for having me," Galdinia replied with a smile.

"Would you like to sit next to me?" Luan asked, pulling out a chair beside him for Galdinia.

"Of course," Galdinia replied, a warm feeling of gratitude filling her. She sat, and Luan quickly took up his place beside the queen.

"He has been very excited to meet you since we received your raven," Ravenna said quietly to Galdinia before she moved to her seat at the end of the table. Picking up her goblet of wine, Ravenna addressed the rest of the room, "Please join us."

Bael followed suit and moved to the other end of the table, where he, too, took his seat. Ilyon and Feyroy sat together opposite Galdinia, while Neryda sat at her usual place beside Galdinia, and Raia beside her. The Queen's Guard filled all but one remaining seat beside Bael.

"Are we waiting on one more?" Galdinia asked.

"My brother, Quill," Luan said, his smile having not faltered since he sat down. "He's been sailing in the bay today, but he'll be here soon."

"We are expecting Quillion momentarily," Ravenna went on to explain, still standing, her goblet of wine in hand. "But we mustn't wait for him. May we begin our evening with a toast?" At this, everyone picked up a cup of wine, except Luan, who held a glass of water with lemon slices. "It is lovely to host our guests this evening." Ravenna pointed her glass around the table at Galdinia and her Queen's Guard. "In light of yesterday's attack, we are grateful for the work of the Queen's Guard in protecting not only Queen Galdinia, but also our home. Many thanks to you all." Ravenna gestured to Galdinia's guards, which garnered nods of thanks. "It has been many years since we have dined with the crown, and we are glad to have the opportunity to do so now. May we all have prosperous days ahead and—"

Ravenna was cut off by the sound of heavy footfalls at the door of the dining room. All heads turned to a young man as he walked through the doors, clad in expensive, albeit casual, dining attire, his dark curls bobbing with each step as he walked across the room, showing little to no concern for the interruption his entrance made. This was obviously Quillion Lidel.

"Sorry I'm late," he practically mumbled as he walked across the room, stopping by his mother's side to quickly squeeze her shoulders and plant a kiss on her cheek. He moved down the table, taking no mind of those seated around it, and sat in the empty chair to his father's right. He hastily filled his goblet with wine and took a deep gulp before putting it down beside his setting.

Galdinia looked at Bael, who appeared imperceptibly impressed by his son's casual actions.

"Hi, Quill," Luan said cheerily.

"Hi, Lu," Quillion replied, his lips barely turning up at the edges as he greeted his brother, not bothering to address anyone else.

"Quillion, darling," Ravenna said from the other end of the table, a gentle smile across her lips, "would you like to welcome our guests?"

Quillion looked up and down the table, and his eyes landed on Galdinia, flicking from her face to her crown and back again.

"Welcome." Not a shred of emotion touched his voice.

If Luan took after his mother, Galdinia thought that Quillion obviously took after his father.

Galdinia glanced at Vega; her eyes were as sharp and deadly as her daggers as she stared at Quillion from down the table.

"As I was saying," Ravenna went on, drawing the attention of the table back to her toast, "may we all have prosperous days ahead and long live the queen."

"Long live the queen!" the table chorused, raising their goblets in the air before each taking a sip. Galdinia noted that while Bael seemed to mumble the words, Quillion did not speak a single one.

"Enjoy your meal, everyone," Ravenna said, taking her seat and gesturing to the spread before them.

Leaning behind Neryda, Raia whispered to Galdinia, "It's people like him that you don't mind calling you Your Highness, isn't it?"

"I get the feeling it would be a miracle to hear those words come from his lips," Galdinia replied, looking carefully at Quillion as he first filled his father's plate and then his own with food.

Galdinia served herself some potatoes and bread to start. Before she could take a bite, though, Neryda reached over with her fork, stabbing one of the chunks of potatoes and popping it into her mouth.

"I don't think we're going to run out, Ner," Galdinia said, brows raised, staring at her friend.

"Have you already forgotten my vital role on this trip?" Neryda asked before swallowing the food. After a few seconds, she said with a nod, "Safe to eat."

"Thank goodness for that," Galdinia said, shaking her head as she turned back to her plate.

"Did she just steal food from your plate?" Luan asked Galdinia quietly, concern lacing his words.

"She's my royal food tester, a very important job."

"Why do you need a food tester? To check that it tastes good?"

Luan's innocence warmed Galdinia's heart. "Something like that."

Soon everyone had an array of food on their plates, and they began to quietly mingle among themselves, and Galdinia learned very quickly just how different Luan and his brother were. Down the table Quillion spoke in hushed tones with his father, looking only between him and his own plate of food, paying Galdinia very little mind as though it were commonplace—or even burdensome—to have the Queen of Crysterra sitting at his table. Luan, on the other hand, barely got any food in his mouth in the first thirty minutes of the meal as he asked Galdinia question after question, absorbed in her presence.

"What is it like to be a Fire Flourisher?"

"I heard about the attack yesterday. Are you okay?"

"Tell me about Elderguard. Is it as beautiful as people say it is?"

"What is your favourite food to eat?"

It didn't bother Galdinia, though. The young boy's enthusiasm to get to know the queen was a welcome change to his father's apathy.

"We have a local bakery in Elderguard, owned by a man named Raff," Galdinia explained as she buttered a piece of bread. "He makes the most mouthwatering cinnamon scrolls. Neryda and I have them once a week at least."

"That sounds delicious!" Luan said, his smile widening. "We don't have many baked goods here. Our speciality is seafood."

"I can see that," Galdinia remarked.

"It gets a bit boring to have the same thing all the time, though," Luan commented. "You must eat all sorts of food in the capital! I bet you have a great cook in the castle."

"I do; her name is Miss Giles."

"Do you have to go to a lot of important meetings?" Luan was quick to change the topic as new questions flowed. "As the queen, I bet you do. Are they really interesting?"

"Quite a few, yes," Galdinia said, trying to quickly sneak a bite of her dinner between answers. "They're not all that exciting, though."

Galdinia thought of how she had addressed the Syndicate before she left the capital, her many conversations with Ryden, and, of course, her father's will reading. She wasn't looking forward to the next time she'd be addressing the Syndicate, and she felt the rise of fear in her chest at the thought of coming home empty-handed with merely the remnants of an assassination attempt on her face.

"But as the queen, they all must be a little exciting," Luan pressed, looking expectantly at Galdinia. "You get to make decisions about the country!"

"That is true, but they can be quite stressful, or worse, dramatic."

"Dramatic?" Luan's face filled with intrigue, a fork of roasted vegetables hanging halfway to his mouth, now forgotten.

"My governor told me about how he got a fork to the hand during a will reading once, and I've had people talk over the top of me and raise their voices in protest. Some of them were even my family…"

Galdinia trailed off. The memory of her aunt and uncle's outrage at her father's will reading halted her thoughts and words. Suddenly, she was back in the drawing room of Elderguard Castle after her father's funeral, and the image of three magnificent jewels sparkled in her mind, bringing her attention back to Ravenna's description of their missing heirlooms. She knew they sounded familiar, but she wasn't able to place them during her initial meeting with the Lidels. Only once had Galdinia seen stones as striking as the ones Ravenna had described, and they had been resting on her aunt's neck.

"That sounds horrible! But how thrilling!" Luan's voice cut through Galdinia's thoughts.

"Edana," Galdinia said with a breath, her brows furrowing.

"Pardon, Your Highness?" Luan asked, his expression pleasant despite the queen's strange behaviour.

"Lord and Lady Lidel," Galdinia said, looking from one end of the table to the other. "I know where your jewels are."

The table quietened instantly, and Ravenna and Bael exchanged a look before fixing their eyes on Galdinia.

Galdinia tried to organise her memories as she cast her mind back to when she saw her aunt and uncle again for the first time in the Crystal Temple before her father's funeral, and then again in the drawing room of the castle for the will reading.

"On the day of my father's funeral, my aunt, Edana, arrived wearing three jewels on a necklace: amber, amethyst, and a starlight crystal. I had never seen anything so beautiful and even wondered where she had acquired them. No one could fabricate jewels that stunning, so I thought they were heirlooms of her family. However, I'm now thinking they belong to you."

The air in the room tightened; what had been a pleasant dinner had quickly turned into what felt like an uncomfortable assembly, much like the ones she had just described to Luan. Galdinia watched as the veins in Bael's neck swelled and heat rose in his face. Outraged and without a word, Bael stood to his feet and left the room with heavy steps.

After watching her husband leave, Ravenna turned back to Galdinia, her eyes disbelieving.

"How is this possible?" Ravenna asked. "How could she have them?"

"I'm not sure," Galdinia said. "But I'm almost certain that she does."

"I have some theories," Ilyon replied quickly, his expression thoughtful.

Before he could elaborate, Bael came storming back into the room with something clutched in his hand. He approached Galdinia and slammed his hand on the table, pushing a piece of parchment towards her.

"Are these the jewels?" he asked, his voice coming out in a breathy rasp.

The parchment was home to a painting of a woman with hands outstretched, who, upon closer inspection, resembled Ravenna with her beautiful curls and regal poise. Above her, floating around her head, were three distinct jewels: one of amber, one of amethyst, and one of starlight crystal. They were each distinct shapes, and the starlight crystal was the largest. Galdinia couldn't have mistaken them; they were the exact jewels she had seen around her aunt's neck.

"Yes," Galdinia said. "Yes, that's them."

Bael brought his hands to his head, the frustration burning through his stony exterior and emanating into the room. He began to pace the length of the table. "How?" he asked no one in particular.

Ilyon, still looking pensive as he craned his neck to glimpse the painting from across the table, answered him. "The Elderwins—those of the Shadowed Coast, that is—are known for interfering with the plans of the crown, particularly for their own gain. My guess is that they sent raiders to intercept the ships on their way to the capital, ransacking them and taking not only your jewels, but also our men and control of our ships, unless they sunk them at the bottom of the Southern Shadow. Either is likely."

"How could they have possibly known about our dealings with the king?" Ravenna asked.

"My aunt and uncle are—were—highly strategic and cunning," Galdinia replied. "My guess is that they had informants in the capital."

"Even in Elderguard we have individuals in high places who aren't as tight-lipped as we may wish them to be," Ilyon explained, agreeing with Galdinia's suspicions. "Twelve years ago, when you struck your deal with the king, Draven and Edana would have worked hard to maintain a foothold in the capital. I imagine they didn't even know what they were stealing—it would have been too easy, unfortunately, for them to stop the ships in the middle of the sea once they knew the date of their travels. It would have been even easier to spread word to both yourselves and the late king that you had each been betrayed."

"But to what end?" Ravenna asked. "Surely not solely for a mysterious deposit that may or may not have been worth it."

"No," Ilyon said, shaking his head, "certainly not. They would have seen an opportunity to cause a rift between the crown and another province, so they took it. The jewels would have been a happy surprise, I'm sure. And wearing the stolen jewels to her loathed brother-in-law's funeral would have been a reward for both of them."

"They would have done just about anything to taint my father's reputation," Galdinia added, her voice taking on an edge of malice.

"If this is true," Bael said carefully, coming to a halt behind his wife's chair, "then the suffering of our people during the famine was not the cause of the capital, but instead Draven and Edana."

"I promise, Lord and Lady Lidel," Galdinia started to say, "I have only seen those jewels on my aunt's neck. My father would have never been aware of the ambush."

"Instead, he quickly assumed we had acted in poor faith," Bael countered with a scowl.

"To be fair," Galdinia returned, "you thought the same of him."

The Lidels sat with this, and they shared a moment of silent communication.

"Do you foresee any way for us to retrieve the jewels?" Ravenna finally asked, breaking the silence.

Galdinia now looked to her captain, whose expression deepened as he considered the request. Was this her opportunity to secure the Lidels as potential allies?

"Extracting them from Elderwin Manor would be a difficult task for anyone," Ilyon explained. "It is a highly fortified stronghold, and given the events on the Sixth Day of Mourning, I can only assume Edana will have made arrangements to protect her home at all costs."

"In saying that," Galdinia said, interrupting her captain, "I can assure the return of your jewels in exchange for your alliance and your help making contact with Lund."

At that, all eyes in the room were fixed on the queen; Ilyon's were surprised, the Lidels' were scrutinising and Neryda's were impressed. At the other end of the table, Quillion rolled his eyes as he took another unbothered mouthful of food.

It's now or never, Galdinia thought, deciding that it was worth gambling to avoid going home empty-handed the next day.

"Your Majesty," Ilyon began, concern in his voice, "I'm not sure we can make such a promise."

"Yes, how exactly do you intend on retrieving them?" Bael asked, staring down the table at Galdinia.

"You needn't worry about that," Galdinia assured him, offering a smile in return. "If you can take us to Lund and assure me that you'll fight with us should we engage in another attack, then those jewels will be returned to you. I must first meet with your allies, though. That is my priority. Valah has threatened an attack by the next new moon, so another conflict may arise before I can retrieve them, but I swear to you that I will."

Galdinia could feel Ilyon staring at her from across the table, but she kept her eyes on Lord and Lady Lidel. Once again, they communicated with each other silently before Ravenna replied.

"We will provide you with an escort to meet with our allies in Lund presently and…" She hesitated but finally said, "And once our jewels are returned to us, the army of The Hook will fight beside the Royal Guard, should you be faced with another conflict."

At Ravenna's words, Galdinia felt the tension within her ease momentarily, and a small smile formed across her lips. Although their alliance was conditional, it was more than she could have hoped for mere minutes earlier.

"Thank you," Galdinia said, her voice thick with gratitude. "I will do everything in my power to recover your jewels."

"Take heed, though, Your Majesty," Bael said, placing a gentle hand on his wife's shoulder, "our friends in Lund are not easily won over, and we cannot guarantee their agreement to align themselves with you. Should you be unsuccessful, we still require you to uphold your end of this bargain."

"Of course," Galdinia replied. "Once I have spoken with them, retrieving your jewels will be my top priority. I swear it."

"We shall make arrangements then," Bael said, his words drawn out. "You and your crew will embark with an escort to the Starlight Mountains in the morning."

"Who exactly might our escort be?" Ilyon asked.

"Quillion will accompany you," Ravenna said.

There was a clattering of cutlery from the other end of the table, and everyone turned to look at Quillion, his knife and fork haphazardly discarded on his plate, his eyes searing into his parents as he finished chewing his mouthful of food.

"I'm to do what?" Quillion's words were full of heat.

"You have maintained much of our relationship with Lund, darling," Ravenna went on, her smile still visible, her voice returning to its airy quality. "And you were planning to travel there later this week, weren't you?"

"That's not the point," Quillion replied, his voice tight and bitter.

"What might it be then?" Ravenna asked.

"It will take at least an extra two days to travel there with such a large crew. It's a waste of time. They'll never——"

"You will escort Queen Galdinia and her crew tomorrow," Bael reinforced, staring at his son. "We won't hear another word about it."

Quillion held his father's gaze for a few gruelling seconds before he pushed himself up from the table. Turning from the group, he walked out the door and back into the manor.

"That was a bit dramatic," Neryda whispered to Galdinia as she took a sip of her wine.

"He doesn't appear too pleased by your plan," Galdinia noted, looking back to Lord and Lady Lidel.

"That isn't of concern to us," Bael said. "You will leave at sunrise, and he will be there ready to escort you whether he likes it or not."

"Very well."

"I look forward to having my jewels in my possession once again, Queen Galdinia," Bael said as he walked back towards his chair, his eyes fixed on Galdinia.

"And I look forward to delivering them to you."

Before she went back to her plate, Ilyon caught Galdinia's eye, his expression one of irritated concern. She could only imagine everything he wanted to say to her right now. She supposed it wasn't the best idea to make strategic plans without first discussing them with her captain, but Galdinia already knew he would have shut them down, and she was getting tired of being told which decisions she should make and when.

Once conversation had started to build again, Neryda leant in and said quietly, "That was brave."

"I'm not returning to Elderguard without allies," Galdinia replied in a whisper, dropping Ilyon's gaze. "It's not an option for me."

"So it would seem," Neryda replied. "I don't think there's any question about how fit you are to rule anymore. If you get those jewels, they'll be kissing your feet in no time."

"There's still a lot to do before that can happen," Galdinia whispered.

"Sorry about my brother," Luan said cheerfully, drawing Galdinia's attention back to their previous conversation. "I guess he's the one that made this meeting a bit dramatic, isn't he?"

"You could say that," Galdinia said carefully. "At least I didn't end up with a fork in my hand."

"He's really great when you get to know him," Luan said, and then his eyes sparkled. "I wonder if I can come with you to Lund! I've gone with Quill before, but I haven't been since before the summer months!"

"I don't know how safe it will be," Galdinia replied, fear rising in her heart at the thought of this beautiful young boy being caught in the crossfire of a conflict. "Your parents will probably need you to stay here to help look after things, anyway. I don't imagine they can do it alone."

"You're right." Luan was thoughtful in his response. "I often go to their meetings with them, though most of theirs are very boring. This was the liveliest one in months!"

"Welcome to my world," Galdinia replied with a laugh.

"Also, we only have a few more days of warm water before the autumn chill really sets in, and I won't want to miss my last chance to swim in the bay for a while," Luan said, a smile spreading over his face once again. "Have you ever gone swimming in the bay before, Your Highness?"

Galdinia spent the remainder of the evening answering Luan's questions and watching his excitement rise with every answer she gave. Every now and then, she would glance around the table, taking partic- ular note of the Lidels; Ravenna was swept up in conversation, but Bael held a scrutinising expression. Once again, Galdinia met Ilyon's eye, and if it was possible, his expression matched Bael's.

She was not looking forward to that conversation.

"I don't think I'll ever eat again," Neryda said as she, Galdinia, and Raia walked down the hallway to their rooms after dinner. Neryda was dragging her feet, as though the meal she had just devoured was weighing her down.

"We all know that isn't true," Galdinia replied.

Although Galdinia had filled her plate with a decent portion of food, she had struggled to finish it all after her agreement with the Lidels was made. While her fear about leaving The Hook empty- handed had subsided, a new unease rose in her stomach: meeting with the leaders of Lund. And this didn't leave a lot of room for food.

Once everyone else had emptied their plates and dessert was

finished, they had gone their separate ways to their rooms, and Galdinia noticed that Bael was quick to leave. Luan, however, did all he could to avoid seeing an end to his time with the queen, standing at the top of the stairs beside his mother, a permanent grin on his face. If it weren't for her avoidance of her captain, Galdinia likely would have stayed much later talking with the young boy whose eyes lit up every time she answered one of his questions.

"Maybe just for tonight then," Neryda amended as they walked down the hallway.

"The fish was exquisite," Raia chimed in as she led the pair down the hallway.

"And the potatoes!" Neryda's voice drawled. "Oh, I could have another five of them."

"I thought you were full?" Galdinia asked, perplexed.

"I'm never too full for potatoes."

As they rounded on the hallway that led to Galdinia's and Neryda's rooms, two hushed yet aggressive voices echoed from an adjacent corridor. Always on guard, Raia slowed in her steps as she glimpsed around the corner, stretching out a hand to stop the other two. Galdinia followed suit and peered in the same direction. Bael and Quillion stood at the other end of the hallway, locked in a quiet disagreement.

"While I recognise your feelings, Quillion, they are inconsequential by comparison," Bael said fiercely. "You will act as escort, you will make contact with Orlon, and you will keep her alive. Do you understand me?"

"Send one of the guards," Quillion retaliated, running his hands through his hair in frustration. "Or maybe you could take her if you're that desperate."

"You know that I don't know the mountains as well as you do. You can get her there quickly and safely."

"And what if I refuse?"

At this, Bael took a step towards his son. "Those jewels may mean very little to you—"

"Nothing—they mean nothing to me."

"Well, they mean a lot to your mother. That amethyst stone is the only thing she has left from her family, and I'll do just about anything to have it safely returned to her." Bael's voice was low and lethal. "So you either need to start caring about them very quickly, or you can break your mother's heart. It's your choice."

Quillion stared his father down. They looked like mirror images of each other, anger and fury rising off them both.

"I'll leave with them day after next," Quillion finally said, conceding. "This rain is due to continue well into tomorrow, and I'm not making this journey any harder than it needs to be."

"You and I both know you could stop a storm if you wanted to," Bael said, his tone one of warning.

"And I don't want to. I'm not wasting my energy on stopping the rain for her." Quillion's voice was fierce.

Galdinia frowned as she turned away from the corner and back into the main hall of the wing.

"He's delightful, isn't he?" Neryda said in a hushed tone.

"What's his problem?" Galdinia asked quietly.

"We should get you back to your room, Galdinia," Raia whispered.

Galdinia nodded, not interested in continuing to listen to such a confounding conversation.

As they went to continue down the hallway, Galdinia was brought to a stop as she ran into a sudden force: Quillion had rounded the corner at such pace, he collided with her. Seemingly instinctively, his hands went to her shoulders to steady them both, stopping her from tripping, keeping her upright. As his eyes focused on who was before him, Quillion relinquished his hands instantly, as though his palms had been burnt.

His face was twisted into such a firm scowl, it almost looked painful. The anger that lay there was striking, catching Galdinia off guard, causing her to wince.

"Oh, I'm sorry," she said politely, the years of royal mannerism training instinctively taking over.

"As you should be," Quillion replied in a deep grumble, his glare sinking in further before he brushed past her and marched towards the stairs to the entrance hall, his frustration fuelling him.

Galdinia stared after him, perplexed.

"Honestly, what is wrong with him?" Galdinia asked, turning back to Neryda and Raia.

"He's very rude," Raia commented before leading Galdinia and Neryda towards their rooms again.

"Maybe he holds a grudge even better than his parents," Neryda suggested, taking Galdinia by the arm.

While this seemed likely, Galdinia knew that couldn't be the entire problem. He had said himself that he didn't care for the missing jewels. Why did he seem to detest Galdinia and her troop?

"I think he's just a spoilt brat," Galdinia said under her breath.

"I'd probably be the same if I grew up here," Neryda said, looking around the vast manor.

"You practically grew up in the castle, Ner."

"Then he has no excuse," Neryda said pointedly as they continued down the hallway.

Galdinia tried to leave the residual anger from Quillion behind them, but between her meeting with Bentley, the promises she made over dinner, and Quillion's reaction to her, she found herself internally wrestling for the remainder of the night.

19

As predicted, the rain continued to drizzle over The Hook the next morning. Galdinia awoke before daybreak, having spent much of the night in and out of sleep. Her dreams were overrun with images of Drystan, who she found herself constantly reaching for but never quite able to touch. She couldn't see his face. Instead he was always turned away from her, slumped on his knees.

In one such nightmare, she got so close that her fingertips grazed his hair, just barely. Galdinia's heart ached at the brief touch. The moment contact was made, though, a pair of gaunt hands reached out from the darkness and took hold of Drystan from the front, dragging him away from her and into the void. Galdinia found herself calling after him, tears rolling down her face, but her cries merely returned to her in pained echoes.

By the time she awoke for the third time, her face was wet, and her heartbeat was shuddering in her chest and ears. She decided to give up fighting her subconscious and watched as the rain trickled down her window, the grey clouds muffling the rising sun. Every time she closed her eyes, the image of Drystan being pulled from her reach was imprinted on her mind. She couldn't decide if she wanted to keep her eyes shut and afford herself the privilege of seeing him, or if she was better off keeping her eyes open so as to avoid having to look at him in such a state.

Deciding the latter was likely better for her already tortured heart, she kept her eyes fixed on the trickling rain, which ran in rivulets down the window.

Galdinia could have been lying there for fifteen minutes or two hours, she wasn't sure, but she wasn't pulled from her trance until she heard what she soon realised to be a piece of parchment being slipped under her door. Dragging herself from bed, she retrieved and read the elegant handwriting:

Queen Galdinia,

Due to the inclement weather, we think it is best you and your group leave The Hook tomorrow. Please join us for breakfast whenever you are ready to do so.

Lady Ravenna

Galdinia wondered if Ravenna had spoken to her oldest son before passing on this note or if the change in departure date had come straight from her and her husband. Either way, Galdinia tried to pretend that the Lidels really thought it would be "best" that they left later out of some sense of concern, rather than inconvenience.

Deciding she'd be better off leaving her room and the distressing visions that encroached on her here, Galdinia turned to the bureau to fetch her hairbrush. Soon, she was dressed in a tunic, riding pants, and boots. She threw her cloak over her shoulders before attaching a small vessel of fire to her belt, feeling all the safer with it.

"Good morning, Your Highness." Vega was standing outside Galdinia's room, ready to escort her to breakfast.

"Good morning, Vega," Galdinia replied, somewhat startled by her presence. "I hope you haven't been waiting long."

"Not at all."

Galdinia could only assume that she had, in fact, been waiting a while for the queen to emerge and that Ilyon had organised for someone to be on guard at her door around the clock.

"Please tell me you've already had breakfast," Galdinia said as they made their way down the hallway.

"Not yet," Vega replied, her voice even.

After a moment's hesitation, Galdinia said, "You didn't have to wait for me."

"I was on guard this morning, so I'll eat when I can." Vega was so matter-of-fact about it. "This isn't something you should concern yourself with, Your Highness."

"If my guards aren't eating, I'm concerned."

"I'm not eating *yet*. I will."

Galdinia gave her a long, hard look before they started to descend the stairs. From what Galdinia could gather, Vega seemed to be an immovable object at the best of times, so her stubbornness shouldn't have bothered her as much as it did.

Realising Galdinia wasn't pleased with this response, Vega finally said, "We eat when we eat. This is not unfamiliar territory for soldiers of the Royal Guard. You may think it odd or counterproductive or even extremely unnecessary, but it isn't. I have gone days with only the herbs in my pack and survived to tell the tale. You needn't worry, Your Highness. We are trained for this."

Galdinia didn't like the idea that she was stopping someone from eating, but she chose not to die on this hill.

"Can you at least forgo the formalities?" Galdinia asked as they rounded on the dining room, which was returned by a questioning frown from Vega. "You can call me Galdinia."

Vega smirked. "We are also trained in how to address our rulers. I will eat while on duty before I address you any other way, Your Majesty."

Galdinia looked at Vega with watchful eyes as they stepped into the dining room. She supposed this was not a battle she would win, at least not today.

Ravenna, Neryda, Ilyon, and Kayd were seated around the table, enjoying their morning meal. And again, the table was filled with mouth-watering dishes—fresh fruits, pastries, eggs, and baked vegetables greeted Galdinia as she sat beside Neryda, inadvertently avoiding Ilyon's eye as she took her seat. She noticed he didn't have a plate in front of him; it appeared he was waiting patiently for Galdinia to arrive, and his plate was long gone.

"Good morning, Your Highness," Ravenna said from the head of the table. "I take it you received my note?"

"I did, thank you," Galdinia replied as she served herself some eggs. "We will depart at sunrise tomorrow then?"

"We think that would be best," Ravenna said with a nod. "Wait out the storm, and then take your leave. You may wish to sail out into the bay today. Not even the rain can dampen the beauty of The Hook."

"I may just do that," Galdinia said with a smile.

"Please take one of our sailboats across the bay, if you'd like."

"Thank you, Ravenna."

She ate her breakfast, chatting quietly with Neryda and Kayd. Given Ravenna's proximity, Galdinia avoided any topics of strategy or the days ahead—despite her friendly demeanour, Ravenna was keeping a close eye on Galdinia and her conversations.

Once they had all eaten—including Vega, to Galdinia's relief—Galdinia thought it prudent to take Ravenna's offer. Training was out of the question with the weather, and she wasn't sure how much longer she would last being cooped up in the Lidels' manor. She was craving fresh air.

After thanking Ravenna for her hospitality, Galdinia and her group took their leave. As they walked out of the dining room, Ilyon silently approached Galdinia and finally spoke to her.

"Your Highness, a word?"

Pausing in her step, knowing she couldn't avoid him for much longer, Galdinia allowed Neryda, Kayd, and Vega to walk ahead of her as she and Ilyon trailed behind. She'd practised this conversation in the quiet morning hours between her nightmares, so she steeled herself before replying. "Yes, Captain?"

"That was quite a promise you made last night," Ilyon said in hushed tones as they walked through the manor.

"It was necessary."

"That may be so, but I'm curious how you intend to uphold it."

"I don't think you'll like the answer I have for you."

"Let's see."

Taking a deep intake of breath, Galdinia finally said, "I don't know."

Ilyon looked at Galdinia, giving her a sidelong glance. "Well, that's better than what I'd thought you'd say."

"It is?"

"Frankly, Your Highness, I thought you might suggest we storm Elderwin Manor and turn it over until you find the necklace."

"That still may be better than no plan," Galdinia replied as they stepped into the entrance hall.

"Neither is preferable." Ilyon turned to face Galdinia as Neryda, Kayd, and Vega stepped out into the rain. "I'm not sure we can keep that promise, Your Highness. Travelling to Lund, then to the Shadowed Coast and retrieving the jewels from Edana may not be possible before the next new moon."

"We can't face Valah without first securing allies, so we'll have to try," Galdinia said. "If this promise can help us secure one—if not two—sizeable groups, then so be it. Allies should be our priority."

The other three had walked on ahead. Galdinia could see that Neryda was using her gift to divert the rain above their heads; instead of soaking into their hair or cloaks or slipping down their armour, the water seemed to instead trickle down an invisible bell jar that was neatly situated around Neryda, Vega, and Kayd. Neryda had sufficient practice in such a skill, often doing so with Galdinia and Drystan when they walked through Elderguard on particularly rainy days. As she watched her comrades walk through the gardens, surrounded by a wall of trickling rain, flashes of the ambush infiltrated her thoughts. She glanced at the short set of stairs before them, up which Vega had practically dragged her.

She pushed these hazy images from her mind and turned her attention back to her captain, not allowing herself to succumb to the fear that lay within her memories.

"These jewels are clearly of high value to them," she said, a lilting strain in her voice. "They may be self-serving, but they obviously hold a lot of value."

"Therein lies my main concern."

"Oh?" Galdinia asked as she and her captain stepped out into the morning air. Seemingly subconsciously, Ilyon created a similar barrier around himself and Galdinia, silently commanding the water from the sky to move around the pair, not a drop landing on them.

"I'm sceptical about their promise of an alliance."

"Why?"

"I hope for securing an alliance in Lund is inconsequential to them. However, keeping you alive to reclaim what is theirs *is* a priority. I'm sure they'd prefer to avoid marring their relationship with Lund by sending them a ruler they tried to have killed barely a week ago, but it's worth the risk. They only care about themselves, and once you serve your purpose, I fear they will forget about you sooner than a breath."

Galdinia knew her captain was being careful with his choice of words, almost skirting around his concerns.

"Ilyon," Galdinia said, turning to look at her captain as they walked, "stop being so diplomatic and just come out and say whatever it is you'd actually like to say."

With a sigh, Ilyon replied, "You are a pawn in their games, Your Majesty, nothing more. If you can't retrieve the jewels, they'll find someone else to do it, and we'll lose their alliance."

"Like I said, Captain," Galdinia said as they descended the steps towards the docks below, the rain still falling around them, "we must first go to Lund and then worry about the family heirlooms. The jewels aren't going anywhere, and as soon as we can afford the time, they will become the priority."

"I hope you're right, Your Highness," Ilyon replied, following Galdinia down the stairs. "I certainly hope they don't go anywhere."

Galdinia watched each step she took carefully, wary of the slippery stones beneath her feet.

"I'm surprised you didn't offer to shift the storm this morning," Galdinia said, balancing herself on a particularly narrow step. "I thought you would have been glad to leave The Hook."

"I thought about it, but I decided our group could do with an extra day of rest."

"And by the group, you actually mean me, don't you?" Galdinia asked, not faltering in her step.

"While I think Kayd's arm is still healing," Ilyon explained, "yes, after the ordeal you've been through, I thought you would benefit from it before we embark on what will be a very tiring journey."

Again, Galdinia could decipher the meaning beneath his words, and it sent an itching sensation across her palms; she wanted to draw on the flame by her side and prove just how easily she could protect herself.

"I could have left today, Captain," Galdinia said, descending the last of the stairs.

"I know you could have," Ilyon replied, "but that doesn't mean you have to. We can spare a day to ensure you have your sharpest wits and clearest mind before meeting with the Lund elders."

Galdinia turned to look at Ilyon, replying, "So it's in the name of strategy then?"

"It always is."

At the bottom of the stairs, Neryda, Kayd, and Vega were waiting for their queen and captain. The royal ship towered over a collection of smaller sailing and rowing boats, each one as beautiful as the next with gold detailing and perfectly crafted oars and sails. One of which seemed to already be occupied by someone.

"Queen Galdinia!"

Luan was leaning over the railing of one of the nearby sailing boats, beaming at Galdinia as she approached the docks. He, too, was bone-dry despite the rain. His protection seemed to span much of the length of the sailing boat, though. Galdinia was surprised that such a young Weaver was able to control something as unpredictable as the rain with ease.

"Hello, Luan!" she replied cheerfully, warmed by his welcome.

"Are you going out onto the bay?" Luan's voice was bright and excited.

"I was thinking about it, but I may be in need of a vessel."

"You can join us!"

"Us?"

The word tumbled out of Galdinia's mouth as Quillion came into view behind Luan, coiling a rope around his arm. This explained the protection of the sailing boat and the sweet-faced boy from the rain.

"Quill and I are about to set sail, and we'd love you to join us."

It was hard not to be softened by Luan's naivety.

Galdinia caught Quillion's eye; he had finished organising the rope and stared down at the queen, disdain covering his features.

"'Love' might be a strong word," Neryda said quietly.

"We don't mind taking another sailing boat," Galdinia replied. "Kayd and Captain Ilyon are perfectly skilled sailors."

"Oh please, Your Majesty, I'd really like to take you myself." Luan's eyes seemed to grow twice their size as he pleaded. "Quill promised I'd get to be captain today, so it would be wonderful if you were my first passenger."

"I'm not sure, Luan," Galdinia commented, hating the prospect of hurting this young boy.

"They may prefer to sail alone," Quillion said to his brother, not quietly enough that Galdinia couldn't hear them.

"Please, Quill," Luan said, desperation in his voice. "I'd really like to spend more time with Queen Galdinia."

After a long pause and through gritted teeth, Quillion finally agreed.

Although Galdinia was quite happy spending more time with Luan—especially when it meant so much to him—she didn't know that she had the energy to deal with Quillion's seemingly unjustified aversion to her and her party. She painted her face with a smile regardless, Luan's beaming expression warming Galdinia despite the weather.

"Right this way, Your Majesty!" Luan gestured to the short gangway, and Galdinia and her companions boarded the sailing boat. "We just need to let down the mainsail, and then we will be off!"

With frustration set deep in his brow, Quillion pulled the mainsail free, letting it billow out into the light morning breeze.

"May I be of service, Captain?" Kayd asked, wriggling his fingers and offering his gift to Luan, who appeared entirely chuffed with this title.

"Most certainly! I think if you stand up at the stern, you'll be able to propel us forward quite nicely."

"Aye aye, Captain!" Kayd saluted the young leader of the boat before moving to his position.

"Queen Galdinia, Lady Neryda, Captain Ilyon, Guard Vega,"

Luan said, approaching them with a grin on his face, "may I suggest you take up positions at the bow of the boat? You'll get a tremendous view of the bay."

"Right away, Captain," Galdinia said with a smile, playing along.

This seemed to only boost Luan's excitement further as he returned her words with a toothy grin. Quillion, on the other hand, looked about ready to throw himself overboard.

Ignoring Quillion's hostility, Galdinia followed Luan's instructions as he called out orders to his new Wind Wielder, preparing to depart. In a few seconds, Kayd's wind was filling the sails and propelling them forward away from the docks.

As they moved out into the open water and turned towards the bay and main town of The Hook, Galdinia was greeted with a new perspective of this beautiful province. Despite the rain and its tendency to dull one's surroundings, The Hook's lavish greenery, mountainous landscape, and abundance of trees were only made all the richer by the fresh rainfall. The rainbow of buildings dotted across the bay was no less beautiful in the rain. Now much closer to the buildings, Galdinia could see that many of them stretched up onto the surrounding hills and cliffs, mimicking the shape of the land masses around them. It was a truly special view, and Galdinia was reminded of why the Lidels rarely left their home.

Galdinia turned to look around her, wanting to glimpse the height of Lidel Manor atop the headland. However, her eye caught something else entirely.

Luan stood barely two inches taller than the helm that he grasped firmly in his hands, looking intently out beyond the bow of the boat, an expression of unbreakable focus on his face. Behind him, Quillion stood in Luan's shadow, his arms outstretched and holding the helm just above his brother's hands. His eyes were also fixed on the water ahead of them as he quietly pointed things out to Luan, making suggestions and guiding him. At one such suggestion—arm outstretched, pointing at something in the distance—Quillion did something that seemed entirely out of character: he smiled.

It paled in comparison to Luan's bright grin, but it was most certainly a smile. He then said something quietly to Luan, causing his younger brother to crack in his concentration, letting out a bright laugh.

Did Quillion just make a joke?

This seemed so foreign and unnatural to Galdinia. But there he was, telling jokes and making his brother laugh. Luan tried to school his expression again, taking his job very seriously, but there was a glimmer in his eye as Quillion continued to make his brother smile. Had someone else described this moment to her, she never would have believed them.

Confounded by this interaction, Galdinia turned back around to observe the town before them as they sailed, the boat creating rippling waves in the green-grey surface of the water.

"Do you want to know something interesting, Your Highness?" Ilyon asked.

"What might that be?" Galdinia replied.

"I'm not keeping us dry right now."

Galdinia frowned at her captain before looking up at the sky above them, where the invisible barrier continued to divert the rain from the deck of the boat, and subsequently, themselves.

"You're not?" Galdinia glanced back at the Lidel brothers before adding, "You don't think he's doing it alone, do you?"

"It would seem so," Ilyon replied before looking beyond Galdinia to Neryda. "Unless you're helping cover us, Lady Neryda?"

"I dropped my shield the moment we stepped on the boat," Neryda confirmed. "I assumed you had a handle on it."

"I thought I may have needed to as well, but it would appear Quillion is capable of maintaining it himself."

"All while he teaches his brother to sail a boat," Galdinia said, unable to hide her amazement.

It was enough of a feat to protect the large boat while it was docked, but to maintain the shield as they sailed, while laughing with his brother, was another achievement altogether.

"I would say that's quite impressive," Neryda commented, leaning against the railing of the boat, "if he weren't so insufferable."

"I'd say it's fairly impressive regardless," Ilyon said, glancing up at the shield that covered the length of the boat. "He is a powerful Weaver."

Galdinia wasn't sure what she'd done to receive such a scornful welcome from the eldest Lidel son, but she couldn't deny Ilyon's assessment of Quillion's gift.

She glanced back at Quillion again, still helping his brother steer the boat. His eyes scanned the water before them and briefly landed on Galdinia. His expression darkened, a crease forming in his fore-head. Then he turned his attention back to Luan, helping him steer the boat in an arc, turning away from the coast and towards the heart of the bay.

20

Stepping into the morning air with Raia and Neryda by her side, Galdinia felt more than ready to leave the opalescent fortress that was the Lidels' home.

After their cruise across the bay the day before, they returned to a hot meal, and then Galdinia took herself back to her room, looking forward to escaping the chill of the water—and of Quillion—and instead basking in the warmth of the fire beside her bed.

The following morning, she was glad to see the clouds had parted, not only allowing for the sun to shine, but also for her and her group to begin their journey to the mountains. The warm rays filtered through the trees, making the shadows feel all the cooler. This was the image of the Lidels' home that Galdinia wished to keep in her mind's eye, not the one filled with fog and blood and blades. The leaves were starting to fade in colour, and Galdinia watched as one caught on the breeze, detached from its branch, and fluttered down onto the dewy grass. Autumn had arrived, though it looked much brighter and warmer in the southern reaches of the country; Galdinia knew colder days awaited them as they travelled north.

Ilyon, Vega, Kayd, and Evander were at the bottom of the stairs engaged in what appeared to be a hearty debate. At the sight of

Galdinia, however, their discussion ended, and they turned to face the queen, the guards standing at attention.

"Good morning," Galdinia said, walking down the stairs, her eyes full of scepticism. "Am I interrupting?"

"Of course not," Ilyon said, standing at ease beside his soldiers. "Are you ready to embark?"

"Yes, we're ready," Galdinia said, nodding to the packs that she and Neryda were carrying. They had taken only what they needed from their belongings on the ship: their warmest clothing, as well as Galdinia's fighting leathers, which she now donned; her bow and arrow; and, of course, her armour, Drystan's helmet safely in her hands. After the attack in The Hook, Galdinia would have preferred to wear her full armour, but Ilyon made a point that they shouldn't draw attention to themselves while on their travels, so both she and her guard had agreed to wear their leathers only, stowing their more defensive garb in their packs. The Lidels had even offered Neryda a set of armour, which, although it was a deep blue grey instead of black and didn't fit her nearly as snugly at Galdinia's tailored set, she gladly accepted. Galdinia's crown would also have to be packed out of sight, but she wasn't quite ready to relinquish it just yet.

"The Lidels' attendants will be arriving shortly with horses for us to travel with," Ilyon replied. "As we anticipate a few nights on the road, they've given us tents and sleeping equipment as well. We don't want Valah to get wind of your movements, so we thought it would be best to avoid bigger towns and villages."

"I agree," Galdinia said with a nod. "And where is our eager escort?"

Ilyon nodded behind Galdinia, back towards the front doors of the manor.

Looking even less enthused about the trip than he had two evenings prior at dinner, Quillion stepped out onto the landing of the manor, his black attire resembling an ensemble that one might wear when mourning. Perhaps he was. Behind him, Ravenna, Bael, and Luan followed, Luan looking cheerful enough for both himself and his brother.

"Good morning, Your Highness!" Luan said, bounding past Quillion and stopping a few steps from the bottom, allowing him to share Galdinia's eye level.

"You didn't need to get up to see us off, Luan," Galdinia remarked. "It's very early."

"I didn't want to miss a chance to see you again before you left!"

"Well, that's very kind. I'm glad you did! It was a pleasure sailing around the bay with you yesterday."

"You'll have to come back soon," Luan said eagerly. "I wish I could come with you!"

"Me too," Galdinia said with a smile.

"There you go," Quillion said as he sauntered down the steps, pointing at his brother. "He can take them instead."

"Oh, can I?" Luan turned to look up at his parents as they stopped on the step behind him. Bael shot his eldest a lethal look, and Ravenna placed a gentle hand on her youngest's shoulder.

"It's a little too dangerous for you to go alone," Ravenna replied gently.

"But I would be with Queen Galdinia and all her soldiers," Luan said, pointing around at the group. "I can just show them where to go!"

"Maybe one day, darling," Ravenna said, pulling her son in close to her side. "Maybe when you're a little older."

"You always say that," Luan replied, scowling as he crossed his arms over his chest. "I bet you let Quill go when he was my age."

"They wouldn't let me out of their sight until I was sixteen," Quillion replied, coming to stand by his brother before reaching out to tousle Luan's hair in a moment of brotherly jest, but Luan leant away, dodging Quillion's hand. "You're already allowed to go into town on your own; I've only had four years of freedom. You'll be traipsing across Crysterra before you know it."

Once again, Galdinia felt taken aback by Quillion's sudden shift in demeanour. She wondered if this more pleasant, thoughtful side was only reserved for his brother.

"I'll try to organise to have you both escort me next time," Galdinia proposed, offering Luan a placating smile.

At this, Quillion's manner altered again. He stood up straight and looked at Galdinia from the corner of his eyes. "If there's a next time."

"Quillion," Ravenna said in a low voice, the closest thing to a warning Galdinia had heard from her since she'd arrived.

"I'll see you in a couple of weeks," Quillion said quickly, leaning to kiss his mother on the cheek and nodding to his father. He reached out and rustled Luan's dark curls before his brother could avoid it again.

It had been one week since Galdinia had received Valah's letter, so she had less than three weeks until the next new moon. Quillion's casual tone about when he'd see his family again reminded Galdinia that by that time, she'd be in one of two situations: she'd either have rescued Drystan or she'd have to live with the reality of Valah's threat. Knowing that every conversation, movement, and decision Galdinia made over the next eighteen days could have very real consequences on Drystan's life brought an impenetrable ache into her chest.

"Bye, Quill," Luan said, pulling Galdinia from her contemplation as he allowed his frustrated exterior to falter for a moment as he farewelled his brother.

As Quillion turned from his family, an array of attendants entered the gardens from a nearby path, each one guiding a horse through the lush trees.

"You will be riding on my horse, Your Majesty," Ravenna said from the steps as a beautiful jet-black horse approached Galdinia. Its contrasting white mane was kept long and plaited down its neck. "Opal is friendly and fiercely loyal; I'm sure she'll take to you quickly."

"Thank you, Lady Ravenna," Galdinia replied, reaching out to pat the horse in welcome. Opal leant into Galdinia's touch, allowing her nose to be scratched by the queen.

"We've also supplied you with a week's worth of nonperishables," Ravenna continued gently. "Quillion has been tasked with ensuring they are evenly distributed during your trip. This should cut down on how much hunting you will need to do."

Galdinia very much doubted Quillion would happily hold up his end of the bargain.

"Thank you, again," Galdinia said, attempting to mask her lack of faith in Ravenna's son.

The remaining attendants approached each of the others, handing over the reins to their new companions. Galdinia noticed, though, that there was still one steed unclaimed.

She had an inkling as to who it might be reserved for.

Noticing Galdinia's gaze, Ilyon approached her, bringing his own horse in tow, while everyone worked at securing their belongings and introducing themselves to their horses.

"Your Majesty, I need to talk to you about—"

"Bentley?" Galdinia asked. "That's what you were discussing earlier, wasn't it?"

"It was," Ilyon replied. "I think we ought to bring him with us. I don't think I trust him travelling back to Elderguard without one of the Queen's Guard on watch with him, but they are not expendable, and I don't foresee asking the Lidels to continue to host him would be taken all that well, so—"

"That's fine. We can bring him."

"What?" Ilyon's surprise shadowed his features.

"Captain," Galdinia said, still patting Opal's snout, "my advice to you is twofold: firstly, please don't tiptoe around me when it comes to Bentley. I agreed to him joining this journey in the first place, so you don't have to pretend that he isn't here. I've come to terms with that unfortunate reality. Secondly, we still don't know what information he may hold, and we'll never learn of it if we don't keep him close. If he hasn't got anything to share, then we can leave him to freeze in the mountains for all I care. Regardless, I think he should stay in our company."

She also thought Bentley could be used as quite a valuable trading commodity, should the opportunity arise, but she chose not to share that with her captain.

"Right," Ilyon said with a nod, pleasantly surprised by Galdinia's response. "Very well said. I'll cease all tiptoeing immediately."

"Much appreciated," Galdinia said, smiling.

"Raia and Evander," Ilyon called across the garden. "Fetch the prisoner from his quarters. Raia, you're on duty to keep his hands weaved; Evander, you're to keep any flames in the vicinity under your control. Understood?"

"Yes, Captain," they replied in unison before walking back up the stairs and into the manor.

Galdinia saw that Luan's frustration had subsided, and he was watching everyone prepare their horses with longing eyes.

"Your Highness," Ilyon said, turning back to Galdinia. "I think it would be wise to avoid bringing any lit flames with us. I know it's a big imposition, and Raia will have Bentley under close watch, but I don't want to take any chances."

Galdinia glanced back at the manor. Although the nearest fire was far away in the depths of the hallways in torches, Galdinia could still feel the edges of its warmth. How long would she have to go without harnessing her gift? Knowing that Bentley could be the key to her rescuing Drystan, Galdinia decided she'd go as long as necessary without it.

"I agree," Galdinia said with a heavy sigh, turning back to Ilyon.

"Evander will carry a supply of flint for campfires or emergencies, but I'll also be asking him to leave his flame behind."

"Better you than me," Galdinia said.

"Here is your own supply," Ilyon said, handing Galdinia a small bag, no bigger than the palm of her hand. It was heavy for its size.

"Thank you, Captain," Galdinia replied.

She tucked the bag of flint into her satchel and brought her attention back to Opal.

"Do you really think Bentley has any more information for you?" Neryda asked quietly, approaching Galdinia from her own horse nearby.

"Honestly, I don't know," Galdinia replied as Raia and Evander arrived at the top of the stairs with two other soldiers, Bentley securely shackled and weaved between them. Galdinia took a deep intake of breath before continuing. "But he could be used as a bargaining chip at some stage, so sending him back to Elderguard isn't a gamble I'm willing to make."

Despite everything that had happened as a result of his selfish actions, Galdinia couldn't help but see the glisten of champagne bubbles in his eyes and hear the bright sound of his laugh when she saw him. It unsettled her that she still had such a reaction when seeing him. Bentley caught Galdinia's eyes as he walked down the stairs and was directed to his horse at the back of the pack. This brief glance sent another jolt into her chest, which she promptly pushed down, denying her heart to linger on the moment. With some assistance from Evander, Bentley awkwardly clambered onto his steed, which was then promptly tied to Ilyon's in front and Raia's behind. If he wanted to attempt an escape by horse, he'd be taking two of the strongest soldiers in the Royal Guard with him.

To distract herself, Galdinia drew her attention back to Opal, and more importantly, the packs that needed to be fastened to her saddle. She followed her guards' lead and attached her belongings with relative ease, buckling one on either side of her steed. The left side pack still allowed some room, reminding her it was time to place her most treasured possessions within.

With a reluctant intake of breath, Galdinia reached up and removed her mother's crown from her head, the Starlight Crystals sparkling in the morning sunlight with a glorious glisten. She pulled a thick square of dark mauve silk from her pack and carefully wrapped her crown within. After retrieving Drystan's helmet from Opal's saddle where it had been perched, she ran her fingers along the inside edge where his name was stamped. The indent of each letter tickled her fingertips, reminding her of what lay ahead on this journey. Galdinia's cautious fingers placed her protected crown inside the helmet before placing both head pieces in the pack, now ready to leave.

Looking up, Galdinia watched as Ilyon spoke quietly to Evander. In response, Evander pulled his small lantern from his waist. It had been perching there since the day they had arrived at The Hook and he had been allowed access to his gift once again. In a swift movement, Evander touched his forefinger to his tongue before squeezing the flame between his thumb and finger, extinguishing the fire and his connection with it. Holding his head tall, Evander clipped the lantern back to his belt, now an empty reminder of his gift.

Pulling her eyes from Evander, knowing full well the emotions that were running through his veins, Galdinia turned her attention back to the Lidels and approached them.

"Thank you for your hospitality," she said, looking from Ravenna's pleasant smile to Bael's unchanging, stern expression, then finally to Luan's eager eyes. "I'm grateful for your help and alliance."

"Don't forget our terms, Queen Galdinia," Bael said.

"Your jewels will be retrieved as soon as possible," Galdinia said with a curt nod. "You can rely on my word."

Galdinia thought Bael wanted to rebut that statement, but his young son spoke too quickly.

"Of course we trust you, Your Highness! I can't wait for you to visit again." He then arched his neck to look across the gardens at his brother. "Be nice to her, Quill!"

At this, Quillion rolled his eyes as he mounted his horse.

"See you soon, Luan," Galdinia said with a smile before turning from the Lidels.

"Ready, Your Highness?" Quillion asked, his voice drawling on her title.

"After you, Quillion," Galdinia said, hand outstretched, waiting for him to lead.

"It's Quill," he replied, his tone unamused.

"Very well," Galdinia replied with a nod. "After you, Quill."

If she had to live with his cloud of resentment and disdain for days on end, Galdinia could call him whatever he wanted, playing along in an attempt to quell his obviously misguided first impression of her. And regardless, she understood the desire to be known by a particular name, which she could respect, even if he showed her such little in return.

With this, Quill led his horse towards the path that ran through the gardens, closely followed by Kayd, then Ilyon, Bentley, Raia, and Evander.

"I'm not sure how I'm going to survive this trip with him," Neryda said quietly as they watched the others trot ahead of them. "It's like we're asking him to battle the seas in the middle of a storm without a crew."

"We are just some great inconvenience to him," Galdinia replied before turning to wave at the remaining Lidels once again. As Galdinia, Neryda, and Vega followed the group down the path, Luan's eager smile and enthusiastic wave were the last things she saw before they disappeared behind a row of trees that ran through the gardens.

"He's infuriating," Neryda went on, trotting closely beside Galdinia. "His family is hosting the newly crowned queen, and he barely acknowledges your existence. And then to suggest escorting said queen to meet with allies—or to simply sail around the bay—is a slight on his busy schedule is just unimaginable. You're the Queen of Crysterra, for heaven's sake."

"You're pulling out the queen card early," Galdinia replied, watching her friend carefully.

"I don't think you've used it enough!"

"Oh?"

"Throw him in some stocks for insubordination," Neryda suggested.

"We did away with stocks decades ago," Galdinia retorted, eyebrow raised.

"Lock him up in a cell or something, then," Neryda replied, shrugging. "Chuck his father in there while you're at it. They can seethe and hate us silently from there."

Galdinia gave her friend a long, hard look.

"You seem quite pressed by this," Galdinia remarked, her lip curling up at the edge.

"Of course I am," Neryda said, frowning in Quill's direction at the front of the pack. "He's insufferable and…" Neryda turned to look at her friend. "Why are you looking at me like that?"

"No reason," Galdinia said with a knowing smile, turning back to face the path ahead of them, watching the line of horses before them as she fell into the slipstream behind Evander. She was closely followed by Neryda and then finally Vega. "You just seem quite concerned with him, that's all."

"I'm concerned *by* him," Neryda corrected, her voice a fierce whisper behind Galdinia.

"I can see that." The grin spread wide across Galdinia's face.

"I don't know what you think you're insinuating, but I don't like it," Neryda hissed.

"I'm not insinuating anything," Galdinia said over her shoulder with a shrug. "He's rude, confident, and unwelcoming, and he's clearly touched a nerve. That's all I'm saying."

"I hope that's all you're saying," Neryda huffed.

With a sly smirk, Galdinia pressed forward with Opal, catching up with Evander as they exited the large, wrought iron gates of the Lidels' property and onto a well-worn road. The road stretched out before them, winding over hills and around buildings as it curved around The Hook. From their vantage point, Galdinia could see much of the bay below them, the water sparkling in the morning sun. Although autumn had started to change the colour of the leaves and robbed the surrounding gardens of many of their flowers, the province's beauty was undeniable.

Galdinia craned her neck to look behind her, admiring the Lidels' manor. For a moment, she thought she could empathise with Quill and his displeasure for leaving such a place, but the expression of contempt he had given her earlier crept through her mind, and any sign of empathy danced away on the morning breeze.

Galdinia watched the back of Quill's head carefully as he crested a hill, leading the group from view of the manor. She felt this would be a long journey.

21

After two long days of travelling, Galdinia and her troop pitched their tents in the clearing of a forest along the northern reaches of The Edges. The cool chill in the air became sharper the further north they travelled, and as the sun set, Galdinia found herself very grateful for the heavy coats and woollen socks that they'd packed.

Their four tents sat in an arc around the clearing: Galdinia and Neryda had their own tents, while Raia and Vega shared, and the men sheltered for the evening in the largest one. Although Galdinia had insisted that she and Neryda didn't need separate sleep quarters, and Ilyon could occupy one of theirs instead, he assured the queen that the more people watching Bentley, the better. To this, Galdinia didn't have an argument.

Surveying the area, Galdinia took in their camp for the evening. They were surrounded by trees on all sides, the thicket of forest and bushes hiding them from anyone that may travel down any of the nearby paths or roads. Even if they were spotted, with their leathers hidden beneath coats and cloaks, they looked like a group of harmless travellers.

While Ilyon and Kayd checked the pegs of each tent, Raia and Vega went hunting for dinner. Galdinia sat beside Neryda at the fire pit that was now ready to be lit, Bentley and Evander perched across from them. Ilyon had questioned whether Bentley should be left in a tent or somewhere further in the woods when they stopped each evening, but it was decided that the closer he was, the easier it would be to keep an eye on him. Galdinia also suggested that forgoing one soldier to guard him wasn't as efficient as having him among five soldiers and two people who would attack him without hesitation, should the occasion arise. Quill, however, seemed inconvenienced at best by the prisoner's presence, and he now lounged in the grass, maintaining the weave of water around Bentley's hands, clearly unimpressed with his new task. Although he didn't appear particularly focused on his duty, the sphere of water around Bentley's hands didn't falter.

Looking beyond the trees around them, Galdinia gazed up at the tops of the mountain range that made up The Edges. They had travelled along their base over the last twenty-four hours, walking in their shadow as the sun slowly set. If her geography skills served her well, an entrance to the Wetlands was just beyond the mountain closest to them, and Drystan could have been as near as one day's journey from her current location. She was the closest she had been to him in two weeks, and at the thought of his proximity, her heart started to shudder in her chest. Galdinia recklessly wondered how quietly she could leave the camp that evening and break off to the Wetlands alone.

This thought dissolved as quickly as it had appeared when the presence of a flame drew her attention back to the camp. Evander had pulled a piece of flint from his satchel, struck it against his sword, and before the spark could even reach the kindling, he had harnessed the beginnings of the fire. By way of Evander's internal command and a snap of his fingers, the fire erupted, dancing over the wood before them. Within two breaths, a full campfire was ablaze in the centre of the clearing. To not only capture the smallest of flames at its onset, but to see it build with such accuracy and speed, was mesmerising to watch. The hairs on the back of Galdinia's neck stood on end as she sat before the element she craved for every minute of their journey, feeling more at ease in its presence. Her thoughts about traversing The Edges alone were quickly replaced by memories and imaginings of fire.

Two weeks ago Galdinia had summoned great spheres of fire outside the capital's gates, but those had been harnessed from a much greater fire that had consumed the gates themselves. She hadn't yet been able to surge a flame from its first spark into a roaring fire, nor had she been able to shrink a blaze to a singular flame. She was still working on this skill, and to see Evander do it so effortlessly made equal measures of hope and envy settle in her chest.

As the fire crackled in front of them, Galdinia welcomed the heat and sense of safety that came with the flames. She had felt almost ravenous for the fire by the time they reached their resting spot the evening before. Today was no different.

Across the flames, she watched Bentley as he looked into the fire himself. He didn't seem as desperate—or grateful—for the flames as Galdinia was. Had the water around his hands dulled his senses? Or did he recognise that he wasn't a match for the surrounding soldiers and didn't even entertain trying to break through his restraints?

"Squirrels?"

Neryda's voice pulled Galdinia's attention away from Bentley and to Raia and Vega, who had returned with a bundle of quail eggs, berries, and four unlucky squirrels.

"I don't think this is the time to be picky, Ner," Galdinia said before thanking her soldiers for their efforts.

"Our pleasure," Raia said, placing the rodents on the ground by the fire. "And they're not as bad as you may think. They're actually quite delicious."

At Raia's words, a memory of a conversation Galdinia had during the Week of Mourning came to her. Bentley had told her about how squirrel was a delicacy in The Edges and was often cooked for hours on end in order to be deemed delicious. Her eyes flicked to him across the fire, and a small smile crept over his lips as he stared into the flames. It would seem that he had remembered their conversation too. Or, the more sensible side of Galdinia thought, he may have simply been looking forward to eating one of his favourite meals.

"Sounds gamey," Quill commented from beside Evander, where he was leaning back on an elbow, whittling a stick down to a sharp point with a dagger.

"If they're cooked properly…" Bentley started to say, but he trailed off as multiple pairs of sharp eyes turned to him. Neryda's were the most lethal. Despite their extended time travelling together, he still hadn't been welcomed into their conversations, and these were the first words Galdinia had heard from him since they spoke in The Hook. It was clear that he was there as a prisoner, nothing more.

"I'll roast them on a spit, and we'll have them with some of the walnuts from The Hook," Vega explained. "Quill, can you fill this pot with water for the eggs?"

Quill looked up from his comfortable position in the grass, communicating with Vega with one look that he didn't plan on moving.

"I'm not the only Weaver here that can find you a water source," he said simply, looking back down at his makeshift weapon.

"You're just the most useless one," Neryda said quietly, rolling her eyes.

"What was that?" Quill asked, glancing at Neryda.

"Nothing," she said definitively. "I'll fetch the water."

She took the pot from Vega and made her way from the circle. Galdinia watched Quill as he looked up at her best friend, watching her saunter away, his eyes harsh.

Once Neryda had returned and Vega had prepared the squirrels to eat—a process that caused Galdinia to choose to eat only berries and eggs that evening—the meal was placed on the flames. While Evander was in charge of keeping the fire rolling as their dinner cooked, Galdinia couldn't help but keep glancing at it. She felt the heat from the flames on her skin and coursing through her blood. She wondered how she'd lived so long without it. As she watched the flames lick at the cool air and disappear in sparks above their heads, her eyes found a pair staring at her: Bentley.

Galdinia looked away from him instantly, seeking refuge wherever else she could find it. She hated that something so comforting had become a commonality between them; as she was tugged by fire, she could only assume that he also felt its pull.

Soon Vega had drawn the food from the fire and split up the portions on small steel plates, handing them around the group. The troop of nine ate eagerly, perched around the fire as the sun set behind The Edges.

"We're hoping to make it to Lund in four days' time, is that correct, Quillion?" Ilyon asked before biting into a boiled egg.

"If we travel from sunrise to sunset, yes," Quill said, still reclining by the fire, his plate of food having replaced his hand carved weaponry. "I can't promise you'll get an audience with them, though."

"We know it's a gamble," Galdinia cut in, "but we don't have many other options."

"Just don't get your hopes up," Quill said with a shrug. "We'll have to leave our horses at a stable at the base of the mountains. The terrain beyond is too much for them. So everyone will need to prepare themselves for a good hike."

"Thank goodness for the hearty dinner," Kayd said, looking at the poor excuse of a meal in his hand: a squirrel leg that was barely longer than his smallest finger.

"By all means, you're welcome to hunt instead." Vega shot him a look, scolding.

"With his aim?" Raia said with a scoff. "We'd starve."

"What you do with a bow and arrow, I can do with a knife," Kayd countered.

"Hardly!"

"You'd probably still beat Neryda," Galdinia said quietly, popping a raspberry in her mouth.

All eyes turned to the queen and her mortified friend beside her.

"Excuse you!" Neryda said, mouth agape.

"I love you, Ner," Galdinia said, "but we all know archery isn't your strong suit."

"Well, *now* they do!" Neryda was incredulous that Galdinia would share such apparently embarrassing information.

Galdinia smirked as she looked around at the group. The air was jovial and light—it felt as though the heavy blanket of pretence was lifting. With this one piece of information, perhaps they would start treating her like one of their own rather than simply as their queen.

"Archery isn't that impressive, anyway," Kayd said, cleaning off the last of his food from his plate. "Swordsmanship takes far more skill."

"Over aiming a lethal projectile at a moving target from across a field?" Raia asked, her eyebrows raised at her cousin. "I don't think so,

Kayd. I shot that squirrel straight through the head. I'd like to see you try to do that with a sword."

"I could take its whole head off in one fell swoop!"

"Wow, how impressive," Raia said with heavy eyes. "Well done accomplishing something a child could do."

"What kind of child is cutting off the heads of squirrels?" Kayd asked.

"I did," Bentley said from over the fire, eating the last of the meat on his squirrel's leg. He had been temporarily released of his watery imprisonment while he ate, but his wrists remained chained.

"Of course you did," Neryda grumbled.

"Not for fun," Bentley assured them, looking around the group. "Squirrel is a delicacy in The Edges, and they run rampant, so hunting squirrels was a twice weekly event for me growing up. We used swords, arrows, baits… anything to capture them."

Everyone around the fire was silent, watching Bentley. Perhaps he was also becoming comfortable in the group. Galdinia was reminded that they were likely in the vicinity of his home, which sat somewhere along The Edges; had they already passed it earlier in the day as they navigated through the thick forest?

Before anyone else uttered a word, Bentley spoke again.

"And you've done a fine job with these ones, Vega." He awkwardly waved the bone in the air with one of his shackled hands before placing the plate on the grass before him. "With the tools and time you had to work with, you managed to avoid the gaminess."

Quill looked sideways at Bentley before turning his attention back to his own food.

"And it is impressive to shoot one through the head," Bentley added, looking at Raia. "They're quick on their feet, especially around sunset. You did well to hit them so cleanly."

Galdinia could tell that Raia wasn't quite sure how to respond. This was high praise from someone from The Edges, but Bentley was still their enemy. His friendly conversation, although one-sided, seemed to catch them all off guard, Galdinia most of all, whose mind was inundated with images of a far more refined Bentley who walked with her through the streets of Elderguard, danced with her at the Royal Feast, and met her in the castle gardens.

"At least we know who the most impressive archer is then," Raia said, breaking the tension and sitting up tall, looking across at her cousin with her head held high.

"I do have to interject, Raia," Ilyon said quietly, glancing up at Galdinia. "There may be someone else who has you beat on that."

Once again, all eyes befell the queen.

Ironically, Galdinia knew she was likely matched in her skills after seeing Bentley's display with the apples during their trip to the Royal Wood with the other suitors. Galdinia decided quickly, though, that this wasn't another moment that Bentley would take from her. She could see the hard outer layer of her Queen's Guard melting away, and she had to take the opportunity.

"Have you been keeping a secret, Your Highness?" Kayd asked, wide-eyed.

"Not a secret, per se," Galdinia said, avoiding Bentley's eyes, though she could feel them boring into her from across the fire. "But my skills may extend beyond hitting large targets in open spaces."

"That's her modest way of saying she's mastered shooting raspberries from their stems," Ilyon said, holding up a berry between his fingers, "while on horseback."

Her guards looked at her with astonishment; even Vega seemed impressed. Galdinia caught Quill's brief raising of his eyebrows, and Neryda beamed beside her. Bentley's eyes were still locked on the queen, a gentle smile on his lips.

"You'll need to join me on our next hunt to show off your skills, then," Raia said, beaming, giddy with excitement.

"Perhaps I will," Galdinia said with a coy smile. Her eyes moved to Ilyon, whose expression was warm and full of pride—or at least as warm as Ilyon could get.

The remainder of the evening, which progressively dropped in temperature, continued in a similar fashion as they finished their dinner, spoke of their plans for the coming days, and Kayd and Raia found themselves in familial squabbles. One such disagreement led Kayd to being given cleanup duty. One by one, Raia, Evander, and Vega made their way to their tents, leaving their plates piled before Kayd. He glowered each time the stack grew.

"Quillion and I need to consult the maps before morning," Ilyon said as he placed his and Quill's plates in front of Kayd. "Please get some sleep soon, Your Highness. You'll need all the energy you can get tomorrow."

"I will, Captain," Galdinia said reassuringly, enjoying watching the fire as it continued to burn in Evander's wake. Given she still couldn't make a direct connection with the flame, Galdinia knew Evander held full control of it from his tent and would continue to until everyone had turned in for the night and it could be extinguished.

Quill followed Ilyon into the men's tent, and Kayd looked down at the mountainous chore before him.

"That's it, I'm freezing," Neryda finally said, standing up. "I'm going to bed."

"Good night," Galdinia said, smiling at her friend, not quite ready to leave the comfort of the fire. Neryda looked from Galdinia to Bentley, then back to Galdinia. "I'll see you in the morning." Galdinia's voice was as reassuring as it could be.

"Don't stay up too late," Neryda said, sending a warning look in Bentley's direction.

"Thank you, Mother," Galdinia replied.

Neryda left the circle and went to her tent.

"I'm going to clean these plates before the gully gets too cold," Kayd said, already looking exhausted by the incredibly simple task ahead of him. "I'll see if Evander can watch—"

"I can stay here with him." The words had left Galdinia's lips before she had processed what she was saying.

"I couldn't ask you to do that."

"You're not. I'm offering," Galdinia said. "We've already established I'm good with a bow," she went on, tapping the bow and arrows that lay beside her, "and he's a much bigger target than a raspberry."

Bentley watched Galdinia carefully as Kayd contemplated his decision. The captain wasn't even thirty feet away, still in control of Bentley's reinstated weave of water, and Galdinia's lethal weapon was easily within reach.

"I'll be back in a few minutes," Kayd assured her before picking up his stack of plates and making his way into the trees, leaving Bentley and Galdinia alone around the fire.

Galdinia looked at Bentley as the fire flickered across his face, sending a warm cast over his features, sharpening the shadows but illuminating the brightness of his eyes. She then looked beyond him, past the trees and to the tops of the mountains of The Edges that lay behind them. Once again, she was drawn to visions of herself travelling around The Edges and through the Wetlands to find Drystan. She could see him so clearly in her mind's eye—he was so close.

"It's not worth it." Bentley's voice—hushed but firm—travelled through the fire to Galdinia.

"Excuse me?" Galdinia said, a frown settling in place as she looked at Bentley.

"You're trying to work out if you can get to him." Bentley said this as though it was obvious simply by the look on her face what she was thinking. Perhaps it was. Or perhaps he was just very good at reading her. She didn't like either prospect.

"No, I'm not," Galdinia pushed back.

"You are," Bentley said confidently. "And it's not worth it."

A heavy pause hovered between them as Galdinia struggled to decipher his expression. It was not full of concern or frustration; he appeared almost indifferent. Had he only been able to seemingly read her mind because he had a similar plan himself? Had he contemplated breaking free of the group and escaping to his home in The Edges?

"You have no idea what you're talking about," Galdinia finally replied. She wasn't sure if she was angry or embarrassed; maybe she was both. She hated that even now, he knew exactly what she was thinking.

"I've already told you what a terrible idea it is to go to the Wetlands, but to go on your own? You wouldn't make it beyond The Edges."

"I've made it this far."

"With a full guard and resources."

"You don't know what I'm capable of," Galdinia said, quickly becoming frustrated.

"Anyone would struggle to traverse The Edges alone, trust me."

"Trusting you is a luxury I well and truly gave up," Galdinia said, casting him a glaring stare.

"Fine," Bentley replied, irritation now embedded in his features;

any indifference he was feeling was a fleeting shadow. "Try to travel to the Wetlands alone, don't tell your captain where you're going. Great idea."

"Why are *you* getting frustrated?"

"Because you keep trying to kill yourself just to save one person!" The ferocity in Bentley's voice rose, and Galdinia was sure he'd alert one of the others in their tents, but no one emerged. "It's exhausting trying to convince you that your life is far more valuable than his."

"That's why we're so different," Galdinia said, her voice hushed. "I don't see anyone's life as less valuable than my own."

"Then you're a fool," Bentley chided. "You're the queen. If anyone can bring Crysterra back to its former glory, it's you. And you're willing to put not only that in the balance, but also your own life, to save *him*."

"Of all people, I don't think you should be the residing voice of reason when it comes to Drystan's life," Galdinia replied, clenching her fists in her lap, trying not to reach out to the flames.

"You're right," Bentley said, lowering his voice. "I honestly don't care whether he lives or dies, and neither does the vast population of Crysterra. On the other hand, I can think of many thousands of people who would be affected by your death." Bentley seemed exasperated. "You can pretend that you're being altruistic all you want, but you and I both know that saving Drystan is a selfish decision. You're willing to risk your own guards' lives to save him."

"I'm not asking anyone else to come with me," Galdinia said, frustration rising in her voice. The fire before them surged, growing minimally larger. Had she managed to momentarily push through Evander's hold of the fire without trying to?

"If you were to disappear tonight, you must realise each and every one of them would come after you," Bentley said, looking around them at the surrounding tents. "Forget about your guards; what about Neryda? You know she wouldn't rest until she found you. Imagine how distraught she would be to see you gone in the morning." Galdinia internally admitted that she hadn't considered the reality of Neryda's reaction before that moment. She knew she'd be upset, but of course she would chase after her too. "They would all set out looking for you and potentially risk their lives to save yours because they know how valuable it is. It's time you started to realise that too."

Galdinia could feel tears starting to brim in her eyes at the thought of her guards, her captain, and her best friend searching for her in the Wetlands. She felt a heaviness land in her chest as guilt wracked her heart.

"You're very important, not only to the population of this country but to the eight other people at this camp, including Quill, even if he hasn't realised it yet," Bentley said, his voice barely a whisper now. Galdinia noted that he included himself in that count. "We need you to stay alive, Galdinia. I need you to."

His words brought with them a vulnerability Galdinia hadn't heard from Bentley before, and it displaced something inside her, pushing her off-kilter. They watched each other carefully, their shared element dancing between them. Despite the tension, neither of them showed any intention of using it against the other. If anything, the flames calmed Galdinia, and she couldn't see them as a weapon in that moment.

Before she could form the words to ask Bentley why her survival was so necessary to him, a rustling came from the adjacent trees, announcing Kayd back into the camp.

"Apologies, Your Highness," Kayd said, stepping back into the fire's light, the now clean stack of plates piled in his hands.

"Of course," Galdinia said, her eyes glassy and her voice thick as she pulled her gaze from Bentley, standing to her feet.

"Maybe we should avoid mentioning this to the captain," Kayd said with a chuckle, looking from Galdinia, then to Bentley.

"Of course," Galdinia repeated. "Good night, Kayd."

With that, Galdinia turned from the fire and walked to her tent, avoiding Kayd's eye and not looking back at Bentley. Stepping into her quarters, her eyes still watery, she knew she would be staying there for the remainder of the night, the idea of escaping for The Edges having floated away with the smoke of the campfire.

22

THE NEXT DAY, THE GROUP CONTINUED TO TRAVEL ALONG THE EDGES and through the northern reaches of the Wooden Province, spending their final night among the trees before venturing into the Starlight Mountains. Given they wouldn't be able to traverse the mountains together, their horses were taken to a nearby stable before they settled in for the evening.

After another night of broken sleep—interrupted by images of a starving Drystan—Galdinia left her tent the following morning and found she was the first to rise. She glimpsed the sun over the camp, hovering through branches, muted by the light morning fog. After filling the pot with fresh water from a nearby stream, Galdinia pulled a piece of flint from the small reserve Ilyon had given her, as well as an arrow from her quiver, before she bent down beside some fresh logs and dry kindling. Evander had taken it upon himself to light the fires on their journey, but Galdinia was ready to try her hand at starting a fire from nothing but minerals, something a young woman who'd lived sheltered in a castle all her life was yet to do herself. Tilting the arrowhead towards the kindling, Galdinia struck the flint against the edge of the arrowhead with a sharp crack.

Nothing.

With a frown, she tried again to create a spark, but the kindling remained untouched. On her fifth strike of the flint against the arrowhead, she finally caused sparks to emanate, but she couldn't grab hold of them with her gift quickly enough to coax them into a proper flame.

Finally, after another six attempts, the sparks finally caught on the kindling, and a tiny flame flickered in front of Galdinia. A grin spread across her face, not only at the success of starting a fire from flint, but also at the presence of the element she felt deep beneath her skin.

The flame heated Galdinia's palms as she sent it dancing over the firewood. She felt each crack and pop in her veins, the sizzling heat resting in her chest and the warming glow of the growing fire comforting her. How she ever survived without her gift before the Sixth Day of Mourning, she didn't know.

Galdinia placed the pot on top of the flames before briefly leaving the campfire to collect quail eggs in the nearby trees. Even as she walked away from the fire, she could sense its warmth in her bones, and she felt she was able to control it from afar, keeping it rolling yet contained. By the time she arrived back at camp with enough eggs for two for each person, the pot was boiling and Vega and Raia were sitting by the flame.

"Good morning, Galdinia," Raia said with a smile, watching the boiling water in the pot closely.

"Your Highness," Vega echoed, nodding towards Galdinia.

"Good morning," Galdinia said, placing each egg carefully in the pot.

"Thank you for collecting breakfast," Raia said, peering into the pot.

"It's the least I can do."

One by one, the rest of her guards joined them around the fire, their belongings packed. Evander brought Bentley in tow, who sat down by the fire, his eyes flicking to Galdinia every few minutes. They hadn't spoken since their late-night conversation by The Edges two nights earlier, and Galdinia continued to avert her gaze; the way in which he perceived her thoughts before she spoke had left her feeling rattled.

At the smell of the cooked eggs, Neryda emerged from her tent. She appeared barely awake as she haphazardly pulled on her boots, her curly russet red hair twisted into a knot at the nape of her neck. Once by Galdinia's side, she took an egg and began to peel its shell.

As the group ate their food, the final member called out to them.

"Are we ready to go?" Quill asked, appearing from the tent with his pack, immediately turning to unhook the pegs and ropes that held up the canvas walls.

"Some of us wanted to have breakfast first," Neryda said, already starting on her second egg.

"No time for breakfast," Quill replied without turning from his job of dismantling the men's tent. "We need to leave in five minutes if we want to make it beyond the first ridge by midday."

"We won't make it very far if we haven't eaten," Galdinia replied.

"If we want to make it to Lund by day after next, we need to leave—"

"We have time to eat first," Ilyon said, cutting Quill off.

"You don't know how—"

"You may be an expert in the mountains, Quillion," Ilyon said firmly, "but I know how to travel with a platoon of soldiers. In order to successfully traverse the mountains, we need sustenance. I intend on seeing my soldiers and our queen through the mountains, not at the bottom of a ravine because they didn't have enough energy to make it. We will leave once we've finished eating."

Quill frowned at Ilyon, standing tall, looking like he was contemplating whether to stand up against the captain or not. Deciding against it, Quill turned from the group, pulling out his waterskin from his pack.

"I'm going to fetch some water." His voice was clipped as he spoke. "Hopefully that gives you all enough time to eat your breakfast. We will leave when I return."

Without another word, Quill walked into the woods and out of sight.

"What's his problem?" Neryda asked, glaring after Quill.

"We just continue to be some great source of irritation for him," Galdinia replied before biting into her second egg.

"He needs time to deflate his ego," Neryda huffed, still looking into the trees where Quill disappeared.

"His priorities are different from ours," Ilyon replied from across the fire. "We hope to see the end of a conflict. He is merely doing as his parents instructed him. He doesn't see this journey the same way we do."

"Maybe he needs to," Vega replied, throwing the remains of her eggshells in the fire.

Within ten minutes, Quill had returned, and their tents were packed down and once again attached to their packs. From now on, however, without the help of their horses, their cargo would be strapped to their backs, and each traveller wore their armour. Before anyone could offer to carry Galdinia's belongings, she hauled her own pack over her shoulders, slipping her bow and sheath of arrows into a buckled loop at the side, ensuring they were easily accessible. Reaching her arm back, her fingers brushed over the rounded edge of her pack where the canvas fabric clung to the edges of Drystan's helmet, within which her crown was still securely sitting. She hadn't removed either, but every now and then she touched this spot to check they were still nearby, allowing a sigh of relief to settle in her chest.

Galdinia watched as Raia moved to the now tepid pot of water beside the extinguished fire, drawing the liquid out and approaching Bentley.

"Is there any way we could forgo the water?" Bentley asked, almost wincing at the thought of his hands being weaved yet again. Galdinia glanced at him sideways.

"And why would we do that?" Kayd asked as he tightened the straps of his pack over his shoulders.

"We are about to embark on what I assume to be not only a precarious and rocky track, but also an increasingly cooling climate," Bentley said, looking up at the mountains before them. "Other than needing my hands to balance, I'd prefer that they don't freeze."

"That would be a more permanent solution to the issue," Neryda said with a shrug.

"I know you all think I'll take any opportunity to attack Galdinia, but haven't I proven that's not my goal?" Bentley looked around at the group. "I've had access to fire for the last four days, both weaved and free, and I haven't once tried to hurt any of you. Surely you don't see me as a threat."

"Do you really want us to answer that?" Neryda asked.

"Keep me tied up to any of you, keep your flames extinguished, have me walk fifty feet away from Galdinia, I don't care," Bentley said, holding his palms out face up, his eyes dashing to Galdinia. "Just please don't weave my hands in water that is only going to give me frostbite in a few hours."

Galdinia looked from Bentley then to Ilyon; the captain seemed to be considering Bentley's request.

"What do you say, Your Highness?" Ilyon asked, leaving her with the responsibility to decide.

Galdinia looked back at Bentley, and she could see the desperation in his eyes. After a few good nights' sleep and keeping the soles of his feet on solid ground, he was looking more like himself again. The shadows around his eyes weren't as dark, and his skin was far less sallow. He was slowly looking more and more like the man Galdinia met in the capital a few weeks ago.

"I want his wrists bound, and I need to be able to see him in my line of sight at all times," Galdinia finally replied. "But you can forego the water, Raia."

Bentley let out a gentle exhale at Galdinia's words, and she thought she saw gratitude in his eyes. Raia dropped the sphere of water she'd had suspended in front of her, and it splashed on the ground, soaking into the grass at their feet.

"If he really wanted to hurt her, he could just push her off a cliff when we get halfway up the mountain," Quill said, tightening the straps of his pack. "That would be much easier."

"Thank you, Quill," Galdinia said, glaring at the man. "I appreciate your input."

"You're welcome," he replied with a smug, sarcastic smile before turning and walking away from the group. "Follow me."

"I don't think it's Bentley we need to be worried about," Galdinia said quietly to Ilyon as Kayd followed Quill.

"Like I said, he doesn't share our priorities," Ilyon said, nodding at

Vega to follow Kayd, followed by Evander and Bentley. "I don't think you need to worry about your safety around him, though."

"If I mysteriously disappear on the mountain, you know who to blame," Galdinia said with a frown, watching Quill as he led the group through the woods towards the mountains. Ilyon stepped forward after Bentley, and then Galdinia, Neryda, and Raia fell in line behind the captain.

"You're fiercely protected here, Your Highness," Ilyon said. "I'd like to see him try."

As the group traversed the mountains, Galdinia was reminded very quickly that her standards of physical strength and endurance weren't anywhere similar to that of her companions. While she slipped on the track, took her time to balance herself on rocky terrain, and found herself becoming short of breath as she climbed ledges and natural staircases of rock, the soldiers around her moved with ease and considerable pace. Given his regular trips to Lund, Quill powered on ahead, often stopping around a corner or at the top of a particularly steep slope to wait for the group, who was keeping pace with their queen and her best friend.

"It must be time for a break," Neryda puffed, almost doubled over under the weight of her pack as she hauled herself up another steep incline. They had been clambering up the mountains for hours without a break, and Galdinia could feel the aching in her legs; they, too, were crying out for a moment of rest.

"We aren't stopping until we reach that ridge," Quill called out from the front of the group, pointing up to the next mountain ahead of them. Galdinia estimated it would take another thirty minutes to reach their destination.

"You may not have a choice at this point," Neryda retorted, her breath coming in heavy gulps.

"Come on, Ner," Galdinia replied, taking in her own deep breaths. "We can do this."

"I just need a second," Neryda replied, breaths deep, a very patient Raia by her side. "You go on ahead. We'll catch up."

Galdinia knew that if she took a break now, it would be very difficult to start the trek again. Given that she'd rather perpetuate her physical pain than hear what Quill might say if she paused for even a second, Galdinia pushed on forward.

As they started to climb another almost vertical incline, Galdinia kept her eyes on Ilyon; he led the way, showing her where to step. The captain easily pulled himself up the muddy trail, using the various jutting rock faces as handholds. In the hopes of mirroring his deliberate movements, Galdinia quickly followed Ilyon, taking hold of the rock as she clambered up. Grasping the rock, Galdinia started to pull herself up the ledge, following Ilyon's previous movements exactly. Once beyond the steepest section, she was able to pull herself up and walk on the rock, only a few paces behind Ilyon.

"Well done, Your Highness," Ilyon said with a short nod of approval before continuing on behind Bentley and Evander.

Galdinia watched as Bentley turned briefly to see her stand up straight after the difficult climb. It was one thing for her to be climbing with the pack on her back, but it was another one entirely for Bentley to have done so with his wrists bound together by a chain. Seeing her glance at his shackles, Bentley smiled, catching Galdinia off guard.

As she went to step forward, following Ilyon, Galdinia's right foot didn't quite take hold; she slipped on the mud beneath her feet, rendering any grip in her soles useless. In a moment, Galdinia's feet slipped from beneath her, the weight of her pack sending her off-balance and to the ground with a painful crash of her armour and a cry of panic. With the help of the mud-slicked stone, gravity pulled her backwards towards not only the face of the ledge, but the drop of the cliff face below their trail.

Frantic, Galdinia scrambled to take hold of the mountain. She tried to dig her feet into the rock as her hands flailed, seeking any grip she could take hold of. She slipped further, her feet now beyond the lip of the ledge, her limbs desperately reaching for a hold. Before she could grasp a piece of the mountain, a tight grip wrapped around her right wrist, quickly followed by another around her left, stalling her descent over the ledge, her legs now suspended in the air.

"Gal!" Neryda cried from below her at the base of the ledge, some twenty feet down.

With her heart thundering in her chest and her pulse nearly deafening her, Galdinia glimpsed up at who was keeping her attached to the mountain.

On her right, Ilyon was crouched, one hand around her wrist, the other balancing himself on a nearby boulder.

On her left, Bentley had wrapped both shackled hands around her wrist, his grip tight and determined. Evander was behind him, holding the back of Bentley's coat, keeping him on the mountain.

Both men were looking at Galdinia desperately. Ilyon's expression was severe and urgent as he held Galdinia in place.

Bentley, on the other hand, looked overcome by fear, his eyes wide and his chest heaving. He searched Galdinia's face for any sign of pain or injury.

"Let go. I've got her," Ilyon said, his voice mirroring his expression.

"Are you alright?" Bentley asked, keeping his shackled hands wrapped around Galdinia's—they were trembling. Galdinia's own heart was thundering in her chest as she tried to make sense of the moment.

"Let her go," Ilyon said, his voice lethal now.

Bentley didn't seem to have any intention of letting Galdinia go until he knew she was safe. He seemed to be becoming all too comfortable with disregarding Ilyon in such circumstances.

"I'm okay," Galdinia said as reassuringly as possible for someone whose feet were dangling off the ledge of a mountain.

Bentley held her stare as long as he could before finally letting go of her hand. The moment Galdinia was free from his grasp, Evander wrenched Bentley back. Ilyon pulled Galdinia away from the ledge, using his grip on the boulder behind him to hoist them both back to even ground.

"Don't hurt him," Galdinia said to Evander almost instinctually as Ilyon helped her to her feet. "I'm okay. He was only trying to help."

Evander now held Bentley closer to him, and behind them Vega and Kayd looked down at the group with wide eyes and ready stances. Beyond them, Quill didn't appear to have moved from his place on the track. He merely stared down at them all, waiting.

"Are you alright, Your Highness?" Ilyon asked, bending to search Galdinia's face.

"I said I'm okay," Galdinia assured him, looking beyond Ilyon at Bentley, whose chains were wrapped in Evander's hand, the scruff of his coat in his other. "Just a bit of dirt and a bruised ego. Other than that, I'm fine."

Although her heart would take some time to calm down, she didn't need to be fawned over again like she had been after the attack in The Hook. Galdinia was more concerned about the potential of her guard classifying her as unfit for such travels than she was by the prospect of slipping over that ledge.

There was a scrambling sound from behind them, and both Neryda and Raia appeared over the ledge in quick succession.

"Are you okay?" Neryda asked, rushing to Galdinia's side in a swirl of worry and heaving breaths before taking hold of Galdinia's face, investigating far more intimately than Ilyon or Bentley had.

"*I'm fine,*" Galdinia said tersely, pulling her face away. "I slipped, but I'm okay. Really."

"But you could have—" Neryda began.

"But I didn't," Galdinia said pointedly, looking from Neryda to Ilyon and Bentley. "I'm alive. Thank you both for catching me. Can we please keep moving now?"

"Yes, can we?" Quill drawled, turning away from the group and walking on along the mountain.

Galdinia glared at Quill as he walked away, and she could feel a fresh wave of frustration sweep over her panicked heart.

"She almost fell to her death," Neryda said, her tone casual. "Nothing to worry about."

"If he slips," Galdinia said quietly to Ilyon, "please don't feel the need to move so quickly to catch him."

"I'm sure I can find far more interesting ways to occupy myself," Ilyon replied in hushed tones, joining Galdinia in staring at Quill as the rest of the group turned to follow him. "Perhaps I'll be distracted by a flock of birds or the formations of a cloud."

Before turning to continue the journey with Evander, Bentley looked at Galdinia for another long moment. The look of fear in his eyes as he looked down at her was an image that would be hard for her to erase from her memory, and a genuine concern was still etched into his expression. Galdinia thought that he must have moved very quickly to evade Evander long enough to reach her. Finally, he turned from her and continued to trek up the mountain.

With a deep breath, her heartbeat now back at an even pace, Galdinia followed Ilyon, continuing to move towards the ridge ahead of them, careful with every step she took.

23

AFTER A BRIEF REST AT THE RIDGE, THE GROUP CONTINUED TO TRAVEL up the mountains for another six hours. It wasn't until the sun started to dip below the lowest surrounding mountain that Quill agreed it was time to find a place to set up camp. He managed to push the group to walk an extra expanse of mountain in order to reach a cave that he knew would be a good resting spot.

"I normally arrive here by night after a half day's journey up the mountains," he said, leading the group into the belly of the cave.

"Some of us aren't as well-versed with the mountains as you are," Kayd said briskly, a stark contrast to his usual amiable demeanour.

"I think that has been made abundantly clear," Quill replied, glancing briefly at Galdinia before hurling his pack off his back and turning to Evander. "Light us a fire, won't you? As soon as we lose that sunlight, the chill will really set in."

In response, Evander stared at Quill, his brows angular and his expression fierce.

"Are you waiting for a formal invitation?" Quill asked, not bothering to look up from his pack.

"It wouldn't hurt," Evander replied, pulling a small bundle of kindling and a piece of flint from his pack.

"It also wouldn't hurt for you to be a little more considerate,"

Neryda said, her voice thick with frustration. Neryda's words caught the young lord's attention, and he glanced up as she came to stand above him. Galdinia watched on expectantly.

"Excuse me?" he asked, his hands paused mid-movement as he pulled a blanket from his pack.

"You have been nothing but hostile since we arrived in The Hook, and for what?" Neryda went on, all eyes on her. "Your family managed to get over their grudge with the capital, but you're still holding on to it with such a tight grip, aren't you?"

"You don't know what you're talking about—"

"Of course I do," Neryda charged on, her irritation building. Galdinia's lips turned up into a smug smirk. "You're a self-centred first-born who's had everything handed to him his entire life. And the minute you were presented with a mere inconvenience—which is to help save your head from an enemy that won't hesitate to cut it off the first chance she gets—you stormed out of the room like a child."

Standing to his feet and glaring down at Neryda with a hot fury, Quill said, "Don't speak to me like th—"

"I'll speak to you however I wish," Neryda cut in, "because it seems reluctant civility isn't getting us anywhere! We were put through hell when Valah attacked the capital, and we shouldn't need to remind you that you are assisting in the defeat of a vicious enemy, but here we are!"

Quill glared at Neryda, his anger palpable.

Without saying another word, Quill marched past Neryda and back out the mouth of the cave, disappearing in the light of the sunset.

"Gods, I can't stand him," Neryda said with a huff, dropping her heavy pack to the ground with a thud. The entire Queen's Guard, Bentley, and Galdinia were all staring at her with a mix of expressions.

"I think you've made that abundantly clear," Galdinia replied, her grin growing. "I'm impressed you held that in for this long."

"I think that was more painful for him than a sparring session with Vega," Kayd said with a smirk.

"He wouldn't have been in any condition to leave the cave if I had it my way," Vega replied darkly, coming to sit around the spot where Evander had chosen to make his fire.

In one swift motion, Evander struck the flint with a blade, and he caught the spark on the kindling. In seconds, the flame was the size of a regular campfire, though there wasn't any firewood to maintain it; Evander was doing that all on his own.

Sitting down beside Vega, brightened by the glow of the fire, Neryda took a deep breath before making a suggestion: "Who's up for a round of Trader's Triumph?"

An hour later, Evander was pulling a pile of coins towards his already impressive stack by his foot.

"I won't have any money left by the end of this trip," Neryda complained, throwing her cards into the pile in front of Raia; it seemed her earlier conversation with Quill was almost entirely forgotten and her only frustration now was with Evander.

"I don't care to admit how many times he has sent me into debt," Kayd said with a shake of his head, dumping his cards in front of Raia, ready to be shuffled.

Evander's smirk was visible, even as he sat in the shadow of the fire behind him. He, Galdinia, Neryda, Raia, and Kayd were sitting in a circle beside the fire, while Ilyon sat by the mouth of the cave, keeping watch, and Vega sat against the wall of the cave, preparing their dinner of vegetables and nuts. The group playing cards insisted that Vega play, but she merely shook her head and took it upon herself to organise their next meal. Bentley was within arm's reach of Vega, although it was clear that he wouldn't try anything while he was so near to her and her knives. Galdinia was starting to believe that he wouldn't be a threat regardless.

"Then why do it?" Galdinia asked Kayd, adding her cards to the pile before Raia started to shuffle.

"Pride, mostly," Kayd replied. "One of these days, I'll beat him, and I'll win back every coin he has stolen from me."

"*Won* from you," Evander corrected.

"*Stolen*," Kayd emphasised. "I look forward to that day. I'll buy a feast for the entire battalion, and I won't invite him."

Kayd glared at his friend in mock anger.

"Your money will be paying for all my own feasts in the meantime," Evander said, the fire behind him surging. The added heat sent a prickle of goosebumps up Galdinia's neck.

"Two can play at that game," Kayd said, smiling as the wind outside was redirected and danced through the cave, swirling around the group. The biting cold wind made Evander's fire flicker and Galdinia's hair shudder around her shoulders.

"We certainly can," Evander said more fiercely, using his gift to expand the fire higher into the air at a mere thought, warming the group instantly. Galdinia revelled in the heat.

"Cut it out, you two," Vega said from across the cave, slicing a tomato on a small board.

Ignoring her warning, and by way of retaliation, Kayd's wind became stronger and more concentrated as it wrapped itself around Evander, forcing him to bring his arms tightly to his sides. Evander was quick to counter, sending a spearhead of fire from behind him, over his head and towards Kayd.

"Enough!" Ilyon called from the mouth of the cave, not bothering to turn and look at his soldiers.

At their captain's word, they both released their gifts; the hovering flame dissipated in the air, and the wind settled, allowing Evander to have free movement of his arms once again, while the cave settled in warmth.

"I'll get you next time," Kayd said quietly with a wicked smirk.

"I'd like to see you try, Breeze Boy." Evander's tone was mocking.

Galdinia couldn't help but be amused by the men. She knew that only brothers fought like that and no one was in any real danger for a single moment. It sent a wave of gratitude through her, glad to be surrounded by soldiers who trusted each other enough to behave in such a way.

"Evander, can you watch him while I cook?" Vega asked, standing up with her board of cut vegetables, moving towards the fire, gesturing at Bentley.

"Yes, please," Neryda said, eyes wide. "That might give me a chance to win."

Before Evander could reply, Galdinia stood to her feet. "I can."

"It's no problem, Your Highness," Evander said before correcting himself at the expression on her face. "Galdinia."

"I'm running low on coins anyway," she said. "Plus, I'd like to see what kind of gale Kayd can produce if you beat him again."

With a wink in Kayd's direction, Galdinia turned from the group and walked across the cave to Bentley. He was sitting against the wall with his shackled hands dangling between his bent knees. He watched Galdinia carefully as she crossed the cave towards him.

She wasn't entirely sure what prompted her to insist on watching Bentley, but she thought it had something to do with a question that had been gnawing at her since her near-death experience that morning. Galdinia leant against the wall beside him, glad to be moving her sore body that didn't appreciate the sudden stagnancy after such an intense day of hiking—and falling, as it were.

"Any scratches or bruises?" Bentley asked, looking across the cave at the group as they started another round of cards.

"Nothing serious," Galdinia replied, stretching her neck from side to side, also watching the group as the bet was quickly raised.

"Good." Although his response was brief, Bentley's tone of relief was honest.

As she let her arms relax by her side, Galdinia slid down the wall, coming to sit beside Bentley, two feet of space between them.

"I'm curious about something," Galdinia said. "Why did you help save me today?"

Bentley paused before replying. "You're not really asking me that, are you?"

Galdinia turned to look at him, frowning.

Bentley's expression indicated his incredulity, and he laughed, which Galdinia did not expect from him. The bright, warm tone startled her.

"One of these days, you'll believe me when I say I don't want you dead," Bentley said, shaking his head.

"You'll have to forgive me for struggling to trust you," Galdinia replied as images of burning books and wild flames invaded her mind, uninvited.

"I know I have a long way to go in earning your trust again." Bentley sighed. "But surely saving you from plummeting to your death helps."

"We're getting there," Galdinia said, an undercurrent of stoicism in her voice.

"At the very least," Bentley said, glancing sideways at Galdinia, the reflection of the fire glistening in his eyes, "I added to Quill's irritation by keeping you alive, so that's got to give me a few extra points."

An unexpected smile tugged at Galdinia's lips as she watched his natural wit return, sitting comfortably on his tongue as he eased beside her. She couldn't ignore Bentley's disarming levity—it was one of the reasons she was so easily drawn to him during the Week of Mourning.

"It certainly doesn't hurt," Galdinia agreed, the humour lingering in the air between them.

Galdinia held his gaze, and she thought she could see the words he was contemplating, the words he didn't know whether he should utter or keep locked away behind his lips—words of care and devotion. Words she wasn't sure if she would be able to believe again.

"I'll take it," Bentley said quietly, resting his head back against the wall, closing his eyes.

Although Galdinia supposed she should be grateful he didn't profess any feelings for her again, an unpleasant weight settled in her stomach.

She watched as his profile glowed in the firelight. She glanced down at his chained hands, noticing he was clenching them tightly into fists before slowly flexing his fingers out straight. He repeated this motion over and over again. Was he in pain? Were the handcuffs causing him grief? But that wasn't it, Galdinia thought. It was his gift.

Galdinia wondered how starved for fire he felt after not being able to flourish for two weeks, stifling his gift in order to prove his loyalty to her. She wasn't sure if she could have survived as long as he had without drawing on her gift. And yet, he still had the strength to rescue her from certain death.

"Thank you," Galdinia said quietly, still watching him.

A small smile flickered over his lips, his unmistakable dimple sinking into his cheek.

"You're welcome," he replied, turning to face her. His light eyes glittered, and Galdinia could again see the person she had been drawn to in the castle gardens the night before she received her gift... the night before he betrayed her.

With a sigh, Galdinia turned to look back at the group playing cards, watching Evander, once again, call out "triumph". Galdinia and Bentley sat in silence, watching the others play three more rounds. Before Evander and Kayd could enter another sparring match, Vega called everyone for dinner. Without looking at Bentley again, Galdinia stood to her feet, collected her plate from her pack, and went to the fire, joining a very defeated Kayd.

"You know you're just putting yourself through misery," Galdinia said, handing her plate to Vega. She piled it up with a thick, fragrant stew of vegetables before scattering it with finely sliced walnuts.

"Yes, but odds are that I'll win one day," Kayd said, passing his plate to Vega next.

"Are you sure about that?" Galdinia asked, taking a seat by the fire and thanking Vega.

"I've beaten him a handful of times, and Raia has twice," Kayd said, sitting beside Galdinia. "So it's bound to happen again."

"Whatever you say," Galdinia replied with a smile, scooping up a spoonful of stew and blowing on it before starting to eat. The meal was aromatic, warming, and exactly what Galdinia needed after the day she'd had.

"Captain," Vega called as she filled Bentley's plate, "do you think Quill will be joining us for dinner?"

"Save him a portion," Ilyon replied, turning from the opening of the cave to join them by the fire. "I can't see him returning anytime soon, but I'm sure he'll be hungry when he arrives back. He needs to cool off."

"He'll freeze at this rate," Raia said before taking a mouthful of food and revelling in the taste. "This is some of your best, Vega!"

"Thank you," Vega replied, filling Ilyon's plate, then her own.

The group spoke jovially as they enjoyed their dinner, the cave filling with warm chatter. Once their stomachs were full and the tiresome day had caught up with them, Neryda, Evander, and Raia cleaned the cutlery, plates, and pot with melted snow, while everyone else set their bedrolls out on the ground around the fire. As the night stretched on, they became increasingly grateful for Evander's fire.

"Please let me take a duty on the fire," Galdinia said to Ilyon, who had taken up his spot at the entrance of the cave once again. "Before you say no, Evander can't possibly stay awake all night to keep an eye on it, and we will wake with frozen noses if we don't keep it going."

Glaring out at the stretch of mountain before them, Ilyon considered her request. With the light of the sun erased from the sky, the mountain ranges were lit now only by the glow of the almost-full moon and the sparkling stars. The moon stood as a daily reminder of Valah's threat, and they were almost two weeks from the next new moon.

"You can do the first shift," Ilyon said, conceding. "You'll need to remain alert for four hours, and then you must wake Evander and let him take over."

"I will," Galdinia replied. "Thank you for trusting me."

"It's not you I struggle to trust," Ilyon replied, peering out into the depths of the cold night where Quill had disappeared.

After a brief exchange with Evander, Galdinia took up her position against the wall of the cave, near the fire, while everyone else tucked themselves under their blankets and got comfortable for the evening. Bentley was the furthest from her, and the rest of her guard and her best friend were strewn between them.

Within a few minutes, everyone was asleep, and a quiet hush fell over the cave, interrupted only by the soft snores from Kayd and Raia.

Galdinia sat and stared into the fire for a time, enjoying being able to freely make a connection with it. She could feel the heat of it travelling through her veins, over her arms, and into her chest. She wouldn't need a blanket that evening.

After an hour of simply enjoying using her gift, Galdinia drew the cards from beside Raia and set them out in front of her, playing a version of Trader's Triumph on her own, hoping to practise some of the strategies Evander had given her on the ship. As her muscles had a moment to rest and she wasn't distracted by winding paths or the dynamics in the group, Galdinia finally had a chance to think about her impending meeting with the leaders of Lund. She ran through what felt like every manoeuvre and rebuttal she may face, each scenario playing out slightly differently. She could be met with open arms or pointed weapons, they could welcome her around a table, or they may refuse her entry and turn them away. Either way, her mind ran through all the possibilities as she played her cards, having silent conversations with herself.

Another hour later, Galdinia heard a noise come from the mouth of the cave. She turned and saw a shrouded Quill walk in from the cold. Galdinia watched Ilyon lift his head, seeing who had entered the cave, before resting it again and going back to sleep.

"You're back," Galdinia whispered as he crossed the cave to the other side of the fire where his pack still lay, blanket discarded on the ground.

"So it would seem," Quill replied, his voice insipid.

"We saved some dinner for you," Galdinia said quietly, nodding towards the plate of food beside his pack. Quill acknowledged it, but he moved to his pack and unrolled his bedroll before lying down and pulling his blanket over him. "You're welcome."

"Don't wait for gushing gratitude from me."

"Don't worry, I'm not."

"Good."

Galdinia watched Quill as he lay with his eyes closed, his chest rising and falling quickly. He must have been freezing outside in the chill of the wind.

"I don't know why you hate us all so much, but it would be easier for everyone if you got over it quickly," Galdinia said flatly, taking a leaf from Neryda's book and speaking her mind. "We still have a long time together on this journey, and I'd prefer it if I didn't have to dodge your snarky attacks."

Quill's jaw tightened at her words. "I don't hate all of you," he said without opening his eyes. "I just hate you."

With that, Quill rolled over, turning his back to Galdinia, the fire, and the others in the cave.

Taken aback, Galdinia forgot about the cards in her hands as she stared at Quill, dumbfounded. Aside from the silent feud between The Hook and Elderguard, Galdinia couldn't imagine a reason for Quill to specifically hate her. Perhaps he held on to that grudge stronger than his parents—or maybe he took after his father even more than Galdinia first thought. After Galdinia wracked her brain, running through every interaction between herself and each of the Lidels, trying to find an answer, she finally gave up and turned back to the cards, now a little distracted as she tried to practise her new strategies for defeating an unbeatable opponent.

FULL MOON

24

OVER THE NEXT TWO DAYS, GALDINIA AND HER GROUP MADE THEIR way steadily across ridges, around peaks, and through the rocky terrain of the Starlight Mountains. The further they travelled into the mountains, the colder the air became, causing all members of their troop to don their warmest layers, wrapping their hands and heads in woollen gloves and hats.

The chill in the air, however, was nothing in comparison to the blizzard that was Quillion Lidel. He remained at the front of the pack and avoided Galdinia's gaze at all costs. Ever since he professed his hatred for her, he didn't contribute to conversation when they made their pitstops for food or at camp, not even to chime in with his usual sarcastic comments. He spoke only to Ilyon, and even that was brief as they confirmed their travel plans at the beginning and end of each day.

For some reason, Quill's silence only irked Galdinia more, causing her to feel an irritation in her hands as she longed for the comfort of a flame as they travelled. This desire was met once they sat around the fire in the evening, and she got to spend a handful of hours keeping it under her control. She found it far easier to tolerate Quill when she was using her gift.

As they walked down into a valley between two large mountains on their sixth day of travelling together, Galdinia knew she wasn't the only one irritated by Quill's demeanour, which was made worse by the desire to sleep in a proper bed and to access a functioning lavatory. Of course the soldiers were well-versed in such conditions (and likely worse than these), but it had been a week and a half since they'd left Elderguard, and they'd spent almost every hour with each other. Galdinia could feel that everyone was ready for a break.

"Captain," Neryda said, calling back to Ilyon, who was bringing up the rear of the group with Kayd. "Do you think we'll make it to our destination today? I can't wait to take these hiking boots off."

"What do you think, Quill?" Ilyon called to the front of the pack, his voice reverberating off the walls of the valley through which they were travelling.

"I don't think asking will get us there any quicker," Quill replied, pushing forward into an increasingly narrow section of the track.

"It's not worth it," Galdinia whispered to Neryda in warning. She knew exactly how her best friend would have liked to reply.

"That wasn't my intention," Neryda said, her voice sickly sweet, a forced smile pressed over her lips. "I just want to know how much longer I have to suffer in these boots."

"We'll get there when we get there." The monotony of Quill's voice echoed around them.

Equally as frustrated by his response, Raia turned to glance at Neryda and Galdinia, rolling her eyes.

"Very helpful, thank you," Neryda replied, sarcasm dripping from her voice.

Quill ignored her as he disappeared from sight, turning around a sharp bend in the rock. Vega and Raia followed closely behind him.

"Don't worry, Gal," Neryda said, pausing as they waited for Evander and Bentley to navigate their way around the bend as well. "I don't think you're the only person he hates at the moment."

"He's the least of my worries, honestly," Galdinia said as she and Neryda manoeuvred around the tight bend. While she wouldn't be opposed to Quill grovelling at her feet and apologising for his insubordination, she had far too many concerns to contend with, namely meeting the people of Lund.

"By my estimate, I suspect we will arrive by sunset today," Ilyon said quietly after he followed Galdinia into the confined valley, Kayd not far behind.

"Now, was that so difficult?" Neryda asked, throwing her hands into the air, somewhat obstructed by the narrowing space.

Quill briefly turned his head, looking at Neryda from the corner of his eye before continuing on ahead along the winding path.

Still distracted by her own fears about their incoming meeting, Galdinia absentmindedly said, "I need to decide what I'm going to say when we arrive today."

While she had been thinking about the looming conversation for the previous few days, she still hadn't decided which stance to take. Should she present herself as a benevolent, yet remorseful leader and focus on making amends for the lost lives on the Sixth Day of Mourning? Or should she assert her newfound power, giving them an ultimatum to join her in a battle?

"Just be yourself," Neryda said, as though she could read Galdinia's thoughts on her face. "Be your gracious self, but don't be afraid to remind them who's queen. You survived a meeting with the Lidels; you can do anything." Neryda smirked at Galdinia as they stepped around another tight bend.

"They may not even agree to meet with me," Galdinia considered, her thoughts freely tumbling from her mouth. "They could tell us to turn around and leave."

This was a scenario she had run through in her mind several times, and each time a new wave of fear broke over her. What would it say about her as queen if she couldn't make amends with Lund?

"I don't think my feet will let that happen," Neryda said, looking down at her now well-worn shoes. "I need to soak them in hot water for at least two hours before sleeping for a day in a real bed."

"Let's hope we don't have to resort to your feet making arguments on our behalf," Galdinia said with a smile.

As they walked around another tight passage of rock, Galdinia felt a strain build in her chest. With the soaring cliff faces bearing down on her, as well as her fears of what lay at the end of their path swimming in her mind, an all too familiar anxiety was creeping through her body.

How would she convince the people of Lund to join her in the fight against Valah after all the bloodshed and their previous vow not to fight alongside anyone beyond the walls of their mountainous home? They had lost so much at the hands of Galdinia's own soldiers.

Steeling herself, Galdinia stepped around another bend into an even tighter space, the rock skimming along the sides of her pack, pressing in on her as tightly as her thoughts.

∾

The sun had well and truly disappeared behind the towering mountain faces by the time the group finally made it to a wide pass, a welcome change from the valley they had been navigating for much of the day. With each step, though, Galdinia felt every muscle in her legs tighten, begging that she stop walking. She'd reached the point that, above anything else, she hoped the people of Lund would welcome her into their city just to give her a chance to rest.

"We have eyes on us," Ilyon said to Galdinia quietly, pulling her attention away from her aching steps.

Ilyon had moved to walk directly behind Galdinia, and she hadn't noticed that his guard was already up, hand resting on the hilt of his sword.

"Where?" Galdinia asked, looking across the wide track they were on.

"Look up."

Galdinia glanced up to the mountain peaks to her left and right. High above them and barely perceptible in the shadows of the mountains, Galdinia could just make out the figures crouching behind boulders and blending in with the ranges in grey and brown cloaks. Without Ilyon's warning, she never would have seen them sitting and watching the group move through the pass.

"Soldiers," Ilyon whispered, his eyes narrowing on the sentries as they continued to walk. "We must be close."

"They knew we were coming, didn't they?" Galdinia asked, sure that the Lidels had sent word of their arrival by raven.

"I imagine that's why they aren't shooting at us right now," Ilyon explained, keeping his hand firmly on his sword, maintaining his close proximity to the queen.

243

Galdinia could now see the bows and arrows that were tightly gripped in their hands, some sticking out from rocks, others partially hidden beneath their cloaks of camouflage. Galdinia kept her hands by her sides, forcing herself not to reach back for her own weapons. These people may have attacked her home, but they were not inherently her enemy, and she didn't need to give them a reason to think they should be.

The group walked around a bend in the pass, and at the end of the track, they came to the mouth of a great cave, at which were stationed two guards.

"Wait here," Quill said to Vega, bringing the rest of the group to a halt halfway towards the cave's entrance.

Quill strode ahead, approaching the guards. They spoke quietly for a few seconds before standing aside. Turning back to the group, Quill beckoned them forward with the nod of his head. Cautiously, they moved forward as a group, forgoing the line they had been travelling in. Galdinia and Neryda were surrounded on all sides by the soldiers, with Quill out front and Evander and Bentley at the rear.

As they walked through the entrance to the cave, the Lund guards stared at Galdinia, their eyes scrutinising and their blades poised at their sides. It seemed she didn't need to be wearing her crown for them to recognise her.

Before them was a long tunnel that burrowed deep into the mountain and was lit on all sides by lanterns filled with Peacelight. It was brought to light in the battle on the Sixth Day of Mourning that the soldiers from Lund were gifted with Peacelight, a gift previously believed to only be given to priestesses at the Crystal Temple. Both Galdinia and the Royal Guard were not prepared for this, as Lund's soldiers used their gift to temporarily blind their opponents. Now, in the comfort of their own city, their gift was used to light their surroundings, and as Galdinia quickly noticed, to calm their inhabitants.

Although her apprehension and fears had only grown the further they trekked across the mountains, Galdinia's heart now eased as they walked through the long tunnel, her pulse steadying in the presence of the Peacelight. She was reminded of the many mornings she spent in the Crystal Temple praying for her father's health, seeking guidance from the Gods. High Priestess Saena often flooded the altar with Peacelight, bringing a calm to Galdinia's otherwise anxious heart.

"It's an uncanny feeling, isn't it?" Raia said from Galdinia's side as they moved through the tunnel.

"I hate it," Vega said, her eyes narrowing on the lanterns around them.

"What's not to like?" Kayd asked, raising an eyebrow in Vega's direction as he turned to look at her. "Instant peace."

"I don't like my emotions being controlled," Vega explained, her tone critical.

Galdinia had gladly welcomed the sensation as they entered the cave, but she did appreciate Vega's sentiments. Could she be truly comfortable in a secluded location with people who could hold some control over her emotions without notice?

"You'd better get used to it," Quill said. "The mountain's filled with it."

Vega frowned as they marched on.

Ahead of them, Galdinia could see a change in the light; the cool glow of the Peacelight seemed to shift, and a warm orange glow emanated from their destination.

Stepping out of the tunnel, Galdinia could see that the orange light of the setting sun was reflecting off the scarp faces of the surrounding mountains. They had stepped into a small blind valley, protected on all sides by mountain peaks and cliff faces. The valley was almost circular in shape, and there were a range of cave entrances that tunnelled into the surrounding landscape. At the centre of the valley, a group of about fifteen people stood in front of a fountain carved from the very stone on which they stood, clad in thick layers of fur and leather. The people seemed to be awaiting their arrival. At the front of the group stood a tall, greying man whose alabaster skin wrinkled at the eyes as he smiled at the group's approach—or, more specifically, at Quill's approach.

Quill walked forward quickly, and to Galdinia's surprise, he embraced the man, who returned Quill's greeting by wrapping his arms around him.

"Quill, it is good to see you," the man said, smiling at the arrival of his ally.

"It's good to be back, Orlon," Quill replied, pulling back from the man. "Do you know where—"

"Quill!" Two middle-aged men stepped out of the group behind Orlon, striding quickly to the young lord.

"Hartley, Phyl," Quill said, once again wrapping his arms around these people who welcomed him warmly. One of the men had tears in his eyes.

"That Peacelight really did a number on Quill, didn't it?" Neryda said quietly, leaning into Galdinia, who was staring at the spectacle of a loving and affectionate young man, someone she hardly recognised as Quill.

"I don't think anyone was expecting that," Raia added, standing close behind the two.

"I certainly wasn't," Galdinia said, watching as Quill pulled back from the embrace, now speaking quietly with his companions. This was so uncharacteristic of the man they had been travelling with for the previous week.

Noticing that most of the remainder of the group, including the man Quill called Orlon, was staring at Galdinia, she felt it was her turn to step forward.

"Hello, I'm Queen Galdinia," she said, approaching the man.

"Welcome to Lund, Galdinia," Orlon replied, bowing his head briefly and smiling pleasantly. "I'm Orlon, one of the Protectors of the Mountains. The correspondence from our friends in The Hook was brief, but I believe you would like to meet with us about an important matter."

"That's right," Galdinia replied, taking note of his omittance of her title.

"You must imagine our surprise when we received word that you wished to visit," Orlon went on, a scepticism resting in his expression. "But we trust our friends, and they assured us that you mean no ill-intent."

"I can assure you that I don't," Galdinia replied. "I simply wish to speak with the elders of Lund."

"As I said," Orlon said carefully, "we trust our friends." His countenance shifted and a benevolence rested on his features. "I imagine you're quite exhausted after your travels, so let's hold off until tomorrow morning to discuss such matters."

They weren't opposed to meeting with her or even refusing her entry into their home. This was going smoother than Galdinia had anticipated.

"We don't want to impose," she replied.

"It isn't an imposition. Otherwise we wouldn't have offered." There was an edge to Orlon's otherwise genial tone, but Galdinia was struggling to decipher it.

"In that case, we would be grateful," Galdinia replied, mirroring his expression. "Thank you for having us stay."

"Of course. Anyone that is a friend of the Lidels is a friend of ours." Orlon gestured briefly to Quill, who wasn't listening but instead speaking to the friends he had reunited with, now away from the group.

That's an overestimation, Galdinia thought.

"We are appreciative nonetheless," Galdinia said with a smile before turning to her group. "This is my Captain of the Royal Guard, Ilyon Trunder, my Queen's Guard, and my advisor Neryda Fleur."

"And who is your companion in shackles?" Orlon asked, looking to the back of the group at Bentley.

"He is a prisoner of the crown," Galdinia explained simply.

"And you brought him here?" Orlon asked, a slight frown creasing his brow.

"He isn't dangerous, but he was far too valuable to leave in The Hook after our brief visit there," Ilyon said, stepping forward to assure Orlon.

"If he isn't dangerous, then why are his hands chained?"

"It's merely a precaution," Galdinia said, hoping to change the topic. The group that stood behind Orlon was watching the exchange closely.

"Let's hope so," Orlon said, the pleasant smile returning to his face. "Let me show you to your quarters; I'm sure you'd all like to rest."

"Thank you," Galdinia said, watching the man carefully.

Following Orlon from the valley, they were guided to another cave entrance to their left. Galdinia noticed that Quill did not follow the group but instead walked away with his companions in the other direction. Orlon led them through a tunnel that ran deep into the mountain, and every twenty feet or so, a new tunnel emerged on either side as though the passages were a complex tree root system.

"This is remarkable," Galdinia said, looking around at the passages that were carved into the mountains. She had known that Lund was an established city of sorts, but this was far beyond her imagination. There was no historical documentation on this community of Crysterra, and given their only allies were the Lidels, Galdinia hadn't learnt anything during her studies about how they actually lived in Lund.

"It's taken many centuries for our people to build them," Orlon said as they continued down the same long tunnel. "These tunnels lead to the sleeping quarters. Every family is assigned their own space. Down there," he said, pointing to a long tunnel off to the right, "is the kitchen and dining wing where we gather to eat together."

"You eat together for every meal?" Galdinia asked.

"Certainly," Orlon replied. "Our dining quarters cannot hold everyone at once, so we take it in shifts, but no one in Lund eats alone. Sharing our resources and time with each other is the bedrock of Lund."

Galdinia considered his words and noticed how carefully he spoke. Their resources and time were shared amongst themselves, not with outsiders. How Valah managed to convince them to fight alongside her still baffled Galdinia. She wondered then how Orlon perceived the time he was spending with her now.

"That's really beautiful," Galdinia replied honestly.

After turning off the main tunnel and down another passage, Orlon stopped at a large wooden door, now deep within the mountain.

"You should find these quarters to your liking," Orlon said, opening the door. "There are enough rooms for you all within, but I ask that you keep someone on watch of your prisoner for the duration of your stay." Orlon eyed Bentley, who stood silently beside Evander and Vega.

"Of course," Galdinia said with a nod.

"You may want to rethink the shackles, though," Orlon said, nodding towards Bentley's wrists. "Some people may come to the wrong conclusion if they see you walking around with a prisoner, especially after the conflict."

"We will take that into consideration," Ilyon replied. Given his tone, Galdinia assumed he didn't intend on following Orlon's suggestion.

"Thank you again for your hospitality. I look forward to speaking with your leaders tomorrow," Galdinia said, changing the subject rapidly.

"I look forward to that also," Orlon said, though there was a hint of insincerity in his tone. "Please join us for dinner in the dining hall in one hour."

"Thank you, we will," Galdinia said with a smile.

Orlon's eyes swept across the tired group before turning to walk back down the tunnel.

Galdinia stepped into their quarters and surveyed the room. The space they were given had a hub at the centre with a handful of armchairs, chaises, and a large table with chairs. Doors to their sleeping quarters were scattered around the outside of the room. It was similar in style to the soldiers' barracks, and the chill of the air reflected this also. With a great sigh of relief, Galdinia laid her eyes on a large fireplace. Beside it sat a great stack of logs, ready to warm the room.

The group settled in, grateful for their own rooms—and beds—to sleep in. The noise of sheer excitement that emitted from Neryda's room when she was greeted by a soft place to rest her head echoed around the cavernous space. Galdinia had to admit that she felt equally as excited about sleeping in a real bed that evening. She had to force herself not to climb into her bed immediately, fearing she wouldn't wake up until after their scheduled meeting the following morning.

After revelling in a long soak in the tub in her room, Galdinia forwent her armour or fighting leathers and donned a far more comfortable ensemble, layering her cloak over her thick woollen garments. She thought about retrieving her crown and wearing it to dinner, but given she wasn't sure how she'd be received by the rest of Lund's population, she decided to leave it safely encased in Drystan's helmet in her pack.

As they convened in the sitting room before dinner, Galdinia noticed that most of the others appeared to have bathed as well, something they didn't have the luxury of on the journey, aside from access to a bucket of water and a dense horsehair scrubbing brush.

Kayd—yawning and still wearing his armour—was the last to emerge from his quarters, and that was only after his cousin thumped on his door, demanding he hurry up.

"What's all the racket for?" Kayd asked, rubbing his eyes.

"It's time to go to dinner," Raia said, scrunching up her nose as she looked at Kayd. "Did you fall asleep?"

"I rested my eyes, just for a few minutes," Kayd said sluggishly. "Let me take my armour off. I'll be right back."

Kayd turned from the room and shut his door behind him.

Looking around the room, Galdinia realised that Quill was still missing.

"Has anyone seen Quill?" she asked.

"My guess is that he probably has his own quarters," Ilyon said, arms firmly crossed over his chest. "And by the looks of it, he had some catching up to do with old friends."

Galdinia wondered again who he had reunited with earlier—who had caused such a sour young man to suddenly become so bright and friendly? She couldn't help but again question his reason for professing his hatred for her a few nights prior. Beyond his rude demeanour, something about it didn't sit well with Galdinia; what had she done in such a short reign to anger him so?

"May I make a request?" Bentley's voice came from across the room where he stood beside Evander. Galdinia had barely spoken to him since their conversation in the cave, so engrossed by her apprehension about their arrival in Lund. Hearing his voice caught her off guard.

By way of reply, Ilyon raised his eyebrows.

"Orlon made it fairly clear I shouldn't be walking around with these on," Bentley said, shaking his hands and shackles in the air. "I think I've well and truly proven to you that I'm not a threat. If I wanted to hurt any of you, I wouldn't do it in a cave in the depths of some of the deadliest terrain, surrounded by a population of people that are likely already wary of our presence."

Galdinia could sense her shields lowering, her animosity towards Bentley slowly dampening. Was this due to his seemingly genuine concern for her life or the Peacelight that surrounded them? She reminded herself that he managed to win her over once, and she wouldn't be made a fool by his lies again. Galdinia and Ilyon shared a look before turning back to Bentley, unconvinced.

"And I don't think you need anything else to mar your reputation around here, Your Highness." Galdinia could tell Bentley was being very precise in his words. "I don't want to be a reason for the leaders not to trust you."

Galdinia let Bentley's words hang in the air before them. Bentley was right; she desperately needed to make a good impression tomorrow, and being seen with a prisoner by the rest of the population wasn't going to help her cause.

"I'll put the chains on the second we return," he said, still holding his hands out in front of him, almost pleading.

"Unlock him," Galdinia finally said, causing Ilyon to look at her again for confirmation. "He's right. We don't need anything else to hinder my meeting tomorrow."

At this, Ilyon nodded and unlocked Bentley's shackles. He rubbed his wrists as the chains came off. Galdinia could see red indents around his wrists from where the metal had been pressing into his skin.

"Vega," Galdinia said, not taking her eyes off Bentley. "If you suspect any foul play, I don't want you to hesitate in using your blades, okay?"

Bentley's expression dropped as he looked from Galdinia to Vega. Galdinia followed his gaze and saw something she hadn't before: Vega was smiling. She was leaning against the mantel of the fireplace, her long braids falling over her shoulders, one hand on the hilt of a dagger strapped to her thigh.

"With pleasure," Vega replied.

Moments later, Kayd re-entered the sitting room, having changed out of his armour and into his fighting leathers and a long cloak.

"I'm ready," he said, a triumphant smile on his face.

"Finally," Raia replied, walking to the door. "Shall we?"

The group walked down the long tunnel and followed Orlon's

directions—and their noses—to the dining quarters. The closer they got, the louder the sound of clattering cutlery, hearty laughter, and exuberant conversation became. Stepping out of the passageway, they found themselves in a sprawling cavern with curved ceilings and lanterns of Peacelight hanging around the walls. The room was full of rectangular tables that ran across the room. Most of the tables were full as people ate their dinner and chatted amongst themselves.

Seeing the arrival of the group, Orlon turned from a table of people he was speaking to and approached Galdinia.

"I'm glad you found us," Orlon said, coming to them.

"It was hard to miss," Galdinia said, looking across the room at the many hundreds of people eating there. A few people in their periphery had caught glances of the queen—some wore expressions of surprise, while others looked confused and hurt by her presence.

"Follow me," Orlon said, walking into the room. "I've saved you a table."

As Galdinia followed Orlon, more faces turned to inspect them, their conversations pausing mid-sentence, forks of food hanging before open mouths.

"I thought that by going without my crown this evening, we might attract less attention," Galdinia said to Orlon, trying to avoid the eyes of those who didn't seem too pleased to see her.

"You don't need a crown when you are surrounded by soldiers such as yours," Orlon said with a wry smile, stopping at an empty table towards the centre of the room.

"No, I suppose not," Galdinia said, looking around at her not-so-subtle companions, glad they'd made the decision to remove Bentley's chains.

"But you're also unfamiliar faces—we all know each other too well," Orlon said before motioning to one of the benches along the table. "Take a seat."

Galdinia, Neryda, Kayd, and Vega sat on one side of the table, and Ilyon, Evander, Raia, and Bentley sat on the other. Orlon took his seat at the head of the table. Before them sat a spread of dishes from baked potatoes to pork, to steamed greens and fresh bread. Galdinia could feel herself salivating at the mere sight of the food—she had seen one too many roasted squirrels in their travels and was ready to dig into a hearty meal.

"Who prepares the food for everyone?" Galdinia asked, managing to tear her eyes from the feast before her to address Orlon.

"As I said before, we share resources here," Orlon replied. "Everyone brings a plate of food to our meals to share. We made a little extra for you all this evening."

"Thank you," Galdinia said, genuine gratitude in her words.

She started to question why she had felt so nervous about arriving in Lund. Aside from a few cursory glances and curious expressions, these people had been nothing but welcoming since they arrived and had not turned her away like she had suspected. Just a few weeks ago, they were fighting in her city's streets, so the fact that Orlon was having a meal with them spoke volumes to Galdinia.

"You're most welcome," Orlon said. "Dig in."

Without need for further invitation, the group loaded up their plates and ate their first substantial meal in a week.

"This is a far cry from the squirrel meat and berries we've been eating," Kayd said, shovelling a mouthful of potato into his mouth.

"Didn't we warn you not to comment on the meals if you didn't cook them?" Raia asked, glaring at Kayd from across the table.

"I'm simply too satisfied right now to care, Raia," Kayd retorted, taking another bite of his dinner, eyes misty in the euphoria of the meal.

As they continued to bicker, Galdinia noticed the empty chair at the other end of the table. She wondered if this was reserved for Quill.

"Excuse me, Orlon," Galdinia asked quietly, reluctantly putting down her cutlery. "Do you know where Quill got to this afternoon? We haven't seen him since we arrived."

With a nod, Orlon pointed to a table not far from their own. There, Quill sat surrounded by people, including the two men he had reunited with earlier. They were all talking jovially, laughing and sharing stories as they ate. Again, Quill looked like an entirely different person; the chill that had surrounded him seemed to have evaporated, and he now emanated a warmth Galdinia could not have ever imagined seeing.

"He is a beloved friend here," Orlon explained as Galdinia watched Quill. "He has been visiting us since he was a young boy. He grew up with our children and would visit for weeks on end a few times a year. He even organised provisions for us during some harder times. Some years back, we had a particularly nasty winter, and the snow was so dense that we couldn't leave Lund to hunt or forage for over a month. Quill brought a battalion all the way from The Hook to dig out the snow. It took them a week to make their way through it."

"Quill was digging as well?" Galdinia asked, struggling to imagine Quill doing hard labour.

"Of course," Orlon replied. "He was the first one with a shovel in his hands."

"He's quite the ally," Galdinia said, still watching Quill. "And who are those two men who greeted him earlier? He seems quite close with them."

Orlon paused, also observing Quill as he smiled at his companions, revelling in their company.

"That's Phyl and Hartley," Orlon said, his voice turning grave. "They adopted their son, Kove, when he was just a baby. Kove is actually Hartley's nephew, but his sister died in childbirth, and Kove's birth father was a man from outside the mountains whose name she never knew. Hartley and Phyl loved him like their own, and he was Quill's best friend. They were inseparable whenever he visited and they practically grew up together, even though they lived so far apart."

"He *was* Quill's best friend?" Galdinia asked, glancing back to Orlon.

"Kove fought in the battle in Elderguard," Orlon said, and Galdinia's heart sank deep within her chest—no amount of Peacelight could have protected her against what Orlon said next. "Hartley and Phyl tried to convince him not to fight, but Kove was headstrong; once he made his mind up on something, there wasn't any stopping him. He left with our army, but he didn't arrive home with the surviving soldiers. Hartley and Phyl were devastated, absolutely shattered. We wrote to Quill as soon as we found out. His mother replied to our correspondence that Quill refused to speak to anyone but would be visiting us when he was ready."

Galdinia glanced back at Quill, her heart aching. While he seemed happy now, Galdinia could only imagine the tears that he had shared with Kove's fathers when he arrived—when he arrived with not only the queen, but with the Captain of the Royal Guard and soldiers who were possibly the cause of their son's death. Suddenly, Quill's hostility and stony exterior came into focus.

"That's devastating" was all Galdinia could say.

"We weren't expecting him to visit so soon after the battle. When we received word that he was coming, I know Phyl and Hartley were relieved."

"I see," Galdinia said with a short nod.

"Quill is like their second son," Orlon said sadly, also watching Quill with his friends. "I know it's a relief having him here with them."

"I'm sure it is," Galdinia said, looking back down at her plate, no longer able to watch the people who had been so personally hurt by the battle.

Galdinia did not speak much for the remainder of the meal. If the Peacelight around the room was calming her heart, she didn't want to know how she would have felt without its power. Her shoulders were heavy, and any hunger she'd felt disappeared in an instant.

She wondered if Quill had ever intended on telling her about Kove. Perhaps that was expecting too much of the situation. As she thought back on their interactions—from their first meeting in The Hook, to his incredulity at the thought of accompanying them to Lund, to his brash disregard for her safety—everything seemed to fall into place. Of course he despised the person who led the troops to kill soldiers from Lund, including his best friend. Except she hadn't. Had she been in Elderguard before the battle broke out, she may have called for a ceasefire when she saw the soldiers from Lund. Galdinia could have taken on Valah head-on and alone. Perhaps then Kove wouldn't have lost his life. Perhaps then she wouldn't have lost Drystan.

"We shall meet with you in the morning, Galdinia," Orlon said, standing to his feet once his plate was empty. "I have to speak with a few of the elders this evening."

"Of course," Galdinia said, pulling herself from her contemplative daze.

"The elders' quarters are across the square from here," Orlon explained. "We will meet you there after breakfast."

"Thank you," Galdinia said simply, still somewhat lost for words. "Oh, Orlon?"

"Yes?" he asked, turning to look back at Galdinia.

"Do you think Phyl and Hartley would accept a gift from the crown?" The words were tumbling from Galdinia's mouth faster than she could organise them. "I know it wouldn't make up for the loss of their son, but I'd like to be able to do something to help support them."

Orlon paused and glanced around the room before speaking.

"Everyone in this room lost someone during the battle," he explained. "It may have been a child, a parent, a friend, a spouse, or a neighbour. If one person from Lund is hurt, we all hurt."

Galdinia cast her eyes down, feeling suddenly foolish for making the suggestion; of course these two men weren't the only ones who suffered irreparable damage at the hands of her soldiers. She felt like a child who was offering their favourite toy to a wounded patient as a means for relief.

"It is a thoughtful gesture, and I'm sure they would be grateful for it," Orlon continued, "but you should know that we are all feeling the pain of the aftermath of that conflict."

With these words, Orlon smiled sympathetically, then turned from the table, through the crowd, and out of view.

Galdinia turned back to her plate, still half full of the warm, comforting food. She couldn't stomach another mouthful.

25

COME MORNING, GALDINIA STILL COULDN'T ESCAPE THE FEELING OF guilt and dread that had settled in her stomach.

She had spent much of the night tossing and turning, unable to escape the watchful eyes of those who surrounded her in the dining hall the night before. In her dreams, she was visited by apparitions of Phyl and Hartley, as well as their son, who appeared to her as a faceless fallen soldier. His parents cried out, surrounded by their people, and they all stared at her as though she was their enemy.

I am their enemy, she thought as she woke up for the last time in the early moments of the morning. *At least to some of them.*

Galdinia had convinced herself that the elders wouldn't have accepted her through the tunnel yesterday if she was considered an enemy by the majority. There were some people who must still believe in her, or at the very least, be curious enough to hear why she had travelled so far to meet with them. Given the heartache in Orlon's words as he described the loss of Kove, Galdinia could only imagine what some of these people thought of her and her soldiers.

Not only had her anxious thoughts robbed her of sleep, but they had also tightened in her stomach, rendering the thought of eating inconceivable. Or was she just afraid of the watchful eyes that would follow her once in the sprawling dining quarters? Regardless,

Galdinia skipped breakfast, assuring her captain and best friend that she wasn't ill and wanted more time to prepare for the meeting. In actuality, she lay still on her bed, staring up at the rocky ceiling, listening to the crackling fire in the hearth that she had stoked in the middle of the night. The only relief she felt was when she drew a ball of fire into the palm of her hand, swirling it around and around.

An hour later, Galdinia's troop returned from breakfast, and she was forced to peel herself from her bed. She had retrieved her crown from her pack and secured it to her head before stepping out into the sitting room, the ball of fire still in her hand.

"Are you ready, Your Highness?" Ilyon asked, standing by the door to the long tunnels. They had decided the evening before that only he and Galdinia would attend the meeting. This was not a time that she felt she needed to make the strength of her group known to their hosts.

Galdinia couldn't speak, but she forced a nod. Without another word from her captain, they walked out into the tunnel.

They arrived at the room Orlon had indicated, stepping into the cavernous space, which appeared to be simply—yet extraordinarily— just that: a cave. The ceiling stretched far above them and was glistening with shards of starlight crystals, giving the room a luminescent glow. Hundreds if not thousands of stalactites hung from the ceiling, looming above them, as though waiting to crash down on unsuspecting entrants. Galdinia had never seen so many starlight crystals before, and the value of this room alone would rival her wealth as queen. She thought that if she could snap even just a handful from the stalactites and deliver it to The Hook, that would suffice as compensation to the Lidels.

In her awe, Galdinia momentarily forgot about the fear and guilt that was weighing her down, mesmerised by the space.

Down the centre of the cavern, carved out of the same rock of the mountain, was a great slab of a table, its base curving down towards the ground. There were about fifteen individuals at the table who were already seated, their eyes falling on Galdinia as she and her captain walked into the room.

"Galdinia and Ilyon," Orlon said from the head of the table, still standing, his arms outstretched. "The elders of Lund, the Protectors of the Mountain, welcome you."

Galdinia looked around the group, recognising them as their apprehensive welcoming party from the day before. Many of their expressions suggested they didn't agree with Orlon in his greeting, and despite the apprehension she felt, Galdinia attempted to speak through the nerves.

"I appreciate you all taking the time to meet with me," Galdinia replied, taking the seat at the other end of the table, Ilyon sitting to her right, leaving a spare chair to her left. "I know it's unusual for those of Lund to meet with the crown, so I do not take this lightly."

At that moment, footsteps came from the door of the cave, and Galdinia turned to see Quill walk into the room. Without a word or glance in her direction, he took the final empty seat beside her.

Why is he here?

"Thank you for joining us this morning, Quill," Orlon said with a smile, which was returned in like. "You are right, Galdinia. We do not make contact with the world outside our mountains regularly. However, we trust our friends, the Lidels, so if Quill believes this conversation to be worth our while, then you have our attention." With this, Orlon took his seat. Galdinia watched Quill's jaw tighten, though he still did not acknowledge her. "When you're ready, Galdinia."

At Orlon's encouragement, Galdinia took in a deep breath, smiling at its peak before starting the speech she had rehearsed for much of her sleepless night.

"I have three things I'd like to say. Firstly, I'm sorry for your losses at the hands of my soldiers in Elderguard." With these words, the eyes of those around her either sharpened or became downcast. Galdinia avoided looking at Quill as she went on. "Our home was under attack, and my soldiers had to do what was necessary to protect it. We were surprised to see your soldiers, so you must understand that just as you are sceptical of me, I, too, am sceptical of you." Galdinia sat as tall as she could in her chair, feeling the weight of her crown like never before. "Regardless of this, we both lost soldiers, and I am deeply sorry to have caused your people pain.

"Secondly, I hope to know the answer to a very important question." At this, every face turned to Galdinia, whether intrigued, angered, or otherwise. "When I say that we were surprised to see you fighting alongside Valah, I mean it. The people of Lund have been nothing but peaceful with the rest of Crysterra, so I could hardly believe my eyes when I saw your soldiers in Elderguard, fighting in the heart of my home. I know just how manipulative Valah can be, so my question for you is: why did you fight for her?"

For the first time in days, Quill looked at Galdinia. His eyes were full of warning. She didn't attempt to decipher his silent message, so she tried to ignore him, looking ahead at Orlon instead.

"To insinuate that we were manipulated by Valah is rather insulting, Galdinia," Orlon said, his tone still pleasant.

"My apologies," Galdinia said quickly, not realising the implications of what she had said. "I didn't mean—"

"We both know the treacherous nature of Valah Pyrin," Orlon went on, disregarding her. "She makes promises, which she promptly breaks. However, our involvement in that battle was based on far more than empty promises."

Galdinia thought it wise to keep her lips sealed.

"Soon after your father's sickness was announced, we were approached by one of her advisors, asking us if we wanted to rejoin Crysterra under a new ruler. We were warned that after the death of the king, there would be an outbreak of conflict, given the lack of a legitimate heir." Galdinia bit her tongue against a reaction; for all his pleasantries, Galdinia was starting to understand Orlon's strong and unapologetic nature. "Of course, we have no interest in leaving the mountains; our people have lived here for four hundred years, and we don't plan on leaving anytime soon. However, we were presented with an interesting proposition: under the new rule of Valah, the Starlight Mountains would be made an official province of Crysterra, and my wife and I would become governor and governess."

"If all you wanted was to be recognised as a province, I'm sure my father would have happily agreed to that. In fact, I'd be more than willing to organise that myself."

Orlon paused before replying. "Galdinia, when do you think was the last time I spoke to your father?"

Galdinia looked at Orlon, hesitant.

"I don't know," Galdinia admitted. "Prior to his death, he hadn't mentioned a visit to Lund recently."

"Exactly." Orlon was greeted with knowing expressions around the table. "I never had the pleasure of meeting your father, nor your grandparents. No one at this table has ever been addressed by a reigning monarch of Crysterra."

Given their intentionally reclusive nature, Galdinia couldn't say she was surprised that her father never made contact with them, though she was sure he would have tried. The fact that no other crowned ruler had met with them in many centuries, however, was unexpected. She looked to Ilyon, who appeared to be holding himself back from speaking.

"It wasn't until one of Valah's advisors shared with us the plans for a Pyrin rule that we even considered becoming a province," Orlon went on. "A ruler has never found any interest in us, the meek and private group in the mountains. So when Valah's advisor proposed a new option, we were intrigued. While we understood that this would mean we would have to recognise whoever was on the throne as ruler, and taxes would need to be paid, it would allow for more trade routes, something we have questioned opening ourselves for some time. We also sought the protection of the crown."

"Elderwins have always protected their people—"

"But we have not been *your* people for centuries," Orlon said, cutting Galdinia off again. "Valah sought us out, she agreed to our terms, and we aligned ourselves with her. She did not manipulate us, no." Orlon's voice became grave as his usually pleasant expression dropped. "She simply lied to us."

Galdinia briefly tore her gaze from Orlon to look at the growing frustration in the expressions of those around her.

"Upon arrival at the Bear Jaws Valley, we were instructed to lead the charge through the Northern Gates, as we were promised that Valah's forces were already within the castle and we had to make a way to move through the capital. We were promised that we were simply entering the aftermath of a battle; this was not true. We were faced with arrows and blades ready to cut us down. We were contending with the elements: tornados of wind, walls of water, and spears of fire." Galdinia felt the familiar guilt clench tight at her heart

—she herself had flourished such weapons. "We were nothing but her battering ram."

"I'm so sorry for your losses," Galdinia whispered. Valah had made the Lund soldiers Galdinia's enemy and Galdinia theirs. If anyone had been manipulated, it was her.

"We were even put in a position where we had to demonstrate our Light Lender abilities." At this, all the shards of starlight crystal that were embedded in the walls and ceiling began to glisten. The sight was beautiful, magnificent even. Galdinia had to remind herself that such a breathtaking gift was used to disorient and blind her soldiers just weeks prior. "As soon as we realised we were fighting a losing battle, we fled to the Royal Wood. I tried to corral our people before any more of your soldiers senselessly killed them."

"You must realise we were trying to protect our city," Ilyon interjected, his voice low but firm. "You killed our people, just as we killed yours."

Ilyon put a voice to the argument that was running through Galdinia's mind. She didn't feel it prudent, however, that she be the one to say it, particularly given the request she would soon be presenting to these people.

"But to be held captive in your city walls after we had retreated, weapons to my soldiers' throats..." Orlon trailed off. "That seems senseless."

"It sounds like my soldiers have been trained well," Ilyon countered. "I have taught my soldiers to take prisoners where possible. We only spill blood when necessary. Fighting was not a necessity so you could claim your province status."

"That may have been our mistake then, but like I said, we had never been approached by an Elderwin before," Orlon went on, the heat in his voice subsiding as he turned his attention back to Galdinia. "I was merely proposed an alternative with the knowledge of a dying king and an inevitable change in the ruling family."

"It would seem the latter didn't eventuate," Galdinia said, sitting up tall again, trying to ignore the ache in her chest.

"Evidently," Orlon replied. "And thus, here we are now. To answer your question, Galdinia, that is how we came to fight alongside Valah."

Every time Orlon failed to call her by her title, Galdinia's fingers clenched around the small concealed flame in her lap. She had gone so long being told she wouldn't be queen; she didn't need to be belittled now that the crown was finally on her head.

"You said there were three things you wanted to speak with us about?" Orlon questioned. "Surely you didn't come all this way just to apologise and ask us why we held an alliance with Valah."

"Yes," Galdinia said, trying to maintain a sense of authority; the only problem was that the majority of the people in this room did not recognise her as a figure worthy of such authority. "After the attack, Valah took one of our soldiers hostage. She has demanded my crown in exchange for his life. Crown or no crown, we don't expect her to go down without a fight. Given the damage done to our army in the battle, we are in need of more allies. We have a provisional agreement with the Lidels, but our forces must be stronger before we engage with Valah."

"And you would like us to fight with you?" Orlon asked, his tone dubious.

"Yes, that's what I'm asking."

Galdinia did not expect what came next: a hearty laugh from Orlon and his companions. The sound reverberated around the cavern, and the echoes mocked her. Galdinia winced against the sound before quickly composing her expression.

"I understand that Valah burnt you with a similar proposition," Galdinia said, raising her voice over the dying laughter. "But I can give you all that she promised, and more, before I leave this table."

Orlon now stood to his feet, his face mirroring the tone of his cynical laughter. Up until this point, he had been reasonably amiable, if not a little guarded, with Galdinia. Now something new seemed to be making itself known.

"Four hundred years ago, our ancestors fled in the wake of a savage battle that led to Pyrin power. Our ancestors were not respected then, so they fortified their new territory." Orlon motioned with his hands to the cave and the people around him. "We have kept our home safe from thoughtless, bloodthirsty leaders ever since. The only contact we have maintained with Crysterra is with our friends in The Hook, who we have had ties with since our ancestors first made their home in the mountains. It wasn't until Valah's advisor made contact with us that we even considered broaching the outside world. Crysterra has never done anything for us, and we haven't done anything for it. That is how we have lived so peacefully for so long.

"When Valah suggested a treaty, we were open to a new way into the future. We thought we had outlived the fear and concerns our ancestors had held. We were ready for the next season for our society. The moment Valah betrayed us by sending us into a heated battle, she demonstrated the true colours that many rulers of the past have: a desire for power that is only fuelled by selfish ambition. We will not fall into that trap again."

"I would never treat you and your people the way Valah did," Galdinia said, her voice low, her gaze firm.

"Perhaps not intentionally," Orlon said, his voice confident. "You will always put your soldiers first, your crown first. If our soldiers were fighting alongside each other, you would protect the Royal Guard before you protected us, even if we were sworn allies."

"I would fight to keep you all alive—"

"I know you think you would," Orlon said, cutting her off, "but you still see us as separate from—perhaps even less important than—your people. This is because we are not truly your people, and we haven't been for hundreds of years."

Galdinia and Orlon watched each other carefully for a few arduous moments.

"If we enter in a conflict with Valah—which feels inevitable—and if she is victorious over us, you risk almost certain death." Galdinia's tone was one of warning. "She will do away with anyone who doesn't align with her. That will include you and your people."

"But if we align with you, we will simply be used to fight someone else's battle yet again. We'd much rather fight on our own terms." Orlon paused before adding, "We have no interest in becoming allies with you or anyone who seeks absolute power, so we will not fight alongside you."

"You must understand, I am nothing like Valah," Galdinia said, a hint of desperation coating her voice. "I don't seek the same power she does."

"But you do," Orlon said, his eyes flicking up to her crown. "You both wish to wear that crown on your head. You both wish to sit on the throne in Elderguard. You both wish to lord over this country, ultimately for your own benefit."

"I wish to serve our country, bringing peace across the provinces. Without my title, there is very little I can do." Galdinia's voice was starting to rise, the pain in her chest fuelling her words. It seemed to reach a dull ceiling, though; the Peacelight quietened her emotions.

"Well, while protecting your crown remains your priority instead of your people, you will not be able to call us allies." Orlon's words were firm and final. "As I said, we will not make the mistake of aligning ourselves with anyone who seeks absolute power. That is the way of fools."

"So we are at an impasse."

"It would seem so."

Galdinia continued to stare at Orlon, aware of the many pairs of eyes that were now staring at her. If she didn't have the support of Lund, she didn't know how she would ever protect Crysterra from Valah. Or rescue Drystan.

"Imagine if you were in my position." Galdinia now spoke to everyone at the table. "Imagine you were given the task of protecting your country, your home, from your greatest enemy, someone who has proven they will demolish anyone who doesn't serve their own agenda. Imagine if you were willing to approach a group who had attacked your home mere weeks prior, putting your own grievances aside because you wanted what was best for your country." Galdinia could feel a heat rising in her cheeks. "If Valah takes the throne, you can say goodbye to your haven in the mountains, to your families, to your lives. Yes, I am trying to hold on to my crown, but only so I can protect the lives of everyone in my country from a deadly enemy.

"Accepting the title of Queen of Crysterra was not a frivolous reach for power—it came with a weighty responsibility that tormented me long before I received my gift. I fought not only with myself but with the Gods to end up in this position today. I would do anything to protect my people, including donning a crown that holds not only power, but contention, authority, and a way forward for unity. The safety of my people was, and always will be, my priority."

Galdinia's voice echoed, and she caught some of the elders

glancing at each other, seemingly considering her words. Even Quill looked sideways at her, a watchful expression on his face.

"You and I are trying to achieve the same outcome," Orlon replied, his voice low and slow. "However, risking the lives of our people to serve someone who seeks a crown of gold and crystals is not how we choose to achieve it." Orlon's voice echoed through the cavern. "For that reason, you will not have the support of Lund's forces."

Galdinia breathed in deeply against the surging throb in her chest. She had to accept defeat.

"Then I cannot guarantee the Royal Guard will protect Lund in light of an attack."

"We can protect ourselves," Orlon said, his tone pleasant and even once again. "We went four hundred years without being involved in a Crysterra conflict, and we will not be repeating the events in Elderguard."

"Nor will I," Galdinia said, ready to leave this futile conversation.

"You and your guards are welcome to lodge in our home for another night," Orlon said, "but that will be the extent of our hospitality."

"We will leave at daybreak tomorrow." Galdinia's words were clipped. "Thank you for your time."

As she spoke, Galdinia stood up and turned from the table, briefly facing Ilyon; he looked solemn, yet stolid. Without bothering to glance back at Orlon or Quill, Galdinia began to walk towards the mouth of the cavern, her captain by her side and flame in her hand.

26

WHILE SHE'D NOT KNOWN HER QUEEN'S GUARD FOR LONG, GALDINIA knew that the moment she walked away from Ilyon, Vega was near.

After leaving the meeting, she marched towards the entrance to Lund, muttering to her captain that she wanted to be left alone and would return shortly, insisting he leave her be. Galdinia didn't turn to see him stop but heard his footsteps halt near the tunnel entrance. She knew, however, that Ilyon would have sent Vega on Galdinia's tail immediately—Vega was quick, quiet, and inconspicuous, and her captain wouldn't simply let the queen wander off into unknown mountains alone. And so, as she rushed through the tunnel, past the guards—who looked at her warily—and was out facing the mountains and the road they had travelled to arrive at her doomed destination, Galdinia knew Vega was somewhere nearby, hiding in the shadows of the tunnel.

Now far enough away from the flood of Peacelight, a rumbling frustration rose in Galdinia, making her cheeks hot and her head swim with the echoes of Orlon's condescending words. Needing to get further away from Lund's entrance, Galdinia found a path that led up into the mountains, which she started to climb awkwardly, her feet slipping on stones, her boots scuffing on the dirt track.

Galdinia didn't know how long she had been climbing when she finally reached a point she could no longer traverse, the steep inclines and rocky terrain blocking her way ahead. Finally, she paused and turned to face the direction she had come.

From her vantage point, she looked out over the Starlight Mountains and was struck by their beauty. Down to her right she could see the edges of Lund encased by this wall of mountains. To her left were sharp cliff faces where the mountains continued to rise. All around her in every other direction were mountaintops glistening in the sunlight. She hadn't realised just how high they had climbed in their travels over the previous days, but from this spot, she was baffled by it. The air was rare and brought with it a sharp chill, which helped to clear the tightening pain deep in her body.

Inhaling a long, cold breath, Galdinia closed her eyes.

What am I doing? she asked herself, reliving the conversation with Orlon over and over again. Orlon's words rang through her mind: *absolute power*.

He thought all she wanted was power for power's sake—power for her own gain. He didn't understand that she was different from Valah. She wasn't selfish like Valah; she wanted nothing more than to give Crysterra a future of prosperity and life, not one of subjugation, which would surely come with a Pyrin rule.

However, yet again, she was looked down upon by the very people she wanted to save.

They don't know you.

Galdinia's eyes flew open.

She didn't know if the voice had come from her own mind or elsewhere, but she looked around and couldn't see another person in her vicinity on this lone section of mountain. How close was Vega? Were there soldiers from Lund on the lookout? Possibly. But after scanning the area and finding no one, she couldn't place the voice anywhere.

Cautiously, Galdinia closed her eyes, and once again, the words came to her: *they don't know you.*

How could they possibly know her, though? They weren't giving her a chance to show them who she truly was or to prove herself as queen.

Give them the chance to.

Galdinia pushed this thought—these words—aside briskly. Instead of seeing her crown as proof of her goodness and worthiness, they saw it as a barrier to trust. Surely travelling all this way to meet with them after they attacked her people was enough proof of who she was.

They don't know you.

Irritated now by these words, Galdinia responded aloud, "I know that! That's the problem!"

Her voice echoed around her, each word reverberating off the mountains and returning to her in a collision of pain and exasperation.

And then there was silence.

Galdinia gritted her teeth, searching to calm her heart and her mind. After a few more breaths, though, the words found her again.

You need to show them why you are worthy of the crown.

These words made her throat thick and caused tears to start springing beneath her lashes. Had she not already done that? Had the Gods not proven her worthy to all of Crysterra with her gift? Did she not make the choice to decline the easy path and instead take up the mantle of queen simply so she could save these people from tyranny?

She recalled the days spent training and seeking answers after her father's death, searching desperately for her gift, as though it were something to be found instead of something that was to be bestowed upon her. She had told herself countless times that she needed to prove herself, and she didn't think she could possibly try to do that again.

"I've already done that." Galdinia whispered the words, her tears restraining her voice.

She had already proven herself worthy to the Gods, and wasn't their opinion paramount? What more could she possibly do to make these people believe that she was worthy of following, worthy of fighting alongside?

A crown is one thing; your actions are another.

What more could she have done? She had spent days travelling across Crysterra with someone who despised her, leading her to meet with people who disparaged the crown on her head and had tried to attack her home. It seemed nearly impossible to prove her merit in any other way.

"I need them to understand who I am as a queen," Galdinia whispered between tears, her voice shaky.

These people were possibly her last chance to not only keep her crown and her life, but also to save Drystan. She didn't know how she could possibly do anything without their support.

They need to understand who you are as Galdinia.

These words hit her ribcage, wrapped around her heart, and lingered there, deep within her chest.

When they were in The Hook, Galdinia spoke to Raia about her distaste for those closest to her calling her by her title. Not only did it keep a barrier between them, but it alienated Galdinia, making her feel like she was somehow more important than anyone else. And yet, she so desperately wanted these people she sought to be her allies to call her queen, and when they didn't, she felt dismayed and belittled.

They need to understand who you are as Galdinia.

Galdinia remembered how much pleasure she took in hearing Bael use her title; it was proof that despite his grudge, he had to recognise her as queen. By his own admission—his own words—he had to lift her up higher above him. And for some reason that brought Galdinia a sense of triumph. On the other hand, Bael's eldest son went out of his way to disrespect her, which angered Galdinia more than she could articulate. He thought of her as some autocratic queen who didn't care about the pain of her people. Similar to Lund's elders, he thought she was selfish.

They need to understand who you are as Galdinia.

But who really knew her? Who really knew the kind of queen she was? They were the people who she had allowed to see her true self— not as princess or as queen but as Galdinia. They were the people she didn't place herself any higher than; the people she chose to surround herself with and trusted with her life. They needed to see and know that version of her.

They need to understand who you are as Galdinia.

Galdinia opened her eyes once again and peered around her. She wasn't sure how long her eyes had been closed, but the shadows of the mountains had shifted considerably in the morning sun. She looked around at her surroundings and saw something shift to her right, beyond a stretch of rock beside the path she had taken.

"Vega?" Galdinia questioned, calling out with a hoarse voice.

After a moment, Vega stepped around the rock face and approached Galdinia.

"The captain asked me to shadow you," she said gently, crouching down beside Galdinia.

"That doesn't surprise me," Galdinia said, wiping a stray tear from her cheek.

After a few moments of silence, Vega finally said, "Are you okay, Your Highness?"

Other than Ilyon, Vega was the only member of the Queen's Guard who hadn't given up the formal titles. Galdinia knew Ilyon did it out of pure respect—he was also one of the most stubborn people she knew, and she didn't think she could change his mind without a direct order. Forcing him to call her by her first name would make him highly uncomfortable, and Galdinia had no interest in doing that to someone she respected so highly herself. It seemed that Vega felt much the same. Neither of them used her title to try to prove something to Galdinia; they simply did it because they knew how hard she had worked to obtain the title and it would be remiss of them not to. Galdinia wondered if Vega had her own journey with searching for her gift and therefore understood the pain and torment behind waiting for one.

"I'm okay," Galdinia said after a long exhale. "A bit battered, but otherwise fine. I assume Ilyon told you about the meeting?"

"The captain didn't say anything, though I could tell by his tone that he was displeased."

"You can decipher his tone?" Galdinia asked, quietly impressed. Ilyon wasn't known for being particularly expressive, and so his tone was often of one note: flat.

"You learn to understand the meaning behind every inflection and every cadence of the voice of the person who is often trying to keep you alive. There's a big difference between a 'go' that means 'hurry' and one that means 'leave'."

"I can imagine that's helpful."

"Very." Vega paused before continuing. "I'm sorry that the meeting didn't go as you had hoped."

Galdinia sucked in a breath and cast her eyes to the mountains before her. "If I'm honest, I'm not entirely sure what I was hoping for, and I certainly have no idea where to go from here."

"If I may, Your Highness, hasn't that been the way for this entire trip?"

Galdinia turned to look at Vega, eyebrows raised. "Meaning what, exactly?"

"You travelled to The Hook seeking an alliance that you weren't positive you'd secure. You seemed ready to turn around and return to Elderguard if you had to, but you managed to align with the Lidels, if tentatively and with caveats. You then came here, unsure of what the outcome would be but determined in your next step forward."

"That's as far as I've come, though," Galdinia said. "There is no plan after this."

"Of course there is."

"Would you care to enlighten me?"

"You know what you're working towards. As much as the captain may like to keep you as far away from Valah as possible, I think we all know he'd be fighting a losing battle trying to convince you otherwise. Your end goal has always been Valah; that hasn't changed."

"But I can't face her without first growing my forces," Galdinia replied. "That would be like stepping into a lion's den unarmed."

"So what are your options then?" Vega questioned. "You can go back to Elderguard now and sit there, waiting. She would eventually come to you, and you could fight her on your home soil again."

"I hope there's an alternative to that option."

"Or you can approach her and her army with the forces you have, knowing that you're meant to be queen, and hope for the best."

"Hope for the best?" Galdinia was surprised by Vega's unusually informal manner of speaking. In fact, she didn't think she'd heard Vega utter as many words in the days since she'd known her as she had in the previous two minutes.

"You were made queen by the Gods, Your Highness. That wasn't an accident, and it certainly wasn't a mistake. If you want to take back what's yours, you may have to take it by any means possible."

Galdinia's thoughts trailed to Drystan again. Although he represented so much more than himself—he was every person Galdinia wanted to keep from Valah's torment—she knew that so much of her heart was at the end of this struggle against her enemy.

"But it may all be futile," Galdinia said softly.

"It could be. We may all die trying," Vega said, her voice calm as she looked across the mountains, her eyes trailing over the peaks and valleys. "But if a battle with Valah is inevitable, why not do it on your own terms? Show her who you truly are, not as queen but as Galdinia."

Galdinia's eyes narrowed on Vega, her words echoing the ones she had heard earlier in the depths of her prayers and pains. "What did you say?"

"You're not the only one the Gods have been speaking to while up here." Vega's lips quirked up in a knowing smirk.

Galdinia returned the expression, and the two shared a quiet moment on the mountaintop.

If she was to prove to her hopeful allies—and enemies—that she was worthy of the crown and title she'd been given, she couldn't spend another second questioning herself.

"Shall we, then?" Vega asked, gesturing to the steep path beside them.

With a nod, Galdinia stood up and started to traverse down the mountainside again, Vega by her side.

27

ONCE SHE'D ARRIVED BACK WITHIN THE WALLS OF LUND AND WAS again feeling the effects of Peacelight, Galdinia approached Ilyon, who was pacing in front of the fountain, awaiting her return. With his hands behind his back and a permanent crease set into his brow, he looked up. A shadow of relief rested on his features as he watched Galdinia and Vega approach him.

"Your Highness," Ilyon said, ceasing in his pacing.

"Sorry, Captain," Galdinia said quickly. "I just needed some time to collect my thoughts."

"I'm glad you took the time, but I'm also glad you're back," Ilyon replied. "We must forge forward with another plan."

"Other than hoping for some miracle of persuasion, I haven't assembled a plan... yet."

"The elders don't seem inclined to budge, do they?" Ilyon asked, watching Galdinia closely.

"I would venture to say they are more stubborn than the Lidels."

"That they are." An irritable voice sounded from behind Galdinia.

She turned to face Quill, arms folded over his chest, his eyes reflective of his words.

She knew she was going to pay for that remark in an avalanche of scowls and snarky comments.

Ignoring Galdinia, Quill turned to Ilyon.

"Nothing can be done," Quill said simply.

"Nothing?" Ilyon asked.

Galdinia frowned as she looked between the men.

"I warned you that this would happen," Quill went on. "The elders are not easily swayed, and after the battle in Elderguard, your hope was misplaced."

"Ilyon," Galdinia said pointedly at her captain.

After a moment's hesitation, Ilyon replied, "I asked Quill at breakfast to join us for the meeting, hoping he may be able to help persuade the elders."

"You were a great help, thank you," Galdinia said, shaking her head and turning back to Ilyon.

"I'm sorry that I didn't want to risk my relationship with my allies and friends for *you*," Quill replied, heated. "Regardless, nothing I could have said would have helped."

"That's convenient," Galdinia replied, a snarky smile spreading over her lips. "Can you at least try to speak to Orlon alone?"

"Did you hear what I just said?" Quill's raised eyebrows mirrored his disbelieving tone. "These are my friends, and you are asking them to risk their lives for the same conflict they were already sorely burnt by. And what's more, you want me, their only contact to Crysterra, to convince them to join you. Quit while you're behind, as it were."

"Actually," Ilyon said, stepping in, "the Queen of Crysterra is making a fair request of you so as to avoid the reign of an oppressor."

Galdinia glanced at Ilyon, a hint of surprise in her expression.

"And they really seemed to care about her title, didn't they?" Quill responded, his voice devoid of emotion.

"That is inconsequential," Ilyon replied. "I'm talking about *you* and *your* duty to the crown."

"My *what*?" Quill's eyes narrowed as he spoke. "I don't have a duty to the crown. I'm doing this on orders from my parents, that's all."

"All the more reason to fight for our cause," Ilyon said, stoic as ever.

"And how did you come to that profound conclusion?"

"Your parents sent you here to help us establish more allies. They did not do that as a favour to Queen Galdinia, but because they know that without more allies, there's no chance of their jewels being returned to them," Ilyon explained, speaking each word carefully. "If we return to the south without so much as a way forward with Lund, I can assure you that your parents won't be too happy."

"That wasn't the agreement," Quill retorted. "You agreed to recovering the jewels in exchange for an escort to the mountains. Look around." Quill motioned to the mountains that surrounded them. "You're here. I've held up our end of the bargain, and you have to hold up yours. The outcome of that meeting has no bearing on our agreement."

"But that won't matter if we don't secure more allies," Galdinia cut in, following Ilyon's lead. "Without a stronger army, I'll be dead before I can retrieve your parents' treasures. Unfortunately, we are each other's best bet moving forward."

"I don't need those jewels," Quill replied. "They are of no use to me."

"But they are of incredibly high value to your parents, particularly your mother," Galdinia said, treading carefully.

"Not to mention," Ilyon cut in, "Valah knows the queen visited The Hook, so if she takes us out in a conflict because our forces aren't substantial enough, she will be coming for you and your family's necks after ours. While I can't promise what will happen to you in such circumstances, I imagine Valah will put your head on a stake at the entrance of The Hook. Though that's just an educated guess."

Again, Galdinia glanced at her captain. She was impressed with his verbal sparring today.

Quill considered their words, frowning at the suggestion that he may lose his head. Galdinia knew he didn't like it, and it brought her joy to watch him squirm.

"I'll speak to him once more," Quill finally said through gritted teeth.

"A good decision," Ilyon said with a nod.

"Your cooperation is appreciated," Galdinia added with a pained smile.

Without another word, Quill left Galdinia, Ilyon, and Vega by the fountain and walked back to the cavernous room from which the elders had not yet emerged.

"That was impressive, Captain," Galdinia said.

"It was necessary," Ilyon replied. "I think we may end up paying for it, though."

"Dealing with a sour Quill is worth it, especially if we secure more allies," Galdinia said. "Ilyon, do you think we have any chance here?"

"Honestly, Your Highness, I'm not sure. It's a risk sending Quill to speak with them again, but I'm not sure we have another choice."

"It may damage his relationship with them indefinitely, but I think that's a risk I'm willing to take," Galdinia replied. "Time will tell."

"I suppose it will," Ilyon replied. "Let's brief the Queen's Guard on our meeting."

With that, Ilyon gestured towards the tunnel that would guide them back to their rooms, and Galdinia took the lead.

Back in the sitting room of their quarters, Galdinia joined her companions who were sitting around the fireplace, resting in the warmth of Evander's rumbling fire. Ilyon had relayed the events of the meeting to everyone while Galdinia sat silently, staring into the flames, reliving every moment of the meeting, questioning every word she'd uttered. She knew Evander would be able to feel her tug on the fire as she used her gift to quell the storm in her.

"Tea?" Neryda asked, standing by Galdinia with a mug of steaming water that had been steeped in berries and herbal leaves.

"Please," Galdinia said, taking the mug from her friend. "Thank you."

Ilyon had finished his recount, and everyone else joined Galdinia in her contemplative state. She sat in one of the armchairs with the mug resting in her lap as Neryda handed out tea to those who wanted it—Kayd, Raia, and Evander. Vega was busy spinning a dagger between her fingers, while Ilyon was pacing in front of the fire. Neryda made an effort to avoid Bentley's gaze as she sat beside Evander on one of the chaises, making a point not to offer Bentley a mug. With a sigh, Bentley stood from his armchair, his shackles clanging together, drawing everyone's eyes—and the tip of Vega's dagger—in his direction.

"I'm just making tea," Bentley said, holding his palms up to those around him. Despite the glistening edge of Vega's dagger, Galdinia thought that it was Neryda's glare that was the most lethal in the circle.

Galdinia didn't say a word, but with a curt nod of her head, she gave him permission to move towards the fire and the pot of tea that was sitting on the hearth, keeping warm. It wasn't until he was back in his seat, cradling his mug, that Ilyon went back to pacing, Vega started twisting her dagger again, and the others relaxed into their seats, sipping on their tea.

"So it wasn't the most successful negotiation then?" Kayd asked from beside Galdinia, bringing the group's attention back to the matter at hand.

"Do you really think that's what we need to focus on right now, Kayd?" Raia asked, frowning at her cousin from across the circle.

"I'm just trying to start the conversation," Kayd replied, looking wide-eyed at Raia.

Disappointment and tension hung in the air.

"We do need to discuss our strategy moving forward," Evander said.

"Where do we even go from here?" Raia asked, looking around the circle, her eyes landing on Galdinia.

"I didn't expect them to refuse us," Galdinia said quietly, staring into the fire. "Of course I knew there was a chance they would, but I didn't actually think they'd leave us stranded."

"Me either," Raia said, shaking her head.

"I did," Vega said flatly, gently passing her dagger between her fingers. "Lund has always been self-serving, much like The Hook. At least they have enough respect not to yield at the promise of sparkling jewels."

"No, all they wanted was a province," Kayd said, scoffing. "A far easier request."

"I can give them the status of province much easier than I can the Lidels their missing jewels." Galdinia's voice was low and tiresome. "I can't even begin to think about how we will retrieve those."

"Let's not," Evander said, taking another sip of his tea. "We should be more concerned with convincing Orlon to accept us as allies before dawn tomorrow."

"It can't be done." Quill's voice came from the door of the chamber as he strode in, closing the heavy doors behind him.

Ilyon paused his pacing and looked to Quill. Galdinia watched him carefully as he walked across the room coolly.

"What did Orlon say?" Ilyon asked as Quill lounged in an empty chair beside Bentley.

"He's not impressed with me, for one," Quill said, leaning back in the chair and stretching his legs out in front of him. "He was surprised by my family's request to bring you all here, but he trusted us. Then he thanked me for the time we wasted, so that was nice of him."

Galdinia watched Quill out of the corner of her eye.

"Anything else?" Raia asked, looking at Quill, hoping to hear more than Orlon's obvious disappointment.

"Forgive me for caring what some of our greatest allies think of me after such a tumultuous conversation."

"At least they're your allies," Vega said, her voice low.

"Exactly," Quill went on, "they are *my* allies. And I'd like to keep them as such."

A heaviness settled on the group, and Galdinia could not bring herself to respond to Quill.

"What else did he say?" Ilyon asked, standing firm with his back to the fire.

"He was actually impressed by you," Quill said, raising his eyebrows in Galdinia's direction. "In his words, you're not what he expected, and while he was disappointed with me, he admired your gall. Well done, Princess." The circle bristled at Quill's misspoken title. "Your Highness, apologies." His tone was sardonic. Galdinia wondered if this was the only way he could stomach talking to her: words drenched in sarcasm and disdain. "Other than that, he merely repeated what he'd said in the meeting." Quill crossed his arms over his chest. "Should a conflict arise with the west, Lund's army will not fight with the Royal Guard, nor will it fight against it. They will merely spectate from afar and let one power take down another."

"Surely they realise the implications if they don't align themselves?" Evander's words came out as a question. "If a battle does ensue and we are victors, they will have burnt their bridges with Queen Galdinia."

"And if Valah wins, well, she'll just do away with them," Kayd said, looking down into his mug.

"It's true," Galdinia said quietly. "If Valah defeats us in a battle, she'll kill anyone who has wronged her in the past, whether intentionally or inadvertently. She wouldn't be able to rule a country that doesn't entirely support her."

"This is what I tried to reiterate to Orlon," Quill said. "The reality is that we can't survive a conflict without Lund's support, but they won't survive a Pyrin rule."

Galdinia noticed that he said "we". Had her and Ilyon's words earlier encouraged him to be more invested?

"But he doesn't seem to agree?" Ilyon asked.

"No," Quill said simply. "He is convinced that they can hole up in the mountains, fortify their walls, and continue to live here regardless."

"They're fools," Bentley said quietly, looking down into his cup. Everyone turned to look at him. "She'll dispose of them the moment she gets the chance to."

"Are you speaking from personal experience?" Vega asked, holding her dagger in one hand now.

"Unfortunately, yes," Bentley said. "She did just that to me, and I wasn't the first."

"She did what to you, exactly?" Vega asked, her eyes full of malice.

"Leaving me for dead—"

"After you led Queen Galdinia to her intended death." Vega's voice was almost a growl.

"Exactly," Bentley replied, matching Vega's expression of loathing. "As soon as Valah thought I'd done all I could for her, she left me to die in a burning room."

Quill, who hadn't been made privy to the reason for Bentley's imprisonment, appeared quietly entertained by the details.

"Every move and decision you made led you to that room that night," Neryda said, angered. "You put yourself in a position to be killed by Valah. Galdinia is lucky to be alive, no thanks to you."

"We don't need to rehash this again," Galdinia said. She would never admit it out loud to Neryda, but she wasn't sure that she entirely agreed with her. She wasn't convinced that she would be alive if Bentley hadn't let her run from the library. Of course, she wouldn't have even been in the library had it not been for Bentley, but when her survival hung in the balance, he made a split-second decision to save her over himself.

"No, we don't," Bentley replied, clutching his mug firmly. "All I'm trying to say is that no one can guarantee their safety when it comes to Valah. She saves those who continue to serve her purpose. No one else."

"What about your family?" Quill asked, looking sideways at Bentley. "Surely they're too valuable to her."

"I have no idea." Bentley stared into his steaming mug, his voice thick with remorse. "Without me, they hold very little consequence to her. I can only imagine she treated my family much like the way she treated me. I don't know if my parents or my siblings are still alive."

Siblings?

Galdinia wasn't aware that Bentley's family extended beyond his parents. She quickly reminded herself that much of what she'd learnt about him during the Week of Mourning was fabricated. She didn't know what was fact and what was fiction.

"The only power they hold is that they are lord and lady of our town and are reasonably well-respected," Bentley went on. "Our township is not large, but they are fiercely loyal. They'll follow my parents' alliance, whichever way it leans."

"That seems perilous," Evander said.

"It is, but when you're desperate to keep your people alive, you'll do just about anything to save them. That's what Valah promised my parents before they sent me to Elderguard."

"They're the lord and lady of a township," Kayd pressed. "How difficult can their lives be?"

Bentley shot him a piercing stare. "This is your first trip beyond the east in a while, isn't it?" Bentley asked, his eyes still sharp. "Most towns west of the Midlands are struggling at the moment. Unless, of course, you come from wealth." Bentley gestured towards Quill. Quill returned with his own rude gesture. "In the east, the position of a lord or lady brings authority and provision. Being a lord or lady in The Edges merely means you're in charge of keeping the people happy with very few resources. We have been long forgotten by a Syndicate who is simply too far away to see the needs of a far-reaching country. Instead, my family trusted Valah's promises, and now they could be dead. As soon as she thought I was dead, I doubt they would have held any value to her. So to suggest that she will dispose of the people who live here as soon as she is able, yes, I am speaking from personal experience."

Bentley looked around the group, his expression hard. Galdinia couldn't deny that she was impressed by Bentley's ability to hold his own in this group.

"Orlon is a stubborn man," Ilyon said, breaking the silence. "I don't think he, or any of the elders, will be convinced that it would be better to join us in a guaranteed conflict in order to avoid a possible conflict alone against Valah."

"Well, there is another way to convince them," Quill said simply.

Everyone turned to face him, and Galdinia's brows furrowed.

"He said he wouldn't serve someone obsessed with power, so you could give up your crown," Quill said, shrugging. Everyone's gazes turned to glares, their eyes saying far more than their words needed to. "Okay, fine, perhaps not."

"There is currently no *viable* option to win them over," Ilyon said, brushing past Quill's hasty suggestion. "We have thirteen days to meet — or at least deal with—Valah's demands; I think our efforts would be best put to use fortifying the allies we do have. The Novus and Ly families should have made contact with Ryden by now, so we can send a raven to the governor to confirm their alliance. I'm not sure that we have time to formulate and execute a plan to fetch the Lidels' jewels though. Our time is limited."

"Say we secure armies in the south and the east," Galdinia said. "Would it be enough to hold off Valah's forces?"

"It's hard to say," Ilyon replied. "I can estimate that each army is—"

"No, it wouldn't be."

Once again, everyone's eyes were drawn to Bentley.

Taken aback, Ilyon asked, "Care to expand?"

"Valah has managed to build herself a significant army in the Wetlands. What's more, she has most of the forces in The Edges behind her, and as we learnt a few weeks ago, she also has a force in the east. Even if Kaedric managed to secure the army of his family's province, I would wager that it simply wouldn't be enough. Not after the losses to the Royal Guard."

"And how do you know how many soldiers we lost?" Ilyon asked.

"I was fighting alongside your soldiers," Bentley said, frowning. "To guarantee a victory against Valah, you'll need Lund's soldiers too." He glanced at Quill. "At the very least you'll need The Hook's army."

"Their army is about twice the size of ours," Quill said, confirming Galdinia's fears. "They're our greatest chance at victory."

"Our?" Neryda asked.

"As soon as those jewels are in my hands, we'll be able to share in the victory together," Quill replied, a sardonic smile on his lips.

"How can we possibly retrieve the jewels *and* convince Orlon to fight with us in less than two weeks?" Raia asked the group.

"I don't think we can," Ilyon replied, his voice grave. "To travel to the Shadowed Coast, lay siege on Elderwin Manor, and retrieve the jewels without risking losing more valuable soldiers seems ineffectual. Not if we want to remain within Valah's timeline, at least." Galdinia sent a pointed glance towards her captain. "Which, of course, we are."

Galdinia had put very little thought into how she planned on retrieving the jewels from her aunt, but it wasn't an option to think they could buy any more time from Valah. Galdinia had naïvely assumed that Lund's elders would be eventually swayed and therefore she wouldn't need to think about the Lidels' jewels until after she had rescued Drystan and defeated Valah. If she was honest with herself, she hadn't thought about Edana since she left The Hook. Galdinia made an educated guess that Edana was likely hellbent on getting her own revenge against Valah, so she had been the least of Galdinia's concerns.

Of course, Galdinia thought, a glimpse of a plan unfolding in her mind.

"What about Edana?" Galdinia asked.

"What about her?" Ilyon questioned.

"She has quite the forces herself," Galdinia said, her thoughts tumbling from her lips as they formed in her mind. "Valah admitted to securing the east in front of my uncle, but I know the army of the Shadowed Coast is mighty. I had assumed they were part of the Royal Guard until they showed up on our doorstep."

"I'm sorry, Your Highness," Ilyon said, looking at Galdinia carefully, "are you suggesting we seek out an alliance with Edana?"

"No, of course not," Galdinia said, shaking her head, trying to gather her thoughts as she spoke. "Edana loathes me and wants my crown for herself. But I could almost guarantee that she is far more occupied with her hatred for Valah right now."

"Then what are you suggesting?" Ilyon asked.

"If we give Edana a time and place that we can guarantee Valah will be out in the open, I wouldn't be surprised if she came for vengeance."

"You mean to say we could use Edana's forces as a proxy army?" Vega asked.

"In a way, yes. Edana's army won't be fighting *with* us, but they certainly won't be wasting their time attacking Royal Guard soldiers when the woman who murdered their lord is within reach. I know my aunt; she will want blood."

"And what if she comes for yours instead?" Neryda's tone was apprehensive.

"Let's hope she doesn't."

Galdinia knew this wasn't a foolproof plan, but she felt they were scrambling for viable options, and this might be the only one left.

"Quill," Galdinia said, sitting up straighter and turning to face the young lord. "How do you think your parents would feel about being able to take the jewels from Edana's neck themselves?

"That wasn't part of the agreement," he drawled in response.

"I'm aware of that, but they may get them sooner if they brought their forces to the same meeting point."

Quill contemplated this, likely considering the benefit of being done with Galdinia sooner than he hoped—not to mention the hope of keeping his head on his neck.

"If it means bringing an end to this inane bargain they've made with you, then they may agree to it, yes."

"Good, please send them correspondence of these arrangements,"

Galdinia replied, not taking his bait; she was too occupied with the unfolding plan to respond to his insolence, so instead, she turned to Ilyon. "Captain, can we ask for confirmation from Ryden about Kaedric and Kell?"

"I'll send a raven today," Ilyon said with a curt nod.

"Assuming we have their support, as well as that of The Hook, we need to send word to Edana and Valah to meet before the next new moon. We will need to meet somewhere away from civilians; I don't want Valah to be able to scurry away in a gale again or hurt any more innocent people."

"The Midcrest Grasslands could work," Kayd suggested. "It's an expansive plain in the Midlands, north of Silkshell. There aren't any townships for at least fifteen kilometres in each direction."

"Perfect," Galdinia said. "We will have easy access back to Elderguard from there too. Ilyon, can we set up a camp north of Bear Jaws to house and train with the Royal Guard?"

"Yes, of course, Your Highness," Ilyon said, though his eyes reflected a concern that did not appear in his voice.

"What's the matter?" Galdinia asked. She knew her captain too well at this point to disregard his concern.

"We are relying on a lot of variables. I don't like variables."

"Neither do I," Galdinia agreed, "but I don't see another way forward. You said yourself that we don't have enough time to organise a plan to retrieve the jewels from Edana, and we can't survive an attack without The Hook's forces. Instead, let's bring both to us. With our other allies, we may have a chance at victory."

"If we had more time, we could—"

"If we had more time, we could do a lot of things," Galdinia said, cutting him off, "but we don't. I'm not willing to risk losing my crown or Drystan to Valah, so we must work with what we have."

Ilyon thought about this, his brows knotting as he considered the situation.

"Kayd, fetch me a raven and some parchment," Ilyon said by way of agreement; immediately, Kayd was on his way to a nearby writing desk. "Evander, once we leave the mountains tomorrow, you will be training with Galdinia to use her gift defensively, even as we travel." Evander nodded to Ilyon, then to Galdinia, whose lips turned up at the edges. "We will reach the valley in five days if our pitstops are brief. Expect little sleep. Once at our camp, we will continue training with our soldiers until we meet with Valah. This isn't enough time by far, but as Queen Galdinia said, we must work with what we have."

There were collective nods around the circle.

"Get some sleep tonight, soldiers," Ilyon said, looking around at the group. "You will need it."

As Kayd handed Ilyon a piece of parchment, an ink pot, and a quill, Galdinia reached out her hand.

"Kayd, I need to write a letter of my own," Galdinia said, preparing herself to write to her enemies.

Galdinia had spent an hour in her rooms, mulling over her words, taking the flame from a candlestick and sending it from one hand to another. The movement helped her think, the fire bringing a sense of comfort to her body. She had paced the length of the room countless times before she finally settled at the desk beside her bed and wrote her carefully considered—yet brief—message to Edana, still rolling the flame in her left palm.

Edana,

Valah will be at The Midcrest Grasslands at dusk in eleven days' time, on the twenty-ninth day of my rule. She will have her army in tow, but she will be yours to do away with. The Royal Guard will not raise their weapons against your forces unless it is necessary that they do. If you take my offer of Valah in bad faith, there will be blood.

And it will be yours that I spill first.

Queen Galdinia Anae Elderwin

Galdinia had questioned the wording many times before she landed on this final draft. She needed to give Edana an opportunity she couldn't decline while also ensuring the safety of her soldiers. It was a risk to suggest two enemy armies meet her, but as long as her enemies also hated each other, she thought they may stand a chance.

Before moving to write her letter to Valah, there was a knock at her door. Moments later, Neryda's face peered around the door, her beautiful russet curls bouncing over her shoulders.

"I thought you might like some company," Neryda said, smiling softly.

"Always," Galdinia replied, and her friend stepped in, coming to sit across from her on the edge of Galdinia's bed.

"How goes the letter to your aunty?" Neryda asked, her tone sarcastic.

"It took me an hour to write five sentences," Galdinia replied, picking up the parchment and handing it to Neryda. "But it's done."

Neryda scanned the page, her brows rising as she finished reading.

"Quite the message of love and endearment," Neryda said as she handed the letter back to Galdinia.

"I thought so," she replied, placing the letter on the desk.

"You've had quite the morning," Neryda said, leaning back on her hands as she made herself comfortable. "How are you feeling?"

"Terrified," Galdinia said with a sigh, placing her elbow against the back of the chair and resting her head in her hand. She continued to tumble the fire around in her free palm. "I can talk about strategy and write letters full of threats of blood, but at the heart of it, I'm petrified of what's going to happen when I have to face her."

"I'd be concerned if you weren't," Neryda replied. "On the bright side, our time with Quill is coming to end."

"I got some answers about why he's been so hostile," Galdinia said, distracted from her anxieties about facing Valah by her newest enemy. She watched as Neryda's attention seemed to tighten on her.

"Oh?"

"His best friend was killed in the battle at Elderguard. He was fighting in Lund's forces."

"By who? You?" Neryda's eyes were wide.

"No, by one of my soldiers."

"They were attacking your city," Neryda replied. "He can't blame you for that."

"I know, but Valah had manipulated Lund's army," Galdinia replied, feeling as though she could finally pull together her thoughts on this situation. "And I can understand Quill's perspective. Of course he would hate the person who led the charge that murdered his best friend. I would hate him if a soldier from The Hook even touched a hair on your head."

"I'd like to see them try," Neryda said with a smirk before lowering her expression, noticing how solemn Galdinia was. "It's not your fault."

"I know that," Galdinia replied, her heart heavy. "But to be even remotely connected to the murder of an innocent person isn't something I think I'll ever get used to."

"That's what makes you such a good queen," Neryda replied with a sad smile.

"I don't know about that," Galdinia said, looking down at the hand in her lap as she twisted and turned the flame. "I'm trying so hard to protect my people and ensure their safety, but what if all this hesitation leads to our detriment?"

"What do you mean?"

"All this planning could be useless," Galdinia replied. "I'm trying to line everything up perfectly, and it may not even work. In the long run, perhaps this will have wasted precious days that could have been used to plan Drystan's rescue."

"Gal," Neryda said, reaching over to place a hand on Galdinia's forearm, "you didn't hesitate to get on a ship to make amends with some potentially very powerful—albeit painful—allies. You then risked your own neck traversing mountains to make contact with, arguably, an even more stubborn group. You have been strategic every step of the way from the moment that crown was placed on your head."

They both glanced at her crown sitting on the desk beside her ink pot and a handful of pieces of parchment.

"But maybe I should have just gone straight to Valah myself," Galdinia said, her voice thick.

"And what? Give her your crown?"

"No—I don't know, but at least I'd be doing *something* productive,"

Galdinia said, her heart squeezing in her chest. "I could have tried to save Drystan myself."

"While I think you are incredibly strong and brave, Gal," Neryda said, squeezing her friend's arm in comfort, "I don't think you'd be able to walk away from the Wetlands alive, with or without Drystan. Valah wouldn't hesitate to kill you on sight, and you will need all the manpower you can get before you face her. Trying to storm her territory alone to save Drystan would be reckless. You're doing the right thing."

"But she could be doing anything to him right now." The words barely escaped Galdinia's lips as she finally spoke out loud the fears that had been plaguing her dreams each night.

Neryda took in a deep breath, holding back her own tears.

"I know," Neryda finally replied. "That's why we have to do all we can to save him, and right now that looks like making allies and bringing down Valah."

"I can't let him die when he thinks I hate him," Galdinia said, her eyes filling with tears. "The last real conversation we had, I told him he should leave Elderguard. I told him I didn't want to hear him speak my name again."

The tears escaped her eyes as she remembered the way she had spoken to him in the barracks hours before the attack; the inescapable expression of pain and heartache on his face was branded on her mind. Neryda pulled Galdinia from her chair and drew her to the edge of the bed with her, holding her close as Galdinia let her tears fall, all the weight of responsibility, exhaustion, and fear overwhelming her.

"He doesn't think that you hate him," Neryda said, sniffing as her own emotions broke through her usually amiable exterior.

"What if he dies and he doesn't know that I love him?" Galdinia said, her tears trickling down her face and onto Neryda's shoulder.

"He knows," Neryda said, pulling Galdinia in tighter, both girls shedding tears for their friend who was somewhere across the country in the hands of their greatest enemy. "He knows."

"It's my fault he's there," Galdinia whispered.

"Only because you care so much about him."

"We have to save him, Ner," Galdinia said, holding the fire in her fist close to her chest, the warmth emanating through her.

"We will."

"And I won't let Valah hurt anymore of my people," Galdinia said, breathing in deep and sitting up straight. "I have to do whatever it takes to save Drystan."

Clutching the flame in her hand, Galdinia swiftly moved back to the desk and pulled a piece of parchment from the pile before dipping her quill in the ink pot. Quickly, before she overthought it, she wrote to Valah.

Eleven days, at dusk on my twenty-ninth day of rule, The Midcrest Grasslands.

He'd better be breathing.

28

ALTHOUGH THE WIND HAD A DISTINCT CHILL AND HER BODY WASN'T quite ready for the trek, Galdinia had to admit that the journey back down through the mountains was significantly easier than the trip up. It took them two days to traverse down the mountains, and after collecting their horses from the stable, the group finally made it to The Vale, a large expanse of green pastures that was flanked by rolling hills and mountains on either side. Galdinia was glad to be reunited with Opal—the horse even whinnied when Galdinia approached her. She had to admit that she was grateful to have some more assistance in their travels.

As they moved down into The Vale, Galdinia enjoyed the expansive, open air before them, relieved to be free of the tight corners and narrow passages of the mountains. If she could see beyond the mountains to the east, she would have seen her family's winter estate. As a child, she and her father often spent a week or two there in the colder months, embracing the crisp climate. How she wished to continue their journey in that direction, where plush beds and enormous fireplaces would be awaiting their arrival. Royal Guard soldiers were put on a rotation to guard the royal family's second home, with a handful of attendants to maintain the building and grounds, so Galdinia knew they could arrive and be well-fed and warmed in minutes, but they didn't have time to take the detour.

"What do you say, Galdinia?" Evander's voice drew Galdinia's attention back to the group as their horses carried them beyond the last foothills and into the lush grasslands before them.

"What was that?" Galdinia asked.

"Now that we've made it beyond the mountains, shall we get some training in?" Evander asked, obviously repeating himself. "We can train as we travel; the open space will make it less haphazard."

He was right; the vast vale that they were now entering would allow for safer training with fire, something they couldn't easily attempt within the mountains where they had to navigate small crevasses and narrow pathways. Although her body was tired from all the travel, she knew she needed every second of training she could get.

"Good idea," Galdinia said, trying to keep the reluctance out of her voice.

"We won't be slowing down," Quill interjected from the front of the group.

"We'll take a break in about two hours," Ilyon said from the rear, "so you'll need to keep up the pace while you train, otherwise you might miss lunch."

"Sounds like good motivation to me," Evander said with a smile.

With that, Evander and Galdinia dismounted their horses and tied them up to Raia's and Kayd's mounts. While the horses were walking at their regular pace, and they were moving gradually downhill, Galdinia realised very quickly that she needed to maintain a steady walk herself to keep up with the group. Evander and Galdinia fell behind the group, leaving enough distance so as not to disturb the horses while they trained.

"Have you ever made a shield with your fire before?" Evander asked, drawing the flame out from the vessel at his hip.

"Not yet," Galdinia said, retrieving her own flame.

After saving her life on the mountain and being surprisingly helpful in their strategising, it was decided that Bentley could be trusted around the fire, allowing both Evander and Galdinia to keep a flame on their person while traversing down the mountains again. He still stared longingly into the flames each evening when they set up camp, but he hadn't made any attempt to harness the small flickers on the other Flourishers' belts.

"As much as fire can be an offensive weapon, it also makes a great shield, especially against arrows and Water Weavers," Evander explained. "Let's focus on stretching and growing the flame to shield attacks."

Evander held out his left hand, and his flame flickered there. With his left hand, he skimmed the top of the flame and created a fist with his fingers before making a swift pulling motion as he dragged the flame up and outwards in all directions. Now no longer small and flickering, the fire had been transformed into a wall of flame that covered his torso and face, its orange edges licking at the air as it moved with Evander's hand—it was suspended in midair yet mirrored his movements. He held his right hand up, unfurling his fingers as though pressing his palm against an invisible barrier, helping maintain its shape and size.

"You make it look so easy," Galdinia said, wide-eyed at how quickly and easily Evander formed his shield.

"You'll get there too," Evander said as he nodded towards Galdinia's hands. "Your turn."

Imitating Evander's actions, Galdinia held out her left palm and used her right hand to draw on the heat of the edges of her flame. She tried to pull at the flame, just as Evander did, and she watched as its edges slowly expanded, but she struggled to make a shape similar to Evander's, much less the size of his. Hers barely covered the circumference of her face.

"It doesn't seem to want to expand much further," Galdinia said, furrowing her brows in concentration.

"Try to connect with the heart of the flame, not just the edges," Evander advised, still holding his shield firmly in his hands as they simultaneously walked down The Vale, keeping their distance behind the group. "Imagine the width of the shield coming from its core."

Galdinia did as she was told, focusing on the centre of her small pane of fire. The middle looked hot, broiling, and deep, while the perimeter was wispy, dancing off into the air. She kept her attention on the heart of her fire, trying to draw the flame further out, using her hands to reflect her mind's intent. While it grew further, she couldn't extend the shield further than her collarbones, leaving her torso exposed. After twenty more minutes of Evander's coaching and Galdinia's striving, the shield had not expanded any further. This training felt reminiscent of her time with Ilyon in the soldiers' barracks, where she spent many hours trying to connect with a gift she hadn't yet possessed. However, now that she had her gift, it was almost even more frustrating that she felt she could only do so much with it.

"At least my face will be safe," Galdinia said with a defeated sigh.

"Am I wrong, or did you produce two enormous spheres of fire just a few weeks ago?" Evander asked, shrinking his shield back to a meagre flame in the palm of his hand.

"Uh, yes, I did," Galdinia said, a question hanging in her tone, her own fire diminishing as well.

"Tell me about that moment," Evander asked. At Galdinia's furrowed brow, he added, "How did you feel? What was it about that moment that you felt you could create something so powerful?"

Galdinia paused in her walking as she looked down at the flame in her hand. She couldn't recall many of her thoughts from that moment, but she could feel every emotion echo deep in her chest.

"I was desperate and hurt and angry." Galdinia's voice was low. "Valah had hurt my people, and she had taken someone very precious to me. I barely even thought about what I was doing before I conjured the spheres; it was instinctual. Something within me knew what I needed to do to protect my home—to protect who I loved."

The image of the glinting blade at Drystan's throat invaded her mind, bringing with it waves of unwanted fear and guilt.

"I see," Evander said thoughtfully before turning to the group on their horses. "Lady Neryda! May we borrow you?"

Galdinia looked up to see her friend slow her horse, turning to face Evander.

"Would you like me to extinguish those flames for you?" Neryda asked with a mischievous smile.

"Not exactly," Evander replied. "But could you tie your horse to Vega's and join us?"

Clearly sceptical, Neryda slowly dismounted her horse before securing its reins to Vega's saddle. She let the group move on ahead of her and waited for Evander and Galdinia to catch up.

"Lady Neryda," Evander began, turning so Galdinia and Neryda were looking downhill at him, "if you can take a position behind the queen, that would be fantastic."

With a questioning frown, Neryda did as she was told and stood behind Galdinia.

"Perfect," Evander said with an approving nod. "Galdinia, please bring your shield up again."

Galdinia raised her left hand and used her right to draw the edges of the flame up and out. Again, it didn't stretch wider than her face.

"It's understandable that you don't have full authority over your gift yet," Evander said, holding out his own flame. Galdinia tried not to take offence to his words. "That isn't to say that you aren't powerful —you certainly are—but you're still relying on your circumstances to tap into that power. So, we are going to try to replicate the emotions that spurred you on outside of the Northern Gates."

Instantly, Galdinia felt a pinch in her chest. The thought of having to relive the experience of seeing Valah threaten Drystan's life only to take him hostage sent heat up her neck and shock waves through her lungs. She was terrified at the memory alone; she didn't know what she would do if she had to do that all over again.

"We're going to keep moving, and I'm going to send flames your way," Evander said, holding up his palm of flame. "But I won't be aiming for you. I'll be aiming for Neryda."

"Excuse me?" Neryda asked over Galdinia's shoulder. "I don't remember agreeing to being scorched today."

"Good thing Galdinia will protect you," Evander said, looking knowingly at Galdinia.

"I'm not sure I can do this," Galdinia said, feeling the weighty ache settle in her chest.

"Of course you can," Evander said, starting to walk backwards in the direction of their group. "You've been up against far worse than me. You can do this."

"What if I can't, though?" Galdinia asked, starting to walk forward as well.

"You'd better work it out quickly," Evander said with a smile. "And Lady Neryda, please keep your gift to yourself during this exercise."

Before Galdinia or Neryda could steel themselves, Evander quickly manoeuvred his hands in a circle, turning his fire in a flaming ball, from which he sent stones of flame towards Galdinia.

"Oh my—" Neryda said, moving in tight behind Galdinia.

Instinctively, Galdinia reached out with her left hand to absorb the flame in her measly shield. Evander was too quick and his grip on the flames too strong, and Galdinia could only absorb his fire into hers; there was no way she could try to take control of it in midair. With every new attack, she moved quickly to catch the flame in her own. Evander had sent out seven balls of fire, all of which Galdinia managed to reach and absorb, but her shield didn't become any bigger. Between attacks, she tried to stretch it again with her right hand, but she barely expanded it beyond her collarbones.

Evander again drew pellets of flame from his sphere and threw his arms out progressively quicker. He had Galdinia moving side to side across the grass as she frantically tried to intercept each attack, stopping the curving flames before they reached her friend. He sent some curling through the air, others a straight shot towards Neryda. After running to catch a pellet that went wide, Galdinia twisted, watching as Evander sent another straight in Neryda's direction. Neryda squeezed her eyes shut and held her hands in tight fists by her side, no doubt fighting the urge to reach for her own elemental weapon. Digging her boots into the grass, Galdinia pushed back in the opposite direction, lunging forward and reaching out with her left hand to catch the flame. As she did so, Galdinia tumbled to the ground, landing in the grass with a heavy thump. But this didn't matter—Neryda was safe.

Neryda bent down to help Galdinia up, who with a groan, got to her feet. Both Ilyon and Bentley had turned at the sound of her fall; the former's eyes were impressed, the latter's concerned.

"You're getting good at catching the flames," Evander said, momentarily pausing his onslaught.

"You're not really giving me any other choice," Galdinia said, wiping grass and dirt from her boots, trying to catch her breath. Her heart was tumbling in her pained chest.

"That's exactly my goal."

"If you want me to extinguish his flame," Neryda started to say quietly, "just say the—"

"That won't be necessary, Neryda," Evander assured her. "This is a training exercise for Galdinia. Your water won't help her harness her gift."

"It might help protect the hair on my head, though."

"That's not our priority right now."

"Well, it should be," Neryda muttered under her breath, her words thinly veiling her concern.

Choosing to ignore Neryda, Evander said, "Now, let's see how you do when you have more than one attack to shield." Evander started to walk backwards again, and Galdinia noticed that Bentley had his head turned slightly, allowing him to keep the corner of his eye on her.

Evander split the sphere into two, and the fire twisted in both palms.

"Gal, I've never had so much faith in you," Neryda said, moving to stand behind Galdinia again, almost crouching. Galdinia knew it took everything within her friend not to draw on her own store of water.

Shaking off her fall, Galdinia sucked in a deep breath, and she focused on the small shield in her hand, hoping to breathe life into it as she exhaled. She felt time slow as she watched Evander throw out both arms, sending his fiery weapons through the air simultaneously, one to the left and the other to the right. The flames arced through the air, and Galdinia knew she couldn't catch one without the other snaking behind her to hit Neryda. In a moment of desperation, she closed her eyes and pressed against the ache in her chest, using both hands to push her flame out in front of her. She felt the heat of the fire course through her, starting in her chest, then moving along her arms, and out through her palms. The hairs on her arms stood on end, rippling with the power that coursed through her body. Planting her feet firmly in the ground, she pushed once more into her fire, her eyes still squeezed shut in concentration.

She didn't hear Evander's fire land. She didn't hear a scream of pain from Neryda. In fact, she could hardly hear anything. Not the breeze in the trees or the birds of the sky. There was a muffled sizzling, and that was all.

Shakily, Galdinia opened her eyes and looked around her in amazement. She hadn't just conjured a shield in front of her and Neryda; she had encased them within a fiery dome. It stretched out and around from Galdinia's hands, encircling their feet and the air around them. She had completely barricaded them inside an impenetrable structure of fire.

"Gal," Neryda said breathlessly, looking around at the dome that stretched a foot above their heads. "How did you do that?"

"I'm not sure," Galdinia said, her heart thundering, her hands shaky. She inspected the dome closer. It wasn't a thick wall of flame, but rather resembled a thin casing of glass, shimmering with the flame, orange and red near her hands and yellow behind Neryda. Not only did she create it, but she was sustaining it, sending the pulsing heat from her body out through her palms. Galdinia looked ahead of her at Evander, who stood ten feet from them, a grin on his lips. The rest of their group had stopped their horses and were watching Galdinia, their eyes wide, some jaws slack. Ilyon, with his firm eyes and subtle smile, looked positively ecstatic. Even Quill had paused to look over his shoulder at Galdinia and her achievement.

"Well done, Your Majesty!" Evander said, his voice muffled by the fire surrounding them.

At her internal command, the flames drew back from their position around them and snaked back into her hands, forming the modest shield she had conjured earlier.

"That was amazing, Gal!" Neryda said, throwing her arms around her best friend from behind, pulling her close.

"I can't believe I did that," Galdinia said, looping her right hand over Neryda's arms while inspecting the fire shield in her left.

"It's incredible what a little urgency and love will do," Evander said.

"Look how much you love me!" Neryda practically sang, squeezing Galdinia tighter.

"Now you'll never doubt it," Galdinia said with a laugh, still baffled by what she had just achieved. Evander went to return the flame in his hand to his hip, but Galdinia spoke. "What are you doing?"

"I think that's quite an accomplishment for today. I don't want to tire you out."

"Oh no," Galdinia said with a shake of her head, a grin growing over her lips. "We're doing that again."

For the remainder of their travels to their next pitstop, Galdinia worked at replicating the fiery dome. At first, she was able to draw it up over her and Neryda's heads again, and then she experimented with expanding its size once they were encased within it, pressing both hands out to either side. She still needed the threat of Evander's attack to fuel her creations, but she was learning to feel for and trust her gift as it surged through her.

Two hours after she created her first dome, the rest of the group had found a shady spot in the tree line to sit to eat lunch as Galdinia, Neryda, and Evander slowly caught up.

"Before we stop, I want to try one more thing," Galdinia said as she drew the flames back to her after expanding them far enough to encompass herself and Neryda, who was now at least two metres behind her.

Galdinia wiped at the sweat on her brow with the back of her sleeve; the cooler climate wasn't doing anything to counter the warmth running through her veins or that of the flames around her. As long as she had control of the flames, they would never burn her, but she wasn't immune to the heat that radiated off them.

"Then you need a break," Evander said thoughtfully as they approached the group by the trees.

"Deal," Galdinia replied, taking in a deep breath. "Ner, stand beside Evander."

Looking at her friend with a pinch of concern, Neryda slowly walked towards Evander, and Galdinia jogged past them both; now she was the one looking uphill.

"At least this means he won't be throwing fire at me now, right?" Neryda asked, her tone hopeful.

"Well, I suppose *he* won't be, no," Galdinia said, a mischievous glint in her eyes. "But I will be."

Neryda's face fell, and Evander's filled with excitement. "Why is everyone enjoying throwing fire at me today?" she asked.

"Maybe because you're an easy target," Quill said, his mouthful of food not quite muffling his words. Galdinia saw that the rest of their party was watching them closely as they ate. Bentley's eyes were fixed on Galdinia and her flames.

Neryda glared at Quill in return.

"Just stand still," Galdinia said, turning back to her targets. Evander and Neryda ceased all movement as they stood side by side. "Kayd, may I borrow you?"

"Certainly," Kayd replied, bounding from his seat on a nearby log, leaving his meal of quail behind.

"I'd like you to start to suck the air from around Neryda and Evander."

Kayd's jovial expectation quickly dissipated and was replaced with apprehension. "You want me to—"

"Take the air from around them so as to cause them to stop breathing."

"Are you sure about that?" Kayd asked.

"Of course," Galdinia said, her confidence now as prevalent as her gift. "I'll stop you, don't worry."

"If you're sure," Kayd said, stretching his hands out towards Evander and Neryda.

"I'm sure," Galdinia replied with a nod. "Valah is a Wind Wielder, and she very much enjoys suffocating her opponents. I need to start planning to combat that."

"You know, Gal," Neryda said, looking at her friend with cynicism, "this isn't any better than the fire."

"I know," Galdinia replied, raising her own hands, starting to build the flames in her palms, "this is probably worse."

Neryda rolled her eyes, and Galdinia watched as her friend planted her feet more securely in the ground, trying to hold firm against the oncoming onslaught. Beside her, Evander still looked excited at the prospect. Galdinia nodded towards Kayd, and she felt the shift in the atmosphere almost instantly.

Neryda's hair billowed around her face as Kayd drew the air from around the pair. Galdinia watched as Neryda squeezed her eyes shut as her bundled fists strained by her side. Galdinia knew that she had mere seconds to stop Kayd's attack before more drastic consequences would surface, and she didn't want Ilyon or anyone else to step in and take charge.

She needed to be able to do this alone.

With that new sense of desperation feeding her gift, Galdinia sent her flames out before her, pushing against Kayd's power. With what felt like her entire being, Galdinia pushed harder into her flames, sending them springing forth around Neryda and Evander, creating another dome around the two of them. This time, however, Galdinia was outside the shield. She maintained the shape around them and watched as Neryda's hair settled around her shoulders, and she took in a deep breath. Both she and Evander smiled from behind the glistening sphere of flames, safe from Kayd's attack.

"Ah!" Kayd's voice rang out, and Galdinia's attention was pulled instantly from the protective dome and to her guard's shout of pain. Kayd's control of the wind ceased as he lowered his head, inspecting his hands closely.

The dome dissipated, and Galdinia was left with a small fire in her palm and a sinking feeling settling in her stomach; her confidence evaporated in the echo of Kayd's voice.

"Kayd?" Raia's voice rang out in concern, rushing to her cousin's side.

Galdinia placed the flame back in the vessel as she hurried to Kayd, Neryda and Evander following her.

"I think some of your flames caught on my wind," Kayd said, his eyes still downcast to his hands.

Galdinia saw that his fingertips had been singed, each one burning bright red.

"Kayd, I'm so sorry," Galdinia said in earnest as Raia pulled the water from her vessel and weaved Kayd's hands. He let out a breath of relief as the cool water encased his burning fingers.

"It's okay," Kayd replied, looking down at Galdinia, giving her a reassuring, yet pained smile. "You didn't mean to."

"I've only ever seen that happen when the Flourisher or Wielder meant to do it, never accidentally," Evander said, a glint of fascination in his eyes.

Was he impressed with her? Surely not.

"That wasn't my intention at all," Galdinia said, looking between Kayd's face and his hands, guilt staining her words.

"I know, Your Highness," Kayd said, smiling more convincingly now. "I should have felt for it sooner and dropped my hands."

"No, I should have—"

"I'm alright, really," Kayd cut her off, his eyes full of reassurance.

The five of them walked to the shade of the trees, Galdinia's heart pounding, partially from the residual exertion and partially from her painful remorse. She couldn't believe she had attacked one of her own guards.

"You'll be fine," Ilyon said after inspecting Kayd's hands. "We'll get some pine sap and sage on your fingers, and you'll be right by morning."

Vega began digging through a satchel of medicines, concoctions, and remedies and pulled out two small jars. After applying the mixture of the two substances on his fingers, Kayd already seemed more at ease.

"Again, Kayd, I'm so sorry," Galdinia said, coming to sit on the log beside them.

"This really wasn't your fault," Kayd said with a smile. "And anyway, I've experienced far worse in training with the captain. This is nothing in comparison to some of his drills."

Ilyon raised an eyebrow in Kayd's direction as he took another bite of his lunch.

"The combat drills are particularly merciless," Evander said, agreeing with Kayd. "I lost an eyebrow in one of my first ones."

"By your own flame?" Quill asked, his tone mocking.

"When you have three Wielders coming at you with their gift, it can be difficult to maintain full control over a fire," Evander rebutted, his voice cold.

"I lost about three inches of hair once," Raia added. "I was paired up with Vega during physical combat training. I couldn't use my gift, just my sword. She took it very seriously."

"You should be glad you left with your head on your neck," Vega drawled, not looking up from her hands as she sliced an orange into segments with a paring knife. "I chose to give you a haircut instead of killing you."

"You did that on purpose?" This revelation seemed to rattle Raia.

"Only because he told me to go easy on you." Vega motioned towards Ilyon with her knife.

"Captain!" Raia exclaimed.

"It was for your own good," Ilyon replied. "You were relying too heavily on your gift, and you needed to practise your physical defensive skills."

As Raia continued to squabble with her captain, Galdinia leaned in closer to Kayd, glancing down at his hands.

"I really am sorry about this. It wasn't my intention to hurt you. I just needed a real threat to be able to create the dome."

"Please stop apologising, Your Highness—"

"Galdinia."

"Galdinia," Kayd said with a smirk. "Like I said, I've seen worse. I also should have been more prepared. You created something incredibly powerful. I've not seen many Flourishers do what you did today."

"That means a lot," Galdinia said, looking from Kayd's hands to her own. "I need to work on doing it without the threat of loved ones hanging in the balance, though."

"You will," Kayd assured her. "But sometimes love is the most powerful driving force."

"That's what Evander was saying earlier," Galdinia remarked.

"And he's right," Kayd said with a nod. "Your gift will become as instinctual as love. That's when you'll be able to harness it as such."

"As instinctual as love." Galdinia looked at Neryda as she stifled a laugh, listening to Raia. "Is that how it feels for you?"

"Every day," Kayd said, his eyes wandering to the other side of the group where Vega sat, smirking down at her orange as she listened to Raia complain about her impromptu haircut. "There's nothing quite like it."

Galdinia smiled as she watched his eyes flicker back to his hands. "Using your gift like that or love?"

"Both."

Galdinia looked around the circle at the people there and how close the Queen's Guard truly were. They had been in battle together, trained together, and likely saved each other's lives countless times. It would be hard not to be motivated to use your gift when protecting and fighting alongside your family and closest comrades. To have that constant source of fuel seemed both fanciful and terrifying. If Galdinia had to watch Neryda stand in danger in order to draw out her gift in such a powerful way, she wasn't sure how long she'd last in battle. But the lure of eventually learning to use her power with such confidence without a frightful threat was too good to ignore.

Across the circle, Galdinia's eyes landed on Bentley. He, too, was enjoying the good-humoured conversation, silently smiling in response as he finished his lunch.

A few weeks ago, on the morning of the Sixth Day of Mourning, Galdinia knew that if she'd had her gift then, Bentley would also have sufficed as a target for her to protect. She would have done anything to protect him from Evander's flame or Kayd's wind. She would have been motivated instantly to keep him safe. As he sat now, more at ease than he had been when they started their journey from The Hook, Galdinia could see the person she had so easily fallen for. Although she knew that she had been motivated by the threat of losing her mother's crown, as well as the heartbreak of being forbidden to love Drystan, her motivations were wrapped in a very real attraction. He had drawn her in with his charm, his wit, and that stupid dimple, but she had been truly enamoured with him.

At this thought, Galdinia reminded herself that he also hadn't stopped her from walking into a room with her greatest enemy. Some part of him—and Galdinia didn't know how much of him—wanted her dead that evening. He hadn't planned on marrying her or keeping his promise. Despite the confessions of affection he had made recently, she knew his first priority was himself and his own life. Evidently, Bentley didn't care about who he hurt along the way.

Bentley looked up from his food and caught Galdinia's eye across the group. His eyes softened as he looked at her. Galdinia could see a hundred thoughts flying around behind those brilliantly bright blue eyes. Was he scheming how to escape? Was he wondering how he could lure Galdinia in again to take her to Valah's door himself?

Or perhaps he was merely enjoying the moment in which he could silently look at her without her avoiding his gaze straightaway.

"We'd better get back on the trail," Ilyon said, standing up, pulling Galdinia's attention away from Bentley—though she could feel her heart lingering longer than she would have liked to admit. "I'd like to make it further down The Vale by nightfall—it looks like the weather may take a turn."

To the east, the clouds were stained a few shades darker, and

Galdinia could see the beginnings of a storm brewing far in the distance.

"Let's go," Galdinia said in agreement, standing to her feet.

With that, the group started to gather their belongings and packed them on their horses. Galdinia watched as Ilyon helped Bentley with his pack, his hands still restrained in shackles but the water well and truly gone. Everyone was becoming more comfortable around Bentley, and Galdinia couldn't decipher how that made her feel, so she turned from them, mounted her horse, and continued down The Vale.

29

That evening, Galdinia found herself going to bed earlier than she had in days. While she was satisfied with all she had accomplished with Evander, her body felt the effects of such rigorous training. From her muscles, to her bones, to the pounding headache, she was more than ready to sleep the moment they set up camp. After a quick dinner, she excused herself to her tent, where she didn't even bother removing her fighting leathers and instead fell onto her stretcher, wrapped her blanket around her, and fell asleep within seconds.

Despite her exhaustion, Galdinia was hurtled into the same dream —or rather, nightmare—she'd been having so often as of recent: Drystan in the hands of Valah. Galdinia's unconscious mind whirled with foggy images of a malnourished and beaten Drystan, slumped on his knees, fighting to stay alive in a dark, shapeless place. As she dreamed, Galdinia's heart tumbled in her chest, sending the sound of its laboured beats thumping into her dream.

As she tried to call out to Drystan, the thundering of her heartbeat silenced her words. He didn't look up—it was possible he couldn't hear her. Galdinia stretched out her arms, but he was just barely out of her reach. She strained forward, willing her hands to reach him in the darkness. She went to take another step, but she couldn't move.

Her legs felt heavy, as though they were tied to the ground; she struggled to pull them forward, but no amount of might or strength released the tension in her feet. She simply couldn't get closer to Drystan.

Suddenly, he looked up at her, aware of her existence, aware that she was there to save him.

"Galdinia." Her name came out as a whisper, but it echoed around her as though he'd yelled it. A smoky haze in the air started to encircle him, swirling in all directions.

Again, she tried to reach him, heaving her body forward, desperate. The harder she tried, though, the foggier her vision and the louder her heartbeat became. It was as though the closer she got, the harder it was to see, hear, or feel anything. As she tried to force her feet forward, Drystan's voice came again, but this time he yelled, every muscle in his body roaring her name.

"Galdinia!"

Galdinia's eyes flew open as she fell out of her dreamscape and back into reality. She realised very quickly, though, that this reality was very different to the one she had gone to sleep in.

Disoriented, the smell of smoke filled her head, and the flicker of firelight encased her, sending light and shadows dancing over the walls of her tent. All she could hear was the blazing crackle of fire and voices shouting and calling at one another. That was when she heard it again.

"Galdinia!" The voice boomed across the campsite, but it wasn't Drystan's voice; it was Evander's.

Finding her physical body again and grasping the fact that she was no longer dreaming, Galdinia shot up from her stretcher. Grabbing her bow and arrows, she frantically leapt out of her tent and came face-to-face with a wild scene.

Across the campsite, balls of flame were being thrown in the direction of their tents. They were being intercepted, however, by Ilyon and Raia. They were sending up walls of water, extinguishing the fire in midair. To her right, Galdinia could hear the uncontrollable neighing of their horses, distressed and afraid, still tied up to the trees at the edge of the forest. To her left, Evander was using all his might to fight against a blaze around two of their tents, though he appeared to be struggling with it.

Their camp was under attack.

"Galdinia, help!" Evander's voice cut through the deafening sound of her surroundings.

Looking to her Flourisher guard, Galdinia realised that the fire he was trying to control was not just surrounding the tents but was starting to engulf them. Galdinia's heart dropped when she saw whose tent was almost being enveloped by flames: Neryda's.

"Neryda!" Galdinia screamed and ran to Evander's side, dropping her bow and arrows, freeing her hands to try and take control of the flames.

Her best friend was caught inside a canvas structure, surrounded by an inferno.

No, no, no, no!

"Someone else is controlling it," Evander said desperately, sweat pouring down his temples, his arms outstretched as he tried to restrain the flame.

It burned Galdinia's eyes to stare into the fire—as long as she didn't have control of it, she would feel its usual effects. With her arms outstretched, she threw her whole body into fighting against the power of the unidentified Flourisher who was maintaining a tight grip on the fire from somewhere in the darkness. Were they in the shadows of the trees?

"Does she have any water in there?" Galdinia called out.

"I don't know!" Evander replied, gritting his teeth against the flames. "But it may not do any good. This is the work of a very powerful Flourisher."

"We need Quill!" Galdinia shouted, glancing around frantically for Quill. Their other Weavers were indisposed, and they needed all the strength they could get against this fire.

Galdinia strained against the heat, searching for any piece of the fire she could connect with, but she was only met with resistance, as though the flame was encased by an invisible wall.

Galdinia looked around them, her eyes wild and her heart thundering. Stumbling from the men's tent, Kayd and Bentley emerged.

Bentley looked alarmed as his eyes darted around the scene. When he saw Galdinia, relief briefly crossed his face.

"Kayd, give us a hand over here!" Evander called out.

"Bentley, help!" Galdinia called, desperate.

Before the words had left her mouth, though, Bentley was already running to her side. Without a second thought, he extended his shackled hands into the air and tried to help his fellow Flourishers calm the fire. Kayd immediately tried to stifle the flame, drawing air away from the uproar, hoping to starve it.

"Are you okay?" Bentley asked her, his voice reflecting the strain of his arms.

"I'm fine, but Neryda's in there," Galdinia said wildly, her chest aching and her throat getting tight.

"We'll get her out!" Bentley called back, his tense effort plastered over his face.

"Someone's got hold of the surrounding air," Kayd said, determination set in his face. "They don't want this fire to go out!"

Desperately, Galdinia continued to push against the flames. Twice, she managed to penetrate the blockage, and she felt the grip of her gift wrap around the force of a section of fire, but just as quickly it was pulled from her grasp, and she lost control again. She was frantic and not nearly as controlled as she had been the day before when Evander was throwing flames in Neryda's direction.

"I've got a hold on it!" Evander shouted, managing to pull on a section of the fire, drawing it away from the tent.

As long as he could hold it, they may have a chance of extinguishing the flame, but they needed water.

"Where is Quill?" Galdinia roared, her voice booming from somewhere deep within her.

Before anyone could answer, the hairs on the back of Galdinia's neck stood on end. She couldn't logically explain what made her move, but on instinct, she dropped to the ground in a crouch. She watched as a ball of flame narrowly missed her, having flown from the forest before crashing into the overpowering fire on Neryda's tent. She didn't have time to react to the growing flame, though, as more fire came hurtling towards her like a cannonball. She dove across the grass, just barely missing the attack.

Scooping up her bow and sheath of arrows, Galdinia scrambled to her feet. Quickly, she attached the sheath to her back and drew on the flame in the lantern at her hip, pulling it out to shield herself from her invisible attacker. In seconds she had manipulated the flame into a shield, holding it against her forearm, just like she would a metal one. She held it up just in time to absorb another attack from the Flourisher enemy hiding in the woods, the force of the blow knocking her back a step.

With bared teeth, Galdinia surged forward, hoping to find her attacker.

One after another, flames were emerging from the depths of the forest towards her. In response, Galdinia lit her arrows on the edge of her shield, hurling flaming arrows back to her assailant. She wasn't quite sure where she should be aiming, given her attacker was somewhere in the trees, so she tried to avoid setting the whole area ablaze. The sounds of the horses echoed across The Vale, now terrified by the ongoing attack.

Again, Galdinia felt the nerves on her neck prickle, but this time she reacted too late. A flame struck the back of her right shoulder, not quite penetrating her leathers but causing her to tumble to the ground as a searing heat travelled over her shoulder.

Her shield was somehow still intact as she stumbled up onto her knees before another attack from the woods came. She was now trying to protect herself from both sides while also sending out her arrows. She could create her dome, but she knew that would only protect her, hindering her attacks. She hadn't yet mastered how to attack while fully shielded, and whoever was ambushing them needed to be brought down.

Over and over again, Galdinia fought against her undetectable assailant, who was hiding somewhere deep in the trees. She listened to her instincts as she used her shield to catch each strike and sent arrows of fire through the woods. Her body was growing tired as she searched for her attacker in the darkness, yearning to find them. In the depths of the forest, she saw a spark of light. Squinting, Galdinia tried to make out the shape of the person hidden there.

"Galdinia!" Bentley's call broke her focus, reaching her before she felt any inkling of an oncoming attack.

With his hands still shackled, Bentley hurled himself at Galdinia, forcing her from her feet and pulling her to the ground. With a painful crash, they landed on the grass, the metal of his chains pressing into Galdinia's side. At the same moment, Galdinia watched two fireballs collide in midair above them, one from the forest, the other from the direction of the tent. The attacker was simultaneously drawing flames from Neryda's tent as they threw them from the trees.

Galdinia looked at Bentley, astonished by what he had just done—once again, he risked his own life to save hers.

"Stop looking at me like that," Bentley said, his voice strained against the pain of their sudden impact.

"Like what?" Galdinia asked, acutely aware that his hands were resting on her middle.

"Like you're shocked that I want you alive!" Bentley said, breathless.

Before she could reply, an ear-splitting screech resounded across the camp. Both she and Bentley turned to the edge of the woods and watched as one of their horses let out a guttural noise before falling in a heap on the ground. The light of the fire illuminated the area, and she saw a cloaked figure pull a blade from the horse's chest, a layer of thick blood dripping from the sharp blade.

The attacker then rounded on one of the other horses, pulling on its reins, stopping it from rearing itself again. They prepared their knife to strike, but before they could harm another horse, a flicker of metal flew through the air and struck them in the neck. They faltered before they fell to the ground, the hilt of Vega's knife glinting in the firelight. Vega moved quietly as she retrieved her knife before trying to calm the distraught horses, the scene around them causing them to panic and tangle in each others' ropes. Without hesitation, Vega used the same blood-stained knife to cut through their ropes, sending the horses running in all directions.

"The flame is still raging—there must be someone else out there," Bentley said before glancing at the fiery shield Galdinia still held on her left arm. "Give me some of that."

"Bentley, I don't think—"

"We don't have time, Galdinia. We have to save Neryda."

While her hesitation was evident, it was brief. Galdinia pulled a portion of flame from her shield and held it out for Bentley. As soon as the flame had left her palm, Bentley used his gift to expand the fire into his own weapon: a sphere of fire blazing with red-hot fury. Before another assault from the assailant could land, Bentley charged towards the forest, sending sharp spears of fire through the air.

Galdinia looked across the camp to where Ilyon and Raia were still fighting off another Flourisher—or two—using their gifts to drown flames and encompass their enemies before they could hurt them. Galdinia pulled herself to her tired feet, ready to continue fighting the flame around Neryda's tent, but a miraculous feeling caused her to pause mid-step: a drop of water landed on her face.

In seconds, the rain had begun. Sheets of water fell from the clouds above—icy cold and desperately welcome. Galdinia watched as the shield of fire and the flames surrounding Neryda's tent succumbed, not able to stand against the torrential rain. Evander and Kayd looked to the sky in utter disbelief as the flames sizzled into smoke beneath the downpour.

In urgent haste, Galdinia threw herself forward and pulled back on the singed tent door, stepping into the partially destroyed shelter. The tent was full of smoke, and she looked around wildly for Neryda. On her stretcher, still cocooned in her blanket, was her best friend, unconscious and barely breathing.

"Ner!" Galdinia called as Kayd and Evander followed her into the tent. Kayd scooped her up in his arms and carried her from the crumbling shelter, bringing her out into the relief of the rain. "Neryda!"

Kayd laid her on the rain-soaked grass, and Galdinia crouched beside her. Droplets of water landed on the bare skin of her face, catching on the soot and becoming ashen rivulets along her cheeks. Galdinia gripped Neryda's arm and tried to shake her awake as tears started to form in her eyes.

"She's probably inhaled too much smoke," Evander said, crouching down to look at Neryda, still unconscious.

"We have to do something!" Galdinia cried, her voice desperate.

"Let me try something," Kayd said, dropping to his knees beside Neryda's head.

Galdinia watched as Kayd held his hands, palms together, over Neryda's face. With great focus, he pulled his hands up in the air, causing Neryda's body to shake beneath his gift. Her torso rose into the air briefly before Kayd lowered his hands towards her face, sending her body back into the grass. Galdinia was both terrified and awestruck as she watched Kayd pull the smoky air from her best friend's lungs, replacing it with the fresh air of the night.

After doing this twice more, Neryda let out a strained cough, shuddering as she sucked in a deep breath.

"Neryda!" Galdinia cried, pushing the wet curls of hair out of Neryda's face.

Delirious and barely breathing evenly, Neryda croaked out, "I think there's a fire."

Galdinia laughed, placing both hands on her friend's face, her tears still trickling down her cheeks.

"You're okay," she said with a smile as Neryda finally opened her eyes, revelling in the feeling of the rain on her skin. "The rain saved you."

"Of course it did," Neryda said quietly, her voice as tired as her expression. "It's the best element."

"This isn't a time for a superiority complex," Galdinia said with a tear-filled laugh.

Neryda coughed again before spluttering, "I think I need to sit up."

Galdinia helped pull her into a seated position and rubbed her back as she continued to cough, finding her even breaths again. How grateful Galdinia was that Neryda was alive and breathing, if only unevenly.

"Why didn't you get out?" Galdinia asked.

"I didn't know what was happening," Neryda explained, raspy. "I was asleep, and then suddenly I couldn't breathe. All I could smell was smoke before I passed out."

"Is everyone okay?" Ilyon's voice called through the rain.

Galdinia turned to see him and Raia, drenched from head to foot, walking across the camp, each holding on to a soldier whose hands were now weaved. The soldiers were dressed in silver armour, the Pyrin crest pressed into their breastplates. A heavy knot of dread formed in Galdinia's stomach, pulling tight and sending a wave of terror through her body. These soldiers were Valah's, and somehow—yet again—they found her. As the soldiers caught sight of Galdinia, their faces filled with hungry disdain and their lips curled into fierce snarls.

"Fine, Captain," Galdinia replied, standing to her feet and looking between the two captured soldiers, trying to maintain some semblance of authority; she would not be left unconscious by Valah's men again. "Your rain saved Neryda from a painful end."

"That wasn't me," Ilyon explained, pushing his and Raia's prisoners down onto their knees. "I was too busy with these two."

Before Galdinia could question the well-timed rainfall, Vega's voice came from the direction of the woods.

"There were three more in the trees, Captain," she said, walking towards the group with Bentley by her side. She was slipping a now clean dagger into its sheath on her thigh. "They're not quite as viable as these two though."

"All dead?" Ilyon asked, glancing to the forest from which they came.

"Yes," Vega replied simply.

Galdinia could see Bentley looking at her intently, his eyes almost that of warning, the still pelting rain trickling down his face. Galdinia frowned at him, unable to decipher what he was hoping to communicate with her.

"And the horses?" Ilyon asked.

"Gone," Vega replied. "I may be able to track one or two of them, but they'll be long gone by now. The fire spooked them, and they would have killed themselves tugging on their ropes. One of the attackers already took one of them down. Sorry, Your Highness."

Opal, Galdinia thought, looking painfully across at the silhouette of the beautiful horse now slain in the grass, wrapped in shadows. A sharp pain tugged in her chest, compounding on the fear that still wrapped her insides.

"My mother isn't going to be happy about that." Quill's voice emerged as he did, walking around from the other side of Galdinia's tent. "I won't be the one to have to tell her about Opal."

In a rush of anger, Galdinia advanced on Quill, her emotions getting the better of her. "Where have you been?" Her eyes were as sharp as her tone as she stopped a foot away, forcing herself not to lunge at him. She quickly decided they didn't need another death that evening. "We were fighting against an immovable flame, Neryda almost died, and you decided to go for a midnight walk? What is wrong with you?"

Quill stared at Galdinia for a second, the rain clinging to each of his curls, which were now flattened down the sides of his face with the weight of the downpour. He tilted his head to the side and frowned at her. "Who do you think sent the rain?"

Galdinia was taken aback. She distantly remembered how Quill had protected his and Luan's sailing boat in The Hook, but pulling a downfall of that magnitude with such precision was something else. The only Weaver she had met that was capable of such a thing was her captain, and he was known in Crysterra for having such a reputation. "You what?"

Quill's frown deepened. "The rain—this wet stuff falling from the sky—that was me," he said, lazily pointing up to the rain. "The moment I smelt the smoke, I ran out into The Vale to get a clear view of the sky away from the trees so I could pull the rain from the east over camp. I'd say it was a roaring success."

Galdinia was stunned. She backed up slightly, her anger suddenly quelling. "You helped us."

"So it would seem."

After another long pause, Galdinia finally said, "Thank you."

Quill didn't reply; he merely crossed his arms over his chest and glared down at Galdinia.

"Speaking of the rain," Neryda cut in, her voice still hoarse, using Evander's hand to stand to her feet, "although I'm grateful for it, can we tone it down a little?"

Given that Quill was still unmoving, Ilyon took responsibility. After passing off his prisoner to Kayd, he reached his hands into the air above him, swirling them around him in wide circles. The rain halted as quickly as it had come, leaving puddles around the camp and everyone within dripping.

"What are we to do with these two?" Galdinia asked, addressing the two prisoners still on their knees in the soaked grass. One of them looked up at Galdinia, his perceptive eyes full of animosity.

"Queen Valah will rise again," he said tersely, his voice spine-chilling.

"Quiet," Kayd ordered, kneeing the prisoner in the back, causing him to avert his eyes again.

"I think Kayd and I may take them to the woods for questioning," Ilyon said, glaring down at the prisoners. To this, their lips curled again. "Vega, you may wish to join us in case they struggle to find their words."

At this, Vega drew her dagger from its sheath again, contempt painted over her face. The second prisoner seemed to recoil slightly at this prospect.

"Captain, there's something you should know," Bentley said suddenly, stepping forward, looking between Ilyon and Galdinia. "Both of you."

At his words, Galdinia felt a similar prickle on the back of her neck as she did when the flaming attacks were hurled her way. She looked sideways at Bentley before looking back at her captain.

"What might that be?" Ilyon asked, moving his hand to rest on the hilt of his sword.

Bentley hesitated, glancing back into the woods before finally speaking. "One of the soldiers in the woods was a Wind Wielder. They were probably the one protecting the fire."

"Okay?" Galdinia was confused.

"It was Kaedric, Galdinia," Bentley said quietly. "Kaedric Novus."

No.

Galdinia was staggered by Bentley's words. Images of a keen smile and sweet demeanour flickered through her mind.

No, it couldn't be.

"Are you sure?" Ilyon asked as Galdinia stood frozen.

Bentley nodded in response.

Galdinia couldn't believe it. While at times a little overbearing, Kaedric had been so kind and sweet to her during the Week of Mourning. He hadn't wanted to do anything other than impress her.

"But he…" Galdinia tripped over her words, her mind reeling. "You're sure it was him? Maybe it was someone else. It was really dark—"

"Galdinia," Bentley said grimly, "it was him. I saw him in the light of my own flame."

"Ryden was sending word to his family when we left Elderguard," Galdinia said, still struggling to process Bentley's words. "Why would they do this?"

"Valah," Bentley said simply, his voice quiet.

"But we were counting on them for numbers. His family is one of our allies. They have been for decades!" Her emotions were brimming once again, her chest constricting.

"It doesn't sound like they're your allies anymore," Quill muttered.

"He fought with us in the battle on the Sixth Day of Mourning," Galdinia powered on, disregarding Quill. "How could he have defected so quickly? And how many of their soldiers chose to join them? Gods, it could be thousands."

"The Royal Guard in the east is at least three thousand strong," Ilyon said, his tone dire.

"I can't believe it," Galdinia said, the shock seeping in.

"And Kaedric was so harmless," Neryda said, frowning.

"Evidently not as harmless as you thought," Quill commented.

Galdinia rounded on Quill again, her eyes heated. "If you haven't got anything helpful to add, could you kindly shut it?"

"Don't worry, I'm leaving," Quill said, making a start towards his tent.

"I can't say I've ever once been worried about you," Galdinia replied, her words clipped.

"Likewise," Quill replied, his voice dark.

"You know, it wouldn't hurt for you to show a little respect." Bentley's voice shot across the group. "She is your queen."

"That's rich, coming from you," Quill said, stopping in his tracks and turning to stare at Bentley.

"You act like you're our enemy, but you're not," Bentley said, rolling his eyes. "It's getting pretty exhausting."

"I'm sorry, but aren't *you* the one in chains?" Quill asked, nodding to Bentley's restricted hands. "There's no 'our' for you. Don't be fooled by their growing trust. You're the real enemy here. You might as well be kneeling next to these two." Quill nudged a thumb towards the two soldiers still silently bowed next to Kayd and Raia.

"At least I'm willing to help the cause."

"And how noble it is to be fighting a losing battle," Quill replied with a sarcastic smile. "There's no hope for her side, especially with a traitor in her midst."

"Please don't speak about me as if I'm not here," Galdinia interjected, her voice hot.

"Fine," Quill replied, turning to face Galdinia. "Whatever you think you're doing by trying to secure more allies, you're delusional."

"Quillion—" Ilyon's words were cut short.

"You've no chance against Valah and barely a chance against your aunt." Quill charged on, his tone sharp, cutting deep into Galdinia. "You aren't nearly strong enough to outlast another fight, you have next to no experience in battle, and your forces are too small. And by the looks of it, they just got smaller. You've had your crown for how long—three weeks?—and you've already made one of your allies defect. You're so desperate for allies at this point, you'll take a traitor! That is quite the accomplishment." Quill's voice edged on its usual tone of derision. "Put simply, you're not good enough to be queen. My parents are fools to trust someone who takes prisoners on holidays with them."

Galdinia glared at Quill, mirroring the hatred in his eyes. She could feel the heat in her chest rise up her neck and into her cheeks. She needed a flame—either to calm herself down or to hurtle at Quill.

"You're out of line—" Ilyon began.

"No, he's right." Galdinia's voice cut off her captain, though her gaze didn't break with Quill's. "Our army *is* too small, I'm somehow losing allies without even trying, I'm not strong enough to take down Valah, and the only experience I have in battle is when *your* allies partnered with a hateful and bloodthirsty woman to try and kill me and my people." Galdinia's words flew from her mouth like fiery arrows. "Bentley may have been on the wrong side at one point in time, but unlike Valah or you, I'm prepared to learn to trust again in order to have another powerful Flourisher on our side and not hers. As you suggested, I can take all the help I can get."

In her peripheral vision, Galdinia noticed Bentley shift in place.

"Good thing you have him on a short leash then," Quill replied, his voice harsh.

"Keep your friends close," Galdinia snarled, taking a small step forward, standing her ground, "and your enemies closer."

"I won't give you the satisfaction." With these words, Quill turned from the group and marched across the camp and into the men's tent.

"Is there any chance we can send him back to The Hook tonight, Captain?" Raia asked as the rest of the camp stood in silence.

"I need to go for a walk," Galdinia said before Ilyon could answer Raia, turning away from the group.

"Do you want me to come?" Neryda asked after Galdinia.

"No," Galdinia said firmly, not turning to look behind her.

"Stay close to camp, Your Highness," Ilyon said quickly.

Without another word, Galdinia strode beyond their tents and out into The Vale, walking across the drenched grass. Once far enough away from the camp that she could just barely make out the shapes of the tents in the darkness, she gave into her emotions and dropped onto her knees, cradling her face in her hands.

Galdinia's heart was pounding in her chest and throbbing up into her ears. She felt like her whole body was rattling with the pump of her heart and the shuddering of her breath. Anger, frustration, fear, and self-doubt were running rampant through her veins. And she wasn't even upset that Quill had belittled her in front of her guards, Neryda, and Bentley.

No, Galdinia was so wracked with pain because she believed every single word he'd said about her.

In less than two weeks, Quill had managed to get under her skin, found her most vulnerable insecurities, and hurled them at her, one at a time. Her sense of inadequacy had been toying with her thoughts, but Quill had a special way of making her feel truly useless. For once she didn't want to draw on a flame or find comfort in its warmth; she never felt so undeserving of her gift than she did in that moment.

Galdinia leant her head back and breathed in a deep breath as she stared up at the sky. The clouds had moved, and peeking out from behind their shifting forms was the moon, inching towards its third quarter. Every day darkness crept across it, a stark reminder that she wasn't anywhere closer to finding a viable way to save Drystan. He was as good as dead if she couldn't build, or even maintain, her army and lead them to end Valah. Perhaps she would never be able to.

Her chest cleaved at the thought of not being able to rescue Drystan, at the thought of him being left to rot in a cell or being tortured beyond recognition. What if she never got to see him again? What if she never heard her name on his lips? What if she became the reason his life was cut short?

"Your Highness." Vega's firm but quiet voice broke Galdinia's thoughts as she silently approached.

"I'd like to be alone, Vega," Galdinia said, looking up at the soldier.

"I can understand that," Vega replied. "I just have to quickly say something."

"I really don't feel like talking."

"Nor do I," Vega said, crouching down beside the queen; Galdinia thought it would be fair to say that Vega rarely felt like talking, so this was their second uncharacteristic conversation in a matter of days. "I feel that what I have to say is important, though."

Galdinia looked at Vega for a moment before conceding. "Fine," she said with a sigh.

"Quill is an ass," Vega began, looking intently at her queen. Galdinia found Vega's word choice sobering. "You know that, I know that, I think even Quill knows that. He doesn't shy away from saying what he really thinks, and he isn't concerned about how he may affect someone else with his words."

"I know all this, Vega."

"On top of this," Vega went on, "he isn't someone who forgives easily—or at all—and he certainly won't move on from something unless all wrongs have been made right." Vega took a breath before her next words. "I say all this to say that I think you need to apologise to him."

"What?" Galdinia asked, incredulity painted over her face and voice.

"Quill has made it abundantly clear that he dislikes you—"

"That's a nice way of putting it," Galdinia remarked with a scoff.

"He believes that you have wronged him in the worst way possible," Vega said, her tone even. "So even though he has been nothing but an ass since we met him, which he's been quite consistent about, I think you need to tell him you're sorry for the loss of his best friend.

He is our direct connection to The Hook and their forces; his parents may be clever, but they won't shy away from hearing Elderwin slander the moment he steps back into The Hook, possibly affecting our chances at maintaining an alliance with them, no matter how conditional."

Galdinia and Vega stared at each other for a few seconds as Galdinia absorbed her words.

"Did Ilyon ask you to come speak with me?" Galdinia asked, frowning now.

"No," Vega said. "I told him I'd meet him in the woods shortly. My words are my own."

"I apologised for the damage of our soldiers when we were in Lund," Galdinia returned. "That should be enough."

"It should be, but it would seem it isn't," Vega replied. "I think he needs a personal apology, alone, away from all the strategy and politics."

"I don't think I can bring myself to apologise to him, not after what he just said," Galdinia said, dropping her gaze to the grass. "And even if I did, he has no interest in apologies or forgiveness. It won't change anything."

"You're right," Vega agreed, "he doesn't seem to be big on forgiveness. But you can't know the impact an apology might have until you try."

Galdinia shook her head.

"He has made me feel so inadequate time and time again," Galdinia said. "I don't think I could give him the satisfaction of inevitably choosing not to forgive me if I did apologise. That's too much power for him."

"Are you worried about giving him more power or losing your own?" Vega asked, her watchful eyes as attentive as ever.

"Can I be worried about both?"

"Of course you can. That doesn't mean either needs to be true. I'd argue you'll find more power in reconciliation, even in just attempting it."

"How did you come to that conclusion?" Galdinia asked, looking up at Vega again.

"Until you do something to prove Quill wrong about you, he'll go on believing whatever he likes," Vega explained. "You take back your own power when you choose not to be intimidated by someone who has a warped perception of you. You take back your power when you prove them wrong."

"He'll think I'm weak."

"I don't say this lightly, Your Highness, but he already thinks that about you." Vega's words lodged themselves in Galdinia's heart, searing her. "You could take back some of your strength by showing him who you really are, not only as a queen but as Galdinia: just, fair, and kind. Maintaining some semblance of an alliance could be a nice supplementary benefit."

Galdinia didn't respond right away. Could she really apologise to such a vile person? Could she really strike up enough nerve to try and reconcile with someone who had hated her since before they met?

"I'll think about it," Galdinia finally said, "but even if I do apologise, my hopes aren't high for reconciliation."

"Neither are mine," Vega answered, standing to her feet. "He's an ass and he'll always be an ass, but he may just become a more agreeable one."

With this, Vega walked back to their crumbling camp, leaving Galdinia to sit and ponder in the grass.

30

THE FOLLOWING MORNING, GALDINIA COULD HARDLY PULL HERSELF from her stretcher.

She had slept terribly as her mind circled the events of the night: her painful dreams, the fiery onslaught, Quill's diatribe, and her exchange with Vega. No matter how many times she tried to convince her thoughts to move on, she couldn't escape the visions of the attack —uncontrollable flames, Neryda's lifeless body, imaginings of Kaedric perpetuating the violence—and the echoes of Quill's hurtful words. Every time she thought she had persuaded herself to apologise to him, she could imagine just how he would respond, which promptly proved it wasn't a good idea. Would he laugh in her face? Possibly. Would he ignore her and walk away? Highly likely. After acting as his personal target to hurl verbal spears and glaring daggers at, she had predicted at least fifteen different responses that she'd likely hear from him.

It was for this reason that she had not yet braved the outside world. She felt trapped under a blanket of fear, feeling as though she were about to walk into a lion's den at feeding time.

The only thing that kept bringing her back to the decision to apologise to Quill was Vega's advice from the previous night: "You take back your power when you prove them wrong". If she could prove Quill wrong at least once, if even for a moment, she could be satisfied.

At that thought, Galdinia took her limited confidence and pulled herself from her stretcher. As she dressed, she prayed to the God of Wisdom, asking for the right words to say, hoping to keep the possibility of a very necessary alliance despite her distaste for their son.

Is that all I want, though? The question rang in her mind as she laced up her boots. If she was entirely honest with herself, she knew she wanted more than an alliance; she wanted peace.

Most of their troop was already awake and milling around the campsite when Galdinia finally surfaced. Neryda was sitting on a log beside the fire, cradling a cup of tea, clearly tired but very much alive and well.

"Morning, Gal," she said, raspy, smiling up at her friend.

"You're okay?" Galdinia asked, standing above Neryda and placing her hands on her cheeks and inspecting her face carefully.

"I was until you put your icy fingers on my face," Neryda said, scrunching up her nose.

"Just checking you've not lost any feeling." Galdinia smiled and pulled her hands from Neryda's fire-warmed skin.

"I certainly haven't," Neryda said, relaxing her face. "You didn't sleep well, though. You were tossing and turning all night."

Given that the walls of her tent had been reduced to little more than singed strips of material, Neryda had pulled her stretcher into Galdinia's tent, sharing her still-standing sleeping quarters for the night.

"Sleep didn't come easy after last night, but I'm fine," Galdinia said, attempting to give Neryda a reassuring smile. Before Neryda could question her further, Galdinia asked, "Do you know where Quill is?"

Making his way to the fire after packing up the largest tent with Evander, Ilyon answered, "He wanted to bury Opal before we left."

Galdinia glanced at the thicket of trees, and she saw Quill, shovel in hand, scooping dirt from a pile into the ground.

"How long has he been at that?" Galdinia asked.

"About an hour."

Galdinia watched as he painstakingly threw the dirt in the hole.

"How did you go with the prisoners last night?" Galdinia asked.

"They didn't give us any information," Ilyon explained. "Vega is usually very persuasive, but even she couldn't get anything from them."

"Where are they now?" Galdinia asked tentatively.

"Dead."

Galdinia looked at her captain, frowning as her stomach tightened.

"They attacked our camp, Your Highness," Ilyon went on, his jaw tight. "They tried to kill you. We couldn't take them as prisoners."

"You took Bentley as prisoner," Galdinia pointed out.

"That was when we were in Elderguard," Ilyon explained. "Given the circumstances, our grace can only stretch so far. Everyone's safety is paramount."

Ilyon's eyes flicked briefly to Neryda before settling again on Galdinia. Although the thought of killing the prisoners made her feel ill, she quickly reminded herself that Neryda had been caught in the crosshairs of an assassination on her own life, so she didn't let herself linger on the thought.

Across the camp, Bentley, Raia, and Kayd were making their way from further up in the woods, their hands full of berries, a few squirrels, and eggs. Kayd and Raia were talking and laughing between themselves; Galdinia noticed that Bentley smiled to himself, not quite joining in but seemingly comfortable in their presence. Glancing down at his hands full of quail eggs, Galdinia saw that his usual shackles were no longer wrapped around his wrists.

"The chains are gone," Galdinia noted, drawing Ilyon's eye to where she was looking.

"I thought that after last night's display of loyalty, we may let him forgo them momentarily," Ilyon explained. "He'll need to be back in them when we reach the Royal Guard camp, but a brief reprieve of freedom may be in order."

"By display of loyalty, do you mean when he hurled me out of the way of flaming balls of fire or when he stood up to Quill?"

"I wasn't aware of the former, so let's go with the latter." Once again, Galdinia was treated to a rare smile from Ilyon. "Is that okay with you?"

Galdinia considered it for a moment and decided perhaps it was time to take Bentley's advice: she had to stop assuming he didn't want her alive.

"That's fine, Captain," Galdinia said before turning back to look into the woods where Quill was still shovelling dirt, choosing in a split second to also heed Vega's advice. If she could see beyond Bentley's actions and learn to trust him, she needed to choose to be the bigger person and apologise to Quill, whether she thought he deserved it or not. "I'll be back shortly."

"Is everything okay, Your Highness?" Ilyon asked as Galdinia made her way towards the trees.

"Hopefully it will be," Galdinia said quickly, not allowing any space to talk herself out of this once again.

Moving into the thicket of trees, Galdinia caught Quill's attention quickly. He glanced up from his work, streaks of dirt smeared across his face, his hands equally dirty. He momentarily paused as he looked at her before continuing to shovel the dirt into the large hole in the ground. Galdinia glimpsed down into it and could make out the shape of Opal lying on her side, covered in a layer of dirt. She was lying four feet down into the ground, her final resting place.

"Quill," Galdinia said, "I need to speak with you."

Quill didn't stop or look up from his work, continuing on as if she weren't there.

"Quill, please," Galdinia said, an ounce of desperation in her voice. She didn't need him to give her a reason to turn around and walk away.

Quill paused in his movement, and Galdinia watched his shoulders rise and fall as he let out a tedious sigh before he reluctantly looked up at Galdinia with bitter eyes. He waited for her to speak, eyebrows raised, looking as though he was already finished with the conversation.

He is one of your people. The words came to Galdinia as quickly as they left. She wasn't sure if it was her own inner monologue speaking or perhaps the words of a power far greater than her own. *He needs to understand who you are as Galdinia.*

"I'm sorry," Galdinia finally said, staring at Quill, the residual pain of what he'd said to her the previous evening bubbling beneath her skin. It took every ounce of effort from her not to let it take over her words. She had to do what was right—no matter how painful—to build her alliance and protect her people.

Despite her apology, Quill's expression remained unchanged, and he did not respond. She had to admit, staring blankly wasn't one of the responses she thought she'd be met with.

"Did you hear me?" Galdinia asked after a pause. "I'm sorry."

"I heard you," Quill said frankly. "I just didn't think it required a response."

Irritated, Galdinia gritted her teeth before replying. "Quill, I'm trying to apologise."

Quill didn't speak for a few seconds, his eyes scrutinising Galdinia.

"That's nice," he finally said. "But do you know why you're apologising?"

"Yes," Galdinia said, only barely maintaining her composure, aware of the delicate subject they were stepping into. She prepared the words she had practised a hundred times in the night. "I'm sorry that my soldiers likely caused the death of your closest friend in a battle where his people were used by a hideous enemy to take the brunt of the attack. I hate that my forces were the cause of such pain, so I'm sorry."

Quill's jaw tightened as Galdinia spoke. He glanced away from her, looking up into the trees that surrounded them.

"That's not why you're sorry," he said between tight lips.

"Yes, it is. I'm very sorry—"

"No, it's not," Quill said, cutting her off, his voice full of poison as he looked back at her. "You're sorry because I'm your only connection to Lund. You're sorry because I've not done a very good job of establishing your alliance with them, and you want me to keep trying because you're getting really desperate. You're sorry because you need me to hate you a little less to keep my parents on your side. You're sorry because you'd say anything to keep your crown. You're not sorry because I lost my best friend, or because I had to watch his parents grieve him, or because an innocent life—among thousands—was lost. You're sorry because you think an empty apology will help you save your own neck."

Every word punctured Galdinia, sending an echo of pain through her body, causing her breath to shorten and her chest to ache.

"That's not true." Galdinia's words travelled on a weak breath. How could he possibly think she was that selfish?

327

"It's not?" Quill asked, his expression stolid. "Then why are you only now apologising to me? Why weren't the first words out of your mouth when we met in The Hook an emphatic apology?"

"Because I didn't know how much hurt had been caused," Galdinia said simply, her voice feeble, her frustration and guilt coursing through her veins; she wasn't sure which was more prevalent at this point.

A pained laugh escaped Quill's lips. "Some of The Hook's greatest allies lost their lives at the hands of your soldiers, and you didn't think to apologise?"

"You're not the only one who lost allies in that attack." Galdinia couldn't stop the words from tumbling from her mouth as she spoke. "The army from Lund cut down my people—both soldiers and civilians. I had to watch as they blinded my army with their gift before driving swords into their hearts and arrows through their eyes. So forgive me if my first words to you weren't 'I'm sorry'."

"The exact same thing happened to my best friend," Quill said, stepping towards Galdinia, his voice low and his expression lethal. "He was found with a Royal Guard's arrow in his chest."

"And for that, I am terribly sorry," Galdinia said, standing her ground as she stared up into Quill's face. "I know the heartache of losing someone you love; my best friend was also taken from me, and now he's somewhere in Valah's clutches."

"At least he's still alive." Quill's voice was firm, but Galdinia could see his eyes starting to become glassy.

"Sometimes I wish he wasn't." Galdinia was taken aback by her own words, and her heart lodged somewhere in her throat. Was she really going to admit a painful truth that she hadn't shared with anyone, let alone Quill? "Drystan was taken by someone who loathes me more than you ever could. Valah knows how important he is to me, and she took him from beneath my nose, using my vulnerability after my father's death to manipulate me." Galdinia could feel her own tears rising. "And he's been in her imprisonment for weeks, and I can only imagine what kind of state he's in. At night I lose sleep wondering if he's still breathing, or when he last ate, or how Valah has instructed her soldiers to treat him—or worse, how she herself has treated him. And in the depths of midnight when I find myself drifting between reality and the dark imaginings of wherever he is right now, in my weakest moments, I wish that she would put him out of his misery." With her words, a tear escaped Galdinia's eye. "Because I'm not worth the pain he is going through right now."

Quill was silent as he stared down at Galdinia, the tension between them tightening.

"But as long as he's being held prisoner because of me, as long as Valah is still a threat to my people, I'll fight to do whatever I can to make sure she is vanquished." Galdinia didn't try to control the quiver in her voice. "That includes going to absurd lengths to build allies— like trying to work with someone who hates me. I need you to realise that I'm not your real enemy. I know you think I am because you see me as a power-hungry heir, but I care far more about my people than my crown, Drystan especially." The tears pooled in Galdinia's eyes as she spoke, and still Quill held her gaze, his expression hard. "So that's why I'm sorry, Quill. I'm doing all I can to save the people of Crysterra—from Elderguard, to The Hook, to the mountains, to Drystan, wherever he is—just like I'm sure you would have done for Kove if you had the chance."

At the mention of his friend's name, Quill lifted his chin, looking as though he was biting his tongue against his thoughts and his emotions.

"I'm sorry for the pain that has been caused to you and to your allies," Galdinia said, her tears now falling silently down her face. "I never want anyone to experience that hurt again, but I can't assure anyone that freedom without allies. Without your family's and Lund's forces, there is very little we can do against Valah. If we want to bring her down and truly avenge your friends and my people, I need *your* alliance just as much as I need your parents' alliance. And more than that, I need your forgiveness." Sniffing, Galdinia stared at Quill through tears. "Please, Quill, we need your help."

Quill's jaw was firm, his eyes shining. Desperately, Galdinia prayed that her words—and painful honesty—had swayed him, if even for a moment.

"I'm not making any promises," he finally said, his voice low and raspy as he spoke against the pain, "but I'll stay in contact with Orlon and try to sway him."

Galdinia released a shaky breath. "Thank you."

"Don't thank me yet."

"Gladly." A hint of a smile flickered at the edge of Galdinia's voice.

After a stretch of silence, Quill finally said, "I'm sorry about your friend too."

"You didn't capture Drystan."

"You didn't kill Kove," Quill said, his voice quiet, "but the acknowledgement helps."

"I just want to save him," Galdinia replied. "I need to. He can't die because of me."

"I understand. Like you said, if given the chance, I would have done anything to save Kove. I'll see what I can do to stop another innocent murder."

"Thank you."

Turning away from Galdinia, Quill continued to shovel dirt into the grave before him. Galdinia quickly wiped the tears from her cheeks, the thought of Drystan catching her by surprise and bringing a fresh wave of anxiety through her. If he was still alive, she may have just increased their chances of rescuing him.

"Can I help?" Galdinia asked with a sniff. "I'd like to pay my respects to her as well."

With a curt nod, Quill agreed.

Without a shovel, Galdinia got down on her knees and used her hands to collect the dirt to slowly cover Opal's body, taking it in turns with Quill's movements. They worked in silence, each one doing what they could to honour Opal, one mound of dirt at a time.

31

"IT'LL BE OUR FINAL ROUND OF TRADER'S TRIUMPH FOR A WHILE, SO you should join us."

Bentley stared up at Kayd for a few silent seconds. Kayd had interrupted Bentley's vital role as dishwasher for the evening and was asking him to join what had become their nightly round of cards. At least, that was what Bentley thought he said—but was he imagining it?

Over the course of the previous two days, as they travelled through The Vale, past Wharf Town, and to the entrance of Bear Jaws Valley, Bentley had noticed a shift in the way he'd been treated within the group. He'd been offered cups of tea after dinner and been included in the preparations for breakfast that morning. This felt like the ultimate confirmation of trust, though: a game of Trader's Triumph, an almost holy ritual among the Queen's Guard. He supposed he should have been honoured.

Glancing around Kayd, Bentley looked to Galdinia, who was sitting beside the fire, listening to their conversation. To his surprise, she gave Bentley a subtle shrug, leaving it up to him to decide his own fate for the evening: he could continue busying himself with his monotonous task, or he could step into the fold.

"Sure," he finally said, discarding the plates.

He'd be back in his chains the next day when they approached the

Royal Guard camp, so he thought he might as well make the most of his freedom. Ilyon told the group he expected the Royal Guard soldiers to be organised at the western entrance into Bear Jaws Valley, ready to train and prepare for their encounter with Valah in a matter of days. Bentley had hoped to go without the shackles altogether, but he could see why Ilyon thought it unwise to allow someone who was in a cell in the barracks just three weeks ago to walk freely through platoons of the same soldiers who captured him.

"Excellent," Kayd replied with a grin.

"I've not got anything to bet with though."

"I'll give you something to start with," Kayd replied before adding in a whisper, "but don't make me regret inviting you by losing it all to Evander."

"Are you sure you've got enough money to share?" Galdinia asked as Kayd and Bentley joined the circle beside the fire. "Have you not lost it all to Evander at this point?"

Galdinia's tone was casual and easy, her words carrying a lightness Bentley had watched bloom over the last two days. Although initially rattled by the attack from Kaedric and Valah's soldiers, Galdinia appeared to hold a greater sense of ease among her guards; Bentley supposed saving each other's lives had a distinct bonding effect. Was he being afforded the same treatment now as he sat with them, ready to play a round of cards that was otherwise reserved for friends and allies?

Aside from the perceptible displeasure that sat in Neryda's eyes as he sat down, the rest of Galdinia's guard didn't seem to mind his participation, and Quill had taken himself to bed early, so Bentley wouldn't be susceptible to his snarky remarks either. He'd noticed that there was even a shift in Quill's demeanour since he and Galdinia had shared a quiet word the morning after the ambush. He still hurled sarcastic comments and sardonic looks—many of which were reserved for Bentley, the one he proclaimed as the enemy—but he seemed to have softened towards Galdinia, making the rest of their journey all the more comfortable.

"Although we aren't all lucky enough to have a vault of gold beneath our own castles," Kayd shot back at Galdinia, a glint of mischief in his eyes, "I do in fact have plenty to go around. Not that it matters. I'll be winning every coin back tonight."

"Sorry, Kayd," Galdinia continued, picking up the cards Raia had dealt, "but I don't think there are enough hours in the evening to make that possible."

Bentley watched Kayd as he looked up at Galdinia with sharp eyes. The rest of the Queen's Guard were painted various shades of impressed. Glancing at Galdinia, Bentley saw a smirk dance over her lips from behind her cards. What he wouldn't give to keep such an expression permanently on her face.

"You're a little too confident for someone who hasn't won many games herself," Kayd said, returning Galdinia's quip.

"If my sums are correct, though, my win to lose ratio is looking far better than yours," Galdinia replied, organising her cards.

"I think you've just painted a nice big target on your back, Your Majesty." Kayd slowly enunciated every syllable of Galdinia's title.

Bentley knew she hated that.

"Likewise," Galdinia replied simply.

"Are you two done with the verbal sparring?" Neryda cut in. "Can we play now?"

"By all means," Kayd said, gesturing towards Galdinia. "After you."

Bentley hadn't noticed, but a wide smile had stretched across his lips, watching the exchange. He forced his face to relax as he pulled his cards up to his face, inspecting and organising them in his hand.

"Your Highness," Ilyon said from where he was sitting on a log beside the group, cleaning his armour. "Can I speak with you for a moment?"

"Is there any way we can talk while I take Kayd's money from him?" Galdinia asked, her tone casual as she played her first card.

"I'd hate to be a distraction," Ilyon replied.

"Don't worry, I don't have to concentrate too hard to actually be able to do that."

Bentley watched as Galdinia caught Kayd's eye from across the circle. He scoffed in response. This sent another smirk flickering over Bentley's lips; he was no stranger to Galdinia's quick wit, and he was glad to be afforded the chance to hear it, something he wasn't sure he'd ever be graced with again.

Ilyon looked around the circle before deciding that whatever he needed to say could be said amongst the group, Bentley included.

"Not to bring the mood down," he said carefully, "but I think we need to discuss our next moves."

After Kaedric's blindside, Bentley, too, had wondered how Galdinia would choose to progress with their plans. In Lund, they had decided that facing Valah without the extra forces of those in the east would be a death wish, but Bentley had held his tongue every time he went to question Galdinia's next movements.

"How do you think we will fare against Valah after Kaedric's betrayal?" Galdinia asked while Raia contemplated which card to discard. "We were already running a risk with the numbers we had, but assuming we've lost the Novus family's soldiers in the east, it seems almost impossible now."

Although she attempted to maintain a lighthearted air to her voice, Bentley could see a shade of fear and uncertainty in her eyes. He had seen something very similar as they sat on the terrace of the castle together; he had been suggesting they marry after knowing each other for only a matter of days. She appeared excited, happy to have a solution to an insurmountable problem, but the doubt in her face as she grappled with her heart was palpable.

Now, he wondered how many questions were plaguing Galdinia as she wrestled with a far more significant decision. Would she consider returning to her original plan to rescue Drystan alone? Bentley decided that he wouldn't be able to sleep that night—he'd be listening for noise from Galdinia and Neryda's tent, going after her if she decided to go on ahead alone.

"I agree, it's not an ideal situation," Ilyon replied, using a rag to buff the chest plate of his armour. "Valah made it clear that she will bring violence wherever she goes, so a conflict feels inevitable."

Bentley played his first card as he watched them both from across the circle.

"But is it foolish that I'm bringing it upon myself in a matter of days?" Galdinia asked, shifting from side to side in the grass.

"At least you're doing it on your own terms," Evander offered, his voice even as he threw a coin into the growing pool of money in the centre of the circle.

"Evander's right," Ilyon added. "Whether in the Midcrest Grasslands, in Elderguard, or the Wetlands, she will try to take your crown."

"And my head."

Bentley swallowed against the pain that rose in his throat at the thought.

"Gal." Neryda scolded her friend, frowning as she took her turn.

"It's true," Galdinia said frankly. "As long as I'm wearing my crown, she'll want to take it all from me."

"It's certainly a factor," Ilyon said gravely, his hand pausing, contemplative.

"While I'd like to keep my head," Galdinia assured the circle, "I also want to mitigate the impact of a battle on not only the wider population but also on our army. We can't afford to lose any more soldiers."

"That will be difficult," Vega said, picking up a new card and discarding one Bentley had been waiting for, which he quickly picked up at the start of his turn.

"Do you think there's any chance of convincing Lund to join us?" Galdinia asked, an air of hope in her voice.

"Honestly, I don't," Ilyon replied. "They made it abundantly clear that they won't cooperate with our plans and priorities."

"All because they see me as nothing more than my crown."

"I don't think they realise just how different their lives will look if Valah had it instead," Kayd pondered, meeting the current bet.

"Not that they'll still have their lives," Raia added quietly.

"Could you appeal to the Lidels once more?" Evander asked, his eyes remaining on the pile of cards before them. "You could request that they use whatever sway they have left to change Orlon's mind."

"One immoveable object speaking to another," Galdinia mused.

"It might be our only chance to build our forces, though," Ilyon added. "If we sent word to them tomorrow morning, they might be able to send their own message to Orlon in time."

"We only have six days," Galdinia said with a sigh, casually throwing a card onto the pile. "I don't think we can rely on changing the elders' minds."

"It's worth a shot, isn't it?" The question escaped Bentley's lips before it had fully formed in his mind. They had invited him to play cards, not to join discussions of strategy, but that hadn't stopped him before, he supposed. "What else have you got to lose?"

"You mean aside from potential allies, her life, and the lives of thousands of others?" Neryda asked, her eyes piercing across the circle as she stared at Bentley.

"I think we've already established that's a threat no matter what," Bentley replied, taking a card from the draw pile, happily finding another he needed. He was only two water cards away from declaring "triumph".

"We don't need to invite it in by hoping for a response from people who don't respect us, only to be left stranded and surrounded." Neryda didn't drop her gaze from Bentley, and he was again reminded of the bond between her and Galdinia. Galdinia had warned him during the Week of Mourning just how fiercely loyal she was; he wasn't sure Neryda would ever trust him again.

"But if we go into a battle without having tried, we will almost guarantee death." Bentley met Neryda's hostility with blatant honesty. "Galdinia said it already: Lund's respect doesn't extend to the crown. Appealing to the Lidels is our best bet."

Bentley was painfully aware of his word choice, including himself in the plans. It seemed Galdinia was too, because she was watching him carefully as the game continued, her eyes seemingly deciphering his own expression.

"I hate to admit it, but Bentley's right," Galdinia replied before Neryda could cut in again. Bentley's lips turned up at the corners. "I'm not running from meeting with Valah. The consequences are far too dire." Galdinia's fingers clenched around her cards as she spoke; Bentley knew she was thinking of the prospect of losing Drystan to Valah's hand. "But if I can try once more to convince the Lidels to vouch for us, we have to do it. Valah is coming for me regardless. I might as well face her with my best chance of keeping my life… and Drystan's."

"And we still have the security of Edana taking the bait to do away with Valah for us," Ilyon said, starting to buff his armour once again.

"Ilyon," Galdinia said, her tone contemplative, "what would your soldiers do if Valah killed me?"

The air around the circle thinned as everyone froze in their movements. It made Bentley uncomfortable every time Galdinia mentioned her potential death, but there was something in her question that felt too pragmatic, too impersonal. A frown set into his brow as he watched her.

Ilyon even appeared momentarily stunned, unable to answer her question right away.

"Firstly, the Royal Guard are instructed to protect you at all costs," Ilyon finally said, finding his voice. "But should their efforts fail, they will do whatever possible to maintain an Elderwin reign."

"As far as I'm aware, I don't have any heirs."

She was trying to be funny, Bentley told himself, but he hated how plainly she talked about her death as if it were a real possibility.

"Your reign extends beyond you to the Syndicate," Ilyon explained.

"So they'll move to Elderguard and protect Ryden?" Galdinia asked, picking up a card and inspecting it carefully before glancing around the circle.

"Exactly," Ilyon continued. "But if that becomes futile, they will scatter to any number of locations around the country where our allies reside. Sometimes fighting isn't as necessary as maintaining a stronghold elsewhere. If all my soldiers are killed, then there's no way to take back an Elderwin rule, as it were. So each battalion will follow the instructions of their commanders, who are made privy to many contingencies." Ilyon glanced at Galdinia. "But that's not something we need to worry about, Your Highness."

Galdinia continued to stare at the card in her hand, contemplative. Bentley tried to decode her expression, hoping to find her thoughts woven in the creases in her brow and the long gaze of her eyes.

"That's good to know," Galdinia eventually replied, a pleasant smile resting on her face as she placed the card—a four of fire—on the discard pile before her.

From the corner of his eye, Bentley saw Evander shift in his seat— he sat up straight and his face relaxed as he looked up at Galdinia, a distinct joy in his eyes. No, it wasn't joy, Bentley realised; it was pride.

"Ha!" Neryda said from beside Galdinia, picking up the card Galdinia had abandoned and shifting it within her own hand. She quickly threw another card into the centre of the circle before laying her hand out in the grass for all to see. She had a straight run of fire cards from two to ten. "Triumph!"

An exasperated sound came from Kayd as he dropped his cards to the ground, revealing he was two cards away from a complete run of wind cards.

"You're kidding!" he said with a huff, dragging his hands over his face. "You practically gave her the win!"

"I don't think it was her goal to win," Evander said evenly, the pride still reflecting in his face. "She just wanted you to lose. You're learning, Galdinia."

Bentley watched Galdinia's own face brighten at Evander's words as they shared a knowing look.

"Only from the best," Galdinia said with a smirk.

"Excuse me," Neryda said, incredulous. "I think we're forgetting who actually won here."

Neryda leant forward and dragged the coins towards her, her eyes hungry.

"Well done, Ner," Galdinia replied graciously as she slung an arm around Neryda's shoulders, throwing her own cards into the pile.

Bentley peered at the cards; all she needed to win was a four and seven of fire, confirming that she had, in fact, let Neryda win.

Bentley glanced at Galdinia as the dancing light of the fire flickered over her face. She looked up, catching his eye, a resolute warmth in her expression.

"Another round?" Evander asked, collecting the cards and beginning to shuffle them.

"I suppose so," Kayd groaned, frowning across the circle at Galdinia. Bentley could practically see the target on Galdinia's back grow.

"One more round for me," Galdinia said, her smug smile still on her lips. "Then I need to write a very important message to The Hook."

THIRD QUARTER

32

The Royal Guard camp was even more impressive than Galdinia had imagined. The day after their final camp as a troop, Galdinia walked through hundreds—if not thousands—of tents that had been set up across the western entrance of the Bear Jaws Valley, sitting perfectly in their neat rows. They walked past soldiers training in combat circles and at archery targets, while others prepared their weapons or brushed their horses' manes. The Queen's Guard's new quarters were at the centre of the camp—if they were attacked while asleep, a few thousand soldiers stood between Galdinia and an attacker.

All morning as they made their way to the camp, an impossibility of a plan started to form in Galdinia's mind. Echoes of their conversation the night prior and information they'd gathered on their travels fell into place, as though on a chessboard. The next moves were still a tangle of complicated decisions, but she could finally see a road ahead to saving Drystan and hopefully the rest of Crysterra.

After settling themselves in their tents—and taking much needed baths—Galdinia and Neryda stepped into the captain's tent and were faced with Ilyon, the Queen's Guard, and Quill, all standing around a table covered in maps. Upon arriving in the Royal Guard camp, Bentley had been resigned to a tent of his own, not far from the

340

Queen's Guard's quarters. He went obligingly, assuring Galdinia that he understood that his apparent freedom could cause a stir among the many thousands of soldiers who could easily recognise the man who had betrayed them in their own home.

"If we send a battalion north, we run the risk of sending the conflict towards those villages," Ilyon said, pointing to the largest map in the centre of the table.

"You're not willing to risk the lives of a few to save thousands more? Including your queen?" Quill asked, arms crossed over his chest.

"The reason for meeting Valah in this location was to avoid such dangers," Ilyon said, not taking his eyes from the map.

"But we'll have a far greater chance of survival if we attack their army from all angles," Quill retorted. "If my parents have agreed to the new terms of retrieving their jewels from Edana themselves—"

"You mean you haven't heard from them?" Kayd asked, staring at Quill.

"They're not likely to put such information in a letter," Quill replied defensively. "I had to be as cryptic as I could in my own. Their silence in return is confirmation enough."

"That's risky," Kayd replied.

"So is this plan," Quill shot back, looking down at the maps. "As I was saying, assuming Edana takes the bait, my parents' army will come in from the west, and then we just need to cover the south."

"We're not sacrificing innocent lives," Vega interrupted, her voice hot.

"And we can't risk moving any closer towards the Shadowed Coast," Ilyon pressed, looking at Quill with stern eyes. "We can't guarantee Edana's army will show, but we also can't confirm they won't attack us if we move too far south."

"It's your funeral then," Quill said, turning from the table, noticing Galdinia and Neryda in the doorway.

"Quill," Galdinia said, causing the rest of her soldiers to turn and acknowledge her. "I need you to go back to The Hook."

"You're not offended by what I said, are you?" Quill asked, rolling his eyes. "I don't want innocent people to die just as much as you, but this is all in the name of strategy."

341

"No," Galdinia said, holding a piece of folded parchment towards him. It was held together by the Elderwin seal. "I need you to get a message to your parents."

"Do I look like a raven?"

"I don't trust a raven with this." Galdinia kept her hand outstretched towards Quill.

"You shouldn't trust him either," Neryda said darkly.

"They'll be taking their leave from The Hook in just a matter of days," Quill went on, ignoring Galdinia's hand and Neryda's words. "Can't someone deliver it to them when they're a little closer?"

"No, I need them to have this information as soon as possible."

Quill stared at Galdinia, his frown deepening. Conceding, he finally took the parchment from her and looked down at it in his fingers. Galdinia could feel the heavy gazes of her guards on her.

"It won't help you to read it before you deliver it," Galdinia warned. "I've stated that should the seal be broken before they read it, our deal is off and their jewels will die with Edana. I don't know him well, but I can imagine your father wouldn't be pleased with his own son costing him his most prized possessions."

Quill stared at Galdinia, eyebrows raised; he almost looked impressed. Almost.

"We'll see you soon then, I suppose," he replied.

"That you will," Galdinia said coolly.

"I'd say it's been a pleasure, but…" Quill trailed off as he looked around the tent.

"The feeling's mutual," Neryda replied, a cynical smile on her lips.

Quill raised a brow at Neryda before turning from the queen and marching out into the camp.

Galdinia joined her guards at the table, staring down at the map too.

"I've never wanted to read a letter more in my life," Kayd commented, smirking at Galdinia.

"Yes, will you be sharing the contents of your note with us, Your Highness?" Ilyon asked, looking across the table at the queen. "By the sounds of it, there's more in there than we discussed last night."

"For now, I'll be keeping it to myself." Galdinia looked around the circle. "It's not that I don't trust any of you, but for me to see if this strategy will pan out, I need to play it close to the chest."

"You're a good student," Evander replied, raising his eyebrows at Galdinia.

"Time will tell," Galdinia said with a meagre smile. "So where are we up to?"

Ilyon held Galdinia's gaze for a long moment before speaking. "Quill had hoped we'd send soldiers north to attack from multiple sides, but I don't think we can risk the lives of civilians."

"I agree," Galdinia said with a nod. "I don't want to put anyone else at risk. If Valah wants a fight, we will contain it to the Grasslands. But I want to meet with her first and try to avoid a conflict."

"Not alone," Ilyon said firmly, staring down at Galdinia.

With a deep intake of breath, Galdinia replied, "No, not alone. You and Bentley will join me."

All eyes flew to Galdinia. This was not the response her closest allies were expecting.

"Bentley?" Neryda asked, her tone mimicking the expressions of her guards.

"He could be used as a bargaining chip," Galdinia said simply. "He could prove to be very valuable."

Ilyon looked at Galdinia carefully, unsure of her plans.

"And what about the rest of us?" Raia asked. "Respectfully, but you're mad if you think we won't be by your side too."

"You'll be on the frontline of our army, ready to lead our soldiers if we need to attack, though I don't plan on things escalating to that point," Galdinia explained; her team was becoming sceptical, and Galdinia needed to quiet their concern. "If I can rely on Edana to show, then she'll take care of much of the onslaught of Valah's army, should a conflict arise."

"Sounds risky," Kayd said on a breath.

"Gal," Neryda chimed in, "Ilyon is right. You can't just walk into Valah's vicinity without your guards and expect her not to hurt you."

"Being without my guards is one of the very reasons I think she may not kill me on sight," Galdinia countered, choosing her words carefully as she spoke. "And you will be staying with them back here at camp."

"Gal, you're not serious—"

"Don't argue with me, Ner," Galdinia cut in, shaking her head. "I'm not going to risk losing you again. Raia, you are to stay with Neryda at all times."

"Yes, Your Majesty," Raia said with a nod.

"No, not 'Yes, Your Majesty'!" Neryda was indignant.

"You can either have your own horse and wait with Raia, or I can replace Bentley with you in the prisoner tent and chain you up. Your choice, Ner."

Neryda glared at her friend but finally agreed.

"Speaking of," Galdinia said, "I need to go brief Bentley on the plan."

"You're going to disclose more of your plan to him?" Evander asked, stunned.

Galdinia could feel the tension in the air sizzling with every passing second. Bentley was integral to her plans, but without a trusting guard, she knew she'd see it all come crumbling down around her any moment.

"Everyone's on a need-to-know basis. You just need to know different things," she finally said.

Before Galdinia could walk from the tent, Ilyon stopped her. "Your Highness, I'm not sure about all of this. I feel like we're going into this blind."

Ilyon held her gaze, a disquieting unease shadowing his features, an expression Galdinia was not used to seeing on her captain's face.

"You just need to trust me, Captain," Galdinia said earnestly. "I'm being the queen you believed I was even before I had my gift."

Ilyon continued to stare at her from across the table, and Galdinia knew it took every strength within him to not only respect her commands as queen but also her intentions as the young woman who'd cried, yelled, and cursed in front of him, on the brink of giving up. She was still that girl—desperate and fierce—but she had a new fire burning within her, one that would do anything to save not only her loved ones but her people. Galdinia watched as Ilyon slowly came to terms with this.

"I trust you," he finally replied, nodding.

"Thank you," Galdinia said gently before turning from the tent.

She quickly made her way to where Bentley was being held, weaving between two rows of tents and avoiding the obvious gazes of the soldiers she passed. Two Royal Guard soldiers were stationed at the entrance and were perpetually standing at attention.

"I need to speak with the prisoner," Galdinia said, standing tall with her crown on her head and her bow and arrows strapped to her back. The soldiers did not hesitate in pulling back the fabric doors and allowing her entrance.

Galdinia stepped into the round tent and was faced with Bentley sitting on the hard ground, his hands weaved and his wrists bound in shackles once again. The shackles were attached to a chain that was fastened to the centre post of the tent. It was driven deep into the ground, keeping Bentley contained.

Bentley looked up as Galdinia walked in, and he squinted against the bright light that followed her in before the canvas doors settled shut. A small smile spread over his lips as he realised who his visitor was.

"They didn't give you somewhere to sleep," Galdinia said, looking around the empty tent, discomforted by the thought of him sleeping on the ground for the next few nights.

"The grass isn't so bad," Bentley said as he stood up, his chains rattling.

"I'll get you a stretcher," Galdinia promised.

"That's really not necessary," he replied, shaking his head.

"I know it isn't," Galdinia assured him. "But I would like to."

"Thank you," Bentley replied, smiling again.

"Before I do, though," Galdinia said, "I need to speak to you about something."

"Your Highness?"

Thirty minutes later, Ilyon's voice came from outside the tent, interrupting Galdinia and Bentley's quiet conversation.

"I'll be out in a moment, Captain," Galdinia called in response before turning back to Bentley.

He was now leaning against the post, staring at his weaved hands, his frown set deep into his forehead.

"Are you sure about this?" Bentley asked, looking up at Galdinia.

"I'm certain."

"And nobody else knows?" he asked, keeping his voice hushed.

"I can't tell anyone else at this stage," Galdinia replied. "Ilyon will have choice words to say about my strategy, and the others won't agree to it. And Neryda—well, I can't even imagine her response."

"So why me?" Bentley asked, a boyish innocence in his voice.

Galdinia was careful as she spoke, choosing each word with purpose.

"You keep telling me to do all I can to keep myself alive," Galdinia explained, "and this is the only way I can assure that while still saving Drystan. My hope is that you won't oppose my plan if it keeps me breathing."

"That still isn't guaranteed."

"It never is, but I think this is my best chance," Galdinia said. "So, can I trust you?"

Bentley frowned as he watched her, pursing his lips, contemplative.

He held her gaze as he finally replied, "Yes, of course."

"Thank you," Galdinia said, releasing a long breath. "Not a word to anyone, understood?"

"Understood," Bentley said with a nod.

"You'll need this too," Galdinia said, unclipping a small lantern from her hip; it housed a tiny flicker of a fire.

"Really?" Bentley asked, raising his eyebrows. "You're going to trust me with a flame?"

"Not to echo your own words, but I think if you wanted to kill me, you would have done it already," Galdinia said, the lantern dangling at her fingertips. Despite the promise of his own fire, Bentley's eyes were locked on Galdinia and not the flame.

"I'm glad you finally believe me," Bentley said.

"Don't make me regret it," Galdinia said as she slowly stepped toward him. "If you get any funny ideas, just remember that if you hurt me, you'll have Neryda and the entire Queen's Guard to answer to."

"A fair warning," Bentley agreed with a nod. "I wouldn't dream of it, though."

Galdinia wondered in that moment what he did dream about. Was his unconscious self plagued with images of his deepest regrets and most fitful fears like her own? Or could he sleep soundly even after everything that had happened between them? Something within Galdinia caused her to doubt it.

"Good," Galdinia said simply before stepping around him to his back.

"What are you doing?"

"I can't have the guards finding it," Galdinia explained as she lifted the hem of the back of his shirt and attached the small vessel to his belt. As she secured it, her fingers brushed against the skin of his back, and Galdinia saw his muscles tighten at her touch. Almost a month ago, when they sat on the terrace and he left gentle kisses on her arms, she was the one reacting to his touch, each press sending jolts of happiness along her skin. Now, she couldn't help but smile at his involuntary reaction as she lowered his shirt over his hips, the floaty material concealing the lantern.

She came to stand in front of him again, and he was watching her carefully, a timidity in his eyes that she'd not seen from him before. Had a rosy pink colour tinted his cheeks? Galdinia chose to spare him potential discomfort by moving on quickly.

"There's enough oil in there to keep it burning until you'll need it, and you aren't to try to control it before then," Galdinia explained. "I assume one of the soldiers outside is a Flourisher. So as long as you don't draw it from the vessel, he won't notice it; his own fire will take too much of his attention to feel this one."

"You have my word." Bentley seemed to have relaxed again, still leaning against the post.

They shared a long gaze, and Galdinia tried to scrutinise his expression. She knew it was a risk trusting Bentley, but he was possibly her final lifeline.

"Bentley, I need to know something," Galdinia eventually said.

"Anything."

"In exchange for accompanying us on this trip, you promised Ryden and Ilyon some great information about Valah's plans after the attack on Elderguard," Galdinia said, watching him closely. "I need to know what that information is."

A small smile flickered over Bentley's lips.

"You know, I never actually promised to know anything about Valah," Bentley said, a gentle reticence in his voice. "I believe my words to them were something to the effect of having information that would keep you alive, and I think I've done just that."

Galdinia stared at Bentley. A few weeks ago, when she so easily wrapped her hand around his throat, hearing this reply would have sent her into a frenzy. Now, however, she couldn't stop the smile from rising on her lips. Of course he'd been calculating with his words; he'd have done anything to help keep the breath in Galdinia's lungs. And that was why she knew she could rely on him now.

"So you have nothing for me?" Galdinia was impressed.

"Sorry, Your Majesty," Bentley said, his voice taking on a gentle sincerity. "It was nothing more than a tactic to help keep you safe."

And there, in his bright eyes, Galdinia saw the same sparkle that drew her in during the Week of Mourning.

"It's both nice and terrifying to trust you again," Galdinia said, candid.

"It's nice being trusted," Bentley returned. "And I don't take it lightly." Bentley's voice was earnest, and a promise settled in his eyes. "I'll keep trying to keep you alive as long as you'll let me. You have my word, Galdinia."

A smile tugged at Galdinia's lips as she held on to the hope that she could rely on Bentley's word. Again, she held his gaze and couldn't ignore the jolt in her own heart as they shared this moment.

"I'll see you soon," Galdinia finally said before turning towards the tent doors.

"Bye," Bentley replied, hesitating before adding, "Gal."

Galdinia paused in the doorway, a smile flickering over her lips, but she didn't turn to look at him again before pushing past the canvas doors.

She didn't have time to linger on hearing Bentley call her by her nickname as she came face-to-face with her captain, who was patiently waiting for her.

"Captain," Galdinia said before turning to one of the guards at the tent. "Get him a stretcher, clean water, and a set of armour."

"Of course, Your Highness." The soldier nodded before leaving his post to follow the queen's orders.

"Armour?" Ilyon asked, raising his eyebrows at Galdinia.

"I'm not sending him out into the grasslands without protection," Galdinia said quickly, not mentioning the contraband flame she'd just left on Bentley's belt.

"And a stretcher and clean water?" Ilyon questioned as they began to walk side by side through the camp. "Is there any reason you're trying to keep a prisoner so comfortable?"

"For the same reason you took away his chains in The Vale and you stopped weaving him in the mountains," Galdinia replied. "We can trust him, and we aren't beyond providing some comfort where possible."

"I see," Ilyon said, looking at Galdinia from the corner of his eye.

"What can I help you with, Captain?" Galdinia asked, changing the subject as they walked down a row of tents. Soldiers became distracted as they watched their queen and captain walk past, most standing at attention immediately, others looking with scrutinising eyes at the young queen. She wondered if friends of Drystan's were among them—were any of them aware of their past together? Although she knew Drystan was far too honourable to share such details with his comrades, she knew their relationship wasn't a secret within Elderguard.

"Are you willing to tell me what was in that letter to the Lidels yet?" Ilyon questioned.

"Sorry, Captain," Galdinia replied, "not yet."

"You're being awfully secretive," Ilyon noted. "I can't say I like it."

"I thought you said you trusted me."

"Of course, Your Highness, but as your captain—"

"Then that's all that matters," Galdinia said, not breaking her stride.

"I fear you're going to propose we attack the Wetlands early," Ilyon mused. "Or perhaps call the Lidels to storm Edana's forces."

"And why would we do that?" Galdinia asked, looking up at Ilyon carefully as they walked beside the area of camp cordoned off for training. "I need Edana ready to take her rage out on Valah."

"Hence my curiosity," Ilyon said as they stopped to watch a pair of Weavers fend off the attack of two Flourishers in a combat ring. The opposing elements crashed together, swirling in an impossible ribbon of fire and water. The water sucked the life from the flame, while the fire simultaneously evaporated the water into a cloud of steam. These soldiers were so evenly matched that they could replenish their own gifts while draining that of their opponents.

"In five days, we will meet with Valah in the grasslands, I will secure Drystan, and Edana's forces will help in attacking Valah's army, should they put up a fight," Galdinia explained simply, watching as the Weavers bore down on the Flourishers with their gifts, extinguishing their flames, inch by inch. "That was our plan, and that remains the plan."

"Except for your secret task for the Lidels," Ilyon noted, watching the battle wage on.

"Assuming all goes according to plan, then my message to the Lidels may turn out to be unnecessary," Galdinia said as the Weavers pressed harder with their water, now getting closer to swirling around the Flourishers' heads. A thin wall of fire now stood between the Flourishers and their suffocation.

"You aren't making this easy for me, are you?" Ilyon asked, his voice stern.

"Actually, I'm trying to make it very simple for you," Galdinia suggested, her voice light. At that moment, one of the Flourishers—with gritted teeth and a strained neck—made an almost imperceptible flick of their index finger and thumb, sending a spark of flame from their wall of fire down to the ground, where it skidded across the dirt and rushed up the leg of one of the Weavers' armour. The howl of the Weaver, caught off guard by the sudden, yet effective attack, filled the immediate area.

"How did you come to that conclusion?" Ilyon asked as they watched his soldiers flail, clearly unaffected by the sight before him. With such a brief, yet painful distraction, the Weavers lost control of the fight, and the Flourishers quickly advanced on them.

"This requires very little strategy from you," Galdinia explained as the Weaver that was attacked scrambled to control his gift once again. "And all you need to do is follow the plan and trust me. That sounds quite simple, don't you think?"

At that moment, the Flourishers got their footing and surged forward across the ring with their fire, ribbons of flames evaporating the water from all angles, sending clouds of steam above their heads. Within three seconds, their opponents were on the ground, surrounded by fire, all water evaporated into the air. A cheer came from one side of the ring, and fellow soldiers celebrated the winners. On the other side of the ring, another group of soldiers were kicking the dirt, frowning at their cheering brothers and shaking their heads. They seemed to be organised by their gifts.

"I suppose so," Ilyon said as they watched the Flourishers retract their fire and help the Weavers to their feet. "But I still don't like it."

"You don't have to," Galdinia said, noticing that coins were now being traded among the spectating soldiers. "But I appreciate you trusting me."

Ilyon looked down at Galdinia from the corner of his eye, inspecting her. That was the closest she would get to a reply.

"So how do I organise to be part of one of these skirmishes?" Galdinia asked Ilyon as a new pair of soldiers entered the ring to face off against the winning Flourishers.

"You don't," Ilyon replied simply. At Galdinia's forceful glare, he went on to explain, "You're the queen, and I will not have my soldiers engage in combat with you."

"You had no problem setting Evander, Vega, Kayd, and Raia on me," Galdinia pointed out.

"They're part of the Queen's Guard. They are highly trusted soldiers and were under strict instructions not to harm you." Before Galdinia could protest about the pain Vega's training sessions caused her, Ilyon said, "Nothing beyond normal training aches, of course."

The next fight in the circle began, and the Flourishers were now faced with two Wind Wielders.

"I'm getting pretty good at building my shield," Galdinia said, watching as the Wielders used their gifts to manipulate the fires and shape them despite the Flourishers' control. "I think I could be a formidable opponent for your soldiers."

The Flourishers tried to penetrate the wall of wind that the Wielders were pushing towards them, but they struggled to surge forward while also keeping their flames from extinguishing.

"I'm sure you would be, but you would also be far too much of a distraction," Ilyon said, watching his soldiers closely. "You'd never get a true fight out of them; they'd be too afraid to hurt you."

"Perhaps when we return from meeting with Valah, then?" Galdinia suggested as she and Ilyon turned from the circle and continued to walk down another row of tents.

Moments later, a cheer erupted from behind them. Galdinia craned her head back to see who had triumphed—the Flourishers or the Wielders—but the throng of soldiers had become too dense, and the winners were blocked from her view.

"Perhaps," Ilyon said, looking carefully at Galdinia before they turned and continued to walk through the camp together.

Galdinia knew he would never agree to such a thing, but she enjoyed prodding him nonetheless.

33

THE NIGHT BEFORE HER RECKONING WITH VALAH, GALDINIA FINALLY managed a dreamless sleep. She wasn't sure if she was so struck by exhaustion after training for days on end since arriving at the camp or if her body simply knew that if any night she needed sleep, it was this one, but she awoke the next day having not been woken by terror-filled images of fiery attacks, blinding fog, or a pained Drystan. She realised that the next time she would see him would be with her own two eyes rather than in her subconscious. At least, she hoped she would.

What if he isn't alive?

Galdinia knew this thought was futile and unhelpful, but she had to maintain some semblance of hope that at dusk today she would see him alive again.

Before long, Neryda joined Galdinia, and they ate boiled eggs and bread together in her tent. Although not quite as nice as her bedroom in the castle, her lodgings were far superior to the stretcher she had been sleeping on during their travels, and the small table and chairs they sat at in the corner of the tent were a lot more comfortable than logs and the grass.

"I didn't realise just how grateful I was for fresh bread," Neryda said, buttering her third slice.

"It truly is a gift from the heavens," Galdinia agreed, sinking her teeth into the fluffy dough and salty butter.

Neryda finished her slice of bread before finally speaking again. "Shall we keep dancing around the topic, or are you ready for me to ask you about today?"

Galdinia let out a great sigh before answering.

"I don't think I'll ever be ready to talk about it," Galdinia said thoughtfully. "I've simultaneously longed for this day and also hoped it would never come. I have to confront Valah and possibly die in the process."

"But…" Neryda encouraged.

"Drystan." Galdinia's heart swelled at the thought of Drystan again. In her mind she could see the sweet boy she had fallen in love with all those years ago, with his kind eyes, jovial sense of humour, and protective embrace. That was who she hoped to see today, but she knew he likely resembled the malnourished and fatigued Drystan of her recent dreams.

"Drystan." Neryda nodded, seemingly sharing in the sentiment of the moment.

"He has been my priority this whole time," Galdinia went on. "Of course I want to keep Elderguard safe, build allies, and do what's right for my people, but if I'm honest, I'm doing everything I can to ensure his safety too. I just can't have him die because of me."

"He won't, Gal," Neryda said gently. "And even if something happens—I'm not saying it will, but we know too well how treacherous Valah is—it's not your fault. You can't be blamed for Valah's actions."

"I know that in theory, but in practice… that's something else entirely."

Neryda paused before speaking again. "He knows you love him, Gal. He does."

These words pulled tight at Galdinia's heartstrings. *Does he, though?* They had left on such bad terms, and she needed him to know that she loved him; she couldn't possibly survive if he didn't know that.

"I'll be able to tell him soon enough," Galdinia said finally, pushing against her fear. She didn't have time to wallow in self-doubt right now.

"That you will," Neryda said with a sad smile. "One more slice?"

"I think it's only necessary," Galdinia said, returning Neryda's smile, though mountains of fear and trepidation lay beneath it.

As the sun lowered towards the horizon in the west, painting the sky in dusky shades of pink and orange, Galdinia gripped her horse's reins firmly in her hand as it walked her across the Midcrest Grasslands. Behind her, the Royal Guard army was standing patiently in rows, awaiting a signal from their queen or captain before they made any movements. She sat tall and strong, her mother's crown on her head, glistening in the light of sunset. Atop their own mounts, Ilyon and Bentley flanked her; she'd tucked Drystan's helmet in the pack attached to Ilyon's saddle for safekeeping.

Had she known a month ago that she would not only be trusting Bentley enough to remove his shackles and the weave of water from his hands but to accompany her to meet with Valah in an open field, she would have buckled over in laughter. Yet here they were, side by side, going to confront the woman who Bentley had previously sworn his loyalty to, in order to save the man Bentley had used as leverage to assure his own safety. As they rode, Galdinia silently prayed that her trust in him wasn't misplaced. She supposed that it was now just a matter of time until she could confirm where his true intentions lay.

In a matter of minutes, he could either be fighting with her or against her.

Glancing sideways at him, Galdinia thought she could finally see the Bentley she first met at the docks on the Second Day of Mourning. His hands were free of restraints, and his hair almost shimmered in the glow of twilight, now no longer matted. He was wearing the armour Galdinia had requested for him, and a bow and sheath of arrows were slung across his back, matching Galdinia's. With his unbound wrists and proper attire, he sat up tall on his horse, looking far more like the lord who didn't hesitate to jump in the sea to save a stranger's life. She hoped that was the man beside her now and not the one who led her into Valah's trap in the castle.

Feeling her gaze, Bentley turned to look at Galdinia. His bright eyes sparkled in the light, and he gave her a reassuring smile before she turned to look ahead of her again. Then her heart stopped.

Across the field, more than one hundred metres away, her enemy was approaching.

Valah was advancing on her own horse, her black cloak trailing behind her in a billowing mass. She resembled a cloud of smoke slowly approaching during a forest fire, signalling its destructive path. Beside her, her advisor Reynard rode on his horse; at his hip was a great sword glinting with each step of his steed.

After slowly travelling closer to each other, both groups halted, now only ten metres of grass between them. It was at this moment that Galdinia noticed another with them. With a rope bound around his wrists, which was attached to the back of Reynard's saddle, a shaky and weak Drystan stepped out from behind the horse, his face down-cast and his breaths coming in heaping gulps.

Galdinia sucked in a desperate breath at the sight of him, her heart sinking and her chest tightening. She squeezed the reins in her hands to stop herself from leaping off the horse and running to him.

He was here, and he was alive.

Noticing they had stopped and he could finally rest, Drystan looked up. Tears had already welled in Galdinia's eyes as her gaze caught his. Shock set into his dark features: dark pools of exhaustion rested under his eyes, his hair was a twisted mess as it fell into his face, and he looked like he hadn't eaten in days. The thick, fraying rope was digging into his wrists, and Galdinia thought that without this anchor, he would have collapsed to the ground. He was broken and weary, but he was Drystan. He was her Drystan.

He looked across at her with eyes of longing and desperation, searching her face for the answers to questions that he couldn't ask. Galdinia did all she could to hold back her tears as she tried to give him a heartening smile, steadying herself with the reins. Her heart screamed at her to run to him, but she had to remember where she was and who she was faced with. If she went to him now, she would have wasted every moment of planning up until this point and she could almost certainly guarantee both of their deaths. His eyes heavy and tired, Drystan looked gravely at Galdinia. She knew he would be angry with her for risking her life like this, but she could hardly think about that.

Steeling herself against her emotions, Galdinia sat up straight, making firm her expression and turning her attention to Valah.

The woman sat atop her horse, looking across at Galdinia as though she were a foul piece of mud stuck to the bottom of her boot. Valah looked down her slender nose, her sharp cheekbones cutting across her face as she pursed her lips.

"Have you finally decided to give me what belongs to me?" Valah asked, using her gift to carry her words over the grass between them, sending her voice snaking up to Galdinia, dancing around her ears, far too close for comfort.

Galdinia forced herself not to react to the invasive experience, though it made her heart quicken and the hairs on her arms shift.

"Do you intend on returning to me what's mine?" Galdinia countered, her words catching on Valah's returning wind. Despite the pain in her chest and the fear in her heart, Galdinia's voice was firm and strong as she addressed her enemy.

At her words, Reynard reached back and pulled on the rope, forcing Drystan forward by his wrists, causing him to stumble as he came to stand between the two enemy horses. Galdinia bit down on her tongue to stop herself from crying out.

"All I want is that piece of jewellery atop your pretty little head," Valah replied, pointing to Galdinia's crown. "Then you can have your lover boy back."

Looking beyond Valah, Galdinia glanced at her army, who was a few hundred metres away. They sprawled over the grasslands, larger than Galdinia's forces by far. She glanced southwest, waiting expectantly for another army's banners to crest over the hills. Still hopeful that hers weren't the only forces Valah would have to fight off, she needed to buy some more time.

"Don't insult me, Valah," Galdinia said, turning her attention back to the woman in front of her.

"Whatever do you mean?" Valah asked, her voice crooning.

"You and I both know that you don't intend on letting me walk away alive, with or without my crown," Galdinia replied.

"Well, I suppose I could send you off to the far reaches of the kingdom," Valah said, looking around nonchalantly. "You'll be left on your own, without any food, supplies, or allies. You can get a taste of what your grandparents did to me when I was just a child. Let's see how you fare in the big, scary world on your own."

"That was an act of mercy," Galdinia spat. "They should have killed you with your treacherous parents."

Valah let out a sharp laugh that echoed across the field and crept its way up into Galdinia's ear, causing her to wince. "Mercy? Don't dishonour their memory like that, Galdinia." Valah turned her nose up again. "I'll admit, some days I wish they'd have just killed me right there in the library. It would have been far easier. But knowing that I'm moments away from dethroning their granddaughter and taking the crown back for the Pyrin name, it's well worth it. I couldn't think of sweeter retribution." Valah snarled as she looked across at Galdinia with bitterness and malice in her eyes. "And no, I don't think I'll exile you like they did to me. I'd like to take your head back to the castle with me and put it on display somewhere, to remind everyone who the true queen is."

Galdinia's eyes shifted to Drystan, who had a look of utter panic on his face. Galdinia's eyes flicked to the southwest again before looking back to Valah.

"Well, Valah," Galdinia said, releasing the reins of her horse and sliding off its back, "let's see just how vile you are."

Reynard straightened up, placing his right hand on the hilt of his sword. Valah's brow creased, and Galdinia saw Ilyon's face snap to look at her.

"Your Highness," he said, releasing a breath, "what are you doing? Get back on your horse at once."

Galdinia looked up at Ilyon and mouthed two words: *trust me*.

Stepping forward a few metres, Galdinia reached up for her crown, grasping the glistening headdress in her hands. Pulling it from her head, she felt her spine extend, relishing the freedom of the extra weight. Galdinia looked at the crown of twisted gold vines and starlight crystals, admiring the beautiful piece of art and symbol of power it had become. Looking up at a sceptical Valah, Galdinia bent down and placed the crown in the grass.

"It's all yours, Valah," Galdinia said, standing up straight.

Reynard looked to his master before gazing back down at Galdinia, still resting one hand on the hilt of his sword, the other holding tight to the rope attached to Drystan, whose expression was full of disbelief. Galdinia didn't dare turn around to look at Ilyon; she already knew that he was glaring at her in utter bewilderment.

"Surely you don't wish me to believe it's that easy," Valah replied, incredulous.

"But it is," Galdinia said with a light shrug. "You want the crown in exchange for Drystan, you can have it. I'm giving you what you want, so now you need to give me what is mine."

"Have you really just been waiting to give me your crown for the last month?" Valah asked, a sickening smile twisting on her lips as she threw a leg over her horse, sliding off her steed.

"I've had to mull over my decision. It hasn't been easy," Galdinia said, her face conveying no emotion, "but it's worth it."

"Worth it?" Valah let out another laugh as she slowly walked towards Galdinia. Reynard's eyes followed Valah closely. "You think giving up your crown and your title for this boy is worth it?"

"I am more than this crown," Galdinia said, her chest tightening as Valah approached, now mere feet away from her. "But you are nothing without it."

"Oh, Galdinia," Valah said, bending down to pick up the crown. "You have no idea what I am with it, though."

Valah lifted Galdinia's crown in the air, inspecting it closely. Her grin grew as she looked longingly into the jewels. She looked like a hungry mountain lion that just caught its prey. Slowly, she raised it to her head, secured it in place, and took in a deep breath.

With a maniacal grin, Valah brought forth a great wind across the field, its power swirling around them, sending both her and Galdinia's hair whipping in all directions. Galdinia took a few steps backwards and forced herself not to draw on the fire at her hip.

Not yet, she reminded herself.

Allowing the wind to still, Valah's arms came to rest at her side.

She looked positively frightening with the crown on her head.

"I've given you what you wanted," Galdinia repeated herself. "Now return Drystan to me."

Demonstrating her complete lack of fear, Valah turned her back on Galdinia to look at Drystan, whose expression was still one of exhausted shock as he struggled to stand up straight.

"You know, I don't think I will," Valah said with a sneer, turning back to look at Galdinia.

"We had a deal," Galdinia said, her emotions on the brink of slipping. She needed to stay calm; for this to go the way she had planned, she couldn't let her composure drop.

"You didn't really think I'd let you leave here with the breath still in your lungs, did you?"

"You can't kill her." Bentley's voice rose from behind Galdinia. She heard his horse trot up beside her, and she glanced up at him. He was sitting just as tall as he had been when they arrived, and his eyes were vicious as he looked at Valah. In response, Reynard led his horse forward by a few more feet, tugging Drystan with him, his eyes locked on Valah.

"Oh, your new pet speaks," Valah said, a wicked smile forming on her lips. "I'm surprised you made it out of that library as more than ash, Bentley. Oh, how far you've fallen."

"I couldn't have stooped any lower than when I was working for you," Bentley replied, his voice hot. "I realise that now."

"I think you'll realise just how wrong you are shortly, Bentley."

"No, I won't, because you won't kill her."

"Care to entertain me?" Valah casually asked. "Go on, tell me why I can't slice Galdinia's blonde head from her shoulders right now."

At her words, Galdinia felt a tightening in her throat; she wished not to hear again about the prospect of losing her head.

"Across all reaches of Crysterra, there are people loyal to the Elderwin name," Bentley said, his voice even and strong as he slipped off his horse and came to stand beside Galdinia. "If you take Galdinia's life, you will be subjected to a ruling that begins out of treason, and the population will see you as the murderous villain that you are."

"You're mistaken," Valah interrupted. "You seem to think that is a title I would cower from, but I welcome it gladly."

"You won't when they turn on you." Bentley's words were impassive. "Imagine the entire capital and half of the rest of the country turning their backs on you the moment they learn of her murder.

They may not have been enamoured with her father, but you'll be hard pressed to find Elderwin loyalists that don't support their queen."

Valah thought on Bentley's words for a moment before responding.

"Thankfully my allies are widespread and far larger in number," Valah replied, her voice becoming frustrated. "I don't have a problem removing every single Elderwin loyalist from Crysterra, nor will they."

"You would begin your reign as a murderer." Bentley scoffed. "Your blood will cover the throne room before dawn tomorrow."

"I'd like to see them try," Valah said, her voice drawling.

As she stood staring at Valah, watching her exchange with Bentley, Galdinia could feel a low rumble rise in her chest. She couldn't tell if it was coming from the desire to reach out to her flames or somewhere beyond her.

"You have another option, of course," Bentley went on. "You could let her live."

"What a brilliant idea," Valah replied, her tone sardonic, clearly becoming tired by this conversation.

"If you let her live and allow those in the capital and beyond to believe that Galdinia willingly gave up her crown, they may simply accept you as their queen. I know it's not in your nature, but this would be the road of least resistance. You may even have the chance to keep your own head."

"But if you kill me," Galdinia interjected, "you'll be following me to the grave. Mark my words."

Valah paused.

"You know, Bentley, I don't think I gave you enough credit when you were in my employ," Valah said, her words long and drawn out. "This is quite a clever plan. Give me the crown, convince me not to kill Galdinia, then attack me when I least suspect it. It's a little predictable but quite clever for you, a measly lord from The Edges. I'll have to tell your parents of your plan—of course you won't get a chance to. You'll be buried in the ground before nightfall."

Galdinia looked up at Bentley and saw his expression shift, a perceptible amount of his confidence falling from his face. She knew it wasn't because of the thought of his own death but rather the mention of his family.

"Oh, did you think they were dead?" Valah asked, her attention now entirely turned to Bentley. "No, the Penrose family is alive and well—all of them. They're back there with my troops, ready to fight, in fact."

"Not all of them," Bentley said, his voice low.

"Of course all of them," Valah said, a smirk on her face. "Your parents were very quick to put swords in their youngest children's hands, especially after the utter disappointment and embarrassment their eldest turned out to be."

"They're children." Bentley's voice was barely above a whisper, but it held a fiery fury.

"I did think of that," Valah said, her tone painfully honest. "But a body is a body. The more swords in my army, the better. They won't survive in a battle for very long, but they may slow down a soldier or two of yours, so it's worth it for me."

"Bentley," Galdinia said, keeping her eyes on Valah. "Don't listen to her. She's lying."

"Galdinia, have I ever lied to you?" Valah asked. Galdinia frowned as she stared at Valah. "No, I haven't. He has." She pointed at Bentley. "But I never have. And on your deathbed, why would I start now? Young Elres and Aster Penrose are among the soldiers behind me, standing side by side with their parents. It was hard to find armour that fit, so I just put them in fighting leathers instead."

At this, Bentley started forward towards Valah, but Galdinia reached out an arm to stop him, grabbing onto his forearm and holding him in place.

"Bentley," Galdinia hissed, her tone one of warning.

"Let's hope a battle doesn't break out this evening. Otherwise they may have to use the swords they were given," Valah said as she drew a long, sharp dagger from her hip. "And there's only one way to guarantee that."

In that moment, Valah sneered at Galdinia as she snapped her fingers with a painful crack. As she did, Galdinia felt her breath lodge in her throat. Suddenly she couldn't breathe. Her hands flew to her throat, suspended in a suffocating vacuum, no air going in or out.

"No!" Drystan's hoarse voice barely carried to Galdinia as he tried to struggle forward, but Reynard held him in place by the rope, a wicked grin spreading over his lips.

"Galdinia!" Bentley exclaimed, turning to face her.

But with another snap of Valah's fingers, Bentley's eyes went wide, his own breath stopping in a heartbeat. Galdinia tried with all her strength to draw in a breath, but Valah's grip on her was so fierce, she couldn't even glean a whisper of a sigh.

Galdinia could feel her face growing warm without the air, grey spots sprinkling in her vision. She staggered to the ground, in such pain that she couldn't even make a connection with the flame at her hip or the one on Bentley's belt. As she writhed against the desperation, almost ready to pass out, the air suddenly flooded back into her lungs as she choked in oxygen. As she blinked, regaining her vision, she could feel a vibration underfoot. They didn't have long left.

Glancing up wildly at Valah, she saw that Valah's hands had been weaved by her captain, whose face had contorted into one of fury and strength, still atop his horse. If anyone's gift could break Valah's, it was Ilyon's.

"Kill her!" Valah screeched as she pulled against Ilyon's gift, desperately trying to break free.

At this, Reynard charged forward on his horse, sending Drystan tumbling to the ground as he was pulled across the grass. Impulsively, Galdinia forced herself to her feet and threw her body into Bentley's, tackling him out of the way of the horse's hooves, sending them both crashing into the ground, still gulping for air.

Without a second thought, Galdinia leant up on one knee and pulled her bow and an arrow into her hands, calling on her flame to alight the tip of her arrow. As Reynard forced his horse into a circle, Galdinia aimed at the horse's rear, sending her fiery arrow at the rope. Whether or not the tip struck the rope, it didn't matter—Galdinia commanded her flame to spread and burn through the rope, singeing Drystan's attachment to the horse, sending him rolling across the tall grass. For a second, Galdinia gazed in the direction he'd landed, but he didn't rise. The tall grass remained motionless.

"No!" Galdinia cried, her voice echoing across the plane.

"Gal—move!" Bentley's voice accompanied his movement as he pulled Galdinia up from the ground just in time before Reynard's horse attempted to run her down once again. This time, though, his sword was free and he was brandishing it; had Bentley not taken hold of her, she would be in a state that would make Valah very pleased indeed.

Before she could attack Reynard, Bentley pulled an arrow from his sheath and nocked it in a second. He aimed carefully before letting the arrow fly through the air, sending it into the gap between Reynard's armour at his shoulder. He cried out in pain, pulling on his horse's reins, causing it to neigh in protest.

"I'll take care of him," Bentley said, taking out another arrow.

He shot it quickly, this time straight into Reynard's left foot, sticking right through his boot. The man roared in agony again, this time falling from his horse and crashing onto the ground in pain.

Looking around, she watched as Valah and Ilyon were in a furious tussle themselves: Ilyon still mounted on his horse, Valah on the ground. She was fighting against Ilyon's water, trying to break her hands free. Galdinia looked around her for Drystan, unable to find him in the tall grass, feeling panicked and disoriented after falling to the ground.

Again, the rumbling Galdinia felt in her chest rose, and the sound of shouts and horses' hooves beat through the air. Valah whipped her head to look to the southwest, where over the crest of a nearby hill, a sea of gunmetal grey tumbled into sight, and banners holding the Elderwin crest came into view. It wasn't Galdinia's forces, nor those of the Lidels, but rather her bloodthirsty aunt's army.

Galdinia took a cautious step backwards as she reached out to the flame at her hip, pulling it from its perch. Somewhere behind her she could hear Bentley and Reynard in a struggle, but she forced herself not to look away from Valah.

"It looks like you have another enemy to deal with before me," Galdinia said, and Valah turned back to Galdinia, her eyes wild, hands straining against Ilyon's gift. "Edana wants you dead."

"I'll take you first—"

With a wild cry of desperation, Valah managed to free her hands of Ilyon's grasp, sending his water flying in all directions. Before Valah could reach out towards the queen with her gift, though, Galdinia pressed both hands out in front of her, transforming the meagre flame in her palm into a great arc around her head, encircling herself in a dome of flame, protecting her from Valah's onslaught.

Valah stopped in her tracks and snarled at the sight of Galdinia's shield. Incensed, she turned away from Galdinia and towards what Galdinia realised very quickly was Drystan's lifeless body, fury seething around her.

"Drystan!" Galdinia screamed, the dome of fire trembling before breaking and returning to a flame in her hand.

Before she could rush forward, an arm wrapped around her middle, pulling her back towards their horses.

"You need to go!" It was Bentley, and he was shouting over the growing sounds of trampling and shouts heading their way. Galdinia glanced at him and saw that he'd left Reynard either dead or unconscious in the grass.

Galdinia strained against his arm, desperately trying to get to Drystan. With only one free hand, his other still holding tightly to Galdinia, Bentley sent a wall of flame out from his own vessel, encasing Drystan, blocking Valah from getting to him. Startled by the flame, Valah's horse reared, while Valah shielded her face from the fiery inferno.

Galdinia watched in stunned silence as Bentley protected Drystan with his fire. She stopped pushing against his arm, allowing him to use both hands to maintain the shield around Drystan, his face firm and heated as he took a few slow steps forward. Without warning, Valah threw her gift in Bentley's direction, seemingly to knock him off his feet or to extinguish his flame. In a reflexive action of distress and anguish, Galdinia threw a wall of flame between the gale-force wind and Bentley, protecting him from the onslaught. The three of them stood there, each holding their gifts with fervour and all the strength they had. Galdinia ground her feet into the grass, glaring at Valah as she continued to press forward, trying with her ardent anger to penetrate Galdinia's fire.

The rumbling from Edana's forces grew as they came closer and closer.

"Your Majesty!" Ilyon yelled to Galdinia. "We must retreat!"

"Not without Drystan!" Galdinia yelled through gritted teeth, her eyes flashing from Bentley to Valah.

"Go!" Bentley yelled at Galdinia, standing firm to keep his dome in place around Drystan, sweat beading at his temples. "I'll keep him alive! You need to go!"

At this, a crash of hooves approached as Ilyon and his horse sprinted towards them—he wasn't giving her a choice. With his arm outstretched, Ilyon reached down for Galdinia, taking hold of one of her outstretched arms and pulling her up from the ground before charging his horse towards Valah. Instantly, Galdinia's wall of flame returned to a mere flicker in her palm.

No! Galdinia thought hopelessly, watching as Bentley became defenceless. With a cry, however, Valah hurled herself to the grass and out of Ilyon's path, the connection with her gift also dropping as she fell to the ground.

With great effort, Galdinia pulled herself up behind Ilyon, and they circled around towards the north, away from Valah, Bentley, the oncoming army, and worst of all, Drystan.

"We have to go back for them!" Galdinia shouted over the whipping wind and crashing hooves, her arms locked around Ilyon's armour. "Ilyon! Take us back!"

Straining to look backwards, Galdinia watched as Edana's soldiers approached dangerously close and Reynard slowly started to rise, holding his sword in the air, inviting Valah's soldiers to charge and join the fight.

"You're my priority!" Ilyon called back.

"But they're *my* priority!" Galdinia shouted, turning back to yell in her captain's ear against the rush of wind, her voice urgent. "Please take us back!"

"I have to get you to safety! Bentley can fend for himself!"

"And Drystan?"

"Bentley will protect him," Ilyon assured her as he pushed his horse forward, encouraging it to gallop faster and faster to the north, away from their enemies and their allies.

Galdinia turned again to look back towards Drystan and Bentley. They were specks now, but she could see a dome of flame at the centre of the field, as well as a billowing mass of black. Galdinia could hear the resounding clashing of metal on metal as the beginning of battle broke out. Voices of anger, fear, and pain rang out over the field as it became washed in deeper dusky hues.

Twisting in the other direction, Galdinia saw that her army had not moved. They still looked on towards the beginnings of the battle.

"What will our forces do?" Galdinia asked. "Their captain isn't there to instruct them."

"Nothing yet," Ilyon called back, still pushing his horse faster. "They've been instructed to keep themselves alive, though, so when they see your crown on Valah's head, they'll be her forces instead."

Galdinia watched them as they galloped further and further away, the pain in her chest rising.

Galdinia turned her head back to the battle she so desperately wanted to rush back to, tears forming in her eyes, perpetuated by the cool wind whipping in her face. She watched through bleary eyes as Valah's army spilled across the field, moving as an undulating mass towards their leader—towards the new Queen of Crysterra.

NEW MOON

34

LAKEBORN WAS A SMALL TOWNSHIP NESTLED IN THE DEPTHS OF THE Midlands, shrouded in trees, positioned beside the Midlands Lake. The autumn chill ricocheted off the water and tumbled through town, bringing with it the promise of a cold winter to come.

Tucked in an alleyway beyond the centre of town sat a small tavern hardly detectable from the street. Only locals regularly travelled through its doors; however, on the odd chance that a traveller found themself in need of somewhere to lay their head in Lakeborn for the night, the two rooms above the tavern were almost always available.

Thanks to this fact, Galdinia and Ilyon found themselves sitting— or rather, pacing—in one such room.

After fleeing the Midcrest Grasslands, Ilyon refused to let his horse stop galloping until they were kilometres from the conflict and they could no longer hear the clashing of metal and the shouts of pain. Despite Galdinia's furious protests to turn back, Ilyon ignored her, forcing them to ride through the night. The moon had now disappeared from the sky, and only the stars provided them with minimal light as the captain navigated through woodlands and past busy towns. Galdinia's mind whirred as they rode, her aching heart screaming at her to turn around, but the further they rode, the more she knew it was too late.

Had she just given up her crown *and* lost Drystan, all in a matter of minutes?

Hours later, they finally arrived at Lakeborn soon before dawn. Ilyon seemed to be familiar with the town, and he took them straight to the tavern, tying up his horse behind the building and shrouding Galdinia in a cloak stored in his riding bag. Before he ushered her away, Galdinia pulled out Drystan's helmet and tucked it beneath the billowing fabric of her cloak.

Once above the tavern and in their room, Ilyon locked the door and slowly turned around to look at Galdinia. All manner of emotions flickered across his face, his once stoic exterior crumbling in a breath. Galdinia could only imagine the thoughts racing through his mind.

"Captain, I—"

Ilyon raised a hand, silencing Galdinia. He took his other hand and rubbed his temples, releasing a long sigh. Galdinia had never seen him like this, and the unpredictability kept her mouth shut. She held Drystan's helmet in her hands, using it as some kind of stability in this moment of simmering chaos.

"You gave up your crown," Ilyon said eventually, not meeting Galdinia's eye.

"Yes, but—"

"You gave it up." Ilyon sounded dumbfounded, as though he couldn't quite believe his own words. "Please tell me you didn't make that decision in the moment."

"Of course not," Galdinia tried to explain.

"So you planned on giving up your crown?"

"Yes."

Ilyon looked across the room at Galdinia now, some sense of his usually balanced self returning.

"And you didn't think to inform me?" Ilyon's words cut Galdinia deep.

But she had prepared herself for this conversation; it was inevitable the moment she'd decided it was worth forgoing her crown.

"You know I couldn't have told you," Galdinia said, her voice quiet. "In no world would you have let me leave camp if you knew my plans."

"You're right, I wouldn't have." Ilyon clenched his jaw, but

Galdinia held her head high. "But why would you give it up at all? We could have fled with your crown. You'd still be queen."

Here we go, Galdinia thought, preparing every reason and thought that she deemed as logical to have led them to this result. "No, I couldn't still be queen."

"Of course you could be. We would have—"

"No," Galdinia said firmly, pressing her palms harder into the metal of the helmet. "She would have killed Drystan the moment we attacked, and I would have been the next to go."

"You don't know that."

"She wouldn't have hesitated, Ilyon. We both know that." Images of Drystan in her nightmares and the one she'd left lying motionless in the grass infiltrated her mind, wreaking havoc on her consciousness.

"But you gave her exactly what she wanted. There was no strategy. We could have planned it together!"

Another wound opened in Galdinia's chest with his words. She couldn't take another moment being underestimated.

"Captain, I respect you beyond words." Galdinia was very careful as she spoke. "I know it likely broke your heart to see me hand over my crown, but imagine, just for one second, how truly difficult that was for me. I did not decide that in a split second or because I thought it would be easy. I did that entirely for strategy's sake."

Ilyon took pause before responding. "I'm struggling to see the strategy."

Galdinia held her tongue against the slew of words she wanted to throw at him right now. For someone who was usually so accepting of Galdinia as a young matriarch, he was choosing the wrong moment to underestimate her.

"We need allies, and we know that without Lund, we will likely never win in a battle against Valah. When we met with the elders, they told us in no uncertain terms that while that crown still sat on my head, they wouldn't align with us, so now the crown is no longer on my head."

Ilyon stared at Galdinia, lost for words. When he finally found them, he said, "You took Quill's advice," referring to Quill's hasty suggestion before they left Lund.

"I did, in fact," Galdinia said with a nod.

"That was brave."

"I know, and possibly a little bit stupid."

"Maybe a little."

"But this may pay off for us," Galdinia said firmly. "And if it doesn't, then I have potentially lost my crown forever."

"But if it does pay off…"

"We'll have to wait and see." Galdinia held her captain's gaze as she continued. "I need to show Crysterra who I am beyond the crown, and I can't do that if Valah decided to kill me. It's all very well and good for me to ask people to join our cause in the Elderwin name, but when they have been burnt by that name in the past—or names like it —I can't expect them to join my cause. Orlon and the elders don't know *me*. They think they do, but they couldn't possibly see past the crown on my head and the power it gave me. This is my chance to prove to them that our cause is one worth fighting."

"This is risky, Your Highness."

"I think you ought to get used to calling me Galdinia."

"You may not have the crown anymore, but you're still my queen," Ilyon said with a sense of finality. "So this was more than a rescue mission?"

"Indeed," Galdinia said with a nod. "Far more than that."

"The Lidels and their army were never going to join us, were they?" Ilyon asked, putting the pieces together himself.

"Not once I sent Quill off with that letter," Galdinia replied.

"I hope you're now willing to share what you wrote in it."

"If we want to stand any chance in taking down Valah once and for all, I'm going to need all the forces I can get," Galdinia explained. "Although I quite liked the idea of the Lidels retrieving their jewels from Edana themselves, I need The Hook's army to stay strong. After Quill's little outburst after the ambush in The Vale, I realised that we simply couldn't survive a battle with our quickly depleting numbers, so I didn't want to risk losing more. In the letter, I told them to hold fast in The Hook, to fortify their province, and that I'd contact them soon about our next movements forward."

"So you're now hoping we can work on securing both Lund and The Hook without your crown?"

"Precisely," Galdinia said with a nod. "I know it's a gamble, but had I not taken it, I can almost certainly assure you I'd have been killed hours ago."

Ilyon pondered her words as he inhaled a deep breath.

"And how does Bentley fit into all of this?" Ilyon asked. "I'm still trying to understand why he was considered more trustworthy than me."

This was the question Galdinia felt the most apprehension about answering.

"In no way is he more trustworthy than you, Captain," Galdinia assured him with a shake of her head. "But Bentley played a necessary role in all of this—I couldn't even trust Neryda to do this."

With the mention of her best friend, Galdinia's gut twisted; she couldn't linger on the thought for long, or she'd rush from the room, take Ilyon's horse, and ride until she found Neryda alive and well. She knew she'd made the right decision for the greater population, and she just had to hope and pray that Neryda was still breathing, protected by the Queen's Guard.

"Is that right?" Ilyon asked, unconvinced.

"Bentley would do anything to keep me alive," Galdinia said carefully.

"And I wouldn't?" Ilyon's voice took on an uncharacteristic air of offence.

"Of course you would. That's all you ever do," Galdinia said quickly, "but I know you wouldn't have agreed to my plans, and you would have likely physically barred me from leaving my tent if you knew what I wanted to do. Bentley, on the other hand, was in no such position to stop me. I needed someone who would follow my plan and help me execute it without question. My apologies, Captain, but for once, you weren't the man for the job."

Ilyon released a tired sigh, the tension between them slowly dispersing as he accepted her explanation.

"I may not entirely agree with your decisions here," Ilyon said with a brief shake of his head, "but I respect your strategy. You could have been dead in the grasslands by now had you not done what you did."

At this, Ilyon's features softened, his pride for Galdinia etched into his expression.

"I'm just trying to survive another day," Galdinia said on an exhale, looking down at Drystan's helmet, the shiny onyx metal reflecting a warped version of her face back at her. "I can only hope the others will too."

"I suspect we'll find out soon," Ilyon said, breaking Galdinia's concentration on the piece of armour.

"Excuse me?"

Ilyon was standing straight again, head held high, his countenance back to its usual steadiness.

"After your secretive meeting with Bentley a few days ago, I could only assume you made a deal with him to help you get Drystan out of harm's way, so I went and had my own conversation with him." Galdinia gaped at her captain. "You're not the only one who can keep a secret," Ilyon continued, a hint of smug satisfaction crawling across his features. "I had to have a contingency plan in case everything went awry. Of course, I didn't expect you to willingly give over your crown, but in the event that we couldn't safely return to Elderguard, I set up a meeting point with him. One of us just had to get you to safety no matter the cost, so here we are."

"Bentley's coming here?" Galdinia asked, wide-eyed.

"He should be."

"And with Drystan?"

Ilyon took in a deep breath and replied, "If they both got out, yes."

Between the waves of anxiety and self-doubt, a glimpse of reassurance shimmered before Galdinia. Could they both have made it out of the battle alive? Galdinia couldn't hold too tightly to that hope—it was made too foggy with uncertainty and disbelief at the prospect.

"So what do we do now?" Galdinia asked.

"You should get some sleep, Your Highness."

"I couldn't possibly sleep right now," Galdinia replied, walking to glimpse out the small window at the sky that slowly warmed even before the sun had breached the horizon. Her humming mind and restless limbs wouldn't let her rest even if she tried.

"We travelled all night. You should try to rest."

Before she could respond, Galdinia's concentration was disrupted by the sound of heavy footfalls out on the landing, followed by a tired knock on the door. Both she and Ilyon stared at the door, and Galdinia's heart leapt in her chest. Before she could rush to the door herself, Ilyon held up a hand, cautioning her. With every restraint in her body, Galdinia stood still across the room as Ilyon moved to open the door a crack, holding his foot behind it, allowing him to inspect who was in the hallway.

Galdinia watched as his shoulders momentarily relaxed before he opened the door.

Stepping into the light of sunrise that was now streaming into their room, Bentley came into view. His lip was cut, his armour was smeared with dirt and mud, and he looked just about ready to sleep for a week. As he stepped through the door, he pulled someone else with him.

Drystan.

Galdinia's throat became thick with tears as he stumbled into the room, hair matted, with sunken eyes, dirty clothes, and barely standing. He was relying entirely on Bentley to remain upright and looked all the more emaciated up close. But he was breathing. He was alive. And he was here.

Gasping, Galdinia rushed forward, discarding the helmet on the bed beside the window before taking Drystan's weight from Bentley, wrapping her arms around his middle and holding him close against her. Drystan's arms crashed around Galdinia's shoulders with a sigh of relief.

"Gal." Drystan's voice was pained and weary, but to hear him say her name again filled Galdinia with a blazing joy she wasn't sure she'd ever feel again.

The tears flowed silently down her face as he used what strength he had to hold her close. Finally, he was within reach again, and in that moment, nothing else mattered. There was no threat, no crown, no battle; there was only her and Drystan with their arms wrapped around each other, and she didn't know if she'd ever be able to let him go.

"Drys," Galdinia said, her tears soaking into his shirt. "I'm sorry. I'm so sorry."

"It's okay," Drystan reassured her, his voice strained. "Everything's okay."

Over Drystan's shoulder, Bentley—weary, drained, and shattered —was leaning against the now closed door, dried blood on his lip.

"Thank you," she said, releasing a breath, barely believing what Bentley had done for her by saving Drystan.

With a pained smile, Bentley nodded in acknowledgement. "You're welcome," he replied, his voice hushed.

"I'll fetch us some food," Ilyon said, a tone of relief in his voice. "You're okay, Bentley?"

"I've certainly been worse," Bentley replied, moving away from the door, lifting a hand to his lip and wiping at it with two dirtied fingers. "I'll come with you."

"It might be good to get him lying down," Ilyon suggested before the two of them walked out the door, closing it behind them.

"Just one more moment," Drystan whispered, clutching on to Galdinia for another long second before finally leaning back to look at her in the face properly. "You're real, aren't you?"

"Gods, I hope so," Galdinia said with a smile full of tears, reaching up to push his tangled hair from his eyes.

He was frail and close to collapse, and yet his eyes reflected racing hearts, the warm glow of summer and all comfort. And suddenly, Galdinia was home.

"There are other versions of you that aren't real," Drystan explained. "You were in my cell with me and in my dreams, but I couldn't hold on to you for longer than a second."

Galdinia imagined Drystan in a dungeon, deprived of sleep and food, hallucinations blurring his vision in his delirium. A fresh wave of guilt crashed over her heart.

"I'm sorry I couldn't get to you sooner," she said desperately, placing her hand on his cheek, making it abundantly clear to them both that they were real and not figments of each other's imaginations.

"Don't say that," Drystan assured her, his warm eyes penetrating his otherwise worn appearance.

"I tried to work out how I could reach you," Galdinia continued, "but I just couldn't. I was so worried about you."

"That makes two of us," Drystan replied, tucking some loose

strands of hair behind Galdinia's ear, his hand coming to rest on her neck.

"If it weren't for me, she never would have taken you hostage. I'm just so sorry for leaving you on your own for so long." The words spilled from Galdinia as she uttered every apology and thought she'd had since they'd been separated during the attack in Elderguard.

"Gal," Drystan said, pressing a finger to her lips, his touch sending a warmth across her skin, "you were with me the whole time—every morning and every evening, in every thought and every breath, you were there with me. I'm only alive because of you."

Fresh tears brimmed in Galdinia's eyes, and Drystan moved his hand to her cheek, using his thumb to catch the tears as they fell. Leaning down, he placed his lips gently against the skin of her cheeks, each tear replaced with a soft kiss. With her eyes closed, Galdinia felt every press of his lips deep within her chest. She held on tightly to his sides to keep herself balanced, her relief of once again holding Drystan in her arms meeting her heavy fatigue. Finally, her heart could rest.

When the tears stopped, Drystan pressed his forehead against hers, and they stood like that for what could have been ten seconds or ten minutes.

"You gave up your crown," Drystan whispered into the quiet, his eyes closed. "And your title."

"I had to," Galdinia replied on an exhale.

"I'm not worth that, Gal," he said, his voice resolute despite his weariness.

"You are worth it a thousand times over," Galdinia assured him, tightening her grip on his torso and holding him closer.

Drystan's eyes fluttered open. "You looked spectacular in it," he said, a delirious smirk crossing his lips.

Galdinia smiled, her eyelashes still wet with tears. "I'll get it back," she said. "But you are worth every crown in every realm. You are my crown now."

With his hands still resting along her jaw, Drystan pulled her forehead to his lips, kissing her the same way he had when he said goodbye to her in the castle's entrance hall when he'd chosen his duty over his heart. Galdinia leant into him, wanting to linger in this moment for as long as their tired legs would allow.

It wasn't until Ilyon and Bentley's returning footsteps sounded that Galdinia guided Drystan to the edge of the bed by the window. He let out a great sigh of relief as he relaxed into the pillows.

Ilyon and Bentley walked in and placed four plates of a questionable looking grey soup on the table in the corner. Galdinia crossed the room, standing beside Bentley as he passed her a bowl. A deep sense of gratitude settled in Galdinia's heart as she took it from him.

"Thank you, again," Galdinia said quietly, the words escaping her lips before she thought of what she wanted to say.

"For the soup?" Bentley asked, looking down at his own plate. Was he avoiding her eyes? "Ilyon paid for it."

"Bentley," Galdinia said gently, causing him to look up at her, a new expression in his eyes. "You know I'm not talking about the soup." She glanced backwards at Drystan, where Ilyon was passing him a bowl and spoon, before looking back at Bentley. "You really have no idea what this means to me."

"I think I have some idea." Bentley's eyes were intent on hers, communicating far more than his words.

"I wasn't sure what would happen, and the fact that you saved him, endangering yourself, it's just—" Galdinia's breath stopped short, a fresh wave of tears threatening to break. "Thank you."

"It was the only way I could guarantee you'd stay alive."

Galdinia frowned at Bentley in confusion. "What?"

"If he didn't live, you would have let Valah kill you, or you would have died trying to kill her," Bentley said in hushed tones. "You had to live, and so did he."

Galdinia held Bentley's gaze, his blue eyes shining in the morning light.

"Thank you for keeping us both alive then," Galdinia replied, a small smile on her lips.

"That's what I do," he said, returning the smile. "I keep you alive."

It might have been her exhaustion that got the better of her, or perhaps stupidity, but Galdinia reached out a hand and placed it gingerly on Bentley's arm, squeezing it briefly. Their eyes lingered on each other before Galdinia turned and went to sit beside Drystan on the edge of the bed.

"Gods, I hate mushrooms," Drystan said, though he quickly sipped the thick grey soup off the spoon. "It's delicious."

Galdinia smiled at his appreciation for one of his least favourite foods. It seemed that very few things could squash Drystan's spirit, and if mushrooms didn't do it, Galdinia didn't know what would.

"How were things looking after you left the grasslands, Bentley?" Ilyon asked, dipping a slice of bread into his soup.

"It wasn't looking good," Bentley explained before his eyes flicked to Drystan. "I'm surprised we even got out."

"We were surrounded," Drystan said between mouthfuls, his eyes bleary.

"Did the Royal Guard stay put?"

"From what I could tell, they didn't move," Bentley replied, shaking his head. "And the heat of the battle seemed to remain between Edana's and Valah's forces."

"Did you see Edana?" Galdinia asked Bentley.

He nodded curtly. "She was on the frontline and practically ravenous. I didn't see a lot after that, though. Edana did exactly what you'd hoped: she distracted Valah and her forces."

"Perfect," Galdinia replied.

"When Valah and Reynard turned their attention to Edana, I quickly pulled him onto my horse, and we made a break for it," Bentley continued, nodding towards Drystan.

"Again, thank you," Drystan said.

"Of course," Bentley replied with a tight smile.

Galdinia could hardly believe the situation she found herself in now with Drystan and Bentley, but she was beyond grateful that both of them sat before her.

"Do you know if Valah survived?" Ilyon asked.

"I'm not sure," Bentley said on a sigh. "The last time I saw her before we got too far away, she was climbing onto her horse and riding back towards her army. Either of them could be dead."

"But they could also still be alive," Galdinia said, staring into her plate.

The four of them contemplated this prospect in silence as they ate their meal.

"So I assume one of you has a good plan for us to get out of here?" Bentley chimed in, finding some energy after a few mouthfuls of food. "I don't imagine you planned on keeping us in this fine establishment for long."

"I wish I could say I had a plan beyond this, but I don't," Ilyon said, shaking his head, his bowl of soup already half-empty. "Your Highness?"

"I have one or two plans," Galdinia replied, a small smile tickling her lips.

"And do you care to share those?" Bentley asked, raising his eyebrows in her direction.

"First thing's first, I'm going to need my Queen's Guard," Galdinia explained, looking around the room at each of the men. "And then we are going to need to retrieve the Lidels' jewels. I have a bargain to uphold."

The end

Galdinia will return in book three of The Crystal Crown Trilogy.

~

If you enjoyed *Crown of Dusk*, it would be greatly appreciated if you could leave a quick review on Amazon and/or Goodreads.

Visit megangilbert.co, or scan the QR code below, to find links to your favourite reviewing platforms.

ACKNOWLEDGEMENTS

When writing the first draft of Crown of Dusk, long before the publication of Princess of Dawn, I had an eerie realisation: my experience of drafting Book 1 and Book 2 curiously mirrored Galdinia's own journey so far.

Now, in case there's anyone out there who may be skipping ahead to read the acknowledgements before the actual book (do these people exist?), this is your warning that you're officially in spoiler territory.

Although the story of Princess of Dawn had been on my heart for quite some time prior to writing it, and I knew it was a story that needed to be told, I still felt that familiar dread of imposter syndrome when writing and publishing it. I was worried my readers wouldn't find me, or—and possibly more terrifying—if they did, they'd think my work wasn't worthy of the crown on the cover.

But then I hit 'publish' and the right people found and resonated with Galdinia's story.

Enter: Crown of Dusk.

You'd think that after writing and publishing a book one might feel a little less petrified about doing it all again. I can confirm that this is far from the truth. More than ever, I felt I had to earn my stripes, bringing a story with as much emotional resonance as the first, satisfying the expectations of those who loved Princess of Dawn, while also setting up for the final instalment of the trilogy. I was wearing the proverbial crown of 'author', and yet I wondered if I truly could do it again as I wrestled with the story and Galdinia's own sense of self-confidence.

For those following the analogy closely: fear not. I'm not handing said crown to a terrifyingly lethal woman as Galdinia did, but this whole process has brought a level of self-reflection I think is necessary for me to be able to complete the trilogy.

Have I managed to squash every moment of imposter syndrome as it hurled itself at me along the way? No, unfortunately not. But have I still managed to write (and now publish) another book in spite of it? Absolutely!

And it truly wouldn't have been possible without so many loving, caring and supportive people around me. A few of whom, I'd like to briefly—and sincerely—thank; however, a handful of words in the back of a book will never do justice for what you've all done for me.

First and foremost, Jesus is the only reason any of this is possible. He gifted me this passion for storytelling, and I never would have thought it possible to publish my words without him.

To Jack, my first reader, best friend, greatest cheerleader, and most effective sounding board. I'm so grateful for your constant support, creativity and willingness to stop whatever you're doing when I regularly ask, "Does this make sense?" You're everything and more than I could ask for in a best friend and husband. Thank you.

To my alpha and beta readers—Miranda, Tash, Jess, Bek and Maisie—and my proofreaders—Mum, Alysha and Jack (again). Thank you for your invaluable feedback and eye for detail when reading this story at different stages, while also sending me your theories and gushing about your favourite characters.

Thank you to my fantastic editor, Katie Wolf, and my brilliant cover designer, David Gardias, both of whom I trust beyond words to help me create a book worthy of being published, both inside and out.

In 2025, I was introduced to a beautiful group of fellow authors who have been a great source of support and inspiration over the last year. I'm so grateful for our girl gang of creatives and the wisdom shared in the group. Thank you to Alaina, Bree, Charlene, Elle, Emily, Jadis, Jess, Jordan, Kathryn, Marie, Sam, Taryn, and Taylor.

Finally, I thank *you*, my wonderful readers. Without you, this book may not exist. Your excitement to see where Galdinia's story will lead —and perhaps the fates of two particular young gentlemen—have spurred me on throughout the writing and editing process. I'm so glad to finally be able to share this story with you and I can't wait for you to see where Book 3 will take us. Thank you for caring about Galdinia as much as I do.

ABOUT THE AUTHOR

Megan Gilbert is a writer, reader, English teacher and peppermint tea drinker from Sydney, Australia. Through her post-graduate studies in creative writing, she has delved into a variety of genres, text types and mediums. Her first love is speculative fiction, particularly fantasy. She seeks to write stories that inspire young and new adults to read more avidly.

Megan is passionate about writing stories for young people, especially young women, through fantasy stories with strong female leads and challenging plots. Having worked with teenagers for many years, she believes it is imperative to provide young adults with stories that promote positive representations of managing mental health and body inclusivity, in particular.

'The Crystal Crown Trilogy' is Megan's first foray in the publishing world and she looks forward to exploring Galdinia's story further in the final book of the trilogy.

You can find out more about Megan, her books, and subscribe to her newsletter on her website:

megangilbert.co

www.ingramcontent.com/pod-product-compliance
Lightning Source LLC
Chambersburg PA
CBHW050112120726
47904CB00004B/1323